Recipe for a Perfect Wife

Recipe for a Perfect Wife

A NOVEL

Karma Brown

VIKING

VIKING

an imprint of Penguin Canada, a division of Penguin Random House Canada Limited

Canada • USA • UK • Ireland • Australia • New Zealand • India • South Africa • China

Published in Viking Hardcover by Penguin Canada, 2020
Simultaneously published in the United States by Dutton,
an imprint of Penguin Random House LLC

www.penguinrandomhouse.ca

*Publisher's note: This book is a work of fiction. Names, characters, places and incidents either are
the product of the author's imagination or are used fictitiously, and any resemblance
to actual persons living or dead, events, or locales is entirely coincidental.*

LIBRARY AND ARCHIVES CANADA CATALOGUING IN PUBLICATION
Title: Recipe for a perfect wife / Karma Brown.
Names: Brown, Karma, author.
Identifiers: Canadiana (print) 20190139935 | Canadiana (ebook) 20190139943 |
ISBN 9780735236240 (softcover) | ISBN 9780735236257 (electronic)
Classification: LCC PS8603.R68435 R43 2020 | DDC C813/.6—dc23

Book design by Elke Sigal
Cover design by Five Seventeen; adapted from the design by Alex Merto
Cover image: © The Advertising Archives/Bridgeman Images

Printed and bound in the U.S.A.

10 9 8 7 6 5 4 3 2 1

Penguin
Random House
VIKING CANADA

For my nana, Miriam Ruth Christie, who was a feminist despite the confines of her generation. A "from the can" cook, she was not known for her kitchen skills but did make a mean Chicken à la King. Which I miss, though not as much as I miss her.

And to all the women who have come before me, thank you for lighting the pathway. For those coming after—especially you, Addison Mae—I'm sorry the work is not done. I hope we've left you with enough to finish the job.

*Art is a hard mistress, and there is no art
quite so hard as that of being a wife.*

—BLANCHE EBBUTT, *Don'ts for Wives* (1913)

Recipe for a Perfect Wife

1

You seem to forget that I am married, and the one charm of marriage is that it makes a life of deception absolutely necessary for both parties.

—Oscar Wilde, *The Picture of Dorian Gray* (1890)

*I*t was late in both day and season for planting, but she had no choice in the matter. Her husband hadn't understood the urgency, having never nurtured a garden. Nor did he hold an appreciation for its bounty, and as a result had been gently irritable with her that morning. Wishing she would focus on *more important tasks* instead, of which there were many, as they'd moved in only the week before. It was true much of the garden could wait—little happened during these later months, as bulbs rested dormant, waiting for the rain and warmth of spring. But this particular plant, with its bell-shaped flowers plentiful, would not be so patient. Besides, it was a gift and came with specific instructions, so there was no alternative but to get it into the ground. Today.

She felt most like herself when she was mucking about in the dirt, singing to and coaxing the buds and leaves. That had been the main reason she loved the house when she first saw it. The garden beds were already prepped, though sparse, and she could envision how they could be transformed into something magnificent. The house itself had felt large and impersonal—especially its many rooms, considering it was only the two of them. However, they were newlyweds still. Plenty of time to make the house a home, to fill it with children and warmth.

Humming a favorite tune, she slid on her gardening gloves as she crouched and, with the trowel, dug out a large circle of earth. Into the hole went the plant, which she held carefully with her gloved fingers so as not to crush the amethyst-colored blossoms. She was comforted as she patted the soil around its roots, the stalk standing nice and straight, the flowers already brightening up the garden. There was plenty of work still ahead, but she lay down on the soft grass, her hands resting like a pillow under her head, and watched the clouds dance in the blue sky above. Excited and ready for all that was to come.

2

Men like a clean house, but fussing about all the time, upsetting the house in order to keep it clean, will drive a man from the house elsewhere.

—William J. Robinson, *Married Life and Happiness* (1922)

Alice

.....

MAY 5, 2018

When Alice Hale first saw the house—impressive in size though dilapidated and dreary from neglect—she couldn't have known what it had in store for her. Her first thought was how gargantuan it seemed. The Hales lived in a teeny one-bedroom in Murray Hill, which required shuffling sideways to get past the bed and featured a bathroom door that grazed your kneecaps when you sat on the toilet. By comparison this house was a sizable rectangle of symmetrical brick with shuttered windows on either side of a red door nestled into a stone archway, the door's paint peeling like skin after a bad sunburn. Reluctance filled Alice as she imagined walking through the door: *Welcome to Greenville, Nate and Alice Hale,* she could almost hear the house whisper through the mouthlike mail slot, in a not-at-all-welcoming tone. *This is a place where young urban professionals come to die.*

The suburb was perfectly lovely, but it wasn't Manhattan. A town a few minutes' drive from the better-known and more exclusive Scarsdale, Greenville was less than an hour's train ride from the city and yet was an entirely different world. Wide lawns. Picket fences, many of them predictably white. Sidewalks clean enough to eat off of. No sounds of traffic, which made Alice uneasy. Her left eye twitched, likely the result of having barely slept the night before. She had paced their shoebox-size apartment in Murray Hill in the dark, overwhelmed by the sense that this—the house, Greenville, all of it—would be a terrible mistake. But things always feel dire in the middle of the night, and by morning her insomnia and worries seemed silly. This was the first house they had seen, and no one ever bought the *first* house.

Nate took her hand, leading her along the sidewalk to look at the house from the side. She squeezed his fingers, followed his gaze as they walked. "It's nice, right?" he said, and she smiled, hoping the twitching eye wasn't obvious.

Taking in the home's facade—the deep cracks in the cement walkway, the graying picket fence that leaned askew—Alice realized why the house was priced the way it was, though still pushing their budget. Especially now that they were living on one paycheck, which had been Alice's doing and still made her stomach ache with guilt when she thought about it. The house was desperately in need of work. *A lot of work.* And they hadn't even gone inside yet. She sighed, pressing her fingertips to her eyelid. *This is fine*, she thought. *It's going to be fine.*

"It's a lot of money," she said. "Are you *sure* we can afford it?" She had grown up with nothing extra and sometimes not even the basics; the idea of a mortgage terrified her.

"We can. I promise," Nate replied. He was a numbers guy, and good with money, but she remained hesitant.

"It has really good bones," he added, and Alice glanced at him, wondering how they were seeing things so differently. "Classic, too. Don't you love how solid it looks?" *Solid.* That was what one got for marrying an actuary.

"Think the Realtor gave us the right address?" If Alice tilted her head *just so,* it looked as though the house was leaning to the right. Maybe they were in the wrong neighborhood and this home's in-much-better-shape cousin existed elsewhere. *Oh, she said Greenwich, not Greenville,* Nate might say as he reread the email from their Realtor.

Alice frowned at the eyesore of a front lawn, the lackluster and overgrown grass, wondering what a lawn mower cost. But while everything else appeared unkempt, the flowers that lined the fence—rich pink blooms that looked like they were made from layers of delicate tissue paper—were gorgeous and plentiful, as though they had been tended to only that morning. She tucked her fingers under one of the flowers and leaned in, its perfume intoxicating.

"One seventy-three." Nate looked up from his phone and at the tarnished brass house number. "Yup, this is it."

"A colonial revival," their Realtor, Beverly Dixon, had said while Nate and Alice listened in on speakerphone the evening before. "Built in the forties, so it has a few quirks, but with gorgeous detail. Wait until you see the stone archway and the classic layout. This one won't last long, I'm telling you, especially at this price." Nate had looked excited as Beverly went on. Alice knew he felt stifled inside their small apartment with its too-few windows and absence of green space and the shockingly steep rent.

Nate had wanted to move out of the city for as long as she'd known him. He wanted a yard to throw a ball around in with his children, the way he had with his dad. To have songbirds and summer cicadas wake him each morning rather than delivery trucks. A fixer-upper he could put his stamp on. Having grown up in a Connecticut suburb with still-married parents—one of which was a stay-at-home mother—and two siblings as accomplished as he was, Nate's vision of family life was naively rosy.

Alice loved their perfectly cozy apartment, with a landlord who handled leaky faucets and fresh coats of paint and a new refrigerator when theirs conked out last spring. She wanted to stay living ten blocks from her best friend, Bronwyn Murphy, whose place Alice escaped to when she needed a break from living in a shoebox with a man. Nate was, to be fair, tidier and more concerned with everything having a place, and there being a place for everything, than Alice was, but he still had minor shortcomings. Drinking juice straight out of the carton. Using her insanely expensive gold-plated tweezers for pulling out nose hairs. Expecting life would give him whatever he wanted simply because he asked for it.

Alice reminded herself she had promised Nate she'd be open-minded, and she wanted to get better at keeping her promises. Not to mention the fact that if they did end up moving to Greenville, Alice had no one to blame but herself.

A few minutes before their agreed meeting time, a Lexus purred up to the curb, and out jumped Beverly Dixon. After grabbing her purse and a folder from the passenger seat, she gently nudged the door shut in a way that told Alice this car was brand-new. Beverly locked the door with her key fob—twice—and Alice looked around, seeing no one nearby except for a woman pushing a stroller across the street and an elderly gentleman pruning a bush a few doors down. Alice thought back to Beverly's earlier comment about the neighborhood. "Crime is nonexistent. You'll be able to leave your doors unlocked if you want!"

Beverly closed the gap between them on three-inch heels, her body balloon-round inside the beige skirt and matching jacket. Her smile was wide and warm, her hand extended long before she reached them, heavy gold bracelets jangling. As she smiled at the couple, Alice noticed a smear of pink lipstick on one of Beverly's front teeth.

"Alice. Nate." Beverly pumped their hands, bracelets clinking like wind chimes. "Hope you haven't been waiting long?"

Nate assured her they hadn't; Alice smiled and stared at Beverly's tooth.

"A real gem." Beverly was out of breath, a slight wheeze accompanying her words. "Shall we head inside?"

"Let's do it," Nate said, grabbing Alice's hand again. She allowed herself to be pulled toward the house even though all she wanted was to drive back to the city and slip into her yoga pants and hide in their cramped apartment. Maybe order takeout, laugh about their temporary insanity at considering a move to the suburbs.

Heading up the front walkway, Beverly pointed out a few details ("gorgeous stone on that archway . . . you won't find anything like that anymore . . . original leaded glass . . ."), and Alice saw movement out of the corner of her eye. A flutter of curtain from the top left window, as though someone was pushing it to the side. She shielded her eyes with the hand Nate wasn't holding and looked at the window, but whatever had moved was now still. Maybe she'd imagined it. Probably—she was more exhausted than someone who wasn't working should be.

"Like I said on the phone last night, the house was built in the 1940s. Now, I know things are a little rough around the edges out here, but nothing a lawn service can't handle. Aren't those peonies stunning? The previous owner had a real green thumb, I hear. What I wouldn't do to have flowers like that in my front yard."

A lawn service. Good grief. They were officially going to become one of *those* couples. The type who desperately wanted plush suburban grass for their kids to play on, and for their golden-doodle to shit on, but couldn't actually take care of it. As they approached the front door Alice's stomach clenched. She'd had nothing to eat aside from coffee and a handful of stale cereal, but that wasn't why she felt ill. This house, and everything it signified—not the least of which was leaving Manhattan—was making her nauseated. Bile coated the back of her throat as Beverly and Nate chattered on about the "bones" of the house and its unique features, including the original doorbell, which still worked. Nate, oblivious to Alice's disquiet, pressed the bell and laughed delightedly as the tinny chimes echoed behind the red door.

3

A modern woman who is of the contentious type is often amenable to love and reason. If she will only listen quietly—a process that is painful to her—you may firmly, rationally, and kindly convince her she is not always in the right.

—Walter Gallichan, *Modern Woman and How to Manage Her* (1910)

Alice

.....

*I*t was dim and chilly inside, and Alice tucked her hands into her armpits as she looked around. Everything was old-fashioned, a layer of fine dust coating the wallpaper Beverly kept referring to as "vintage," as though that was somehow a plus. An old desk was pushed up against the front window, and what seemed to be a sofa was hidden under an off-white sheet in the living room's center.

"Do either of you play?"

"Sorry?" Alice asked, not sure what Beverly was referring to.

"The piano." Beverly lifted the lid of a black piano, tucked away at the back of the living room, and tinkled a few keys. "Dusty and out of tune, but it seems in great shape otherwise."

"We don't," Nate said. "Though maybe we could learn?"

Alice doubted that—neither of them was particularly musically inclined, and she was fairly certain, after listening to him sing in the shower for the past couple of years, that Nate was tone-deaf.

From the living room they entered the kitchen through a rounded doorway. The kitchen, much like the rest of the house, clearly hadn't been updated for decades: peach cupboards; an ancient fridge that was somehow still running, its hum like the roar of a freight train; an oval Formica and chrome-legged table with four robin's-egg-blue chairs nestled into it set against the far wall. There were still dishes stacked in the open corner cupboards—the kind you'd find at thrift shops and antiques markets, opaque white with flowers and swirls. The house was listed "as is," meaning it came with everything inside. They might be able to get some money for the dishes. They were *vintage*, after all.

"What's this for?" Alice asked, pointing to a small rectangular metal insert beside the sink. She lifted the lid and peered inside.

"Oh, that's a garbage hatch," Beverly said. "They were used to hold vegetable peelings or to scrape off dishes after meals." She opened the cupboard directly below, where a shallow pan—rusting slightly in its corners—rested. "Then you would clean out this pan. It was really very handy, and every good kitchen used to have one."

"Smart," Nate said, opening a few more drawers and cupboards, finding such things as a metal cookbook holder behind one door, hooks for pots and pans lining the back of another cupboard, and a pullout board that Beverly explained used to be a work surface for homemakers who wanted to sit while they prepared food.

Nate was so engaged, so obviously excited, that Alice tried to look past the state of things and see what this house could become. Maybe it was exactly what they needed. Things had been tense these past few months, which Alice accepted was entirely her doing. So she was the one who had to make the sacrifice, even if it meant subscribing to a life that felt alien.

Perhaps she could throw her restless energy into making the house a home, as Beverly kept saying. Strip away the "vintage" wallpaper, though the thought made her want to weep because there was so damn much of it. Knock down the walls separating the rooms. Create one big open space so the light from the windows could stretch from front to back. As she tried to imagine the positives, Nate whispered how great the front window would be for writing. "Picture a bookshelf beside the desk to hold all your novels, once they're written." Maybe. She could pivot. It had always been one of her greatest skills and why Alice was typically tasked with the most difficult clients at her firm. "All in, all the time" had been her mantra.

"I bet it's a great neighborhood for jogging," Nate said, no doubt imagining the miles they could run together on the weekends. *Tick, tick, tick,* she could almost see the boxes in Nate's mind. Maybe she could get serious about jogging again, covering miles on the quiet tree-lined streets, never worrying about getting hit by a car if she stepped off the sidewalk.

Beverly nodded with fervor. "Oh, there goes someone now," she said. They all looked out the living room's front window at a woman jogging past the house. The timing was so precise it seemed the jogger might have been a Beverly plant.

"You were just saying how much you want to get back to running," Nate said. "At least until there's a baby." He placed a hand on Alice's stomach and gave a rub.

"Oh, are you expecting?" Beverly asked, a little gasp escaping. Nothing like a kid on the way to add urgency, to make the house seem better than it might have otherwise. "This is a lovely neighborhood for young families. And we haven't been down there yet, but there's a full-size washer and dryer in the basement, so when those mountains of baby laundry come you won't have to leave the house."

"We are not expecting," Alice replied. Quickly, firmly. She was not pleased Nate brought it up, to a perfect stranger no less. The state of her uterus was a private matter, and besides, they had only recently agreed to start trying.

"Not yet," Nate added by way of correction, giving one final rub and a tap before taking his hand off Alice's stomach, where her T-shirt now clung to her middle in a most unflattering way. Alice used to be easily thin, the ability to drop a size as simple as drinking green juice and coffee and eating nothing but bone broth and watermelon for a week. Plus, work had been deliciously all-consuming, offering no time to ingest enough calories to soften her frame. But unemployment had done the trick. Nate loved her new curves, told her women who are too thin have trouble getting pregnant. When she'd asked where he'd heard that, Nate said he couldn't recall exactly. Alice suspected he had a few pregnancy sites bookmarked—Nate Hale was nothing if not prepared.

"Do you work, Alice? Outside the home, I mean?" Alice was offended by Beverly's question, as though she appeared like someone who lacked industriousness. *I'm twenty-nine years old,* she wanted to say, haughtily. *Yes, I work.* But that wasn't true, not anymore. Her stomach clenched again, this time with a longing like an itch she couldn't scratch. She missed work; the pace, the challenges, the paycheck . . . even the too-high heels, which she sometimes slipped on to walk around the apartment after Nate left for work because they made her feel more like herself.

"I was in public relations, but I quit my job recently. To focus on other things," Alice replied.

"Ali's writing a novel," Nate said, and Alice resisted the urge to shush him. If only he knew she hadn't actually started the novel. Or about what really happened with work.

Beverly's eyebrows rose at the mention of a novel, her mouth forming a firm and round O. Alice imagined that Mr. Dixon, if there was one, probably enjoyed that mouth quite a bit. "Well, isn't that fantastic," Beverly said. "I wish I could write. But grocery lists and real estate listings are about as far as my skills go." She smiled wide—pink tooth on full display—and Nate said he was exactly the same, would stick with his numbers and charts.

"What's it about? Your novel?" Beverly asked.

"It's, uh, about a young woman in public relations. Sort of *Devil Wears Prada*–ish."

"Oh, I loved that movie!" Beverly exclaimed.

"Anyway, I'm just in the beginning stages. We'll see." Alice tucked a stray piece of hair behind her ear, wanting desperately to change the subject.

"Ali doesn't like to give too much away." Nate rested his hands on her shoulders and gave a gentle squeeze. "Writers need to keep some secrets, right, babe?"

"Oh, of course," Beverly said, head nodding emphatically. "Now, should we head upstairs?"

"After you, ladies," Nate replied, gesturing with his hand up the staircase.

"So, a writer . . . how exciting, Alice. I for one love to read." The stairs creaked as Beverly stepped onto the first tread. She looked back over her shoulder, holding tight to the railing. The staircase was narrow and steep, requiring them to climb single file.

"What do you like to read?" Alice asked.

"All sorts of books. Anything, really. Though police procedurals are my favorite."

Police procedurals. Huh. That was unexpected. Alice looked out the window in the first bedroom they walked into and at the house next door, which from this angle was partially obscured by the branches of a large tree. It seemed in decent shape by comparison to the one they were considering making their own.

"What can you tell us about the previous owner?" Alice asked. They moved into the larger bedroom, where two single beds were made, though only for show, it seemed. Slices of bare mattress poked out from where the simple coverlets hadn't been pulled down far enough. And the closets were empty when Alice opened them, the night tables free of clutter, and the washroom without toilet paper.

"The house has been empty for just over a year," Beverly replied.

"A year?" That further explained the lawn, the peeling front door, the layers of dust, and the tomb-like feeling of the rooms, with their dark corners and long shadows and musty smells that tickled Alice's nose. The house felt abandoned, like someone had gone out for milk decades ago and then simply decided not to come back. "So why is it just now on the market?"

Beverly jangled her bracelets, cleared her throat. "The owner passed away and left the house and her estate to her lawyer to handle. She had no family, apparently." She frowned, then brightened. "That's why it's priced so well. It had been listed a bit higher earlier in the year, but no nibbles. So, back on the market and in your price point. Which is fantastic!"

Even Alice, with zero knowledge of home improvements, understood this house was in their price point because it would be a major project. Probably new wiring, and likely plumbing, too, along with asbestos removal if they did any significant renovations, like taking down walls. Maybe they'd replace windows when they could budget for it, to reduce the electricity bill. And every square inch needed a facelift.

"Is there anything else we should know?" Alice asked.

Nate bounced on one leg and the floor creaked under him. "Floors are good," he said. Alice glanced at the hardwood under her feet as Nate continued to bounce. "Are they original?"

"I believe they were redone some years ago," Beverly said, opening her folder and running a finger down a sheet of paper on the top of the pile. "Yes, here we go. New floors in 1985."

"Still retro!" Nate said.

"So, anything else about the house, Beverly?" Alice asked, ignoring Nate's eagerness for the moment. "I would really hate a surprise, especially with how much work we're looking at."

Nate, all smiles, looked at Beverly, certain there was nothing more. He loved the house, wanted the house.

"I don't need to disclose this, but you're a lovely couple and I can tell you're keen, and, well . . . the previous owner, she . . ." Beverly's voice trailed as she tapped a glossy fingernail against the folder, her brows knitting together. "Apparently she passed . . . in the house." Beverly's mouth turned down further; she wished to get back to discussing vintage wallpaper and newish floors and good bones and down payment options.

"Oh. In the house . . . What happened?" Alice asked.

"Cancer, I believe." Beverly looked stricken, now worried the Hales might be the type who would never buy a house with that sort of history.

And that was exactly who they would be. Greenville, and this house, didn't suit Alice or Nate. She needed to get them back to Manhattan—even if these days the city made her feel like a failure. "I see." Alice rubbed her hands up and down her arms as though to dispel a chill. "That's *interesting*." Her tone implying that by "interesting" she meant "concerning."

"Again, it was some time ago now," Beverly said, seeing her commission flying out the leaded glass window in front of her.

"I'm not sure I'd call a year 'some time ago,' Beverly." Alice frowned at their Realtor, her own lips turned down in mirrored response.

"Well, to be honest, these days it would be hard to find one of these old houses that didn't have a similar history."

Alice turned to Nate and gave another little shiver, lowering her voice. "I don't know, babe. It's sort of creepy."

"Is it?" Nate asked, looking from Alice to Beverly. "Creepy, I mean? We're not exactly superstitious. And like Beverly said, it was over a year ago, so any ghost living here has likely upgraded its accommodations."

Beverly tittered and Nate chuckled and Alice knew her moment was over.

Nate gave his wife a hopeful, questioning look, his expectation obvious. After Alice nodded (it was slight, but it counted), he turned to Beverly. "I think we're interested. Very interested."

4

Nellie

....

JULY 19, 1955

Meat Loaf with Oatmeal

....

1 pound ground steak (round, flank, or hamburg)
1 cup Purity Rolled Oats
1 medium onion
1½ teaspoons salt
⅛ teaspoon pepper
1 cup milk or water
1 egg, slightly beaten

Mix all ingredients, place in greased loaf tin, and bake in slow oven (300°F) for 45 minutes. Serve hot or cold. One tin of concentrated tomato soup is a pleasant addition to any meat loaf.

*N*ellie Murdoch buttoned her dungarees—which she wore only to garden because her husband, Richard, preferred her in skirts—and tapped the Lucky's white-and-red-foil cigarette package on the table against her hand. Sliding the slender cigarette into her mother-of-pearl holder and lighting it, she sat in one of her new chairs—robin's-egg blue, like cloudless summer skies—at the kitchen table and smoked, flipping through the latest *Ladies' Home Journal*. Richard kept trying to get her to switch to gum (he'd inherited a chewing gum business from his father, the original Richard Murdoch), or at least to a filtered cigarette, suggesting they were healthier. But Nellie hated all the lip smacking that came with chewing gum and loved her Lucky cigarettes. She liked how smoking changed her voice, made it a little huskier and certainly more interesting when she sang. Nellie had a beautiful voice, though sadly the only time she used her gift was at church, or in the bath, or to coax out flower petals. Filters promised to remove throat irritation, as her doctor and the magazine advertisements told her, and Nellie wanted no part of that.

Picking a piece of errant tobacco off her tongue, Nellie stopped at the "Can This Marriage Be Saved?" column in the magazine and scanned the three points of view: the husband's, the wife's, and the therapist's. The husband, Gordon, was overwhelmed with his financial responsibilities and irritated that his wife continued spending money on things like expensive steak for dinner, clearly not aware of his stress. The wife, Doris, felt ignored by her husband and his silent treatment and would cook him this expensive steak to try to make him happy. Nellie shifted in her chair, crossed her legs, and drew deeply on her cigarette, imagining what advice she would offer this couple who had been marinating in marriage for more than a decade. One, she'd tell the wife to quit cooking for a week and see how that helped her husband's stress. Two, she'd suggest to the husband he might try talking to his wife rather than expect her to read his mind.

She quickly scanned the therapist's advice, which amounted to: *Doris should know her expensive dinners were only making things worse for poor, worried Gordon, and therefore her as well;*

Gordon should not be expected to have to tell Doris how he's feeling . . . she should just know. The way any good wife would.

Nellie—who had been Mrs. Richard Murdoch for barely a year—snorted, sympathetic to Doris and Gordon's plight but certain she would never have to write away for such advice. From the moment Richard, eleven years her senior, plucked her from the crowd at the supper club and declared she would be his wife, Nellie had felt lucky. He might not have been the most attractive compared to her friends' husbands, nor the most doting, but he certainly had his charm. Richard had swept her off her feet that night—quite literally, as he picked her up in his arms and carried her to his table once he heard it was her twenty-first birthday, plying her with expensive champagne and adoration until she was tipsy and enchanted. In the two years since, Nellie had discovered that Richard was not a flawless man (was there even such a thing?), but he was an excellent provider and would be an attentive father. What more could a wife expect from her husband?

She stubbed out her cigarette and tapped the holder to release the butt before pouring a glass of lemonade. It was getting on, and she knew she should start dinner soon. Richard had asked for something simple tonight, as he was ill with one of his bad stomach spells. He'd suffered a terrible ulcer a couple of years earlier and it continued to flare up now and again. There'd been a great sale on ground hamburger this week and she'd bought enough for a few meals. Richard kept telling her she didn't need to scrimp, but she had been raised to spend wisely. To be thrifty wherever possible. Despite Richard's family's money—which was now their money, since his mother Grace's death only four weeks after their wedding—Nellie still liked a deal.

She pulled her mother's bible—*Cookbook for the Modern Housewife*—the spine soft thanks to years of use, its pages covered in the spots and stains of meals past, from the shelf. Singing along to Elvis Presley's latest, "Hound Dog," Nellie sipped her lemonade, thumbing the pages until she found the one she was looking for, dog-eared and well used. Meat Loaf with Oatmeal, the note *Good for digestion* written in her mother's pristine handwriting beside the ingredients list.

Setting the cookbook aside, she finished her glass of lemonade and decided it was time to get to the garden before the day got away from her entirely. It was scorching outside and a hat would probably be wise, but Nellie liked the sun on her face. The smattering of freckles she'd accumulated already this summer would have horrified her mother-in-law, who valued unblemished skin on a woman. But the impossible-to-please Grace Murdoch was no longer around to offer her opinions, so Nellie headed outside without a hat.

Nellie loved her garden, and her garden loved her. She was the envy of the neighborhood, her flowers blooming earlier than everyone else's, staying full and bursting long after others were forced to clip flower heads and admit no matter what they did they would never have flower beds like Nellie Murdoch's.

Though everyone was dying to know her secret, she claimed there was no secret at all—merely time pruning and weeding, and an understanding of which blooms liked full sun, which thrived in wetter, shady spots. Nothing extraordinary about it, she'd say. But that wasn't entirely true. Nellie had from an early age mucked about in the garden with her mother, Elsie Swann, who spent more time among her plants than with human companions.

Through the warm months Nellie's mother was gay, funny, and ever present in her daughter's life. But once the flowers died with the end of the sunny season, turning to a mass of brown mulch covering the garden soil, Nellie's mother would retreat inside where no one could reach her. Nellie grew to hate those cold, dark months (she still did), her mother glassy-eyed at the kitchen table, unaware how much her young daughter was trying to do to keep the household running. To keep her no-good father from leaving them, the way her grandfather had left her mother and grandmother years ago.

Elsie taught her daughter everything she knew about gardening and cooking during those swatches of light woven between her dark moods. For a while things seemed good, Elsie always coming back to herself after the snow melted and the days grew long shadows. Nellie and her mother were an unbreakable team, especially after her father left, finding the cheerfulness of a younger, less complicated woman more palatable to his needs.

Sweat trickled between Nellie's breasts, well encased in her brassiere, and pooled in her belly button and in the creases behind her knees. Perhaps she should have worn shorts, and she considered going upstairs to change out of her dungarees. *Never mind,* she thought. *This heat is good for me.* She sang softly to the plants, stopping to caress the tubular magenta petals of the newly sprung bee balm, a favorite of hummingbirds. "Even a plant needs a gentle touch, a gentle song, Nell-girl," her mother would say. Nellie wasn't as green-fingered as Elsie, but she did learn to love her flowers as much.

Once the garden was weeded and the blooms lullabied, Nellie trimmed a few herb sprigs, macerating a flat parsley leaf with her gloved fingers and holding it to her nose, the smell green and bright and satisfying.

Back in the kitchen Nellie washed and chopped the parsley and added it to the meat mixture, along with a sprinkle of the dried herbs she cultivated in her garden and kept in a cheese shaker in the cupboard. She glanced occasionally at the meat loaf recipe to ensure she hadn't missed anything. Despite having made this recipe dozens of times, she liked following the steps precisely. Knew it would result in a meat loaf perfectly browned on top yet still juicy inside, the way Richard liked it.

Nellie hoped his stomach had improved as the day wore on; he'd barely been able to get his breakfast down. Perhaps a batch of fennel and peppermint tea with dinner might help—iced, because he didn't enjoy warm beverages. She hummed to the radio as she trimmed a few mint leaves, hoping Richard wouldn't be late for dinner again tonight. She was bursting with wonderful news and couldn't wait to tell him.

5

To be a successful wife is a career in itself, requiring among other things, the qualities of a diplomat, a businesswoman, a good cook, a trained nurse, a schoolteacher, a politician and a glamour girl.
—Emily Mudd, "Woman's Finest Role," *Reader's Digest*, 1959

Alice

.....

MAY 26, 2018

*A*lice's head screamed with the shrill beeping of the moving truck as it backed into the driveway. *Their driveway.* Long enough to fit two cars, three if they went bumper to bumper. Only a couple of hours earlier she and Nate had made multiple trips from their eighth-floor apartment to the truck, filling it with their worldly possessions—which had been scrunched into their Murray Hill apartment like Tetris blocks but easily fit into the truck's cavity, with room to spare.

The night before, their last in Manhattan, Alice's best friend, Bronwyn, had thrown them a moving-out party to which she wore all black, including a lace-veiled funeral hat she'd picked up at a consignment shop. "What? I'm in mourning," she'd said, pouting when Alice raised her eyebrows at the hat. Bronwyn was at times melodramatic—when she and Alice were roommates she'd once called 911 when a mouse ran out from behind the oven—but she knew Alice better than anyone, and Alice understood that while the hat *was* a bit much, the sentiment was fair. A year earlier Alice would have scoffed at leaving the city for the "country," but things, and people, change. Or, as in Alice's case, people make one tiny error in judgment and completely fuck up their lives and then have no choice but to change.

Putting her hands to the sides of Bronwyn's face, Alice had said, "I'm not dead. It's only Greenville, okay? Change is good." She held back hot tears, hoping her wide smile hid her worry.

Bronwyn, seeing right through her, repeated, "Change is good. This city is overrated anyway," then suggested they get drunk, which they did. Around midnight they escaped Bronwyn's crowded living room—their friends shoulder to shoulder in the cramped, humid space—and shared the last of a bottle of tequila on the fire escape, until Alice's words grew slurry and Bronwyn fell asleep, head in her best friend's lap.

So after a very early alarm and some dry heaving and not enough coffee, Alice was cotton-mouthed and in a foul mood and she wanted the truck to stop beeping. Or maybe what she really wanted was to lie down on the overgrown and weedy driveway and let the truck run her over, ending her hangover. Alice chuckled, imagining how Beverly would spin that story for the next potential home buyers.

"What's so funny?" Nate asked, nudging Alice.

"Nothing." She shook her head. "I can't believe we're here."

Nate glanced her way. "All good?"

"Fine. Except my head feels like it's going to explode."

"Poor baby." Nate cradled an arm around her shoulders and kissed her temple. He rubbed his free hand over his face, squinting in the bright sunshine. His sunglasses were on top of his head, but he didn't seem to remember. "I'm seriously hungover too."

The truck had mercifully stopped, the backup alarm finally quieted.

Alice tipped his sunglasses onto his face. "Think we can pay them to unpack everything so we can go to bed?"

"I think we should save our pennies," Nate replied, and a spike of guilt hit Alice despite his mild-mannered tone. His salary was good—much bigger than Alice's ever was, maybe ever would have been—and would jump significantly after his next, and final, actuarial exam in a few months. Plus, he was a responsible investor and saver, but it was his paycheck alone that would have to float them, at least for now.

"You're right," Alice said, rising on her toes to kiss him. "Did I mention how much I love you, even though you forgot to brush your teeth this morning?"

Nate clamped a hand over his mouth, laughing softly, and Alice pried it away.

"I don't care."

She squealed as he dipped her, both of them fumbling as her hand, looking for something to grasp, caught the arm of his sunglasses and ripped them from his face. Nate shifted to catch the glasses, dropping Alice to the sidewalk in the process. They lay side by side, Alice laughing so hard she couldn't make a sound.

"Are you okay?" he asked, cradling her head so it wasn't resting on the cement. He grinned when he saw she was writhing in laughter, not pain.

"Mostly," Alice murmured, then smiled and placed his sunglasses back on his face. Nate pulled her to her feet, both of them brushing bits of gravel from their jeans when Beverly's Lexus pulled into the driveway.

She stepped out of the car, this time with jingling silver bracelets adorning her mostly bare arm. The skin under her biceps flapped as she waved, and Alice clutched her own arms, surreptitiously seeing how much skin she could squeeze. She made a note to do push-ups later.

"Ali! Nate! Hello!" Beverly was carrying a package in her other hand, the excess of clear cellophane wrapping jutting out in all directions from a pale yellow ribbon tied around it. "Today's the big day. You must be excited!"

Beverly beamed as she thrust the basket toward Alice, who was unprepared for how heavy it was and nearly dropped it.

"Oh, careful there," Beverly said, putting a supportive hand underneath Alice's. "There's a lovely bottle of wine you won't want to waste on these flowers." Patches of dandelions sprouted up from the cracks in the pavement. Beverly might be equally useless in the garden if she qualified these weeds as "flowers."

"Thanks, Beverly." Alice tightened her grip on the gift. A sprig of cellophane scratched her chin, and she shifted the basket into the crook of her elbow. "You didn't have to do this."

Beverly waved away the words. "Don't be silly. This is an exciting day." She handed Nate the keys for the front door. "I think you're going to be very happy here. Very happy indeed."

6

It is up to you to *earn* the proposal—by waging a dignified, common-sense campaign designed to help him see for himself that matrimony rather than bachelorhood is the keystone of a full and happy life.

—Ellis Michael, "How to Make Him Propose," *Coronet* (1951)

Alice

.....

Alice and Nate were in bed in the unfamiliar master bedroom, mildly tipsy after finishing Beverly's gifted bottle of wine. They lay under a duvet on their mattress, which they'd plopped on the floor, too tired to put the frame together. The only light came from a bedside table lamp plugged into the far wall. Alice's body ached; every muscle from scalp to feet begged for a massage, or at the minimum a hot bath. She thought about the rust-ringed, almond-colored tub and decided a shower would probably be good enough tonight, if she could muster the energy. There were no blinds on the windows yet, and without the glow of traffic or the hundreds of lit window squares from neighboring buildings, it was unbelievably black skied outside the house. And quiet. So quiet.

Remembering the box she'd placed by the bedroom door earlier, she reluctantly shimmied out of the bed's warmth and padded over to it. "I have something for you," Alice said. "It's just a little thing, so don't get too excited." She pulled an oblong parcel, wrapped and tied with a gold bow, out of the larger cardboard box. Settling on top of the duvet, her legs tucked up under her so her nightshirt covered her knees to stem the chill, she handed it to Nate with a smile. "Happy housewarming, my love."

He looked surprised and shifted to sit beside her as he took the box. "What? I didn't get you anything."

She gave him an incredulous look. "You bought me a house."

"*We* bought this house." Nate nuzzled his chin, which with a shadow of a beard was like fine sandpaper, into Alice's neck and planted a soft kiss. She didn't correct him, didn't remind him it had been mostly his savings that had gone into the down payment.

"Open it," she said.

Nate shook the parcel and something heavy shifted inside. His eyebrows rose with curiosity, and he ripped off the bow, followed by the wrapping paper. Lifting the lid of the white box, he pushed aside the tissue paper Alice had nestled around the gift and gave a big, joyful laugh.

"Like it?" Alice asked, grinning.

He kissed her, twice. "I love it." He held the polished wood handle in his right hand, pretended to hammer a nail into the air in front of them. "It's perfect." Nate ran his fingers over the rustic hammer's handle, where Alice had had inscribed into the wood, *Mr. Hale*.

"I'm so glad, because it's nice to have a matching set." She went back to the box by the door and pulled out her own identical hammer, though on its handle it read, *Mrs. Hale*.

"You are the best," he murmured, still smiling. "Thank you. Now let's hope I don't smash too many fingers."

"Same." She laughed, pausing briefly before adding, "We may be in over our heads here, you know."

"I know. But at least we'll go down together." He took the hammer from her hands and placed it beside his on the floor next to the mattress. "We can christen those tomorrow." He nudged her backward until she was flat on the mattress, his hands tugging her nightshirt up so his palms rested on her bare skin. Alice shivered, from the room's chill and the tickle of Nate's thumb lazily circling her belly button.

"We're going to make a life here, babe," Nate murmured. "I'm going to take care of us."

Nate Hale and Alice Livingston met in Central Park, midway on the running path that circles the reservoir. He was running toward her but she didn't notice him, as she was frantically trying to get dog feces off her shoe. Nate was a "real" runner—he had the GPS watch, the moisture-wicking shirt with stripes of reflector tape sewn into the seams, one of those Lycra water belts, and the bouncy stride of someone who found jogging fairly effortless. This was only Alice's second attempt. Though later she would come to appreciate it, at this particular moment Alice hated everything about jogging.

When Nate first noticed Alice she was hopping around on one foot—her soiled shoe hanging from its laces, pinched between her fingers, from her outstretched arm.

"Everything okay?" Nate slowed his pace as he got to Alice. He was nice-looking, with a good head of hair that appeared as though it would stick around for at least a couple more decades. Long, dark eyelashes. Slim build, and a six-pack to boot, which was hard not to notice—first when he pulled up his shirt to wipe sweat out of his eyes, and later that afternoon, up close in Alice's bedroom.

"I stepped in something." She forced back a gag.

"Here, give it to me." Nate held out a hand, and Alice gladly passed the shoe to him. He walked a few feet to a green swath of grass under a tree. "I'm Nate, by the way," he said over his shoulder as she limped after him, toe-touching with her shoeless foot. "And I'd shake your hand, but, well." He grinned and Alice noted his great teeth.

"Alice," she replied. "And thank you. You saved me from losing my breakfast."

Nate crouched, sliding the bottom of her shoe back and forth over the grass, firmly, like he meant business. Alice waited nearby, sorting out how she was going to get home with only one shoe because obviously the one in Nate's hands would be going in the closest trash can. After inspecting the sole, Nate rubbed it again on the grass and took one of the miniature water bottles from his belt. When he squeezed a stream of water onto her shoe, the fouled water ran off the rubber sole and Alice turned to the side and heaved—this time embarrassingly losing the few sips of Gatorade and half a banana she'd had before she left her apartment into the grass at her feet.

Fifteen minutes later they sat on a nearby bench, both shoes back on her feet (Nate had done an excellent cleaning job), enjoying an ice pop he'd purchased from a cart to get something back into Alice's stomach.

"So, tell me, Alice, what are three things I should know about you?"

"Hmm. Outside of knowing dog shit makes me throw up?" Nate laughed and Alice looked contrite.

"Sorry about that, by the way."

"It's fine," Nate said, taking a lick of his ice pop, which was melting quickly in the day's rising temperature. "You made today's run much more interesting." He smiled, and Alice, though mortified by her weak stomach, enjoyed his flirty banter.

"So, three things?" he asked.

"One, I'm in PR and I work too much but I love it. Two, I'm not really a runner despite how it looks." She gestured at her shoes and jogging shorts. "This is only my second run, actually."

"And what do you think? Do you want to be a runner, Alice . . . what's your last name?"

"Livingston. And that remains to be seen." She laughed. "I would not count today as a great success."

"And three?" Nate was finished with his ice pop by now, the wooden stick between his teeth as he leaned back against the bench, watching her intently.

Alice blushed under his stare, a warmth coursing through her body that had nothing to do with the humidity or her prior exertion. "Three . . . I don't generally eat ice pops with strange men in Central Park."

Nate smirked, and it was adorable. "Well, this is the first time I've bought an ice pop for a woman who threw up at my feet, so I guess we're both in unfamiliar territory."

"Funny guy," she murmured, chuckling. Alice tried to keep up with the melting sugary ice and failed, its stickiness all over her hands.

Nate took one of his water bottles and said, "Hold 'em out." Alice did, and Nate squirted the water, then lifted his shirt to dry her hands. For a moment his touch lingered, and then he smiled, looked away, and busied himself with putting the bottle back in his running belt around his waist.

"I don't know if you want to give this running thing another try—I know the shoe incident might have been a deal breaker," Nate said, a deeply serious look on his face that made Alice laugh but then cringe as she held a hand to her stomach. "But I'm out here a few times a week at least and am happy to, you know, give you some pointers if you're willing to risk it."

"Are you asking me on a jogging date, Nate . . . Wait, what's *your* last name?"

He held out a hand, and she took it. "Nate Hale. Runner; actuarial analyst, which is a fancy way to say I work with numbers; and overall nice guy with a rescue-the-damsel-in-distress weakness."

Thirty minutes later their naked bodies were pressed together in Alice's shower, running shoes haphazardly kicked off by the front door and a trail of shorts, T-shirts, a sports bra, and underwear leading to the bathroom. Alice didn't typically invite guys she had just met back to her apartment, but Nate was different. She knew it right away.

It wasn't long before Alice was spending most nights at Nate's place and Bronwyn started asking—somewhat grumpily, as up until Nate, Alice had insisted she was *not* relationship material and Bronwyn, similarly minded, imagined them living together for years to come—if she should find a new roommate.

Alice had met Bronwyn Murphy a few years earlier, both of them junior PR associates hired only a week apart, and they'd bonded over their fear of, and worship for, their boss, Georgia Wittington. Though Alice would have called herself "ambitious," Bronwyn had been rabidly so. For her, Georgia and the firm were merely stepping-stones, and she had a fully charted timeline for when she would advance within Wittington or leave without a glance back. When a promised promotion from Georgia didn't come through, Bronwyn gave her notice. She'd begged Alice— by then her roommate—to come with her, but Alice hadn't wanted to give up her seniority, expecting soon to be rewarded for her hard work and loyalty. Now Bronwyn pulled in twice what Alice had at her top salary, and had a coveted "director of publicity" title from a competing firm.

"It's going to be hard to find someone who understands my needs," Bronwyn had said, following Alice around when she came back to their apartment briefly to pack a few things to stay at Nate's. "Someone else might want to use the oven, for, like, roasting a chicken." Alice had hugged her friend—Bronwyn currently used their oven to store her shoe overflow.

"You're all *settled* now." Bronwyn sat heavily on Alice's bed and watched as she tucked a few pairs of underwear into her weekend bag. "I miss fun Alice! She always made me feel better about my choices."

"She's still here! You're overreacting, Bron. Yes, I have a boyfriend. But I am still your best friend and will never abandon you. Don't worry."

"Fine," Bronwyn grumbled, helping Alice fold a couple of T-shirts. "But if you go all *Stepford Wives* on me . . ."

A few months later Alice officially moved in with Nate, and six months after that, during an early-morning jog through the park, Nate proposed. Beside the same bench where they'd shared ice pops, pulling the diamond ring from a tiny zippered pocket inside his running shorts and getting down on one knee, causing passersby to cheer and shout out well-wishes.

Alice loved Nate. Deeply. Initially it scared her because she hadn't been expecting it and her past experience hadn't prepared her for it. Her last serious relationship was with a colleague, Bradley Joseph, who was charming and successful and very much into her, but who also, as it turned out, was a control-freak bastard. At first it was small stuff: he didn't like the hemline of her dress (too short) or the color of her lipstick (too bright); he bemoaned her weekly drink night with her work friends, suggesting he was taking their relationship more seriously than she was; he never asked her about work, preferring to talk about his own accolades instead.

Initially she dismissed it all, explaining his behavior as that of a confident guy with a bit of an ego, but nothing to be concerned about. Until he punched a hole in the wall of her apartment, inches from her head, after she said she couldn't attend his brother's wedding because she had a 104-degree fever. Alice broke up with him on the spot, but Bradley turned her off the opposite gender enough that she didn't go on another date for more than a year. Until she met Nate.

"What about Nate made me say yes? It's simple, actually. Life with Nate is better than life without him," Alice had said at their wedding reception, holding a glass of chilled champagne in one hand, Nate's hand in her other. He kissed her, her gulp of champagne wetting his lips as their teary-eyed guests clapped, and Alice thought, *There will never be a moment more perfect than this one.*

7

Nellie

....

SEPTEMBER 15, 1955

Chocolate Chip Cookies

1 cup soft shortening or butter

¾ cup brown sugar

¼ cup granulated sugar

2 eggs

1 tablespoon sweet milk

1½ cups flour

½ teaspoon baking soda

½ teaspoon cloves

¼ teaspoon salt

1 cup semisweet chocolate pieces

¼ cup coconut

Cream shortening, adding sugars gradually until combined. Beat eggs with milk, and add to shortening mixture. Sift together flour, baking soda, cloves, and salt and add to shortening mixture. Cut chocolate into small pieces and stir into dough with coconut. Drop rounded teaspoonfuls of dough onto greased baking sheet, about 2 inches apart. Bake in moderate oven (350°F) for 12 to 15 minutes.

*N*ellie settled the cookie tray on the back seat of the two-door Chrome Yellow Studebaker—the car had been Richard's choosing, but he'd let Nellie select the color, which reminded her of the yellow hybrid tea roses from her mother's garden—and got in herself. She ran her hands down her black dress to release the creases, adjusted her gloves, and stewed as she waited for Richard. They had argued all morning, he demanding she stay home ("pregnant women should never attend funerals") and Nellie countering she would do no such thing. She was perfectly healthy and would not miss Harry Stewart's funeral because of one of her late mother-in-law's silly superstitions. "How would that look?" Nellie had asked, because Richard was concerned with such things. She had marched out to the car, cookies in hand, leaving him no choice but to follow.

As Richard pulled up to the church, Nellie took in the large group of black-clothed people gathering for the funeral. Harry Stewart was one of Richard's best salesmen and had died riding the train to work the previous Friday morning. He'd been seated, though slumped to the side and leaning against the train's interior wall as though deep in sleep. It was only when the train braked hard—pitching Harry forward into another commuter's lap—that someone realized something was horribly wrong. Harry was thirty-six, a year older than Richard, and father to four young children. "Heart attack," Richard had said, looking as shaken as Nellie had ever seen him. Likely imagining himself in Harry's place, his death going unnoticed for some time while fellow passengers read newspapers, smoked cigarettes, and carried on banal conversations.

The fear hooded Richard's eyes all that week as he dealt with his shocked employees and helped Harry's widow make funeral arrangements, the cost of which Richard covered personally. Nellie tried to imagine if it *had* been Richard on that train, dead in an instant when his heart ceased beating. Would she be standing on the church steps like Harry's wife, Maude, was right now? Pressing a church-bazaar embroidered handkerchief to puffy, desolate eyes? But Nellie couldn't put herself there. Not because she couldn't imagine the grief, but because she and Maude Stewart had little in common.

Maude's four daughters stood in a row beside her like Russian nesting dolls, from the oldest and tallest to the youngest—four or five, by the looks of her. Maude had made a wise choice about whom she married. Harry had been a kind man who loved his children, wife, and God, in that order. Nellie had met him only a few times, but she could see it instantly—the warmth in his eyes when they were introduced, the way he never walked ahead of his wife, always beside her. Nellie glanced at Richard now, taking in his dour expression, a worm of unease wriggling in her belly. He placed a hand to his jacket, on the left side of his chest, and his scowl deepened.

"Are you all right?" Nellie asked.

Richard ignored her, stepping out of the car and opening Nellie's door. She took his arm, and they walked side by side toward the widow Stewart and her sad, nesting-doll children on the church steps.

Nellie clamped her glossy fingernails into her palms through the service, her breath returning to normal as soon as they stepped back outside the heavy church doors. She loathed funerals. Could barely stomach how trite and predictable those left behind made grief look. Somber faces, quiet murmurs of consolation, and silent tears streaking rouged cheeks, dabbed by linen handkerchiefs balled into fists. Through the entire service,

Nellie would wait for a tortured wail to burst forth from one of the front rows, proving the importance of the dead's life. Occasionally there would be a gasp or ragged sob, perhaps the odd swoon, and Nellie would be glad for it. She would appreciate such an overt display if it were her in that coffin at the front of the church. But funerals were not for the dead; they were for the living.

After the graveyard service, they drove to the Stewarts' home for the luncheon. Nellie glanced at the tray in the back seat, the cookies meticulously plated in perfect rows. Richard had questioned their luncheon contribution, suggesting cookies were not hearty (or impressive) enough for the occasion. "You're such a good cook, Nellie," he'd said, but she knew what he really meant. He didn't think cookies made the right kind of statement for the Murdochs.

But Richard knew nothing of feeding sadness—that was women's work—or how far a simple chocolate chip cookie could go to lift one's mood. Besides, Nellie had already dropped off a chicken casserole for Maude's freezer the evening before when she attended the wake, without Richard, who was once again suffering stomach pains. The fourth time that week. He'd promised Nellie he would see Dr. Johnson soon, but when she pressed him again he told her it wasn't any of her concern. Not her concern! She was his wife; who else's concern would it be?

As they drove, Nellie thought about how many casseroles and cold-cut trays and jellied salads would adorn Maude's dining table and knew the cookies would be welcomed. "Everyone feels better after eating chocolate," her mother always said.

Once inside the Stewarts' house, packed to the eaves with mourners, Richard stuck beside Nellie, his hand firm on her low back. They found Maude resting in a wing-back chair in the living room, a large photo of the Stewart family, with amazingly identical smiles, perched on the table beside her.

"Oh, Dick. Nellie. Thank you for coming today," Maude said, the skin on her face sallow and hanging. "And thank you again for the chicken casserole, Nellie. We were sorry to miss you, Dick. Hope you're feeling better?"

Richard tensed beside Nellie, his fingers pinching the skin at her waist through the dress. She knew better than to pull away.

"Perfectly well," Richard replied, his voice louder than necessary as if to prove it. He smiled warmly at Maude. "Harry was a great man. Damn, damn shame. Please accept our deepest condolences to you and your girls. Whatever you need, Maude, don't hesitate to ask. Harry was an important part of our Murdoch family."

They exchanged polite niceties for a minute longer, as one does in these situations, before moving on to the dining room under the guise of fixing a plate of food.

"You were not to tell Maude Stewart about my condition," Richard hissed in her ear. Nellie kept the smile on her face as she walked toward the table, where she noticed with great satisfaction only half her cookies remained. But that bubble of righteousness soon popped once they found a quiet corner with plates of food they would barely touch and Richard started in on her again. "You were supposed to say there was an emergency at the plant."

An emergency at the plant. Richard's business was chewing gum—what possible emergency could there have been? Not to mention, the wake had been full of Richard's employees, who knew as well as she did no such emergency had occurred. "I'm sorry. I forgot."

"You forgot?" Richard pressed the edge of his plate sharply into her breast. It hurt, and instinctively she pulled away, unfortunately smacking her elbow on a chairback as she did. Her plate tilted, and a wobble of jelly salad toppled onto the broadloom below.

"Goodness," Nellie said, putting her plate down and crouching to wipe up the spill.

"Let their girl get it, Nellie." Richard's voice was low, but there was no mistaking his tone.

Her heart beat faster as she stood, depositing the soiled napkin on her untouched plate.

"It's time to go."

"We can't leave yet, Richard," Nellie replied quietly. "We only just arrived."

"Say you're unwell. That's expected in your condition."

"Fine." She started toward Maude but stopped when Richard didn't follow. "Aren't you coming?"

"I'm going to get the car." He held his lips tight against his teeth, the way he did when he was angry. A look Nellie had become all too familiar with in recent months, as the Richard she'd met at the supper club vanished, an ill-tempered and fickle one taking his place. She was about to apologize again for revealing his illness to Maude, but one of Richard's plant managers clapped a hand on his shoulder and he turned away from Nellie with a ready smile and confident handshake. It still surprised her, the ease with which he turned it on and off.

Nellie took this opportunity to go back to Maude and offer her excuse: "a bit woozy from being on my feet for so long, so Richard's insisting I get to bed." Maude was kindly concerned, suggested a mug of scalded milk and nutmeg and a pillow under her feet once she got home.

"That sounds perfect." Nellie gave her a warm smile. "Please let me know if you need anything, Maude. I'm only a short drive away."

"You're very kind, Nellie." Maude held her hands and glanced around. "Where has Dick gone?"

"To get the car."

"He's a good man," Maude said, wistfulness and envy

coloring her words. She wiped a few tears. "You're very lucky to . . ." Her voice broke, and Nellie gently squeezed Maude's clasped hands. "You hang on to him, you hear?"

Nellie assured Maude she would and made her exit, taking a deep breath once she was outside the Stewarts' house. But her lungs filled less easily as Richard parked at the curb outside the house. The doting husband, the good man she was lucky to have. *You hang on to him, you hear?*

Richard made a show of coming to retrieve Nellie, and she played into it, as she knew he expected. Leaning on him to prove her wooziness as he led her gently back to the car, his arm tight with concern around her shoulders. Such loving care surely noticed by a few curious eyes from inside the house. This was the Richard she'd first met, the one she missed, and she let herself enjoy his comfort if only for a moment.

Once he'd settled Nellie into her seat and started driving, his mood went black again. Nellie sensed the shift, like a cool breeze you know is coming but still shiver from when it hits your skin. Richard didn't speak or look in her direction, and Nellie knew he'd likely brood all evening, berate her again, and after a whiskey or two find his way to forgiveness and the good husband he believed he was. She wished to rewind time to first thing that morning, when she awoke to Richard gently kissing her on the forehead, his palm caressing the gentle hill of her growing stomach. A man with two faces, her Richard.

Nellie stared out the window, was thinking about dinner and whether she could thaw the pork chops in time, when Richard reached over and dug his fingers into her thigh.

"Oh!" She was shocked by his sudden, painful grab. "Richard. Please. You're hurting me."

He didn't look her way, his fingers clamped around her thin leg. "I can't have my workers thinking I'm ill, Nellie."

"I told you I was sorry. I didn't mean to cause any problems.

Now, please, let go of my leg." But his fingers dug deeper, squeezing as though trying to pop the bones right out of her skin. Nellie knew there would be a bruise tomorrow, though tucked well under her skirts and dungarees so no one else would see it. Richard had never outright hit her, but this would not be the first bruise Nellie had endured in their marriage. However, he hadn't touched her in anger since he found out she was pregnant—she naively believed his prior angry outbursts, and rough fingers, had everything to do with his frustrations. Richard wanted a child more than anything else, and Nellie's inability to conceive during their first year of marriage had been a great source of tension.

"I can barely stand to look at you right now. Maybe I should make you get out of the car, walk home. What do you think about that, Eleanor?"

Nellie's shoes were already pinching, her feet swollen with pregnancy. "I'm sorry, Richard. Please don't make me walk." Nellie's father had once, four miles from home, brought the car to a screeching halt and demanded a then five-year-old Nellie and her mother get out of the car. He was belligerent, having drunk too much at dinner, and Nellie had moments earlier kicked the back of her father's seat, her little legs bored and restless. Nellie and her mother were forced to walk home in the dark, Elsie snapping the heel on her only good pair of shoes when she picked up her half-asleep daughter and carried her the last mile. Nellie's father had been a cruel man, but she couldn't believe Richard, no matter what she'd done, would leave her on the side of the road—especially in her condition.

Despite his threat, Richard didn't slow the car, but he also didn't let go of her thigh, no matter how many times she apologized. Suddenly a jagged pain tore through her stomach, and with a gasp she doubled over and cried out.

"What is it?" Richard's hand popped off her thigh and her leg tingled as blood pulsed to the capillaries no longer under strain.

"I'm . . . I'm not sure." She could no longer hold the tears back. The pain was dreadful.

"I'm taking you to the hospital." Richard made a move to turn the car around.

"No! Please, we don't need the hospital." The only place Nellie wanted to go was home. "It's easing. Only a cramp. I overdid it yesterday in the garden and didn't sleep very well last night."

He glanced between Nellie and the road, foot hovering between brake and gas pedals. "Are you certain? You look quite pale."

Nellie nodded and pinched her cheeks, straightening as best she could. She still pressed her hands to her stomach, which continued to roll with bands of cramping, but forced the tension to fall from her face. "It's better now."

The car lurched forward as Richard stepped on the gas pedal. "Well, let's get you home and to bed."

"Thank you, Richard," Nellie managed. He didn't deserve her decency, but he expected it. Even in pain, Nellie understood her role—the wife who bowed to her husband, who apologized for things out of her control, who made his life easier even if it made hers harder. The perfect wife.

8

Nothing destroys the happiness of married life more than the lazy, slovenly wife.
    —Mrs. Dobbin Crawford, *Bath Chronicle* (1930)

Alice

.....

MAY 27, 2018

*O*n Sunday Nate ran errands and Alice wandered the house, trying to get a feel for it. In the city, they could grab sundries at the nearby bodega, only twenty paces or so from their building. Here in Greenville picking up milk and bread and other necessities required a plan and a car, which Alice was nervous about. She wasn't the most confident driver (she hadn't driven in a decade, since moving to New York), but out here she was trapped without a car. The only thing twenty paces from their house was the street corner.

Alice puffed out her cheeks as she stood in the living room, hands on her hips. She released her breath in one long hiss, shaking out her shoulders. Trying to relax. The dim, cavernous room overwhelmed her, and the floorboards creaked under her feet as she walked, the sound rattling her nerves. Alice texted

Nate to find out how much longer he would be. *I'm freaked out being alone in the house,* is what she wanted to write, but instead she typed out, Don't forget the bleach.

She should have gone with Nate, as he'd suggested. "To get the lay of the land," he'd said, tapping the car fob against the grocery list in his palm. "Come Monday you're going to be the one doing all this. Don't you want to know how to get everywhere?" This was part of their deal—Nate was taking care of their expenses by commuting into work every day, and Alice would take care of things at home. The split sounded simple, even if Alice didn't fully grasp what "take care of things at home" meant.

In her mind, she remained the woman she used to be: alarm at 5:00 A.M., fully caffeinated and at her desk by seven. Managing clients and putting out fires, then picking up takeout and meeting Nate at home later in the evening. Never once worrying about whether the fridge was full or the bathroom clean or the bed made.

Alice walked into the kitchen, which by comparison to the rest of the house was bright and cheerful and made her feel instantly better. She donned a pair of rubber gloves and started cleaning. Her efforts were halted by the discovery of two dead mice behind the rattling fridge, decomposed nearly to their skeletons. Shuddering, she lay the delicate remains on a paper towel and googled whether dead mice should go into the compost or garbage in Greenville.

After disposing of the mice, Alice got to work on the kitchen surfaces, scrubbing off a year's plus worth of grime. She'd only gotten as far as scouring the countertops and inside a few of the drawers—which were off-center and screeched when she opened them—by the time Nate returned.

After setting the paper grocery bags on the table and giving her a kiss on the top of her head—the only part of her she said didn't feel covered in kitchen grime—he opened the refrigerator door, then looked at her over his shoulder. "Didn't get to this yet, huh?" It needed a good scrub, with soap and water (he had forgotten the bleach), but that wouldn't happen before the perishables had to be unpacked.

"I found some dead mice," Alice replied, shrugging nonchalantly even though she felt deflated at his comment. The countertops were pristine and the kitchen smelled fresh and clean, lemon and lavender oils masking the previously stale air. Sure, she probably should have tackled the fridge first, knowing Nate was bringing home groceries to put in there. She sighed, frustrated with herself. In her work life results had been easy to identify and measure. What did one get for scrubbing the kitchen, aside from a (temporarily) gleaming countertop?

"Don't worry about it. We can do it later." Nate shut the fridge door, reached into one of the bags. "Now, this can't compare to the hammers, but I got you—well, us—a sort of housewarming present. Close your eyes."

Alice did, eager with the promise of an unexpected gift, and the paper crinkled as Nate dug around inside a bag. "Hold out your hands," he said, and again, she did as he asked.

He placed something in her palms, a rectangular object without much weight to it. She opened her eyes to find a pink-and-white box in her hands. Staring back at her was a smiling baby peeking out from under a white blanket, surrounded by the promises *Identify your 2 most fertile days! No more guessing!*

"Oh . . . thanks." Alice set the box aside and started unpacking one of the paper bags.

"That's it? 'Oh, thanks'?" Nate crossed his arms, frowning as he watched her swivel from counter to fridge and back, making quick work of the unpacking. "What's up?"

She set the butter, then the milk on the one narrow shelf (old refrigerators were unbelievably limited on space) and hip checked the door closed. "Nothing. All good."

"Well, it doesn't seem like all is good." His forehead creased. "What's wrong?"

What was wrong was that Alice was disappointed. An ovulation kit as a housewarming present? She folded the paper bags and stuffed them into a bin under the sink before responding. "It's just . . . it wasn't what I was expecting. An ovulation kit seems presumptuous, or something."

"Presumptuous?" Nate exclaimed, barking out a short laugh to cover his confusion. As a risk analyst he was hardwired to try to predict the future, and so using an ovulation test seemed perfectly logical—*why wouldn't you want to know your most fertile days if you are trying to get pregnant?*

Alice sat at the table and pulled the box toward her. "Don't you think it sort of takes the fun out of it? Why can't we do it the old-fashioned way?"

Nate pursed his lips. "Ali, we agreed we'd start trying once we moved. You *told me* you were ready." His tone was mildly accusatory, and fair enough, Alice had said pretty much exactly that. And she *did* think she was ready. She'd be thirty by year's end, and now that they had the house, with its extra bedrooms and full-size laundry, it seemed time to start trying. However, it remained a novel idea Alice was still adjusting to. Six months earlier if talk of starting a family had come up, Alice would have replied, "Talk to me in five years." It wasn't that she didn't want children; she simply wanted other things—like a "director of PR" title—first. At least until she screwed it all up. Now she wasn't at all sure what she wanted.

"I told you I was almost ready," she said, quickly adding, "And I am! But there's so much work to do. On the house." She swept loose tendrils of hair into the elastic holding back her ponytail. "I don't want to worry about my ovulation schedule, too."

"Fine, Alice. That's just fine," Nate grumbled. He banged around the kitchen, doing unnecessary things like shifting the loaf of bread from one end of the countertop to the other, opening and closing the cupboard doors without taking anything out. "Where the hell are the water glasses?"

"Top right, above the sink." She *could* have been more receptive to the gift, even if she would have preferred a nice bottle of wine or a stack of takeout menus to choose from for tonight's dinner. Pushing back from the table, she stood behind him as he let the tap run, waiting for the water to get cold. "I *am* ready."

Nate filled the glass before turning. She smiled gently, wound her fingers through his when he set the glass on the counter. "But maybe first we can get rid of the god-awful wallpaper and hire an electrician and figure out how to warm this place up a bit? It's so damn cold in here." She shivered for dramatic effect, and Nate, conceding, pulled her into his chest and rubbed his hands across her back.

"Are you sure?" he asked. "Like, really, really sure? I mean, I thought this was the plan, but I don't want to—"

"I'm sure." She took a step back so she could reach the ovulation kit on the table. "How many tests are in here?"

"Twenty." He pointed to the top corner. "A month's worth, apparently."

Alice noticed the seal had already been broken. "It's been opened."

"Yeah, that was me. I wanted to read the instructions."

"I should have known." Alice laughed. "Okay. I'll start peeing on these first thing tomorrow."

Nate shook his head. "Too soon. It's only cycle day seven. We're aiming for day twelve."

"How do you know it's day seven?"

He shrugged. "I pay attention."

"Huh." If Alice was surprised her husband was monitoring her menstrual cycle with more accuracy than she was, she shouldn't have been. He was a planner and a good partner—naturally he would take a team-effort approach.

"Flowers probably would have been a better choice, huh?"

"Nah, we have plenty of flowers in the garden," Alice replied. "I look forward to putting this to good use in five days."

"Which means . . . we have a few practice days, right?"

"Mmm-hmm. I like where you're going with this." Alice allowed Nate to pull her into the living room. She felt dirty and would have liked to take a shower first, but she felt badly for her less-than-enthusiastic response. With all the flux in her life over the past few months, Nate had been her constant. She couldn't allow her anxieties to come between them.

Alice cast her eyes at the floral sofa, which had come with the house and was in surprisingly decent condition. "This looks like as good a place as any."

Nate nodded, not taking his eyes off her. A moment later Alice lay on the sofa in only her bra and jeans and Nate was on top of her, his weight resting on his elbows. Under him she was satisfied for the first time all day.

"This certainly qualifies as the old-fashioned way." Nate reached between them to unbutton Alice's jeans and she pressed down into the firm cushions to give him more access. He traced a finger along the side of her face, down her jawline and neck, between her breasts.

"I love you, Mrs. Hale," he murmured as he bent to follow his finger's trail with his lips.

Alice leaned her head back against the sofa's padded arm. "I love you more, Mr. Hale."

Alice was up too early on Monday, sun streaming through the drapeless windows before seven. She tried to go back to sleep but instead ruminated on her to-do list: *We need curtains. And maybe a white-noise machine because it's too quiet. And this ugly wallpaper has to go. Along with the miniature, loud fridge, and rusty bathtub, and the drafts,* she thought. *But I don't mind the sofa. Even with the gaudy flowers. The sofa can stay.* Nate sighed beside her.

At his sigh she rolled onto her back and discovered she was alone in their bed. Remembered Nate had probably already left for the office, now that his commute was so much longer. Alice stared up at the ceiling at a long crack she hadn't noticed before, considered maybe the house had sighed through the crack, discontent that its new owners knew little about how to care for it and didn't appreciate its many charms.

A loud bang shattered the quiet, and Alice sat straight up, clutching the duvet to her chest, heart pounding as she stared at the bedroom door, which had slammed shut. She didn't have long to come up with a rational explanation (a strong breeze from the open window?) before the second bang. The bedroom door's heavy brass handle fell off and hit the hardwood floor, rolling noisily across the wood until it was stopped by the baseboard.

With a groan Alice sank back into her pillow and crossed her arms over her face, adding yet one more item to her growing to-do list.

9

Harbor pleasant thoughts while working. It will make every task lighter and pleasanter.

—*Betty Crocker's Picture Cook Book*, revised and enlarged (1956)

Alice

.....

JUNE 2, 2018

$\mathcal{I}$'ve forgotten how cold it is out east." Alice's mom pulled her wrap sweater, which looked like it could double as an area rug, tighter and tucked her chin deep inside its cowl neck. "Aren't you chilly?" She frowned at her daughter's outfit: jeans and a thin long-sleeved T-shirt, bare feet.

"Mom, it's seventy-eight degrees." But that was outside. Inside it *did* feel colder, as though the air-conditioning was on full blast, except that the old house didn't have air-conditioning.

"No wonder I'm cold. It was eighty-six when we left."

Alice swilled her coffee and murmured, "Yes, California's weather is different from New York's." Her mom, Jaclyn, and stepfather, Steve, had been staying with them for exactly eighteen hours, nine of which they spent sleeping, and Alice was already mentally crossing off the days until they headed back to San Diego. She had tried to dissuade them from coming ("a nearly thirty-year-old married woman does not need her parents to help her move"), but her mother had been insistent and Alice had given up when her mother's email arrived with their already-booked flight details.

Her mom placed her steaming mug of tea, her third—matcha, which she brought with her despite Alice's assurances she could get it for her in New York—on the nightstand and settled into a deep lunge in the guest bedroom, her legs and arms like spindles that bent and straightened with surprising ease despite the sweater-rug.

"So how was your first week of vacation?" her mom asked, moving through a series of stretches on the yoga mat she'd rolled out on the floor.

"I'm not on vacation, Mom. I quit, remember?" Alice frowned, thinking about work. Missing it desperately. Wishing she'd had the good sense to keep her mouth shut that night with Bronwyn, rather than torpedoing her career.

"Oh, you know what I meant, honey." Her mom flowed into a downward dog. "When I was your age I would have given anything to quit my job, bang around a big, beautiful house all day, puttering and fixing and whatnot."

A couple of her friends had essentially said the same—Alice was lucky to have Nate and his salary—though if pressed, they wouldn't have been able to say what one does with an extra fifty hours a week of unscheduled time. Everyone Alice knew worked, *had* to work.

"You could always try out a few hobbies while you're figuring things out," Jaclyn said. "Like painting or gardening. Or maybe cooking?"

"Hmm. Maybe . . ."

"Have you heard about this sous vide trend?" Alice's mother

described a particularly moist flank steak she'd had prepared this way a couple of weeks earlier.

"Yeah, I've heard of it." Alice yanked a stray thread from her T-shirt's hem, sighed.

"Trust me, honey, take advantage of this time before the kids come." Jaclyn made the comment briskly, as though offering advice to a friend rather than her daughter, who knew it was pointless to take offense. Her mother was not one to see things from Alice's perspective.

"And give yourself a break. Change is hard." Jaclyn moved into a headstand, forcing Alice to look at her upside down. "Are you taking your vitamins?"

Her mother liked to remind her how as a child she was always catching sore throats and stomach bugs with the changing seasons, or when beginning something new, like starting middle school. "Vitamins are for kids, Mom." She wasn't in the mood to be mothered, particularly by Jaclyn.

Jaclyn breathed deeply as she stretched. Alice closed her own eyes and counted to ten in time to her mother's loud nostril breathing. "Not true, honey. Vitamin D is a must in this sun-starved climate."

Alice's answer to "Are you close with your mom?" was always, "It's complicated." The two women were so physically different that if Alice hadn't seen the pictures of her mom holding her moments after her birth she might not have believed they shared DNA. Where her mother was fair, Alice was dark. Where Alice was small-bodied but had a tendency toward thickness without calorie deprivation, her mom was long and angular and lean. In the sun Alice went lobster red, her mother golden brown.

People often asked if Alice took after her father. She did, physically, but her dad had been absent so long she couldn't say if they shared any other characteristics.

During the ten years Alice's parents were together, her father floated between a variety of jobs—mechanic, farmhand, insurance salesman, yoga instructor—and one day when Alice was nine years old, he floated right out the door on his way to his landscaping job. He didn't come home for supper, nor was he there by the time Alice was ushered up to her room for bedtime. She remembered creeping back downstairs hours later and sitting in the chair by the living room window, where she waited until she fell asleep. But the sun rose, and still, her dad hadn't come home. Her mother cooked them breakfast—eggs, sunny-side up, and slightly fermenting orange juice bought on sale.

"When will Dad be home?" Alice had asked.

"I have no idea," Jaclyn replied matter-of-factly, busying herself with plating the eggs. "When he's ready, I suppose."

Alice, confused and upset by her mother's impassive statement and indifferent tone, had started to cry. Despite his fickle nature, Alice loved her father. She was still innocent enough to see only the good in him: he had a handlebar mustache and would wiggle the ends one at a time like a cartoon character to make her laugh; he let her have a whole doughnut rather than having to share it; he taught her to swim at the community pool near their apartment, leaving time for the underwater tea party Alice typically requested.

"Stop crying." Jaclyn had slid the plate of jiggly eggs toward Alice. "And eat your breakfast. You're going to be late for school." Alice had gulped down her sadness along with those runny eggs, and Jaclyn had said nothing further to comfort her young daughter. That was the first time Alice distinctly remembered being disappointed in her mother.

A year after Alice's father left, her mom met Steve Daikan at a fitness convention. She had been an aerobics instructor for years and Steve ran a successful string of fitness centers in California. Six months later she packed them up and moved them across the country to Steve's sprawling ranch-style house in San

Diego. Alice found California too hot, too predictable without the change of seasons, and so when she turned seventeen she hopped on a plane back to New York for college. Alice loved her mother but longed for a more straightforward relationship, like the one Nate had with his parents. It wasn't easy being a single mother, Alice understood, but it also wasn't easy being raised by someone juggling so many priorities.

"Jaclyn, where's the charger?" Steve popped his head into the bedroom.

"In my carry-on. Side pocket."

"Okeydokey." Steve turned to Alice. "Morning, kiddo. How was your sleep?" Like her mom, Steve was superfit, especially for sixty, his tanned biceps bulging in his T-shirt.

"Good, thanks," Alice replied, getting up to hug him. "How about you?"

"Fantastic," he said. "I'm here for work gloves. Nate said you had a set for me?"

"Right. Let me grab them." Nate and Steve were working on restabilizing the stone walkway and prepping the driveway for repairing. Alice and Nate had been in the house now for a week, and the list of what needed to happen was growing daily and at an alarming rate. "Here you go." Alice handed Steve the gloves from the hardware store bag in the corner of the room, pulling off the price tag as she did.

"Thanks, kiddo."

"Sure thing. Mom—I'm going to go grab the drop sheets. Be right back."

Her mother hummed lightly, still lunging, and nodded with her eyes closed. Steve reached over and gave Jaclyn's butt a light slap with the gloves and her eyes popped open.

"Steve!"

He laughed and kissed her deeply, and Alice left them to it.

Shortly after Nate proposed, Alice went to San Diego for a

long weekend to visit and had asked her mom—both of them tipsy on crisp white wine, which was the reason Alice had opened up to her mother—what the secret was to her still-happy relationship with Steve.

"Twice-a-week sex, minimum," her mother had said without hesitation, which made Alice wish she had never asked, followed by, "And choosing the right person." Alice had nodded, feeling thoroughly confident and slightly smug that, unlike her mother, she had gotten that part right the first time.

"Nate, where did you put the drop cloths?" Alice leaned out the front door, the warmth of the day a welcome contrast to the chilliness inside.

"Basement. Left-hand corner, by the bikes," Nate replied, swiping his arm over his forehead, already slick with sweat. He had a shovel in hand, and Steve was carrying a large square of stone over the grass like it weighed next to nothing. "Want me to get them?"

Yes, please, she thought, but then shook her head. Though the dank, dark basement freaked her out, she would have to go down sooner or later—the laundry hamper was overstuffed.

"You guys need anything? More coffee? Water?"

"We're good," Nate said, pointing to the small cooler to the left of the steps. The two were back to work before Alice had even shut the front door.

She flicked on the basement light and peered down the rickety stairs with trepidation. The single bulb cast barely enough light to see where she was going. Alice took a deep breath, the stale mustiness filling her nose as she stepped gingerly, the plank wooden steps groaning with age. As her feet hit the rough concrete floor, her phone's flashlight beam picked up a scurry of something fast-moving and Alice yelped. A large silverfish slithered by as it searched for the safety of the shadows, finding solace under the washing machine. "Gross," Alice muttered, a shiver moving through her.

The plastic sheets were stacked in the corner as promised, and Alice grabbed the packages, tucking them under her arm, eager to leave the damp chill and silverfish and whatever else hid in the basement of this old house. Her heart beat fast and her underarms were fear dampened, and in such a rush to get back upstairs, she didn't see the wooden skid until she'd tripped over it.

Winded, she gasped and gulped on the ground. Otherwise she was okay, though she would have an impressive bruise on her shin by the next morning. She sat on the floor until she caught her breath, shining the flashlight over to what had tripped her. Three boxes were stacked in a pyramid atop the small wooden skid. Alice could tell by the sagging cardboard walls, the corners soft and losing their angular shape, that the boxes had been there a while. She kneeled and read the writing on the top one. *Kitchen,* someone had written in thick, flowing black-inked cursive.

They must have belonged to the previous owner. Alice considered leaving them as they were, letting Beverly know in case someone ever came looking for the boxes, and whatever they contained. But curiosity overruled, and Alice tucked her phone under her chin and gently lifted the flaps.

Shining the light into the open box, Alice ran her eyes along the spines of a slew of magazines, maybe two dozen—all *Ladies' Home Journal,* with dates ranging from 1954 to 1957. Lifting one out, Alice sat on the edge of the skid and flipped through its pages, her basement fears forgotten for the moment.

There were advertisements for cigarettes, stockings, refrigerators, beer ("Don't worry, honey, at least you didn't burn the beer!"), all the colors muted, the ink matte, unlike the glossy magazines of today. She cringed when she got to an ad for

Velveeta cheese, a picture of a casserole where corners of grilled cheese sandwich popped up through an orange soup like cresting icebergs. "That's disgusting," she muttered, flipping a few more pages.

Setting the magazine to the side, Alice looked back in the box. Some sort of book lay flat at one end, half-hidden by the stack of magazines. She pulled the book out and flipped it over so she could read the cover.

COOKBOOK FOR THE MODERN HOUSEWIFE

The cover was red with a subtle crosshatch pattern and distressed, the book's title stamped in black ink—all of it faded with age. Bordering the cookbook's cover were hints of what could be found inside. Alice tilted her head as she read across, down, across, and up the cover's edges. *Rolls. Pies. Luncheon. Drinks. Jams. Jellies. Poultry. Soup. Pickles. 725 Tested Recipes.*

Resting the spine on her bent knees, the cookbook dense yet fragile in her hands, Alice opened it carefully. There was an inscription on the inside cover. *Elsie Swann, 1940.* Going through the first few, age-yellowed pages, Alice glanced at charts for what constituted a balanced diet in those days: milk products, citrus fruits, green and yellow vegetables, breads and cereals, meat and eggs, the addition of a fish liver oil, particularly for children. Across from it, a page of tips for housewives to avoid being overwhelmed and advice for hosting successful dinner parties. Opening to a page near the back, Alice found another chart, this one titled *Standard Retail Beef Cutting Chart*, a picture of a cow divided by type of meat, mini drawings of everything from a porterhouse-steak cut to the disgusting-sounding "rolled neck."

Through the middle were recipes for Pork Pie, Jellied Tongue,

Meat Loaf with Oatmeal, and something called Porcupines—ground beef and rice balls, simmered for an hour in tomato soup and definitely something Alice never wanted to try—and plenty of notes written in faded cursive beside some of the recipes. Comments like *Eleanor's 13th birthday—delicious!* and *Good for digestion* and *Add extra butter.* Whoever this Elsie Swann was, she had clearly used the cookbook regularly. The pages were polka-dotted in browned splatters and drips, evidence it had not sat forgotten on a shelf the way cookbooks would in Alice's kitchen.

"Alice?" Her mom was at the basement door, calling down the stairs. "Did you find the drop cloths?"

"Yes. On my way up," Alice called back, placing the magazines inside the box and grabbing the drop sheets. She turned to go upstairs but stopped, deciding to take the cookbook with her. Maybe she could give cooking a try, like her mom had said. Tucking it under her arm, she maneuvered carefully back up the rickety stairs, relief coursing through her as she left the basement's gloom. Setting the cookbook on the kitchen table, she took a last look at its cover, curious if this Elsie Swann was also the woman she had to thank for the many layers of wallpaper she was about to spend the next few days removing.

10

Nellie

....

OCTOBER 14, 1955

Chicken à la King

6 tablespoons butter

½ cup minced green pepper

1 cup diced mushrooms

2 tablespoons flour

½ teaspoon salt

1 teaspoon paprika

1½ cups rich milk, scalded

1 cup chicken broth

3 cups diced cooked chicken

1 cup cooked peas

1 teaspoon onion juice

¼ cup slivered pimento

2 tablespoons sherry

Toasted bread for serving

Melt butter and cook green pepper and mushrooms until tender. Blend in the flour, salt, and paprika over low heat until smooth and bubbly. Add milk and chicken broth gradually, stirring constantly over low heat until sauce thickens. Gently stir in cooked chicken, peas, and onion juice. Just before serving, add pimento and sherry. Serve with buttered toast points.

I think we should reschedule." Richard sat at the kitchen table with a glass of stomach-settling albumen drink in front of him. His stomach was "off" yet again, but it wasn't for this he thought they should cancel the dinner party. Nellie lifted the lid on the pot of chicken simmering in the lemon and parsley water, happy to see it was nearly cooked.

"You're not up to this, Nellie."

"I told you, the doctor said I'm fine to get back to things." She tied her apron tighter around her narrow waist, puttered around the kitchen, organizing bowls and platters and checking off items on her list as she hummed to the radio. Plated canapés. Shrimp cocktail. Hollywood Dunk. Lettuce salad with Roquefort dressing. Chicken à la King. Baked Alaska. Canceling was not an option: they were expecting three couples, and the dinner had been planned for well over a month now. Before Harry Stewart died, before the car incident where Richard's angry fingers had left a deeper bruise than Nellie expected. Before Nellie miscarried the baby.

It had happened while Richard was dining in the city with some bigwigs who boasted they could get Murdoch's gum in every soda shop from New Jersey to California. It was only one day after the funeral, and while Richard had been hesitant to leave her, he eventually conceded when she assured him she was fine. His dinner had gone quite late, and he'd ended up staying the night at the hotel, so he wasn't there when Nellie lost their baby.

When Richard arrived home the following morning and learned about the miscarriage, he had raged at Nellie. For going to the funeral, when he explicitly asked her not to, for not calling someone to take her to the hospital, for her general carelessness. Until he caught a glimpse of the bloodied towels balled up in the bathtub. There had been much blood, and it was so sudden and painful that Nellie had curled up on the towels in the bathtub, sobbing until sleep overtook her. She awoke near dawn still in the bathtub, shivering and heartsick, and had meant to clean up the towels before Richard came home.

"Oh my God, Nellie." Richard blanched as he took in the scene, put one hand to his heart and the other to the bathroom's doorframe. Was he thinking back to the car and perhaps blaming himself, remembering his forceful grip, the cramp that doubled her over? Nellie hoped so; it offered some solace to her heartbreak.

Later, Nellie would bleach the bloodstained towels white, except for one she would wrap up with satin ribbon and bury in the garden, under her pale blue forget-me-nots. "True and undying love, Nell-girl. Forget-me-nots are the flower of remembrance," Elsie had said one late afternoon as they weeded side by side, singing church hymns in harmony (Elsie an alto, Nellie a soprano). She pulled back some heavy foliage, showed her daughter the darker, damper parts of the garden the delicate blooms liked best. "They thrive beneath the shadow of these more handsome flowers," Elsie had said, fingering the joyful tulips perched above. Then she swept a hand across the blanket of miniature blue-skied blooms underneath. "Forget-me-nots may be small, but they are mighty."

It was the truth the doctor had said she was fine to get back to things. Dr. Johnson was on vacation, so she'd seen a colleague of his, the ancient Dr. Wood, who wore a tufted toupee and seemed unable to remember her name. She'd made the appointment two days after the miscarriage, and while Richard insisted he was going too, Nellie—wanting to be alone—suggested his employees needed him more than she did. "I'm fine," she'd said. "I promise I'll tell you word for word what the doctor says." So, while Richard caught the train to Brooklyn, believing she was being examined, Nellie instead consulted Dr. Wood about a barely-a-bother rash on her hand. After glancing at the mild rash, he suggested picking up some Mexsana powder at the pharmacy.

"That redness and itching should be gone in a couple of days, Mrs. Murray," Dr. Wood said, eyes on his prescription pad.

"Murdoch," Nellie said. "Mrs. Murdoch."

The doctor glanced up, his toupee slightly askew. "Isn't that what I said?"

"Oh, I must have misheard you."

"Ah, well, that's fine." The doctor finished writing out the medical powder's name, the pen wobbly in his shaky hand. "Mexsana is great for diaper rash, too."

"I'll keep that in mind."

The doctor, his bushy gray eyebrows knitting together as he handed her the note, asked, "How old are you again, Mrs. Murray?" She didn't bother correcting him this time, tucking the paper she planned to dispose of later into her handbag. He knew precisely how old she was, all her pertinent information in the file in his hands. But being childless at her age, two plus years into her marriage, Nellie understood the prying; she was an enigma in her sewing circle and church groups, at the Tupperware parties full of women in various stages of pregnancy, young children hanging off their mothers' skirts.

"Twenty-three." She waited for the inevitable comment; something about not waiting too long to start a family. But Dr. Wood didn't address it, nodded at her response before saying,

"Almost twenty-four, I see here. I'll leave a note for Dr. Johnson. I'd expect that rash to be gone in a few days."

The dinner was a success, as it always was in the Murdoch house. Nellie loved hosting parties, especially themed ones, though her husband did not share her zeal. When she'd prepared a Hawaiian buffet earlier in the year, their guests had fawned over her efforts but Richard had thought it was tacky. "What's wrong with a simple roast?" he'd said, scowling at the ferns and pineapples and bananas Nellie had decorated the table with to make it more festive. Reluctantly he'd put the lei, which she'd painstakingly made for each guest with crepe paper flowers, around his neck only after everyone else had done so.

Tonight, Nellie had put on quite a spread: a vegetable platter to start things off, with radish roses and olives pierced with embellished toothpicks and fresh tomatoes from her garden; canapés and shrimp cocktail and Vienna sausages and deviled eggs; then her Chicken à la King, and when they were all nearly too full to eat another thing, Baked Alaska for dessert. The conversation had been pleasant, the men discussing the upcoming election and General Electric–Telechron's new "revolutionary" snooze alarm clock, the women swooning about Elvis Presley and gossiping about Marilyn Monroe's recent wedding to Arthur Miller, which everyone agreed was an odd pairing.

The miscarriage wasn't mentioned, even when the women were alone, huddled in the kitchen to peer at the Baked Alaska in the oven. Nellie was both grateful and blue about this. She desperately missed being with child: the roundness of her belly, the fullness from deep within, the thrill of what was yet to come. During the evening, not one of her friends said anything more specific than "You're looking well, Nellie," because no good-mannered guest would mire the merriment of a party with such unpleasantness.

After the meal, Nellie had taken the women through the steps in making the Baked Alaska as they sipped their gin-and-lime cocktails—"But how can ice cream go in the oven?"—while Richard plied the men with cognac-based sidecars and talked politics and business in the living room. The guests had left stuffed with good food and flushed thanks to the flowing alcohol, Nellie's reputation for being the dinner party hostess all the wives wanted to emulate intact.

She was pleased by how nice a time everyone seemed to have, and even Richard had been lifted out of his earlier mood, the gaiety of company and the cocktails bringing out his renowned charm. And for the first time in weeks his stomach appeared not to turn on him after dinner—he even had a second helping of dessert, and required no bismuth.

"Well done, Nell-baby," Richard murmured, coming behind her and wrapping his arms around her waist, kissing her softly in the divot between neck and shoulder. "I'm proud of you."

"Good heavens, for what?" Nellie asked, spinning slowly to face him, feeling warm from the gin.

"For all of this, after what you've been through," he said, gesturing to the table, still cluttered with dessert dishes and half-drunk glasses of wine and crumpled napkins. He moved his body closer to hers, gently caressing her cheek with his fingers. "You amaze me, Nellie."

She smiled and, disarmed by his genuine compliment, leaned in and kissed her husband. She didn't typically initiate intimacy, and Nellie felt Richard's body change against hers. "Did the doc say it was all right to, well . . . are you fine to, uh, get back to everything?" he asked.

One would think Richard Murdoch would have no problem

asking for what he wanted. In fact, he usually didn't ask. And Nellie found his hesitation, his uncertainty in this moment, oddly arousing, the way it had been early in their courtship. Back then being with Richard was intoxicating. He treated her like a prized rose, handling her gently, nurturing her delicate petals, proudly putting her on display in the fancy clothes and expensive jewelry he lavished upon her.

No man, including her father (perhaps especially her father), had ever fawned over Nellie the way Richard did in those early days. She had been young and naive, but she also wanted desperately to believe she was worthy of such affection.

Nellie nodded demurely, and Richard gave a sly smile. "Good, good. Coming up?" He leaned back to loosen his tie, but he didn't take his eyes off hers. Nellie glanced at the table, taking in the mess.

"Look, leave the dishes for the girl." Their girl, Helen (though Richard never referred to her by name), was scheduled for cleaning tomorrow. Nellie usually took that time to weed her garden, or visit with her neighbor Miriam, or do her marketing in town, because she was uncomfortable being in her home while Helen was there hard at work. Also, having someone underfoot all day was extra work in a different way—Nellie had things to hide.

"I will," she replied. "Though I'd like to write a few things down first."

"Now?" He was perturbed.

Nellie wasn't worried; he would be fine as soon as she slipped out of her dress, let him wind her stockings down her long, slim legs.

"Can't it wait until tomorrow?"

"I promised to give the dessert recipe to Gertrude, and I'd rather do it now, while it's fresh in my mind."

Richard watched her with drunk eyes, his mouth slightly open. "Don't make me wait too long, baby," he said, his voice thick.

"I won't." Nellie hadn't been intimate with Richard since before the miscarriage—the loss of the baby had wreaked havoc on her body and soul—but she was not one of those frigid wives she'd read about in her magazines. She would give herself to her husband tonight, and the warm glow of gin and the pleasure of a successful party meant she might even enjoy it. Besides, Nellie wanted a child as much as Richard did, and the sooner the better.

After Richard went upstairs, Nellie poured another small juice glass of gin, which she sipped at the kitchen table, pen in hand. She would write out the Baked Alaska recipe for Gertrude, as promised, but not until tomorrow. Nellie had something else to compose tonight. She took another sip of her drink and smoothed a hand over the paper, then started writing.

11

Your mind can accomplish things while your hands are busy. Do head work while dusting, sweeping, washing dishes, paring potatoes, etc. Plan family recreation, the garden, etc.
—*Betty Crocker's Picture Cook Book*, revised and enlarged (1956)

Alice

.....

JUNE 8, 2018

Alice sat on the floral sofa, her legs bouncing as she tried to sort out what to do.

The phone call was a shock. Thankfully, when it came Nate was already on the train to work and her mom and Steve on a plane, likely somewhere over Kansas. Every minute closer to the California warmth her mom hadn't stopped mentioning all week.

Finally alone, Alice planned to go for a jog (even if Greenville's streets were less inspiring than Central Park) and then do some writing. She was bored of her restlessness, so that morning after everyone left she gave herself a much-needed pep talk. "You live *here* now, so deal with it. You can fix up this house and write the bestselling novel of your dreams, and make it all look easy. This is hardly the most challenging thing you've had to do, Alice Hale. Get your damn running shoes on and stop acting like you don't know how to get shit done."

She was tugging on her socks when her phone rang, and her throat parched at the name on the screen. Alice's instincts told her to ignore it (she had nothing to say to her), yet suddenly her phone was to her ear. "Hello?"

"It's Georgia."

Alice stood up quickly, mouth open but nothing coming out.

"Georgia Wittington?" As if she wouldn't recognize her voice. Alice could picture her old boss: sitting in her corner office at the Wittington Group, her sharply angled bob hanging just so, her reading glasses (purple frames, designer) pushed into her hair while she stared out the floor-to-ceiling windows. The ones she complained endlessly about ("too much light," "can't see my screen," "too hot in the summer") but liked the status of—only very important people had such big windows.

"Yes, I know." Why was Georgia calling? For a moment Alice thought maybe she was going to apologize for how things went down. To admit projects were falling apart without her, and would Alice consider coming back? The idea of that pleased her, even though she'd never give Georgia the satisfaction of actually accepting.

"Listen. We have a problem."

Alice wanted to remind Georgia that *they* stopped having anything the moment she was fired.

"How can I help you?" Alice kept her tone light, as though what had happened hadn't destroyed her.

"It's James Dorian. He's suing."

"Oh, well. I can see how that is a problem." She cleared her throat, still pacing the living room in circles. "For *you*." It was satisfying talking to Georgia like that. Like she was no better than a pesky telemarketer. She had spent so many years trying to emulate her, feeling lucky the great Georgia Wittington had chosen to mentor her.

There was a sound of exasperation from Georgia, who was certainly busy and had better things to be doing. Alice knew all of Georgia's disapproving tones, having heard them enough times over the five years they'd worked together, and her Pavlovian response kicked in. Sweat beaded in her armpits and on her upper lip.

"Obviously I wouldn't be calling you if I didn't have to. If you weren't part of this."

Alice stopped pacing. "Part of what?"

"You're named in the lawsuit, Alice."

"What? Why?" Alice sputtered. But she knew exactly the *what* and the *why*, and sat heavily on the sofa as dread filled her belly; James Dorian hadn't been drunk enough to black out their conversation that night, like she'd hoped.

"He's suing the Wittington Group, but you're named in the suit."

"Georgia, I no longer work for the Wittington Group."

Her ex-boss tutted with irritation. "I have to take another call, but I need you to come to the office. Meet with our attorneys for the discovery process."

"Fine," Alice mumbled, wondering exactly how she was going to explain this to Nate. Especially if it turned into something bigger than an unpleasant and ill-timed meeting with Georgia and her legal team. "When?"

"Monday. Eleven."

"Georgia, that's not really—"

"Perfect. See you Monday."

After Georgia hung up, Alice took shallow breaths, trying to quell her rising worry. The house exhaled through its cracks as a gust of wind lapped the facade, and Alice shivered despite the heavy cardigan she wore over her T-shirt. She was desperate for a distraction and, strangely, for the first time in years, longed for a cigarette. The feeling of nicotine hitting her bloodstream was particularly soothing to jangled nerves. Alice had smoked in college and then sporadically until she met Nate, and hadn't had a cigarette since.

Alice rummaged through the front hall closet, a tiny rectangle of space that held only one row of shoes and exactly three coats. Shedding her sweater, she crouched, reaching for her sneakers, and quickly slipped them on. Then she grabbed a ten-dollar bill from her wallet and zipped it into her tights. Not bothering to lock the door, Alice sprinted down the sidewalk, knowing there was a 7-Eleven a few blocks away.

Out of shape, the 7-Eleven more like a dozen blocks away, Alice soon got a stitch in her side and opted to walk versus run home. The pack of cigarettes was bulky inside the band of her tights, and the sharp edges dug into her skin. She had no intention of actually smoking a cigarette, yet knowing she had the option relaxed her. Another pep talk ensued, though whispered this time as she walked the tree-lined sidewalks. "James Dorian got what he deserved. You don't owe Georgia *anything*. Nate does not need to know any of this. James Dorian got what he deserved. . . ."

Alice was less rattled by the time she got home, until she tried to open the front door and it wouldn't budge. Trying harder, she grasped the handle and wrenched it to the right. Then the left. *What the hell?* Stepping back, she put her hands on her hips and scowled. She had purposefully left the door unlocked so she wouldn't have to carry her keys. She was sure of it.

Grunting with frustration, she tried the handle again, twisting it left and right, and threw her shoulder against the door. Nothing. "Stupid old house," she muttered as she stomped around its side and to the backyard, the long grass tickling her bare ankles. At least it was a nice day. Warm without feeling muggy, the air fresh and full of the sounds of chirping birds, a nice respite from the somber, cold house. *It really is peaceful here.*

The backyard was good-size, the gardens carefully designed so someone standing exactly where Alice was—on the square of patio stones, back facing the house—would get eyefuls of bountiful blooms and greenery. Roses lined the fence to the left, pink and yellow mingling in such a precise pattern it was almost as though the flowers understood their order. A wooden shed tucked in close to the house held gardening tools—shears and spades and trimmers, stacks of paper garden bags for trimmings.

Alice took the cigarettes out of her tights and sat in one of the plastic garden chairs. Tapping the packet from one hand to the next, she noted glumly that weeds were already pushing back through the soil between the flowers, despite her mom's efforts over the week. She wished the gardens could be someone else's responsibility—there was just so damn much of it.

"I should just rip it all out . . . ," Alice said, closing her eyes and tipping her head back.

"Hello there!" Startled, Alice dropped the pack of cigarettes. Glancing sharply to her left, where the voice came from, she saw the next-door neighbor, a dirt-covered spade in her hands and a flurry of white curls poking out from underneath a large-brimmed sun hat.

"We haven't officially met," the elderly woman said, slipping off a gardening glove and extending her hand over the fence. "I'm Sally Claussen."

Alice stood quickly and walked over to the chain-link fence separating the yards. "Nice to meet you, Mrs. Claussen." They shook hands. "I'm Alice. Alice Hale."

"Please, call me Sally. Mrs. Claussen was my mother's name." The map of wrinkles on her face deepened in a gratifying way as she smiled. "Welcome to the neighborhood, Alice. Where are you coming from?"

"Manhattan. Murray Hill specifically."

"Ah, a city girl," Sally said. "Things are a bit different out here, aren't they?"

"They certainly are. I have no idea what to do with any of this." Alice gestured around the yard. "The extent of my gardening skills is a fern named Esther I somehow kept alive during college."

"I'm happy to give you a few tips, if you want. Though be warned these roses have resisted my hard work and dedication until recently. I didn't think they were ever going to bloom!" The roses weaved in and out of the fence between them, a sea of pink and yellow polka dots if she stood back far enough.

"My gardens won't win any awards, but luckily the only ones who care are me and the honeybees." She winked, and Alice decided she liked Sally Claussen.

"I may take you up on that. So how long have you lived here?"

"A while, on and off." Alice waited for her to elaborate, but she didn't. Sally placed a hand to her brow and shielded her eyes, the bendy brim of her sun hat flipping up slightly with the breeze. She pointed toward one corner of Alice's garden. "While I think of it, make sure you wear gloves if you touch those ones there."

Alice glanced in the direction Sally was pointing. "Which ones?"

"The foxglove," Sally said. "That pretty purple flowered one there, beside the hosta. It's toxic for us but is a great deer deterrent. They won't touch it."

"There are deer here?"

"Yes, but they're private creatures. Sometimes at dusk or dawn you'll see them. They especially love the hostas."

Alice thought the supposedly toxic plant seemed perfectly harmless. The flowers resembled bell-shaped slippers, grouped in satisfying lines that hung from the main stalk as though weighted from their centers. "This one? It's actually quite pretty."

"Isn't it?"

"The previous owner must have loved it. There's quite a lot." Alice noted aside from the bunch in front of her, it grew in two other spots in the garden.

"It seems she did," Sally said. "The plant also has another name; maybe you've heard of it? *Digitalis purpurea*."

"Doesn't sound familiar."

"They use foxglove to make digitalis, the heart medication." Sally put her glove back on. "But touching any part of the plant—leaves, flower, stem—with bare hands can cause a whole host of trouble. I once treated a child who made a salad out of the leaves. Managed to eat one leaf before her mom stopped her, but she was hospitalized for a week."

"I think things were safer in Manhattan."

Sally laughed. "You might be right there."

"So you were a physician?" Alice asked.

"A cardiologist. It was a wonderful job."

Alice thought Sally's patients had probably loved her.

"Now I'm a full-time gardener and part-time baker. Though I'm not as good at either of those as I was at medicine." She glanced at Alice's garden chair, pointedly drew her gaze to the pack of cigarettes. "You'll have to excuse my forwardness—at my age you simply say what you're thinking—but are you trying to quit, Alice?"

"Oh, I don't smoke. I mean, I used to. A while ago." Alice shrugged, seeing the combination of kindness and pity on Sally's face. "These are just in case of emergency."

Sally raised her brows. "I see. What's today's emergency?"

"A work thing." James Dorian's face came to mind. "It will be fine."

"I had a lot of smokers on my caseload, as you can imagine,"

Sally said. "And the only ones able to kick the habit were the ones who found something they enjoyed more. Something to distract them until they got over the urge of the habit."

"Good advice." Alice accepted that she was now a smoker in Sally's eyes. It was easier than trying to explain what had prompted her to have a pack of cigarettes in hand. "What do I owe you?"

"How about you quit those things and we'll call it even." Sally put a hand on her narrow hip, her beige khakis bunched at her tiny waist. "I guess I should get back to it. These roses won't prune themselves. But I'm happy to continue chatting."

Alice smiled, watched as Sally snipped the flowers' thorny stems. "You didn't say before, but how long have you lived here?"

"This was my childhood home, but when I left for medical school Mother stayed on." She pruned another few stems, gathering them in her hand before tossing the bunch into the paper yard-waste bag nearby. "Moved back about thirty years ago, after she died. I only meant to stay long enough to sell the place. But, well." She smiled. "Here I am." Alice wanted to ask if Sally had been married, or had any children. If she lived alone.

"Did you know the owners of our house?"

"Not well. They moved in after I went away to school. My mother was quite friendly with the wife. Eleanor Murdoch, though she went by Nellie." Sally kept on pruning, bending to get to the underside of the bush, her body agile for its age. "She kept to herself. Taught piano and voice lessons to children out of her living room for years. In the summer, I often heard her singing with her students, through the open windows. Beautiful voice." That explained the piano, which was no longer covered in dust thanks to Alice's cleaning, but still out of tune. "She was quite a stunning woman, and Mother often spoke of her green thumb. Those roses at the front of your house are certainly a testament to that."

"My mom said our garden was in good shape considering the state of the rest of the house. Someone who knew what they were doing had clearly been taking care of it."

"Nellie gardened early in the morning, nearly every day, but after she became ill she hired a landscaper to do the work. They stayed on even after she died, which is why your gardens are still so lovely." Sally placed the cut roses in a neat pile on the grass. "For years we lived side by side after I moved back, but we rarely spoke except for the odd pleasantry. A comment on the rainfall, or a coming cold snap. She once taught me how to bathe my peonies to get rid of the ants. That was the longest conversation we ever had."

Alice remembered the notation in the cookbook. *Eleanor's 13th birthday—delicious!* "I found some old magazines and a cookbook that I think belonged to her. Or someone she knew. Do you know the name Elsie Swann?"

"It does sound familiar, though I can't place why. My mind isn't as reliable as it used to be." Sally straightened and arched back slightly, rubbing her lower back absentmindedly.

"It's fine. I had a thought I'd try to return the cookbook."

"I suspect if someone left it behind it wasn't something they needed anymore."

"Maybe so," Alice murmured. "Well, it was nice to officially meet you, Sally. And I should get back to work myself."

"And solving that emergency."

"Yes. That too." Alice swiveled to look at her house and then, remembering she couldn't get inside, sighed. "But I seem to have locked myself out, so I guess I'll work on my tan until my husband gets home."

"Check under that pinkish rock by the back steps. I can't promise it's still there, but I remember that's where Nellie used to leave a spare key."

Alice lifted the granite rock, realizing it was fake—it was light, hollow when she tapped it. A small trapdoor in the rock's bottom opened to reveal a key. "I'm glad you were out here, Sally."

"Happy to help," Sally said. "And it was lovely to meet you, Miss Alice."

The two women exchanged goodbyes, and Alice scooped up the pack of cigarettes, assuring Sally they were going straight in the trash; she didn't want to disappoint her new neighbor. Back at the front of the house, Alice slid the key into the lock and before she could turn it the door creaked open, as though it hadn't been fully closed in the first place. She let go of the key—still lodged in the lock—as the door yawned open. "What the hell?"

Carefully she stepped into the house, a quick left-and-right glance to make sure it was empty. Satisfied she was alone, she opened and closed the door a few times to see if it was sticking. It wasn't. Alice fiddled with the lock, wondering if perhaps she had locked it from the inside when she left. After a few attempts, the mystery of the locked door remaining unsolved, she slid the cigarettes to the back of the desk's top drawer (she'd throw them out later, before trash day) and tugged on her sweater to combat the room's deep chill—*how can it be so nice outside and so freezing inside?* Her laptop was paces away, but she didn't feel inspired and so settled on the couch with the old cookbook instead.

It fell open at a recipe that must have been a favorite, judging by the number of spills on the page. Bread and Cheese Pudding. Alice scanned the ingredients, snuggling deeper into her sweater. Bread crumbs, cheese, milk, and eggs. Dash of paprika, which she was fairly certain she didn't own. There was a notation beside the recipe: *Perfect for after church. E.S.* And underneath in blue pen, *Sprinkle with 1 tbsp of Swann herb mix.*

Alice set the cookbook on the kitchen countertop, then took the butter, milk, eggs, and cheese from the fridge. After checking, and confirming, that she did not have paprika, she added extra black pepper as a compromise and a sprinkle of dried basil to replace the herb mix she couldn't find an ingredients list for. Because cooking for oneself was not a necessary life skill in the city (and having been raised by a mother who could barely make eggs edible), Alice was generally useless in the kitchen. But she wanted to be better, so it was time she figured a few things out. Not the least of which was how to cook a decent meal. Besides, Alice had been responsible for some of the Wittington Group's most important clients; she could certainly get dinner on the table by the time Nate came home. The pudding came together easily, and Alice, feeling accomplished despite its simplicity, gave herself a virtual pat on the back and popped the casserole dish into the oven, curious as to how a sixty-plus-year recipe would turn out.

12

Nellie

....

JUNE 11, 1956

·

Busy Day Cake

½ cup butter

⅓ teaspoon lemon or vanilla extract

1¾ cups granulated sugar

2½ cups sifted Purity Flour

¼ teaspoon salt

2 teaspoons baking powder

1 cup sweet milk

4 egg whites, unbeaten

Cream butter until it is soft and creamy, and add flavoring while creaming. Add sugar. Sift together flour, salt, and baking powder and add to butter mixture, followed immediately by the milk and unbeaten egg whites. Stir mixture quickly and gently until it is well blended. Spread carefully into well-greased 7 x 12-inch cake pan and bake in moderate oven (350°F) for 60 to 65 minutes. Allow baked cake to set for 20 to 25 minutes before removing from pan. Cool and spread with any desired icing.

*N*ellie held tight to the cake carrier's handle with one hand, shutting her front door with the other. It was nearly noon, but Katherine "Kitty" Goldman—the hostess for today's Tupperware party, starting at 12:00 P.M. "sharp"—lived only a block away, so Nellie knew she had plenty of time to make the short walk.

It was a fine day, and the warm breeze felt wonderful. The skirt of her mint-green dress swished as she walked, her feet content thanks to her decision to wear flatties. Everyone else would be in heels, but Nellie didn't care much about fitting in. Plus, her kitten heels would be back on tonight once Richard got home from work, so she'd enjoy the comfort now.

She made her way up the front walk, slowly so her free hand could stroke the peonies' bountiful pink blooms framing the Murdochs' front garden. Nellie murmured sweet lullabies to them as she did, nurturing the flowers the way she would a child if she were ever lucky enough to have one. Turning onto the sidewalk, she eyed her roses—yellow, stunning—which were her pride and joy, and on full display for the neighborhood. Soon she'd have to deadhead them to allow for a second bloom cycle. Roses were a lot of work, but they gave much in return.

Nellie passed by the last of her roses, nestled behind the white picket fence that squared off the Murdochs' yard, and noticed her neighbor Miriam Claussen tending her own front garden. Miriam was bent over a large bunch of peonies, her back to Nellie, cutting the flowers low on the stem and neatly piling them on the grass beside her like fallen soldiers.

"Hello, Miriam," Nellie called out. "Your peonies are exquisite this year."

"Oh, hello there, dear," Miriam said, her voice strong, lightly musical. Even though Miriam Claussen was in her late fifties, her mind and attitude were those of a much younger woman. Age had not been as kind to her body, however. She straightened with some difficulty, gardening shears in her hands, which were thick with arthritis. Knuckles as big as the knobs on Nellie's dresser of drawers. "That's high praise coming from you. This splendid weather we've been having has certainly agreed with them."

Miriam tilted her sun hat to see better and then knitted her brow, taking in Nellie's cardigan sweater, buttoned up to the top and excessive for the day's predicted temperature. "Are you quite well, dear?"

"A touch of a tickle." Nellie cleared her throat, tugging on one sleeve of the sweater, hoping it covered what it needed to. "But I'll be fine."

"I'm glad to hear it, dear." She was always pleased to see Nellie, and the feeling was mutual. Miriam would often bring over cakes or cookies or, on occasion, a casserole, clucking at Nellie for being wisp thin. Mr. Claussen had died some years before, and their only child, Sally, was in medical school, so Miriam had no one left at home to enjoy her cooking. Nellie had never known a woman so ambitious as to become a doctor and wished she and Richard had moved in before Sally left home. She would have loved to ask her what it was like to do exactly as she wished. "I could never hold that child back from anything," Miriam had once said about her daughter. "Good thing too. Because Lord knows that's what we're supposed to do with our girls."

Nellie sometimes daydreamed of a different life than the one she had; a less stifled one, where she could be more than the childless Mrs. Richard Murdoch. If she had married Georgie Britton instead, the sweet boy she was steady with until his father got a job in Missouri and moved the family, maybe by now she would have children and the reverence of motherhood. Or perhaps if she had never met Richard she would have lived in a quaint little apartment in the city, with only a small kitchen table and one chair. A hot plate, no oven to fill. Like her high school chum Dorothy, who wanted to be an architect and never much cared for men. Maybe Nellie could have sung advertisements on the radio; she would have liked that. Or maybe she would have gone to school to become a music teacher. If she hadn't been so keen to be married, frankly believing it the gateway to a pleasing and bountiful life, Nellie might have discovered the secret to happiness.

Miriam made her way to where Nellie stood by the picket fence, removing her gardening gloves as she did, revealing angry-looking hands—red and inflamed, her fingers crooked. Nellie's own hands were smooth, fingers long and capped off by rounded nails that held a good dollop of shiny polish.

"How are your hands today?" Nellie asked, though it was clear they were anything but good.

"Fine, fine." Miriam waved away the concern. "Nothing a little cider vinegar won't fix." Nellie knew Miriam bathed her hands most nights in a bowl of warm apple cider vinegar, claiming it eased the pain, though her daughter often chastised her for this home remedy. But Miriam didn't like pills, didn't like doctors, even if her own daughter would soon become one. Bert Claussen had done everything right, going to his doctor when he fell ill without Miriam having to nag him much. But they hadn't found the cancer until it was too late for poor Bert.

"I'm headed to a Tupperware party over at Kitty Goldman's place, but why don't I come by a little later this afternoon and help you finish up?"

"You're so kind to offer, Nellie, but I'm sure I'll be fine," she said, swatting her gloves against a nearby fence picket to get rid of the loose dirt. "You best be on your way. It looks like you have your hands full there."

"My mom's Busy Day Cake," Nellie said, lifting the carrier slightly. "With lemon frosting and some violets from the garden

I sugared." Her mother had often made the cake for social gatherings, telling Nellie everyone appreciated a simple cake.

"It's only when you try to get too fancy do you find trouble," Elsie was fond of saying, letting Nellie lick the buttercream icing from the beaters as she did. Some might consider sugaring flowers "too fancy," but not Elsie Swann—every cake she made carried some sort of beautiful flower or herb from her garden, whether it was candied rose petals or pansies, or fresh mint or lavender sugar. Elsie, a firm believer in the language of flowers, spent much time carefully matching her gifted blooms and plants to their recipients. Gardenia revealed a secret love; white hyacinth, a good choice for those who needed prayers; peony celebrated a happy marriage and home; chamomile provided patience; and a vibrant bunch of fresh basil brought with it good wishes. Violets showcased admiration—something Nellie did not have for the exhausting Kitty Goldman but certainly did for the simple deliciousness of her mother's Busy Day Cake.

"Oh, how very lovely, Nellie." Miriam's voice was wistful, and Nellie understood the loneliness behind her tone. She felt it too, for different reasons. "Just lovely."

"I'll save you a piece. I'll bring it over later along with my gardening gloves. All right?"

Miriam seemed pleased. "I'll send you home with a casserole for supper. I made a little more than I needed today." Nellie wondered how long it took to become accustomed to cooking for one. She suspected that after spending so many years with someone the way Miriam and Bert had, one always made enough for two because not doing it was harder.

"Oh, and before I let you go, tell me. What's your secret for getting rid of the ants?" Miriam asked. "I love a vase of peonies on my kitchen table, but those blasted ants end up everywhere. I even found some inside my butter dish last week!"

"Give them a bath," Nellie said.

Miriam cocked her head. "A bath? The ants?"

Nellie laughed, but kindly. "Fill a sink with warm water and a few drops of dish soap, and give the flowers a bath. They'll bounce right back and there will be no ants."

"You are so wise, Nellie Murdoch." Miriam tugged her gloves back on. "Maybe you should run a class for those of us with black thumbs at the church. I bet you'd have a packed house."

"I like to keep some secrets for myself. And for my favorite neighbor," Nellie replied with a wink. "I'll see you later?"

"I'm looking forward to it," Miriam said. "Enjoy your party. I hear Kitty has a spiffy new kitchen." She leaned closer, one hand coming up to shield her mouth as though she was sharing with Nellie a great secret. "Not that she needs it. That woman couldn't boil water if her life depended on it."

Nellie chuckled. Kitty was a ditz, notorious for her lack of kitchen skills (they would likely be served cold sandwiches today, perhaps a jelly salad of some sort) and her wagging tongue, all of which made her someone Nellie had little time for.

"I'll bring back a full report." Nellie was looking forward to her visit with Miriam later, much more so than to this darn Tupperware party. All those gossipy women fawning over pink- and peach- and yellow-hued plastic bowls, talking about how a casserole dish would change their lives. Nellie waved to Miriam and set out on her way, her armpits slick with sweat, and wished she wasn't wearing the cardigan. But no matter how sweltering the day got, or how many times she had to explain she was coming down with something, taking the sweater off was not an option.

The first time Nellie outright lied to her husband about something that mattered coincided with the first time she discovered a lipstick stain on his shirt collar—a gaudy, dark red color that would never graze Nellie's delicate lips.

It was a couple of weeks before the Tupperware party, and Nellie's garden had finally woken up, the days growing longer and warmer. The peonies were nearly ready to burst; Miriam's lilac bush had exploded with lavender-hued flowers whose heady perfume stretched a half block away; and the lilies, tall as they reached to the sun, bloomed fiery orange. Nellie had been anxious to get to her garden that morning and so had put off Richard's laundering—her least favorite of the household tasks. But the next morning, when Richard realized his "lucky" shirt (identical, as far as Nellie could tell, to all his others) hadn't been pressed for that day's important meeting, he had grabbed her forcefully. The bruise left behind—deep purple dots in a line along her arm, the shape of Richard's fingertips—lingered longer than the others had, which was why Nellie had been forced into a sweater the day of Kitty Goldman's Tupperware party.

When Richard had finally released her arm that fateful morning, he tossed the shirt at her feet and demanded she do her "goddamn job." Nellie dropped to her knees, clutching her arm, while Richard glared at her with disdain. She waited on the bedroom floor until the front door shut before picking up Richard's discarded shirt, which was when she noticed the stain. Nellie stared at it a good long while, her heart rate increasing as the realization of what it meant settled in.

Later that day she dialed Richard's number at work, holding his soiled, deceitful shirt in her hands. "The rabbit died," Nellie said the moment Richard's girl, Jane, transferred her call. "The rabbit died, Richard."

"What? You mean . . . ?"

"I suspected it," she said, trying to infuse as much joy into her voice as she could. "But I didn't want to say anything until after my appointment this morning, and oh, Richard . . . I do hope you're pleased?"

"Pleased? How could I not be?" he boomed with delight, before quickly lowering his voice. "And, Nellie, I'm sorry about, uh, earlier. Sometimes you make me so . . . Well, never mind that. You have made me a happy man today. A very happy man." And he sounded it. All puffed up, she could imagine it, standing on his tiptoes to make himself seem grander than he was. Probably opening a bottle to pour something in celebration, already waving at Jane with her red, painted-on lips to find a booze-hound colleague to share the news with.

"I'm glad," she'd whispered, clutching his shirt tighter, wishing she could rip it to shreds. "You've been so patient, Richard."

There was nothing Richard wanted more than progeny, specifically a son to carry on the family business (as if Nellie had any control over gender), and the diamond tennis bracelet he presented her with later that night was his way of proving it. As was his kinder, gentler nature, which he seemed able to turn on and off with disturbing ease.

That evening, after clasping the bracelet around her delicate wrist, Richard made her put her feet up on the sofa and cooked them eggs for dinner, though they were rubbery because he left them in the frying pan too long. After taking her plate, not noticing she'd barely touched her eggs, Richard added another pillow under her feet and gave her a serious look.

"I expect you'll take better care of yourself this time?"

"Oh, I will," she assured him. "I most certainly will."

13

Don't expect life to be all sunshine. Besides, if there are no clouds, you will lose the opportunity of showing your husband what a good chum you can be.

—Blanche Ebbutt, *Don'ts for Wives* (1913)

Alice

.....

JUNE 11, 2018

*A*lice woke to her phone buzzing on the nightstand. A text from Nate, who was already on the train.

Don't forget the lawn company. Good luck with your lunch!

She squinted bleary-eyed at her phone's screen: *8:07 a.m.* Exhausted—her anxiety about Georgia, her anger at James Dorian, and her guilt about lying to Nate squashing any chance at falling back to sleep—Alice stared at the ceiling crack, wishing she could stay in bed. Call in sick today on her life.

Rather than admit her meeting with Georgia, and everything that had led to it, she'd told Nate she was going into the city to meet an editor friend to get a few novel-writing tips. "That's a great idea," Nate had said. He'd asked then how the writing was going, and she'd kept things vague, offering, "It's coming along." The truth was Alice had yet to write a thing.

But it wasn't only the writing that was stalled. Despite their efforts and dollars spent trying to spruce it up, the house remained disgruntled with the Hales. Already a half-dozen things had gone wrong: first, there were the flickering lights, which led to a large electrical repair bill estimate (they decided to live with the flickers); then the newel-post came loose, followed by two of the stair treads, requiring vigilance when going up and down so as not to take a tumble; next, a bird hit one of the bedroom windows and cracked the glass—double paned, antique, expensive to replace; the chills and drafts continued, and it was decided new windows could be the answer but there was no budget for that. And finally, only yesterday, the bathroom tap came off in Alice's hands, soaking the floor and requiring a supremely costly Sunday-afternoon plumber. Even Nate, eternally positive, had finally agreed things could be going better with the house.

While in Murray Hill the beginning of a new week would bring the sounds of harried, jam-packed city dwellers getting to and from, in Greenville things remained quiet. No honking. No sounds of pedestrian traffic marching on below. A few bird whistles mingled with the sound of a rumbling truck in the distance. . . .

Alice sat straight up in bed. *The garbage.*

She wasn't used to the rhythm of suburban life. Rather than a garbage chute, they had two large bins in their garage, one for trash and one for recycling, which Alice was supposed to remember to put out Monday mornings. She'd forgotten entirely last week, had gone back to bed as soon as Nate left and slept right through the trucks worming their way through the neighborhood. Combined with a week of heat, the trash stank up the entire garage, and Alice had promised she wouldn't forget this Monday.

Tugging on the jeans she'd abandoned on the floor the

evening before, she quickly zipped them up and pulled a sweater over her head before racing down the stairs, nearly wiping out on the wiggly tread, swearing as she did. Slamming her feet into her flip-flops, she threw open the front door and then noticed the bins lined up neatly at the end of the driveway. Her phone vibrated in her back pocket.

I put the garbage out. Remember I'm home late—study session.

Alice tapped back a quick response. On it with the lawn. I'll wait up for you. Xo

She ran a hand through her messy tangle of hair, pulling her fingers to the ends and gathering the stray strands as she did. A few got caught in the clasps of her wedding band, and she tugged those out as she perused the lawn. The grass was long, and patches of sunny dandelions and other weeds poked up through the green here and there.

"Good morning, Alice." Sally Claussen was on her front stoop. "Trash usually gets picked up by eight fifteen, but sometimes it's closer to eight thirty," she said, opening her own garage. "I like to wait until the last minute because of the squirrels and raccoons." She disappeared inside the garage, was back a moment later lugging a large bin. "They can make a terrible mess. Smart critters, those raccoons. I've seen them pry open locked lids."

"No kidding," Alice said. "Here, let me get that for you." She took the bin's handles from Sally. "Just this one?"

"Yes. Thank you." Sally wore beige slacks with a navy belt, and a light blue blouse with three-quarter-length sleeves, her white hair pulled back neatly in a low bun. She had a narrow silk scarf tied around her neck—blue and green polka dots—and the entire combination was well put together and stylish. Alice, by comparison, was a disheveled mess of denim and wrinkled cotton.

Alice carried the bin to the end of Sally's driveway, and it bumped against her thighs with each step. Sally walked beside her. "I wanted to ask, do you use a lawn company?"

"There's a young man a couple of blocks over who runs a summer business. He's a student in the city but lives at home with his parents over the break. I'll give you his number. Good prices, hard worker."

"The outside work feels like a full-time job." Alice set the bin down and brushed her hands on her jeans. "So, yes, I'd love that number."

"I'll get it for you right now. Do you have time for a coffee?"

She thought about Georgia and James and the attorneys whom she had to face in only a couple of hours. "I wish I could, but I have an appointment. Maybe tomorrow?"

"Tomorrow it is."

Alice scowled at her lawn. "It would be a lot easier if I liked doing this stuff."

Sally nodded. "You might surprise yourself. I have to say the gardening has grown on me over the years."

The garbage truck turned onto their street, the screech of brakes interrupting them. Sally waved to the man who jumped off the back of the truck, and he waved back. "Morning, Ms. Claussen," he said, taking one earbud out, tucking it swiftly under the brim of his ball cap. He had a trim beard and a dimple when he smiled, which made him look younger than he likely was.

"Hello, Joel. How are the girls?"

"Doing great. Eva learned to tie her shoes, and Maddie won her soccer game yesterday."

"Good for them!" Sally clapped her hands together with delight, as though they were her own grandchildren. "Joel, this is Alice Hale. She and her husband moved in recently."

"Nice to meet you, Alice," Joel said. "Welcome to the

neighborhood." He swiftly emptied the trash cans, then held one in each hand. "Want me to run these back up for you, ladies?"

"Thanks, I can do it," Alice replied, then, after Joel swung himself back onto the truck and waved goodbye, added, "He seems like a nice guy."

"Oh, he is," Sally said, fiddling with the ends of her scarf. "Handsome, too. I always enjoy trash day."

Alice laughed, liking Sally more and more.

The drive to the Scarsdale train station took fewer than five minutes, a quick hop across the Bronx River. Alice was getting better at driving; the suburbs offered a tranquil experience for those nervous behind the wheel, thanks to wide streets and an overall languid pace. As Alice pulled into a parking spot near the station, she marveled again at how quaint Scarsdale was. Tidy brick and stone storefronts, with colorful awnings and flags flying from antique-looking light posts. Perfectly placed trees and manicured green spaces. Outdoor café patios dotted with a smattering of white umbrellas to shield patrons from the beaming sun. It made her envious, how perfectly pulled together this town was—so unlike her current life.

The train ride went too quickly for Alice, and an hour later she stood in front of the Wittington Group's building on Broadway in her suit and highest heels, trying to muster the nerve to walk through the door. With a deep breath that did little to quell the acid rolling in her stomach from a too-large coffee and from the truth she'd been hiding for months, she squared her shoulders and marched into the building.

"Oh, hey, Alice," Sloan McKenzie, the receptionist, said when Alice pushed through the heavy glass doors of the Wittington Group's offices. She beamed a sugary smile Alice knew from experience wasn't genuine. "I'll let Georgia know you're here."

Sloan busied herself calling Georgia, and Alice waited by the desk, marveling at how straight Sloan's hair was, nary a wave or stray strand in sight. Alice remembered her regular blowouts and frequent wax appointments with a whiff of longing, self-consciously tugging at her hair's ends, which had flipped up with the humidity. It had been only a few months since she'd graced this office daily, but already Alice felt out of step and uncomfortable in her business attire.

"She'll be a few minutes. You can take a seat if you want," Sloan said.

"I'm fine standing. Thanks." Her shoes pinched her toes and a nasty blister was brewing on her left heel and she really needed a washroom. The coffee had worked its way to her bladder, and her stomach was bloated inside the unforgiving waistband of her skirt, whose zipper was now one deep breath away from splitting. Sitting would only make everything worse.

"Up to you." Sloan shrugged, back to typing whatever she had been working on when Alice arrived. Probably something on social media, or maybe a note to her colleagues: *Guess who's standing in front of me right now?? Alice Hale!!!! She looks like shit, FYI!!*

Alice texted Bronwyn—who was on a business trip to Chicago for a couple of days—so she appeared as busy as Sloan was, but she didn't get a chance to finish it before Georgia appeared.

"Thanks for coming in." Georgia said, her tone laced with disapproval. It had been nearly five months since they'd last seen each other and the mutual animosity remained palpable. "Please hold my calls."

Sloan said she would, then gave Alice a sympathetic smile, but again, it seemed fabricated.

Alice tried to keep up, limping with her blistered heel, but trailed Georgia—whose heels were as high, if not higher. Soon they were at the large meeting room not far from Alice's old office. There were two dark-suited people already inside, a man and a woman—the attorneys, Alice presumed—and a small plate of dried-out-looking pastries.

Georgia didn't bother introducing the others in the room, so Alice decided to name them Tweedledee (woman) and Twee-dledum (man) in her mind. "Before we start I'd like to remind you that I expect discretion here. Please try to keep what we discuss in this room between us. I hope you can manage that . . . this time." She glared at Alice, who withered as she took her seat, setting her phone facedown on the table.

The female attorney, Tweedledee, spoke first. "So, as I be-lieve Georgia has already mentioned, Mr. Dorian has named you in the suit, Mrs. Hale, and he claims—"

"Alice is fine," she said, interrupting.

The woman nodded, continued. "He claims he was having a private conversation, in a hotel room paid for by the firm he em-ployed. The same one that signed a nondisclosure agreement."

Alice cleared her throat, tried to calm her pounding heart. "I've been out of the game for a few months, but does a drunken chat with your publicist really count as a privileged conversation?" The attorneys ignored the question, and Georgia muttered some-thing under her breath. Alice knew the contract terms as well as everyone else in the room.

"On the note of alcohol," Tweedledum said, flipping through a few pages in the folder in front of him, "James Dorian says he asked for water—repeatedly—and that Mrs. Hale, Alice, kept giving him vodka instead, saying it would relax him for his speech."

"That's bullshit!" Alice lurched forward, slapped her palms

against the shiny mahogany table, which looked like a surfboard. She had spent many hours huddled around that table, and despite the unpleasantness of the current meeting, a wave of nostalgia moved through her.

"Alice, calm down." Georgia sighed and looked at the male attorney as though to say, *See what I've had to deal with?*

"Mr. Dorian claims you put words into his mouth. He had mentioned his student, uh—" The man paused to find the name. "Robert Jantzen, was hired to help him with the book as a fact-checker and in a minor research capacity, and you misconstrued his role. He mentioned you had been drinking to excess, as well."

"Again, complete bullshit." Alice's head whipped between the attorneys and Georgia. "Georgia, you know what James is like. He's a drunk. And I tried to keep him as sober as I could." She pressed her fingers to her closed eyes, counted to three as she inhaled as deeply as her skirt allowed, which wasn't enough to quell her light-headedness. Alice was frustrated by how meek her voice sounded when she continued. "Besides, you told me to 'take care of him' and do whatever was necessary to make him happy."

Tweedledee looked up from her papers, frowning. "What did you mean by that, Georgia?"

Georgia waved a hand. "Nothing. Alice tends to be overly dramatic during crisis situations."

The male attorney spoke before Alice could defend herself.

"Alice?" He faced her. "Care to elaborate on that last part?"

"Let's just say James Dorian likes his booze, and *I was told* to make sure we always had vodka and bourbon—his favorites—on hand."

"Told by whom?"

"By Georgia," Alice said. "But it was a balancing act, because James got handsy if he drank too much, you know?"

Tweedledum raised an eyebrow, glanced at Tweedledee, who leaned forward, her gaze piercing Alice.

"'Handsy'?" The attorney narrowed her eyes.

Alice looked at her, confused another woman didn't understand what she was saying. "You know, a bit touchy-feely. The drunker he got, the higher the probability his hands would end up on your knee, or somewhere else."

"Alice, did James Dorian make any unwanted advances without your explicit consent?"

Alice barked out a laugh. "Is that a real question?" James Dorian's hands-on ways were no secret at the firm, or more generally within New York's publishing world.

"If there was some sort of sexual misconduct, well, that could change things," Tweedledum said to his colleague, who nodded as she took a few notes. Alice felt the shift in the room, Georgia's sudden fidgeting with the top of her water bottle. Twisting it repeatedly as she stared at Alice, her expression difficult to read.

"I assure you, nothing sinister happened," Georgia said. "I would never put an employee in that sort of situation. James Dorian is a pompous ass who likes his liquor, but sexual misconduct? Never."

Alice stared at her former boss. "Georgia, come on. You and I both know that's not true."

There was a long moment of silence, and then the woman attorney said, "Have we missed something here?"

Georgia sighed, finally uncapping her water bottle and taking a sip through the straw that popped up. She was a pro, and Alice knew Georgia was trying to work out her spin before she spoke.

"Georgia?" the woman asked.

Alice watched her former employer sip at the straw, waiting for her to respond, which was when she saw it: the uncharacteristic alarm in Georgia's expression—subtle, likely undetected by those who didn't know her as well. In a flush of satisfaction, the never-rattled Georgia Wittington unsteady, Alice acknowledged how powerless she had become these past few months . . . and how badly she wanted to change that.

14

Be a good listener. Let him tell you his troubles; yours will seem trivial in comparison.

  —Edward Podolsky, *Sex Today in Wedded Life* (1947)

Alice

.....

JANUARY 9, 2018

*I*t happened earlier in the year, at an event where one of the Wittington Group's best clients, the mega-bestselling author James Dorian, was up for yet another award. And Alice had been tasked, like always, with making sure James showed up and made it to the stage when his name was called.

The Wittington Group had booked a pre-party room for James at the hotel where the literary awards were being held, so he could relax before the event but also so they could be sure he wouldn't be late. James arrived already drunk, and with a pointed interest in Alice's smooth, taut legs under her skirt. James Dorian had been married for twenty-five years, but that was beside the point. He loved the power he presumed came with his status, which occasionally meant a valuable, career-boosting endorsement for an up-and-coming writer and at other times meant his hands landed in inappropriate places.

"Do not leave his side," Georgia had barked out as she left the office for her blowout. "Whatever he wants, you give it to him." She was fairly certain Georgia didn't literally mean *anything*, but then again Alice wouldn't have put it past Georgia. She was ruthless when it came to business.

While Alice didn't care much for Dorian or his ego or his sloppy hands, she did care about the promotion Georgia had been dangling in recent months. *Director of publicity.* The title meant James Dorian would no longer be her problem—he would be relegated to a lowlier publicity manager—and Alice would get a decent salary hike, both things she coveted. But tonight she would do the job asked of her and babysit Dorian until she delivered him to the awards ceremony.

"Why don't you join me?" James said, patting a spot beside him on the hotel room sofa. "Get yourself a drink." Alice poured water into the crystal glass, sat beside him. His breath was boozy and bourbon spiced as he leaned toward her, resting one hand on her bare knee. This she was used to, sadly, and she didn't let it bother her.

"We have to be downstairs in five minutes, James," Alice said, taking a sip of her water. "Perhaps we should make that the last one for now?" She glanced at the glass in his other hand, which was tipped at a precarious angle, the dark amber liquid threateningly close to the edge.

"Now, now, Alice," he slurred. "I know Georgia wants you to make sure I'm happy." He drained the glass, smacked his thin lips. "And I'm not done yet." He held out his glass, and she begrudgingly filled it once more.

Alice handed him the glass, and he took it, patting the sofa again as he did. She sat with a restrained sigh, and he settled his palm on her thigh, tucked a lazy finger under her skirt's edge. "This is nice, isn't it?" he murmured.

"Can I get you anything else before we go?" Alice asked, her voice strong, her words purposeful. Dorian's fingers continued making lazy circles on her upper thigh. "James?"

"Georgia should watch out for you." He pulled his hand away to waggle a finger, cocking his bushy eyebrows tinged with wiry gray hairs. "You're twice the publicist she is, and I suspect you're going to knock her right off her fucking pedestal." He made a sweeping motion, and his drink spilled on Alice's lap. She jumped up, the pooling liquid draining off her skirt.

"Shit." She opened a bottle of sparkling water and used a linen napkin to dab at the spot. Dorian seemed unaware of what he'd done; he kept talking and swinging his glass around.

"You're a good writer too. Show plenty of promise. Maybe I should be the one to watch out." He chortled into his glass, amused with himself.

"Mmm-hmm," Alice mumbled, only half paying attention. James was often free with his praise when he was drunk, but it didn't usually amount to much, she had learned.

"I like you, Alice. There's something different about you. You'd make a great character. You're soft and sweet on the outside . . ." His fingers reached for her, but she was far enough away to avoid his touch. He stood, swaying, and poked her breastbone with a sharp finger, hurting her. "But not on the inside. No. You're hard in there. Calculating. You have secrets, all locked up. I can tell."

Alice stepped back so his finger no longer made contact. "Is that right?" She was so done with James Dorian. She couldn't wait for that director title; she had earned it a hundred times over.

"Tell me one of your secrets, Alice."

Her phone buzzed in her clutch, the sound of it reverberating on the glass coffee table. Likely Georgia.

"I don't have any secrets."

"Everyone has secrets!" He laughed, delighted by her resistance. Feeding on it. "I'll tell you one if you tell me one."

This was typically how their interactions went. James uninterested in doing what was required of him, trying to change the game ever so slightly. They'd also had a similar conversation a few weeks earlier, at a dinner with Georgia and his agent, where they'd discussed the plan for his next venture—a screenplay he'd been promising to write for a year but hadn't yet gotten to. While Georgia went to freshen up in the ladies' room and the agent took a call, James asked Alice to tell him something that scared her and he promised to do the same. She made up some bullshit about a plane crash—she had fears, but that wasn't one of them—and he told her his was being irrelevant. *So predictable,* she'd wanted to say.

"We have to get down there. We can talk secrets later."

He pouted, crossed his arms over his chest. "All work and no play makes James a very dull boy."

He poured more bourbon into his glass, then filled another one, which he handed to Alice. He generally stuck with vodka until later in the evening, so the addition of bourbon this early on meant things were going to get messy.

"If I tell you a secret, do you promise to come downstairs with me?" Alice asked.

He took a gulp of the bourbon, nodded.

"Fine." Alice sipped her drink. The bourbon burned, but she didn't mind the flavor. "I ran over the neighbor's cat when I was sixteen and told everyone it was the FedEx driver." She tipped her glass back, finished the drink so quickly her eyes watered. "I'm allergic to cats. It might not have been an accident."

James stared at her, a small smile playing on his lips. "Really?"

"Really," Alice said. It wasn't entirely true. It was her high school friend who drove over the cat (by accident, backing out of the driveway too fast, the day after she got her license), and then blamed her elderly neighbor. But when her friend's dad reminded her they had security cameras trained on the driveway, she'd had to confess.

"See?" James said, pointing his glass toward Alice. "You *are* hard on the inside. And I'm getting hard just thinking about it." He said the last part quietly, as though he never intended Alice to hear it. But she did, and it took everything in her to not walk out the door.

"Okay, drink up and let's go." Alice's phone continued to beep and buzz. They were late, and James Dorian was not going to keep her from this promotion.

"Don't you want to know my secret?" he asked, eyelids drooping as he drained his glass. *Damn.* She'd have to water down his next few drinks if they had any hope of getting through the ceremony. "It's a good one."

"Sure," she said, grabbing her purse and checking her phone. *Georgia.* "Tell me your secret." She typed back a quick response, letting Georgia know they were on their way. She expected to be underwhelmed by whatever Dorian said, so she was barely paying attention. He was one of those men who believed everything he did was fascinating. He was a brilliant writer, she'd give him that, but the rest of him could use an upgrade.

"Sit, sit," he murmured. Alice contemplated telling him there was no time to sit; they had to go. But curiosity won out and so she sat. He rested his hand back on her thigh, tickling her skin through the skirt's fabric.

"James," she said, warning in her voice. Her phone buzzed again. "So what's this secret?" Alice was impatient, irritated by his fingers and by Georgia's constant texts.

"Oh, it's a good one." His hand slid higher.

"Stop it," Alice said, her jaw tense as she clenched her teeth to prevent herself from spitting in his face, or telling him exactly what she thought of him. There was a moment of tension between them before James shrugged, letting his hand drop.

"Christ. Take it easy, Alice." He got up from the couch, swaying like a flag in a stiff breeze, and walked to the full-length mirror. "So, my book, *Widen the Fall?*" he said, trying to straighten his bow tie as he looked in the mirror, making it more crooked. *Widen the Fall* was his most famous novel, published eight years earlier, which launched him from a highly acclaimed yet soft-selling novelist to his current status of world-famous, award-winning author.

"What about it?" Alice held her impatience in check. Georgia was getting more pissed with every passing text. Alice needed to speed things along and went to stand beside James so she could straighten his tie.

But he turned and leaned close to her, rested his hands on her shoulders (letting one settle too close to her breast), and used them to prop up his weight. She flinched but engaged her muscles to hold him up. Alice raised her eyebrows. Waited.

"I didn't write it." He released her all at once, putting her off-balance. The he clapped his hands together and said, "Okay, let's go."

"Wait. What do you mean you didn't write it?" she asked, steadying herself. But James was rifling through his pockets, talking to himself under his breath as he did. Completely oblivious now that he had her undivided attention. "James, what do you mean you didn't write it?"

"I didn't write it. It was my idea, and I had an outline obviously." *Sure you did.* "But I paid this college kid in one of my classes—Robbie Jantzen—who was desperate for a grade I would never give him otherwise and was a total suck-up. But he was talented. I could tell right away, and I knew," he started, holding up one finger, "I knew he could do it. Raw talent. Terrible judgment, but an excellent writer."

"Does Georgia know about this?"

"Now, come on, Alice. Don't tell me I misjudged you." He gave her a wry look. Yes, Georgia knew. She didn't take on clients whose narratives she couldn't control, and being able to do that well meant knowing their secrets.

Alice stood motionless, taking in what James said. That his most famous work—the one the *New York Times* called "brilliant and cunning and sure to become an American classic"— was in fact written by a twenty-something college student with a debt to pay and a hard-on for the elusive A grade James Dorian never handed out.

James put his finger to his lips and let out a long *Shhh- hhhhh*. "But don't tell anyone, sweet Alice. Maybe one day you and I could collaborate on something. You want to write a novel, right?" Alice couldn't remember ever having shared that with him. "Oh, don't look so surprised. All you girls want to write a goddamn novel. As transparent as your short skirts and desperate ambition." Alice pressed her lips together, wishing she could tell the loathsome James Dorian where he could stick his assumptions. But he wasn't wrong, at least about the ambition when it came to writing—Alice had on occasion imagined her name printed on the cover of a book, had been playing around with a loose idea set in the public relations world.

"Anyway, I bet we could come up with something fantastic." He swayed again, fiddled with the fly on his pants. Alice looked away. "I have to take a piss. Be right back."

James went on to win his award, and Georgia gave Alice a loaded look after they stuffed the semiconscious author into the car service limo, smiling as she said, "That was your ticket, my dear."

Alice burst into the bedroom when she got home, woke

Nate up, and told him the promotion was hers. He was so proud of her. "No one deserves this more," Nate said. Alice agreed and, feeling altogether powerful and accomplished, gave Nate a blow job without any added encouragement.

But then Alice made a grave mistake. It was so stupid, actually, she was still trying to sort out how she let it happen.

She and Bronwyn had gone shopping the evening after the award event, trying on dresses for a friend's upcoming wedding in side-by-side changing rooms shortly before the store closed. Alice had already filled her best friend in on her latest James Dorian story and, thinking she and Bronwyn were alone, confessed the *Widen the Fall* ghostwriting secret. She did mention she couldn't be sure it was true—James was drunk and generally couldn't be trusted in that state—but imagine if it *was*? How the mighty would fall. They'd laughed somewhat cruelly and when they came out to show off their dresses were shocked to find another person in the changing room area. A woman around their age, who gave them a quick look before leaving the room. At which point Alice had gasped and turned to Bronwyn, clutching her friend's hands. "Oh my God. Do you think she heard me? Did I actually say his name? Shit. Did I say his name?" Bronwyn assured her she hadn't, or at least she didn't think so, and even if she did, who cared? They made their purchases and went to have dinner, and by the next morning Alice had forgotten all about it.

At her performance review the next day, Georgia did give her a promotion of sorts—a few thousand dollars extra on her salary, an office with a window, and the promise she could soon ditch babysitting James Dorian, but, "For now, I need you to keep doing what you're doing, Alice," Georgia had said. "He likes you. And a happy James is what we want."

Alice had been at first shocked, and then furious. She asked about the director position. "Like I said, keep doing what you're doing and it will be yours within a year," Georgia announced, before kicking Alice out of her office to take a call. *A year?* No. She couldn't.

She strode back into Georgia's office and waited for her boss to finish her call, like she had every right to barge in and interrupt.

"James Dorian didn't write *Widen the Fall*." Alice spoke calmly, folded her hands in her lap so Georgia couldn't see them shaking. "But I suspect you already knew that."

"What the hell are you talking about?"

"He paid one of his students. Some Robbie Jantzen. Apparently, a great writer," Alice said. "James spilled it the other night. Drunk and loose-lipped as usual." While her insides quivered—she had never spoken to Georgia like this before—she was fierce on the outside.

"You won't say anything," Georgia said, her voice not carrying its usual bravado. She pushed her shoulders back, hardened her expression. "You wouldn't."

"Oh, I might, actually. But it's entirely up to you." Alice leaned forward, held Georgia's gaze.

"What do you want, Alice?"

Alice rested her forearms on the desk, her sweaty palms sticking to the papers stacked there. "I want the promotion you promised me. Director."

"No."

"No?" Alice was confused, certain her strategy would work.

"No, Alice, I am not going to let you blackmail me—or blackmail our biggest client. You know why I didn't give you the job?"

Alice stared at Georgia, her heart beating furiously.

"Because you aren't good enough. Not yet, anyway. You have to earn it here. I've always made that clear, Alice."

Without another word Alice walked out of Georgia's office and into the washroom, unsure if she was going to throw up or burst into tears. Shaking, she splashed water on her face and then, once composed, told Sloan she was sick and going home. She didn't look well, pale-faced and red-eyed, so it wasn't a hard sell. Curled under her duvet a few hours later, she almost didn't answer her phone, but when it rang for the fourth time she begrudgingly picked up to Georgia shrieking, "What did you do, Alice?"

Confused, Alice had bolted out of bed. "What are you talking about?"

Turns out, as terrible luck would have it, the woman in the changing room that evening with Alice and Bronwyn was a *New York Post* reporter, and she had, in fact, heard everything. *What are the fucking chances?* Alice thought, as Georgia continued to yell at her. This reporter's editor was an acquaintance of Georgia's and, as a professional courtesy, had called her before they ran the story. The reporter had been able to quickly corroborate it thanks to Robbie Jantzen, who was glad to finally take credit where credit was due—especially because his debut novel had recently published (to little fanfare) and he believed any publicity was good publicity.

Georgia hung up on her after only three minutes, her parting words being, "You're fired, Alice. I'll have your things sent to you." Stunned by how swiftly things had fallen apart, Alice sat with her phone to her ear for another couple of minutes in shock. Her career was over—Georgia, well connected in Manhattan's publicity world, would see to it. And once the *Post* story ran, everyone would know what Alice had done; she was upset, but she was also deeply humiliated. The repercussions of this one stupid blunder would cling to her like pet hair on black pants—there for all to see, including her husband, who up to this point believed her wise and talented and certainly not someone who would screw up her career by sharing gossip in a changing room. And with sudden clarity, she understood she had to get ahead of the story. Quickly. Like she had been trained to do, she prepared her spin, starting with Nate.

Early the next morning, she snuck out of their tiny bedroom while Nate slept and ate a big bowl of cereal, before sticking her finger down her throat, leaving the bathroom door open so Nate would hear her throwing up. When he came in to check on her she told him she had to quit because Georgia was verbally abusive and denied her the promised promotion despite everything Alice had done for her (for James Dorian), and she couldn't deal anymore. Alice was sick from the constant negativity of the office, her stomach wrecked from the stress.

Nate was appropriately concerned, encouraging her to file a complaint with human resources. Alice resisted, said she wanted to move on, and declared she was finished with the dishonesty of public relations. At that Nate reminded her, as good husbands do, that she was too talented for such a lack of appreciation.

"My smart girl," he murmured, dampening a washcloth in cold water and pressing it to the back of her neck as she hung over the toilet bowl. "This is for the best, babe. Now you can write that book you've always talked about. And who knows . . . maybe it's a good time to start working on the baby thing?" He sounded pleased; life was so straightforward from his perspective. As though he believed Alice could simply turn off her drive, or shift it without breaking stride. An unnerving heaviness filled her at the realization that she might have overshot her plan, and she threw up again—this time without any effort.

When the news hit, Alice's messages blew up. Had she known James Dorian was a con, having worked so closely with him for years? How could he have gotten away with it? And from Bronwyn, a pointed text after Alice hadn't answered her six calls, which read, Was it that woman in the changing room?? She ended up telling Bronwyn but made her swear not to say anything—*to anyone*—until she could figure things out, because she'd already lied to Nate and didn't want to compound the problem.

James Dorian swiftly went from literary darling to pariah. Not only were there demands for him to return awards, but his most current book suddenly disappeared off the publisher's schedule, and Robbie Jantzen sued for damages. Alice stuck to her "I quit" story, and because she wasn't named in the *Post*'s exposé (a small miracle) she remained an anonymous source in James Dorian's decimation.

"Wow, your timing couldn't have been better," Nate declared when he read it, never suspecting Alice's part in it. "Glad you got out of there when you did."

Looking back, the lie was slight and mostly harmless—more an omission than a lie, really. It would have been easy to tell Nate the truth because it *had* been an honest mistake, a moment of poor judgment on Alice's part that snowballed into disaster. And she might have confessed—despite her pride—had it not roused something in her, a curious yet intoxicating feeling of control that would pave the way for more significant lies with more perilous consequences. Alice was a good secret keeper, as long as it suited her.

15

Nellie

....

JUNE 11, 1956

Bread and Cheese Pudding

2 cups soft bread crumbs

4 cups milk

1 tablespoon butter

¼ teaspoon baking soda

A dash of paprika

2 cups grated cheese

5 eggs

1 teaspoon salt

½ teaspoon pepper

Scald bread crumbs with milk, and add butter, baking soda, salt, pepper, and paprika, then combine with the cheese and slightly beaten eggs. Pour into greased baking dish and set in larger pan one-third filled with hot water. Bake slowly for 1 hour in 350°F oven.

Richard was late coming home, and dinner was growing cold. But no matter—Nellie actually liked the cheese pudding best chilled, straight from the fridge. Plus, she was happy to have a few moments alone. She'd had a piece of the Busy Day Cake with Miriam only a couple of hours earlier and so still had no appetite for dinner. But she knew Richard would come home expecting a warm meal on the table. She slid a piece of aluminum foil over the casserole dish, pinching the edges to hold in the heat.

Tonight's dinner had been one of her mother's regular dishes, often served for Sunday luncheon after church. It was dead easy and filled with simple ingredients a prepared housewife typically had on hand. Nellie liked to add a few of her own special touches, like a teaspoon of ground rosemary or sage, or maybe some fresh herbs from the garden. She twisted the lid off the cheese shaker jar that held her homemade herb mix, a Swann family recipe. It was less than half full, and Nellie made a note, as she set the jar on the table, to dry more herbs tomorrow for another batch.

Hearing the car pull in, she sliced a piece of cake for Richard's dessert, carefully arranging the sugared violets even though he wouldn't notice or appreciate the effort when he finally arrived home.

"Nellie?" he called out. The front door slammed. Nellie paused, hands held taut above the cake. She tried to determine his mood from the tone of his voice. Sometimes it was hard to tell.

"Baby?" There it was, the best clue. The use of his preferred pet name. Richard was in a good mood tonight, and she guessed why based on how late he was. *Jane.* Or more likely, Jane's tight sweater and long, stocking-covered pins she liked to display with short skirts.

"In the kitchen," Nellie replied, removing the aluminum foil and cutting a serving of the cheese pudding, adding a sprig of parsley for color. She set it at his spot and placed the cake beside it, turning the plate so the violets were at the top left corner. As Richard came into the kitchen, Nellie was fixing him a drink, an old-fashioned, and she offered him her cheek. When he leaned in to kiss her, she smelled unfamiliar perfume.

"Looks good, Nellie," he said, moving his tie clip lower to prevent the fabric from going into the cheese pudding. He shook some of the herb mix onto his pudding, then took two large bites followed by another sip of his drink before he noticed she had an empty plate in front of her. Richard gestured with his fork. "You aren't eating?"

"I'm a tad queasy," Nellie said.

His brow furrowed. "Perhaps Doc Johnson can give you something? Dan Graves said Martha was awfully ill, but Doc gave her a pill that fixed her right up." Martha Graves had been at Kitty's party that afternoon and had shared as much when Nellie used nausea as the excuse for not eating much. "Well, at least you'll stay thin," Martha had said, looking with envy at Nellie's tiny frame while running her hands over her own puffed-out belly. "The doctor gave me something called thalidomide and it worked wonders!" Martha had laughed, though self-consciously. "Too well, *some* might say." Nellie knew Martha's "some" meant her husband, Dan, and she held back her desire to tell Martha exactly what she thought of a man who would criticize his wife while she was carrying his child. Instead, Nellie told Martha she looked beautiful and healthy, and Martha blushed with delight.

"I don't think that will be necessary," Nellie replied. "I had cake and coffee with Miriam not long ago. I'll eat a little something later." She longed for a cigarette, but Richard didn't care for smoking at the table, so instead she poured a glass of lemonade and sipped it slowly.

"How was your day?" Nellie asked, like she did every day over dinner.

"Fine. The usual. Got stuck in a late-day meeting." Richard worked long hours at the gum plant, had a hand in every part of the business. But he seemed to believe she fell for his lies—*my sweet and naive Nellie*. A wife can always smell another woman on her husband. Would Richard think her clever—or foolish—for imagining these "meetings" had nothing to do with gum at all?

"I hope the cheese pudding is warm enough." Nellie watched him take another large bite. "I foiled it, but it has been out a while."

Richard stopped eating, his expression stone-faced, and Nellie held her breath. But a moment later he relaxed, obviously deciding not to respond to her veiled jab about his lateness. "I like what you've put on top here. This red stuff. Quite flavorful."

"Paprika," Nellie said. "I'm glad you like it."

"So how was your day, Nell-bear?" Richard asked, mouth half-full of pudding. "What did you get up to?"

"Some gardening, and I baked the cake for Kitty Goldman's Tupperware party I mentioned last night. I saved you a piece." Nellie pointed to the cake slice, but he barely glanced at it.

"Oh, you were at the Goldmans' today? How's their new kitchen?"

To someone who didn't know him, Richard's tone sounded politely curious. But Nellie knew better—he had never liked Charles Goldman, Kitty's husband. "He's a shuckster," Richard mumbled when his name came up, referred to Charles's booming hardware store as "Mickey Mouse," even though it was anything but, and drove the extra few minutes to Scarsdale to avoid shopping there. Nellie had no idea why Richard didn't care for Charles Goldman, though she suspected it had everything to do with jealousy.

Richard was a very successful man, but Charles was the *most*: a handsome fellow who ran a booming business and was quite affectionate with his wife, holding her hand in public and telling her how beautiful she looked whenever she walked into the room. Kitty wasn't deserving of such a husband—she was a gossipy, vapid woman who was mean-spirited on the best of days. Like at today's party, after poor Martha lamented her unfortunate pregnancy-related weight gain, Kitty had offered to make her a plate so she could rest her swollen ankles. When she brought it over she had whispered, loudly enough for everyone in the room to hear, "I left off the deviled eggs, because I know you're watching your figure." The deviled eggs had been Martha's contribution and were her favorite, but she'd stammered a thank-you as she took the plate of vegetables and jelly salad, looking as though she wished the ground would swallow her whole.

Nellie treaded lightly with her response to Richard's question, for fear he would demand they begin a kitchen renovation soon. She loved her kitchen the way it was, had no desire to uproot her life by making everything a mess in the one room in the house that was truly hers and hers alone.

"To be honest," Nellie began, standing to serve Richard a second helping of the pudding, "it was dreadful. The design, the colors. All of it, chintzy." Actually, the Goldmans' kitchen had been quite lovely. It had been the company that was dreadful. But Nellie went because what else would she do all day? The garden took up some time, as did the chores and errands required to keep the household running smoothly, but for much of the time Nellie was bored. Restless. At least these get-togethers meant she had to bake or prepare something, which always lightened her mood.

"I hope you rested today. Put your feet up." Richard frowned. "You know, you should have Helen come more often. I don't like you working so hard in your condition."

Nellie gave a patient smile. But she didn't want Helen underfoot all day, nor did she like paying for something she could easily do herself. Besides, cooking and gardening were pleasurable, which Richard wouldn't understand.

"Speaking of, I didn't realize we were announcing our news quite yet." Nellie sashayed over to the other side of the room and cracked the window, sliding her Lucky Strikes and cigarette holder from the kitchen drawer. "I had hoped to tell Martha and Kitty myself." What she really meant was she had hoped to tell them nothing at all; her deception had only been intended for Richard. She took an ashtray out of the cupboard and placed it in the sink, taking a long pull on her cigarette.

"Richard, please remove that scowl from your face." She took another drag, blew it out. "Dr. Johnson told me it was fine to smoke. He said it was relaxing for his patients who are in the family way."

Richard held up his hands as he leaned back in his chair. "If Doc Johnson says it's fine, that's fine by me. And I know we talked about keeping the news to ourselves for now, and I'm sorry, Nell-bear, but Dan Graves was asking after you when we rode the train together, and I couldn't help myself."

Richard pushed back from the table and stood close to Nellie, lifting her so she was perched on the edge of the countertop. "Don't let it rattle your cage, baby. It's good news, so why shouldn't we share it?"

"You're right. We absolutely should," she murmured, softening her expression with some effort. "I'm not cross. I promise."

He used his hands to open her knees so he could settle his hips into her circle of space. She didn't resist him (what was the point?), but then felt him tense and pull back slightly as he hesitated, unwilling to risk anything this time. His hands remained on the curves of her behind, gently caressing through the fabric of her skirt. "This is okay, right?"

"I won't break, Richard." It was easier to give in, so Nellie set her cigarette holder in the ashtray in the sink and placed her palms on the kitchen's countertop, anchoring her body so she didn't fall backward. This moved them closer together, and his desire, hot and demanding, pressed into her.

"You always know how to razz my berries, baby." He ground his pelvis against her and leaned in to kiss her neck, his mouth hot and sloppy. The perfume scent was stronger now, nauseatingly so. Nellie was about to feign illness to extricate herself when Richard moaned, but not with pleasure, and a moment later he retreated, leaving Nellie splayed on the countertop, a single tail of cigarette smoke rising from the sink beside her.

"Richard? What is it?" He hunched forward, a pinched look on his face.

"I'm fine," he said between clenched teeth. "My damn ulcer. It's nothing."

Nellie shimmied off the counter and took a last pull on her cigarette before stubbing it out. Richard's stomach was an ongoing problem, but he seemed to be getting ill more often these days. She kept at him to see the doctor about it, but Richard didn't want to bother going in for something so trivial. "Nothing an Alka-Seltzer won't fix," he always said. If he didn't get relief from the fizzy water, he would try a dose of milk of magnesium, or maybe some bismuth.

"Why don't I make you an albumen drink?" Nellie opened her cookbook even though she knew the recipe by heart. She often made it when his stomach acted up. "You go rest and I'll bring it to you."

Richard nodded and clutched his belly, sucking in a pained breath.

"Off you go," Nellie said, ushering him out of the kitchen. He groaned as he settled onto the green velour sofa, and Nellie set the washing bucket beside him in case. Then she separated the egg white, saving the yolk in a small glass dish—she would use it tomorrow—and with her rotary hand blender beat the white until it formed glossy but soft peaks. Squeezing lemon juice into the egg whites, Nellie added a heaping tablespoon of sugar and stirred it all together until it was smooth enough to drink.

"I'm going to take a bath," Nellie said after handing Richard the albumen drink. "If you need anything else, just holler."

Richard grimaced as he sipped the white foam from the glass. He was pale, and a thin sheen of sweat clung to his face, beading at his hairline and above his upper lip. He had loosened his belt and tie and definitely appeared quite unwell.

"Thank you, baby," he said, his voice thin and reedy from pain. "Take your time. I'm fine here."

After retrieving her robe from her bedroom closet, Nellie went into the bathroom and ran a bath. Locking the door, she undressed and glanced at herself in the mirror, critically taking stock of her various parts. Flat stomach, nothing growing inside to stretch it out. Breasts high and full, nipples erect with the chill of being out from the warmth of her brassiere. Her skin was smooth, slightly tanned and freckled where she hadn't covered it during gardening. Nellie slid into the bath water and positioned each foot on either side of the tap. She shimmied close to the faucet so her knees bent deeply and the stream of water hit directly between her legs. As the water caressed Nellie in ways Richard never did, the tension built in her abdomen. A fluttery feeling took over her body, and her limbs began to tingle. Nellie's body soon tensed under the water and she shuddered from head to toe. She let her head drop back so her hair fanned out around her, the noises she made drowned out by the rushing water.

.

Richard was expectedly heartbroken when she told him ten days later—after she scrubbed another lipstick stain out of another shirt collar—she had lost the baby, and his uncharacteristic tears both invigorated and saddened her. She didn't want to be the sort of wife who lied to her husband, especially about such a thing as this, but he had given her no choice. Besides, her guilt was allayed by her belief that she would fall pregnant soon enough. They would have their child and Jane (or whoever replaced her) and her god-awful lipstick would be forgotten.

Richard didn't ask many questions this time, remembering the horror of the bloodied towels from Nellie's miscarriage, only, "Are you certain?" She said she was but promised to make an appointment with the doctor. Instead, she went to Black's Drugs, the pharmacy in Scarsdale, and perused the tubes of lipstick, pausing at the bright red ones, wondering what kind of woman believed she had a right to another's husband. Nellie finally settled on a soft seashell pink tube, which she purchased along with a cold bottle of Coca-Cola, her fingertips leaving imprints on the frosty green glass, not dissimilar to the fingerprints Richard had left on her arm.

16

Woman's sexual response is so general and diffused that frequently she does not even know that she is being aroused, and even more frequently is quite unaware that her behavior is arousing the boy beyond the boundaries which she herself would wish to maintain.

    —Evelyn Duvall and Reuben Hill, *When You Marry* (1953)

Alice

.....

JUNE 11, 2018

*G*eorgia finally answered the attorney's pointed question. "Look, I knew Alice could handle James Dorian. I never would have put her in that position if I thought otherwise."

To that point Alice reiterated that Georgia knew exactly what and who James Dorian was, because they had discussed the issue on multiple occasions. In fact, when Georgia first assigned Alice to James it came with a not-so-subtle warning: "He likes his booze and young women who are not his wife."

After Alice shared this quote, the room was silent for a moment, and then everyone was talking at once. Georgia called Alice histrionic and childish and implied she was misremembering the conversation; the attorneys tersely asked Georgia if there had been other sexual assault complaints about James Dorian; Alice stated to no one in particular that she was going to the washroom. Once alone in the stall, she went to text Bronwyn again, but she'd left her phone on the meeting room table.

When she returned, Georgia's face was tense with frustration. Her plan had been to pin this on Alice: the rogue employee, whom she had fired for reasonable cause (breaking her nondisclosure), would take the fall. But now with sexual misconduct hanging in the air, at a time when powerful men were finally being exposed and branded with damning hashtags that ruined reputations, Georgia had few options.

There would be others who came forward too, Alice knew, if she went public—she was hardly unique when it came to James Dorian's wandering hands. Hell, Georgia probably had stories of her own. Plus, he'd had a long career, both in academics and in publishing, and the Wittington Group was not the first firm to represent him. But even though it was tempting to nail James Dorian and Georgia to the wall, Alice wasn't naive. She would not come out unscathed. There would be sympathy from some, perhaps job offers at other firms with better scruples, and certainly much discussion about predatory, powerful men and what to do about them. There would also be the question of culpability: *Why did Alice wear short skirts for her meetings with James? Why would she agree to be in a hotel room alone, knowing Dorian's reputation? Why did she continue to serve him alcohol? How much vodka did she herself consume? What did she think would happen?*

When Alice said she had no interest in taking things further, Georgia seemed relieved. As for James and his lawsuit, he *had* been quite drunk, but Alice suspected not enough to forget the feel of her thigh against his uninvited fingers.

"I assume I'm free to go?" Alice asked, gathering her things.

"Yes," the female attorney said, giving her a tight smile as she thanked her for coming in. "We'll let you know if we have any other questions. Is this the number where you can be reached?" She read out her cell number, and Alice nodded. Georgia followed Alice out of the room, closing the door behind her as the attorneys huddled over their notes.

"I know the way out," Alice said, not interested in spending another minute with Georgia.

Her ex-boss nodded, tersely said, "Thanks for coming in today."

Alice started to walk away but turned back and flipped her phone around so Georgia could see the screen. Georgia's eyes grew wide, moving from the screen to Alice's face. Alice tapped the red button to stop the recording and closed the voice memo app, then tucked the phone safely into her purse. "In case you're ever unclear on the order of events today, let me know. I recorded the entire meeting and am happy to refresh your memory as needed." Then she walked—head up, shoulders back—down the hall and past the reception desk, ignoring Sloan's half-hearted goodbye and the bleeding blister on her heel, feeling more like her old self than she had in months.

"How was your lunch?" Nate asked late that evening as Alice gently flipped the tattered and food-drop-stained pages of Elsie Swann's cookbook, looking for something to bake for coffee with Sally the following day. *Banana bread? Oatmeal bars? Chocolate chip cookies?* Alice was nervous about baking—it necessitated such precision— so she needed something easy.

"What lunch?" Alice murmured, focused on a recipe for sugar cookies. But the notation, *Lousy,* was written in what Alice now recognized as Elsie Swann's hand. She turned the page and glanced through a recipe for brownies.

"With your editor friend. Didn't you go into the city today?"

"Right, sorry." She checked for cocoa in her pantry as Nate opened the fridge for a bottle of sparkling water. No cocoa, so no brownies, but she did have chocolate chips. "Good. It was a quick coffee, actually, because she had another appointment. But I had lunch afterward with Bronwyn." The fib slipped out easily, and as soon as it did Alice wished to take it back. To tell Nate the truth about how she'd spent her day, if for no other reason than to share how satisfying it had been to one-up Georgia Wittington. But revealing the truth about her day meant exposing the more significant truth she'd been keeping from Nate. If she didn't confess, the shame of her professional misstep could remain buried and, therefore, benign.

"Where did you go?" Nate asked, swigging water from the glass bottle.

"Hmm?" Alice stood on her tiptoes, pulling out small boxes and spice bottles. *Baking soda. Cinnamon.* Check. *Cloves?* She dragged a hand deeper into the pantry until her fingers pulled out the remaining bottles at the back of the cupboard. *Cream of tartar. Another cinnamon.* Bingo. *Ground cloves.* "Oh, we went to that Italian place. On Seventh."

"Trattoria Dell'Arte?" Nate said. He groaned. "Did you have the lobster carbonara? I miss the lobster carbonara."

"Um, yes." She gathered the bottles and boxes and bag of chocolate chips on the counter, reread the recipe, avoided making eye contact with Nate. Worried he'd see her flushed cheeks and awkward smile and realize something was up.

"What are you making?" Nate asked, picking up the bottle of ground cloves, apparently sensing nothing amiss.

"Chocolate chip cookies." Alice opened drawers to pull out everything else she needed. Bowl. Wooden spoon. Measuring cup. She found a never-before-worn apron in one of the drawers and put it over her head. "Can you grab the butter out of the fridge?"

It was as hard as a rock. She tried pressing her fingertips into its surface, leaving shallow indentations in the foil wrapper as the butter yielded little. "I'll need to wait for this to soften."

"You can grate it."

"Like, with a cheese grater? Really?"

Nate nodded. "A trick I learned from my mom. Works like a charm."

"Huh, who knew?" She took the cheese grater out of the dishwasher—the only new appliance in the kitchen—and got to work, following the recipe in the cookbook precisely.

"I've never heard of putting cloves in chocolate chip cookies," Nate said, watching her measure and add and stir. "Where did you get the recipe?"

"From that cookbook in the basement." Alice kept her eyes on the page. "I'm having coffee with Sally in the morning, and I don't want to show up empty-handed."

"Look at you, baking cookies from scratch for our elderly neighbor. I think the suburbs are agreeing with you, babe." Nate was pleased Alice was making an effort, reading into this sudden swing to domesticity from a woman who had previously complained if she had to do more than open a can of soup. He wrapped his arms around her waist from behind and planted a kiss on her neck, murmuring how sexy she looked in the apron.

"If you make me mess up these measurements you're going to be eating a lot of terrible cookies," Alice said, shifting away, but affording him a smile.

She pressed the slippery butter against the grater's sharp holes, careful to keep her knuckles out of the way. "Meant to ask, how did you make out today without your laptop?"

"What?" Nate frowned, focused on his buzzing phone.

"Your laptop. You left it at home?" The grating trick worked beautifully, the shards of butter piling up inside the metal tri-angle.

"Oh, right." He scrolled through his screen for a moment, then tucked his phone in his back pocket. "I was in meetings most of the day, but we used Drew's to study."

"Do I know Drew?" Alice ran through the faces of Nate's colleagues but came up blank. She put the grater in the sink and rinsed her buttered fingers under warm water.

Nate shook his head. "She's only been there for a couple of months."

"Drew is a woman?"

"Yeah, like Drew Barrymore."

Alice wiped her still-oily fingers on a piece of paper towel. "Does she look like Drew Barrymore?"

He smirked, swatted at her behind. "No, she does not."

"Okay, get out of here. I need to finish these cookies before I fall asleep into this grated butter." It was nearly 11:30 P.M. and Nate had been home for only half an hour, which was typical these days between work and preparing for his upcoming exam.

"Okay, okay," Nate said, kissing her cheek as he walked by and into the living room. The light went on and the floorboards creaked as he moved through the room, settling onto the couch with his study notebooks.

She scooped the grated butter into the bowl, measured the baking soda, and stirred in the chalky, past-their-prime chocolate chips. As she did her belly fluttered as she thought back to her meeting with Georgia, who was probably still shocked by how much she'd underestimated Alice.

The call from the Wittington Group's attorney had come a few hours earlier, around dinnertime. Alice was finishing a tomato-and-cheese sandwich alone in the kitchen, as Nate wouldn't be home until much later. She didn't answer the call but let it go to voice mail, checking it once she had a glass of wine in hand. The attorney's message informed her that James Dorian would not be going forward with the lawsuit, and the matter was closed. She left her number, but Alice deleted the message.

Now, hours later, distracted by her internal postmortem about the meeting and her relief about James Dorian, as well as not burning Sally's cookies, Alice didn't notice that the chill in the house had abated—her cardigan, resting over the chair at her writing desk, where it had been since the day before, no longer needed.

17

Don't keep your sweetest smiles and your best manners for outsiders; let your husband come first.
—Blanche Ebbutt, *Don'ts for Wives* (1913)

Alice

.....

JUNE 12, 2018

*S*hortly after midnight, moments after the cookies came out of the oven, Alice and Nate had argued. And not just a short-lived and snappish argument, but the sort that makes a couple go to bed in silence with backs to each other, a chasm of purposeful space between them. It started when Nate came into the kitchen to make a coffee, where Alice was transferring the hot cookies to a cooling rack, and let out an irritable sigh.

"What's up?" Alice asked, glancing up from the cookie tray.

"Nothing," he said, his tone cagey. "Tired, I guess."

"Me too," she replied. "I'm going up the second I get this done."

"It's just—" He sighed again, and again Alice moved her focus from cookies to Nate, waiting for him to finish the sentence.

"Aren't you going to clean up first?" he asked.

Alice looked around the kitchen, at the dough-crusted bowl and butter-oiled grater, the trails of flour. Chocolate chip bag open and spilled next to the spice jars, mixer paddles unwashed and discarded in the sink. Eggshells littering the countertop. The kitchen was a mess, but what difference did it make if she cleaned it up tonight or in the morning? "I wasn't going to."

Nate's jaw tensed, and he nodded before taking out the coffee grinder and beans from the cupboard. But then he made a big show of trying to find space for them on the countertop between the eggshells and flour, and Alice let out a frustrated groan.

She shoved the grinder and beans at him so he was forced to take a step back with them nestled in his arms. Nate stared at her, brow furrowed, as she furiously stacked the dishes in the sink and wet the dishcloth.

He's overworked, Alice reminded herself. *Tired and impatient, and you can easily end this before it goes completely sideways.* But she didn't say anything, pumping liquid soap into the mixing bowl and running the hot water. Tears pricked at her eyes and she pressed her lips together.

"Ali." Nate put the beans and grinder on the table, rested a hand on her elbow, and tugged gently. "Sorry. I'm just stressed about . . . It doesn't matter. Tomorrow is fine."

Tomorrow is fine? Yes, Alice had made the mess, but in Murray Hill Nate would have been just as likely to clean up as Alice (if not more so)—back when neither one of them was keeping tabs, both equal players.

"No, *I'm* sorry," Alice said, voice quaking as she spun out of Nate's touch to put away the chocolate chips, spices, and sugar. "I'll do better next time."

"For fuck's sake," Nate murmured, pressing his hands to his eyes. Alice felt badly—he *was* working all day and then spending his evenings studying. It wasn't too much to ask for a clean kitchen so he could make a late-night coffee without eggshells and flour and dirty bowls in the way. "What are we even fighting about?"

"I don't know," Alice whispered, losing her battle with the tears. But she refused to turn around so Nate could see. Unlike Alice, he had been raised by a stay-at-home mom who continued doing her sons' laundry long after they left home and had dinner on the table every night by seven. And while he spoke fondly of his childhood and revered his mother for all she had done, Alice—perhaps foolishly—never considered that Nate might expect the same of her.

Nate sat at the table, wrapping the cord around the coffee grinder and closing the bag of beans. "Ali . . . will you look at me, please?"

She didn't turn her head, and he let out a ragged breath. "It's fine. I just want to get this done and go to sleep," she said.

He stayed put for another couple of minutes, watching as she washed and dried the mixing bowl, continuing to ignore his presence, then grumbled, "This is bullshit," and got up and left the room. Shortly after, Alice, hating herself for letting things escalate but too tired to fix it, went upstairs, and though she hadn't fallen asleep when Nate joined her two hours later, she kept her eyes tightly closed. In the morning he whispered, "I'm sorry," into the softness of her neck, and she apologized too, though she didn't feel much better.

"I just miss you," she said.

He held her, promised to be home for dinner—he could study afterward—and she promised a great meal "and a clean kitchen," which made him laugh softly. They were okay, Alice told herself. Then Nate got up to shower and she lay alone in bed, chilly without his body heat, thinking about how a baby would fit in their current life. Nate was never home and Alice was always alone. *Like a round peg in a square hole.*

"There's something I can't place. Not cinnamon, I don't think," Sally said, taking another nibble of the cookie. "It actually reminds me of my mom's chocolate chip cookies. I haven't had one in too many years to count."

Alice smiled. "You're tasting the cloves. It's a recipe from that old cookbook, the one I found in our basement? It has Elsie Swann's name in it, whoever she was." Alice took a sip from her mug. Sally made a great cup of coffee. "I've cooked a couple of recipes out of it. It's been sort of fun. I am not a chef and definitely not a baker, but I sort of see the appeal."

"Nothing beats homemade, Mom always said." Sally popped the last bite of cookie in her mouth and murmured how delicious it was, adding, "I wonder if Elsie Swann might have been Nellie's mother. The name does sound familiar, and cookbooks used to be passed down from one generation to another, often as wedding gifts to help the new wives. I'm sure there were many who married completely unprepared." She brushed a few crumbs from her fingers, then peeked into Alice's near-empty mug. "Can I give you a warm-up?"

"Please." While Sally went to fill up Alice's coffee, she stretched her legs and looked around the living room. There was a photo of a young Sally, her wild curls longer and dirty blond rather than white, standing arm in arm with an older woman who could have been her twin, save twenty-five years or so. Alice glanced at the other photos adorning the hutch and fireplace mantel—all of Sally at various stages of her life and medical career. In one she appeared with a swarm of smiling children standing on a patch of dusty red earth, a note in the corner reading *Ethiopia, 1985*. In another a young Sally held a framed medical school diploma in her hands and wore a deep blue cap and gown, and in the final one on the mantel she was dressed in what appeared to be a flight suit and bottle-round goggles.

"I went skydiving on a whim," Sally said, coming to stand beside Alice. "It was in New Zealand, in the seventies, and let's just say it was an era of spontaneity."

Alice smiled, then glanced back at the photos. No signs of a family, and she couldn't help her curiosity. "Did you ever have children?"

Sally shook her head, but there was no sense of melancholy at Alice's question. "Never even married," she said. "Not that you need to be married to have children, but no. My work was my child." She pointed to the picture from Ethiopia. "I spent some time in Africa with Doctors Without Borders in the eighties, and there were so many children who needed care and love, so I put any maternal energy I had into them."

They sat in the upholstered chairs across from the fireplace. "I might have married if the right man had come along, but I was committed to medicine, and no one was as fascinating or satisfying as that," Sally said. "How long have you been married?"

"It will be two years October fifteenth." Alice thought back to the unseasonably warm fall day when she became Mrs. Alice Hale. Remembering as she stood, sweating lightly, in her strapless sheath gown, hair in soft waves held back by glossy pearl pins, feeling beautiful under Nate's adoring gaze. Things had made a lot more sense back then.

"Do you and Nate hope to have children?"

"Yes. Soon, I think," Alice said, shrugging. "But the house is taking a lot of energy. And I'm trying to write a novel. Life feels high-maintenance right now, which is crazy because in some ways I have nothing but time."

Sally watched Alice, ever perceptive. "Ah, you're young," she soothed. "Plenty of time for a family. So, tell me about your writing. Is this your first novel?"

"It is. I have to say, I'm not making much progress yet." A sliver of guilt snaked through Alice. *I've not written one word, actually.* It wasn't that she hadn't tried; rather, it was proving more difficult than she'd expected. Turns out writing a book took more than simply wanting to do it.

"A touch of writer's block?"

"Something like that," Alice replied. "I'm waiting for a flash of inspiration. Or maybe a muse to show up on my doorstep."

"Such an interesting vocation, writing. Being able to create a whole world with nothing more than your imagination." The skin around her eyes crinkled deeply as she smiled. "If I had a single creative bone in my body, I might have considered it after I retired. Everyone needs a hobby for their twilight years."

"You could still do it. I bet you have a ton of stories from all your years in medicine. Traveling the world. Skydiving on a whim."

"Ah yes, skydiving. I'm terrified of heights, actually, but I had some help that day. A *different* sort of brownie—with a special ingredient, if I remember correctly." Sally chuckled.

At Alice's age Sally had been traveling the world, saving lives, eating pot brownies before jumping out of a plane—things women typically didn't do in those days. Shouldn't Alice be more like the young Sally rather than arguing with her husband about cleaning up the kitchen? "Speaking of writing, I should get back to it. But this has been really nice. Thanks, Sally."

"Thank you for those delicious cookies. Mine always burn on the bottom." Sally opened her front door, and Alice gave her a hug, which the older woman returned warmly. "Good luck with your book, Alice. I hope you find your creative muse. Or perhaps she'll find you."

A few hours later a knock at the door made Alice jump from the couch, where she'd fallen asleep. Elsie Swann's cookbook was on the coffee table, fanned open to a recipe for Pineapple Chicken Alice was considering for dinner. The pile of *Ladies' Home Journal* magazines previously in her lap tumbled to the floor as she stood. She was confused, adrenaline from her sudden wake-up making her heart pump furiously. Shaking off the dizziness, she stepped over the magazines and went to answer the door.

Sally stood on the front stoop, two stacks of envelopes held together with elastic bands in her hands.

"Hi," Alice said, smoothing down her hair; she hoped she didn't look too awful. "Come in. Just doing a bit of research. Uh, for my book."

"Thank you, but I'm on my way to a tennis lesson." Sally was dressed in tennis whites, a racket in a carrying bag over her shoulder and a sun visor nestled into her white hair. "But after we chatted about that cookbook you found, I went through some of my mom's things because the name Elsie Swann sounded so familiar. I thought perhaps she had lived in the house before the Murdochs moved in and that Mother might have had an old picture. It was a very social neighborhood in those days."

Alice took the stacks from Sally. The envelopes were yellowed with age and flimsy. "I found these on my hunt in the basement. They're all addressed to Elsie Swann but unopened. The return address is your house, to an *E.M.*, who I'm guessing might have been Eleanor Murdoch?" Alice tilted her head to read the address on the top letter, the cursive writing slanted sharply to the right.

"I'm not sure how Mother ended up with these but thought they might be of interest to you. Might answer some questions about the history of your house."

The letters all appeared sealed, curiously missing postmarks showing they had been through the mail system. "Thank you, this is great."

"You're most welcome," Sally said.

Alice ran a finger over the address on the top envelope, an unexpected thrill coursing through her. "Are you sure? They were your mom's . . ." Her voice trailed because she really didn't want to give them back, suddenly desperate to know what was inside the dozen or so envelopes.

"I certainly have no use for them, dear. They're yours now."

Alice smiled. "Maybe there's a story in here. For my book. Old letters that were mysteriously never mailed?"

"Well, perhaps a muse *did* show up on your doorstep today," Sally said. A taxi pulled up to the end of the driveway. "Oh, there's my ride. I'm off. Happy writing, Miss Alice."

A few minutes later Alice sat back on the sofa and unwrapped the brittle elastic, which had no stretch left in it, taking the top letter off the first stack. She hesitated briefly, feeling a hint of guilt at reading someone else's private thoughts—even if that person would never know—but intrigue won out, and she slid her finger under the flap. It released easily, the glue long desiccated. Alice unfolded the two pages of delicate cream paper and began to read.

From the desk of Eleanor Murdoch

October 14, 1955

Dearest Mother,
   I hope you are well and enjoying this lovely patch of weather we've been having. The birds are singing like it's the middle of July, and it has been so warm my dahlias continue blooming! I'll be sure to bring you some next time I visit. Things are fine here. I've been spending much of my time in the garden, preparing it for its winter rest. With so much early rain, the slugs

were horrendous this year, and my poor hostas are full of holes as a result. I tried vinegar spray and sugar trails, but neither were particularly successful, and I may have to accept these pests as one of a gardener's many challenges.

This evening I hosted a dinner party, which went splendidly. I had Chicken à la King and Baked Alaska on the menu, and my guests were quite impressed that ice cream could go in the oven. I'll surely be writing down the recipe for a few of them.

Richard is keeping busy with the plant, though he has been under quite a strain. One of his sales managers passed recently, which was a terrible shock for everyone. I've done what I can to help soothe the pressures, but I fear it isn't always enough. His stomach ulcer has also been acting up, though the albumen drink seems to provide some relief. I do wish he'd see a doctor about it, but you know how stubborn men can be. Speaking of, I should finish up and head to bed. It's late and Richard is waiting up for me, so I don't want to keep him too long. I have learned that patience is not one of his virtues!

There have been some disappointments of late, but I expect to have excellent news to share soon! However, I will stay mum for now so it can be a wonderful surprise. I will visit soon, Mother. Please don't worry after me, for I am well and taking good care.

Your loving daughter, Nellie xx

18

Nellie

....

JULY 2, 1956

*T*he garden was bursting because Nellie hadn't been culling the flowers, or pulling the weeds, as frequently as she needed to. There had been nearly a week of heavy rain, which had made it difficult to spend time outdoors and turned the garden beds into a sopping mess. Plus, she was supposedly "recovering"—her fictional miscarriage keeping her housebound and Richard more mindful to her comings and goings.

But the plants could only be so patient with her, and so after Richard left for his train she tidied the house, planned her marketing list, and got to work on the garden. She whistled as she weeded, not minding the dirt on her knees and the scratches from the thorns, nor the insects that crawled up her bare legs and required regular swatting. It was a beautiful day, and Nellie Murdoch was hopeful in a way she hadn't been in a while.

Things with Richard were better, and Nellie was happy. He had been more considerate lately, home for dinner on time for the past two weeks and even cleaning up the breakfast dishes that morning. The cloying perfume scent Nellie had become accustomed to was absent from his shirts and jackets, and his hands were gentle on her body in a way they hadn't been in some time. And as Nellie's last round of bruises faded, so did a touch of her contempt for her husband. She wasn't certain his kindness would last, but she hoped it might. Perhaps there were rosier days ahead for Nellie and Richard Murdoch.

These pleasant thoughts, along with a particularly overgrown section of the garden, so distracted Nellie she didn't hear Richard until he was standing directly behind her.

"Eleanor," he barked, and she jumped.

She turned quickly, a gloved hand coming up to shade her eyes.

"Richard, my goodness," she said, her hand going to her chest. "You scared me." Nellie stood, a handful of garden trimmings still in hand. She dropped the weeds and fiddled with her shorts, knowing he wouldn't like how much leg was exposed. "What are you doing home?"

Had she lost track of time? Maybe it was nearing dinnertime . . . but the sun was directly overhead; Richard shouldn't be home for hours yet. "Are you ill?"

Richard glowered at her, and she realized he was angry. A quivering started in her muscles, her body filling with adrenaline, preparing to flee.

"What is it? What's wrong?" Maybe she was imagining things. Maybe—

WHACK!

His knuckles across her cheek, her jaw—hitting so hard her head ricocheted to the side and her teeth clamped tightly and a ringing filled her ears—left her stunned. He had never hit her like this before. Certainly not on her face, where it would leave a mark difficult to explain away. She gasped and put a shaky hand to her throbbing cheekbone, her glove rough against the rawness of her skin. The ringing in her head subsided, but the pain lingered.

"Do you know who I ran into today?" Richard asked, standing so close—too close—to her. She curled her body in slightly, trying to protect herself. Thought briefly about the trowel near her feet and how quickly she might be able to pick it up if necessary.

Nellie shook her head at his question, because she couldn't find her voice. She shivered violently despite the sun's warmth.

"Dr. Johnson, that's who. Did you know he had a daughter living in Brooklyn?" Again, Nellie shook her head. "She's recently engaged, and he was on his way into the city to visit, so we sat together on the train. Had a good, long chat."

Richard stopped for a moment, walked over to the garden shed where the shovel Nellie had used to dig out a particularly entrenched dandelion patch leaned against the door. He came back to where Nellie stood, hand still to her cheek, and set the shovel's sharp edge against the soil, pushing hard until it sliced into the dirt. "He's an interesting fellow. A bit boastful, maybe, but solid nonetheless. And he's taken quite a shine to you, I'll say. Was quite concerned about how your rash had healed."

Nellie was cold all over, a numbness spreading through her body. She knew what had happened without Richard saying another word. Yes, Dr. Johnson was a professional man and would never disclose the nature of Nellie's medical visits to anyone. Except to her husband, because the husband always had a right to know what was happening with his wife.

I'm worried about Nellie, Richard would have said to Dr. Johnson as the train picked up speed after leaving the Scarsdale station. *Sick about it, actually.* He would look it, too. Slightly green around the gills, sheen of sweat on his forehead. *What can we do so this doesn't happen again?*

Dr. Johnson would surely have been confused about Richard's excessive concern, the anxious tone to his voice. He would worry his colleague Dr. Wood had missed something with Nellie, be silently frustrated with the old doctor's stubbornness and wish he would retire already. *Is the rash much worse?* he would have asked Richard. *Did the Mexsana not work? Tell Nellie to call my secretary. Happy to take another look.*

There would be a pause in the conversation. *Rash?* Richard would finally have said, as confused as the doctor had been moments earlier.

Yes. On her hand? Dr. Johnson would have replied, casting a doubtful look toward Richard as his sweating intensified. Maybe Richard wasn't well, he would think. Perhaps he should suggest scheduling a visit to see him at the office . . .

The miscarriage, Richard would have said, so quietly that the doctor would have had to lean in to hear him. *There was so much blood, so much . . .*

Dr. Johnson, less confused now but reluctant to come between a husband and his wife, would have shaken his head. *I'm sorry, Dick, but I'm not sure what you're referring to.*

Richard Murdoch hadn't even gone into the gum plant that morning. Instead, when the train arrived at the station he said his goodbye to Dr. Johnson, paced and stewed on the train's platform calculating his next move, and caught the next train back home. And now he was standing in front of Nellie looking like he might kill her.

Nellie took off one glove so Richard could see her hand. No longer carrying any signs of a rash. "It's fine now. See? But it was kind of Dr. Johnson to worry after me." She held her hand out, the shaking of her arm making it look like a leaf in the wind. Richard ran gentle fingers over the unblemished skin Nellie presented him. He bent and kissed her hand softly, and his fingers—tender moments earlier—pressed hard into the soft and vulnerable spot between her thumb and pointer finger. Squeezing, as though he was trying to separate the bones.

"You lied to me, Nellie." He squeezed harder, twisting her thumb, and she yelped. "Was there ever a baby?"

"I didn't lie." Nellie tried to pull her hand away, but Richard held fast. "I did lose the baby, Richard. I swear to you. You must remember all the blood! The towels in the bathtub I used to clean myself up! But you're right. I didn't go and see Dr. Johnson about it. I was ashamed, Richard. Ashamed my body failed me. Failed us, again." Nellie thought he might break her hand. "That really hurts. Please. Let. Me. Go."

"You expect me to believe anything you say now?" he hissed, though he did let go of her hand.

Nellie stumbled, and Richard picked up the shovel, marching over to the garden. At first, she was confused but soon became panicked that he was going to dig up her beautiful rosebushes. But when she realized what he intended to do with the shovel, her heart nearly stopped.

"What are you doing?" She took a few cautious steps toward him.

He ignored her, the shovel sliding through the earth, piercing the swath of blue forget-me-nots like a hot knife through butter.

"No!" Nellie ran at Richard, yanked on his arm. He swatted her away like a pesky fly, focused on the task. "Please, stop. Richard, please." He remained undeterred. Tossing chunks of earth to the side, crushing the flowers.

"I saw you out here, burying that damn towel," Richard said, huffing with exertion. "I bet it wasn't even your blood. Probably got it from the butcher. Huh? Have you been lying to me all along?"

"I'm not lying." Nellie was sobbing now, her breath catching in her throat. "The . . . baby . . . *our* baby is in that towel, Richard. If you don't believe me, go ahead and dig it up. You'll see."

He stopped, the only movement in his body his heaving breaths forcing his shoulders up and down. Leaning heavily on the shovel, he rested his head on its handle. "You embarrassed me today, Nellie. And I can't allow that."

"Nellie? Is everything all right?" Miriam had suddenly appeared in her backyard, was up against the fence between the two properties, garden shears in hand.

Richard stood, looked around at the forget-me-not destruction. He stepped toward Miriam, blocking her view of Nellie as he did, and placed the shovel behind him. "Mrs. Claussen, how are you today? Lovely day for some pruning, isn't it?"

"Certainly is." Miriam shifted to get a better look at Nellie and at what Richard had done to the garden. Her voice kept its pleasant lilt, suggesting she hadn't heard or seen what had transpired between Richard and his wife. "Nellie, love. I was wondering if I might bother you for a minute? If you're not too busy? I'm still having a heck of a time with these ants. My peonies are in a sorry, sorry state, and I need to make a bouquet for a dear friend."

Richard wouldn't know the peonies had already reached full bloom and were browning; Miriam was giving Nellie a much-needed escape. "I'd be happy to," Nellie said. "Richard and I were just finishing up here."

He glanced at her sharply but rearranged his expression as he turned back to Miriam. "She's all yours." The smile stayed put. Charm back on like a spotlight. But Miriam Claussen was no fool. "I'll leave you to it," he said. "Nellie, I don't expect to be home for dinner tonight."

Nellie nodded, smiled back at him, though it took everything in her to make the muscles in her face do what was required. "We'll see you later tonight."

He paused at the garden shed, leaning the shovel back against the door. "Yes, you will." Turning to Miriam he gave a short, friendly wave. "Hope to see you again soon, Mrs. Claussen. Good luck with the ants."

A moment later he was inside, the door closed behind him, and Nellie took in her first full breath since Richard had surprised her.

Miriam kept the smile on her face, but her voice carried deep concern. "Nellie, honey. Are you hurt?"

Nellie rubbed her hand against her cheek. "How much did you hear?" She didn't even want to think what Miriam might have seen. Though part of her hoped for a witness so the incident couldn't be rewritten for a more palatable history of the marriage between Mr. and Mrs. Richard Murdoch.

"Don't worry about that," Miriam said. She opened the gate in the fence between their yards, softened her voice. "Why don't you come over for a bit? I'll make you a compress and we'll have some coffee."

Nellie hesitated. Coffee sounded good, and Miriam's company and comfortable living room a much-needed reprieve. But Richard could be petty and malicious, and she wasn't certain his anger would stay confined to Nellie. If he believed his wife was confiding in Miriam . . . "I'm not sure that's a good idea." She glanced back at the house, could almost feel Richard's steely gaze on them.

Miriam clucked at her trepidation. "Of course it's a good idea." She scowled then and Nellie knew she'd seen it all, heard everything. "That man is no good. No good at all," she whispered, ushering Nellie through the gate and into her yard.

"I know." Nellie was exhausted and wrung out by the altercation, and leaned into Miriam. "But he's my husband."

"Well, he doesn't deserve you. He's got something coming, you mark my words."

19

Housekeeping accomplishments and cooking ability are, of course, positive essentials. In any true home, every wife should take a reasonable pride in her skill. Happiness does not flourish in an atmosphere of dyspepsia.

> —Reverend Alfred Henry Tyrer, *Sex Satisfaction*
> *and Happy Marriage* (1951)

Alice

.....

JUNE 13, 2018

The first letter, dated the middle of October 1955, was written by Nellie Murdoch to her mother, who Alice now knew was Elsie Swann. It was two pages of humdrum stuff, at least from Alice's perspective: a dinner party where she served something called Baked Alaska; garden slugs; her husband Richard's stomach ulcer, which was acting up. The second and third letters, dated a few weeks apart, contained similarly mundane details.

Disappointed, Alice set the letters aside and called Bronwyn, but the call went to voice mail. A few seconds later she got a text back from her friend saying she was in meetings all day, chat later? Alice missed meetings, or at least her old schedule, which had been frustratingly harried at times but also the foundation of her identity. The confidence from her encounter with Georgia had since faded, and she was back to feeling unmoored. Who was she if not a crackerjack publicist at a top-tier firm? A so-far-failing novelist, a hopeless gardener, an amateurish cook.

With a sigh Alice set her phone—which rarely lit up with messages other than those from Nate, Bronwyn, and her mother these days—on top of the letters and decided to look for this Baked Alaska dessert. Checking the cookbook's index and flipping to a page near the middle, she found the dessert's photo—a dome-shaped layered cake—and scanned the recipe, whose main ingredients were ice cream, egg whites, and sponge cake. *Impress your guests!* the description promised, with Elsie Swann's familiar handwriting beside it: *Fancy and delicious,* and directly underneath, Nellie's own notation (which Alice now recognized thanks to the letters): *Success! Dinner with the Graves, the Reinhardts, the Sterlings—October 14, 1955*

Baked Alaska

9-inch-round layer of Egg Yolk Sponge Cake

2 quarts strawberry ice cream

6 large egg whites

½ teaspoon cream of tartar

1 cup sugar

Make sponge cake and set aside to cool. Pack strawberry ice cream in a round bowl (about 1 inch smaller than cake layer) and place in freezing compartment of refrigerator. Shortly before serving time, make meringue by beating egg whites with cream of tartar until frothy. Add sugar gradually while continuing to beat until meringue is stiff and glossy. Place cooled cake on baking sheet and loosen ice cream from bowl, then invert over cake and remove the bowl. Cover the ice cream and cake with the meringue, ensuring it reaches the baking sheet to create a meringue seal so the ice cream won't melt. Place in very hot oven (500°F) for 3 to 5 minutes, or just until meringue is lightly browned. Slip dessert onto serving tray and serve at once.

Checking her phone (no messages) Alice saw it was close to three. She had promised herself she would write for at least an hour before starting dinner, so she left the cookbook open at the dessert recipe and sat at the desk, determined to make progress.

Alice set her hands on the laptop keys and waited for something to happen. She thought about her interaction with Georgia—what could be more *Devil Wears Prada*–ish than that?—but all that came to mind was Nellie, and what she might have been doing on a Wednesday afternoon. Based on the letters so far, Alice envisioned a predictable trifecta of cleaning, cooking, and gardening. She wondered what that would have been like— when a clean house and a meat loaf in the oven fulfilled expectations. Would it have been a relief, the simplicity of it? Or dispiriting to know that's all there would ever be?

Pushing thoughts of Nellie aside, Alice forced her fingers to type, words turning into sentences, and soon enough she had her first two pages written. But when she paused to reread, she scowled and promptly deleted all of it. Discouraged, she closed her laptop and headed back to the kitchen.

Having already settled on a dinner of chicken thighs in a pineapple-barbecue sauce, she thought the Baked Alaska dessert would be a nice surprise for Nate—he loved ice cream. The chicken recipe was easy, and ten minutes later it was in the fridge marinating. After washing her hands, Alice donned an apron and started on the Baked Alaska.

She was worried about the dinner. Not the meal itself, but the conversation she planned to have with Nate after it. While she gathered the dessert ingredients, she rehearsed what she'd say: she wanted to wait a few more months before they got pregnant. She would barely be thirty by that time. Nate would likely be upset, but she hoped he'd come around to see things from her point of view. Like Sally had said, they were still young.

Alice opened the freezer to see if there was enough ice cream. No strawberry, but there was a quart of chocolate. As for the cake, she opted for a premade Entenmann's loaf, which she trimmed and stacked onto a baking sheet until she had something resembling a round base. The ice cream was solid, so she set it out for a few minutes, using a spoon to scrape off the top layer, letting it melt on her tongue while she waited for the rest to soften. Alice flipped through the cookbook, noting that jellied salads seemed particularly popular in those days, and shuddered at a recipe that called for lemon gelatin and canned tuna.

Fifteen minutes later she had eaten the top third of the ice cream and the remainder was soft enough to pack into a small mixing bowl. She placed the bowl in the freezer and padded back to her desk, where she sat staring out the window for an hour, making no progress on her book.

Nate was supposed to be home at six thirty, seven at the latest. An hour later he still hadn't arrived, and Alice texted him.

On your way? Dinner about to come out of oven.

No response, and still no Nate by eight thirty. Alice fumed as she poured her second glass of wine and pushed the overcooked, cold chicken and shriveled pineapple chunks around her plate. She called him, but his phone went straight to voice mail, which was when worry overtook irritation. Alice checked for news of train delays or accidents. Nothing. Maybe he had been hit by a car riding his bike home from the station? Rattled and anxious, she paced the living room while she finished the wine. Just as she thought maybe she should go look for him—but she couldn't drive, two glasses of wine in—a text came through.

Sorry, babe. Study session went late, grabbing bite here. Rain check on dinner?

She stared at the text for a full minute. *Rain check?* She imagined Nate at the office with Drew, who probably had plenty of important things to do each day, eating takeout and laughing between bouts of focus. Nate having completely forgotten about his wife and dinner waiting for him at home.

She seethed about Nate's lack of consideration as she whipped the egg whites until glossy peaks formed. With some difficulty, as it was frozen solid, Alice transferred the dome of chocolate ice cream onto the loaf base. As she covered the whole thing with the egg-white meringue, trying to make the cloud-like layer even, despite her heavy-handedness, she fervently whispered the things she would say to her husband when he finally came home.

I would have appreciated a call. I was worried.

Did you have a nice time with Drew?

Rain check? You don't "rain check" dinner with your wife!

I hope you don't mind your pineapple chicken cold . . . also, I don't want to have a baby right now.

Still mumbling in frustration, Alice bent to keep an eye on the meringue dome in the oven. At four minutes the peaks *were* golden, but there was also a pool of brown liquid seeping out from under the cake base. Alice promptly took the dessert out and frowned as she poked the droopy meringue. Surely this was not what Nellie had labeled "Success!" It looked inedible. Using a large kitchen knife, she cut a slice in the dome's surface and quickly transferred it to a plate. The piece itself was relatively intact, but the moment she removed it, the rest of the dessert collapsed. She tried to hold one side up with the knife, but the other side buckled, and so she let it go.

Alice took her plate and stood at the kitchen sink, staring into the darkened backyard while she finished the piece of Baked Alaska. Then she left her plate and fork, unrinsed, on the counter beside the remainder of the dessert—by the time Nate arrived home, hours later, all that would be left was a pool of melted chocolate ice cream with a sodden cake island in its center—and went to bed, her mind made up.

20

Nellie

....

JULY 7, 1956

Mint Sauce

....

1½ tablespoons confectioners' sugar

3 tablespoons hot water

⅓ cup finely minced mint leaves

½ cup very mild wine vinegar

A couple drops of green vegetable coloring

Dissolve sugar in hot water. Cool sugar water then blend in minced mint leaves and wine vinegar. Add green vegetable coloring. Let stand for half an hour and serve cool. Makes 1 cup of sauce.

*T*he best time to harvest herbs was after the early-morning dew dried, and Nellie had a long list of things to do, starting with her herb garden. While the sun rose higher and Richard kept sleeping, Nellie used her kitchen shears to trim leaves and stalks from her herb plants to later dry for her seasoning mix.

Rosemary. Sage. Parsley. Dill. Lemon balm. Mint. Marjoram.
Snip, snip, snip went her nimble hands, swathed in gardening gloves to prevent scratches.

It had been nearly a week since Richard had hit her, and Nellie had since accepted her marriage was at best unsustainable, at worst perilous. The Richard she met at the supper club—the charming man who showered her with attention and gifts and made her believe happiness was ripe for the taking—no longer existed. In truth, he had vanished on their wedding night, when Richard roughly pushed himself inside her, his small hands selfish as they ripped her beautiful pale blue nightgown in his haste, the delicate pearl buttons flying off like popped corn. That was the moment Nellie began her education on what it meant to be Richard Murdoch's wife. This would be a life where the most important thing she could do was stand by his side, take care of him, give herself over to him bit by bit. He needed her to look pretty, cook him hot meals, open her legs to him without feigning a headache or lady troubles. She was to keep her opinions to herself while also keeping his dozen or so white dress shirts sparkling and clean of other women's lipsticks. But Nellie had wanted a baby badly enough that despite all this she remained patient if not vigilant, hoping her efforts wouldn't be for naught.

Nellie knew leaving Richard would not be simple; it came with repercussions, both financial and social, and therefore, she needed a plan.

Satisfied with her work, she stood and arched back slightly to stretch her cramped muscles. It was turning out to be a beautiful day, and Nellie, not quite ready to go inside, slid a cigarette from the carton and set it between her lips. She sat on the grass and smoked languidly, the herbs piled on a dish towel by her feet.

Tomorrow, Sunday, was Richard's thirty-fifth birthday. She was planning his favorite meal—lamb chops with mint sauce, which she would make today, along with mashed potatoes, green peas, and peach cobbler. Nellie would wear her prettiest dress, adding to it a spritz of perfume and her most convincing smile, and they would have a nice meal.

As she smoked the cigarette, the sun adding another layer of tan on her outstretched legs, she decided Monday would be the day. She would tell him she had to go visit her mother, whom Richard had never met—her dementia made her incredibly agitated with strangers, Nellie explained when Richard had asked once about joining her. She would pack only a small valise for the trip, into which she would bury the envelope of dollar bills she'd been squirrelling away.

Nellie had been clever, and careful, the way her mother taught her to be. Whenever she went to the market, she would buy only what was on sale, pocketing the extra from her weekly budget and sliding it into magazine spines, where Richard would never think to look. Sometimes when he had too much to drink, or was ill and delirious with stomach pains, Nellie would help herself to a little more as she emptied his pockets to launder his clothes. And when she went to the bank to get money for her dresses or beauty items or necessities for their home—areas Richard allowed Nellie to have near complete control over—she would take slightly more than she needed. It was amazing how much one could save with careful scrimping.

Yes, she would leave Richard on Monday. She would go see her mother and, after that, figure out what to do next. Nellie was resilient and capable, and she would land on her feet. Leaving her beloved house and cherished gardens and dear friend Miriam would pain her greatly. But it had been Miriam who had given her the idea, and Nellie knew she would understand.

"You're a beautiful woman, Nellie. Smart too," Miriam had said, pouring them both a coffee after she rescued Nellie from her backyard standoff with Richard. "And my Lord, can you cook! There isn't a thing you can't do, dear, if you put your mind to it."

"Thank you for saying that, Miriam," Nellie had replied, the shaking finally subsiding, though her jaw continued to throb. Miriam had made a chamomile poultice, heating the dried buds in warm apple cider vinegar before squeezing out the liquid and wrapping the moistened flowers in layers of cheesecloth. Nellie held the soothing, fragrant compress to her cheek. "But I'm not sure that's entirely true."

Miriam had frowned, regarded Nellie with a look that was sympathetic but not at all pitying. "You can always stay with me if you need to. I'd love the company."

Nellie nodded, wrapping one hand around the warmth of her coffee cup. Knew that could never happen because of how much it would anger Richard, putting Miriam at risk as well.

"You could say I needed the help, for a few days anyway. Maybe I've caught my death of a cold, or my arthritis has flared so badly I can't boil water?"

"You're a good friend." Nellie grasped Miriam's hand, squeezed lightly.

"I have some savings," Miriam said, reaching into the drawer of her buffet table. She handed her a thick envelope, Nellie's name written in black ink on its surface. Nellie felt ashamed at her own weakness, wondered how long Miriam had been keeping this envelope of cash for her.

"I'd like you to have it, honey. I want to help." Nellie was filled with gratitude at the offer but would never take Miriam's money, despite the older woman's insistence. Nellie assured her she had some savings of her own tucked aside—not a lot, but enough to get her away from Richard.

It was nearly ten in the morning when she took the last drag on the cigarette. Nellie wanted to get the herbs drying and the mint jelly started so there was still time to market before she had to get ready for their evening. They had a dinner party to attend, at the Graveses'. Richard had been sulking about it all week, knowing he'd have to talk to the "shuckster" Charles, who was surely invited, as the Goldmans and Graveses were close friends. Nellie wasn't any more interested in socializing with Kitty, but she did enjoy Martha's company and at least it meant she and Richard wouldn't be alone.

That only left Sunday—his birthday—to get through. They would attend church, and after the luncheon Richard had plans to go bowling with a few of the men in the neighborhood. While he bowled, Nellie would prepare dinner and then treat Richard like a king all evening, ensuring he suspected nothing. The next morning, she would leave under the guise of a quick trip to visit her ailing mother, and that would be the last time she ever saw Richard Murdoch.

Nellie stubbed her cigarette out on the patio stone and took the herbs inside, bundling them loosely with string so they had space to breathe while they dried. She laid the newspaper-lined tea towel flat along the top of the refrigerator, setting the bundles of herbs gently on the towel. Turning her attention to the mint sauce for Richard's birthday dinner, Nellie chopped the fresh mint, adding a few other green herbs for flavor. After dissolving the sugar into the hot water, she smoked another cigarette while she waited for the mixture to cool. Then she added the finely chopped mint and herbs along with the vinegar and vibrant green coloring. She managed to get slightly more than a cup of sauce, and after pouring it into a jam jar, tucked it into the back of the refrigerator.

Later, they got ready for the dinner party in silence, both of them seemingly lost in thought. At the last minute, Nellie switched her shoes, preferring a higher heel with the dress she'd chosen. Richard wasn't pleased, his mouth taut, his hands shoved into his pockets as he watched her slip on the heels. He didn't like her added height, as they would be nearly eye to eye now. But he didn't say anything, simply gestured for her to walk out of the bedroom ahead of him. As she reached the top of the staircase, Richard a half step behind her, Nellie glanced down and was glad for the change. The heels made her legs look even longer under her skirt.

But she should have been more careful, more attentive to her surroundings and less vain about her outfit. Suddenly unbalanced, she gasped as she tipped forward off the top stair. Unable to stop the momentum, Nellie tumbled down the staircase like a rag doll, and though Richard had been right behind her only moments earlier, he didn't grab for her before she fell.

21

Don't expect your husband to make *you* happy while you are simply a passive agent. Do your best to make *him* happy and you will find happiness yourself.

    —Blanche Ebbutt, *Don'ts for Wives* (1913)

Alice

.....

JULY 12, 2018

What is the right outfit to wear to your estranged father's funeral? Alice stared at the black sea of clothing strewn across the guest room bed, paralyzed by indecision. Eventually she chose a skirt and jacket off the top, and paired them with a sleeveless white blouse and black flats. She dressed slowly despite being late, while Nate, long ago ready, paced the living room, waiting for her.

It had been raining for three days straight, but the moment Alice stepped from the car and onto the cemetery's soggy green grass, the sun came out. A woman behind her whispered, "Oh, Greg always loved a good silver lining," as the sunbeams cast a glare on top of her father's glossy coffin. Alice kept her head lowered, but she did not cry. Nate wrapped an arm around her shoulders.

Alice was relieved at how easily she blended in—another black-outfitted mourner, anonymous in the crowd. She wondered if those around her knew Greg Livingston had a daughter. If they could see a resemblance between Alice and her dad. Likely not, she decided, as no one gave her more than a polite but reserved smile.

Sure enough, the sun didn't stay long (much like her father, she thought), and soon a swath of umbrellas opened, like colorful dots against the otherwise gray sky. Alice had no idea who all these people standing in concentric circles at the grave site were, but her father clearly had friends who cared about him. Alice wanted to be glad for that, but realizing all these strangers knew him in ways she didn't cut deeply. Greg Livingston had left and never once tried to get in touch, at least as far as Alice knew. No birthday cards, no Christmas presents, no phone calls to check in. Jaclyn also had no idea where he was, so it wasn't like Alice could have reached out even if she'd wanted to. As she grew up, her father became a faded memory she rarely invoked.

Because of this, Alice hadn't wanted anything to do with the funeral. "Why should I go?" she'd said to Nate on Sunday night, four days earlier, when Jaclyn—still Alice's father's emergency contact—had called to let their only child know he had died. "We're basically strangers."

Apparently, he had moved from Florida and back to New York State at some point earlier in the year, and was working odd construction jobs for the summer. He had settled only fifteen miles from where Alice and Nate now lived, close enough that they might have even passed each other at a grocery store, or on the trains going back and forth. Would she have recognized him, not having seen him in nearly twenty years?

Greg had been alone when he died, her mother told her. In a one-bedroom apartment that probably had little food in the fridge but a well-stocked liquor cabinet. "What happened?"

Alice had asked, her breath catching despite her best efforts to stay unaffected by this news. Nate, unaware of the news at that point, had looked over at her, the shift in her tone causing his forehead to crease with concern.

"An accidental overdose, apparently."

"Of what?" Alice asked. Pause. "An accidental overdose of what, Mom?"

Jaclyn heaved a sigh. "Does it really matter, Alice?"

"Yes, it matters."

"Well, they said it was Valium. He was probably having trouble sleeping again," Jaclyn said. "Greg was never a good sleeper." The silence hung heavy between the women for a moment. "Alice? Are you still there, honey?"

"Yes," Alice had said, as Nate set a supportive hand against her back. "Now what?"

Jaclyn went on to say she hoped Alice would go to the funeral. Reminded her to up her vitamin C intake to counteract the physical effects of this news.

"Why?" Alice had asked, about the funeral, not the vitamin C, because she was truly incredulous at her mother's request. Jaclyn said she would have flown up but Steve had rotator cuff surgery scheduled the day after, and she needed to be home.

Alice was the only one left to go, and so she went. She held her own umbrella against the rain, and an ache in her gut spread through the rest of her body like tentacles; soon every part of her hurt. Like she was feverish with a flu, her body struggling to rid itself of some virus trying to take over. Maybe she should have listened to her mother about the vitamins, she thought, as the sense of sickness spread.

Later, Nate found Alice lying on the living room floor, still in her funeral ensemble. Hands stretched overhead and eyes closed;

the only movement was in her chest, which rose in measured breaths.

"What are you doing?" Nate asked, sitting on one end of the sofa so he could see her face. His voice carried worry, though he kept his tone light. She wanted to be alone. Though lying in the middle of the living room floor was not the most inconspicuous place to rest when one wanted solitude.

"Does it feel warmer in here?" Alice asked.

"Warmer? I don't know," Nate replied. "I guess so?"

"Don't you think that's weird? I mean, this room used to be freezing. I had to wear a sweater all the time. And now it's warm."

"Do you want me to open a window?" Nate asked.

"No. I like it." Alice's eyes remained closed as she took in a long breath, appreciating the moment of serenity.

"Do you need anything? A glass of water?"

"In one of those magazines it said if you feel tired to lie on the floor with your eyes closed for five minutes."

Alice didn't see Nate's smile because her eyes were shut. "Which magazine?" he asked.

"One of the old ones I found in the basement, with the cookbook. From the fifties."

Nate's knees cracked when he crouched, and his arm pressed against hers as he lay on the floor beside her. Things hadn't been quite right between them since the night Nate blew off dinner—despite his apologies, promises to make it up to her—but it was a lot of work, staying angry. They lay in silence for a while, only the sound of their breath filling the space between them.

"Do you want to talk about it?" he finally asked.

Alice shook her head. "No."

"Okay." The blissful quiet enveloped Alice again. "It's all right to be upset, Ali. He was still your father."

"In title only," Alice replied. She opened her eyes, stared at the plaster ceiling covered with fancy swirls and tiny crests that proved excellent holders for spiderwebs. She should probably take a broom to it tomorrow. "I'm going to start dinner."

Nate rolled onto his side toward her, bent his elbow, and rested his head in his palm. "I thought we could order in tonight."

"Already thawed the chicken." Alice sat up slowly and wrapped her arms around her knees. Her head was fogged, probably because she hadn't yet eaten today, and she waited for the dizziness to pass. "I think the house likes it when I cook."

There was a pause from Nate, and then: "You mean, because it smells good?" He sat up as well.

Alice took a breath in, let it out. Still light-headed. "That too."

Nate shook his head, laughed gently. "I'm confused."

"I know it sounds nuts, but ever since I started making recipes from Nellie Murdoch's old cookbook, the house feels warmer. And we haven't had a house disaster in over a week." Alice stood, felt okay. "The kitchen tap doesn't drip anymore, and even the fridge has gone quiet. Did you notice how quiet it is?"

Nate's mouth opened and closed; then he smiled and got to his feet as well. He rubbed Alice's back, her jacket bunching slightly as he did. "I think you need some sleep, sweets."

"Go in the kitchen and listen," Alice said as she walked to the stairs, wanting to change before making dinner. She slipped her shoes off before she started up, Nellie's last letter outlining a nasty slip and fall down this very staircase—the last thing Alice needed was a broken ankle, or worse. "You'll see. It doesn't rattle anymore."

Nate put his hands on his hips, frowning as he watched Alice climb the stairs, creaking with each step. Then he went into the kitchen and waited, counting to ten . . . then twenty, listening for the reliable clunks and clatters of their antique refrigerator. But it had gone quiet, after all.

From the desk of Eleanor Murdoch

July 18, 1956

Dearest Mother,

I'm sorry I'm unable to visit as planned. This broken ankle is keeping me tied to home, and I'm convalescing with an ugly plaster cast on my leg that the doctor feels will have to stay on for some time yet. I'm not typically prone to clumsiness, but the unfortunate combination of a new pair of heels and freshly polished stairs resulted in quite the dramatic fall. It was most upsetting, but the pain has now eased, thankfully. I do hope to be relieved of this plaster sooner than Dr. Johnson has suggested. My accident also ruined Richard's birthday dinner—I had made a most gorgeous batch of mint jelly to go with lamb chops—but I'll make it up to him soon enough.

Helen, our girl, is staying in the guest room for a couple of weeks to help out, but I fear she won't be able to manage the garden too. It's going to be an awful mess when I'm finally able to get back to it, with all the rain we've been having recently. I wish you could be here—the garden and I would be so lucky to have you! I did manage to cut and dry enough herbs for another batch of herb mix before my fall, and my lovely neighbor Miriam is coming over to help me make it while I'm off my feet. I'd hate for Richard to go without, as he really does love the added spice on his meals.

His stomach pains had been improving, but the last few nights he's been quite unwell. I've had Helen prepare some of your tried-and-true invalid meals, though they seem not to be making much of a difference yet. My own appetite is down, which I suppose is good, as I spend so much time lying about these days, and getting thick in the middle will only make things worse.

Will send more news soon. Kisses and all my love.

Your loving daughter, Nellie xx

22

Nellie
....

JULY 18, 1956

*N*ellie scowled at the bulky plaster of paris cast on her leg, perched on top of a sofa cushion. At least she had painted her toenails before her accident. The wooden crutches leaned beside her as she wrote on her lap, using a stack of magazines to keep her correspondence paper from creasing. She folded the finished letter carefully, lining the edges up and licking the envelope flap to seal it. She wrote out her mother's address in its center and her own at the top left corner before setting the envelope on the side table within reach.

"Would you like me to mail that for you, Mrs. Murdoch?" Helen came into the living room to collect Nellie's barely touched lunch. "I can pop by the post office on my way to the market this afternoon. It's no bother."

"Please, Helen, call me Nellie," she replied, like she did every time Helen called her by her mother-in-law's name, Mrs. Murdoch. Helen, who was a head taller than Nellie, with large eyes that always looked surprised, nodded at the request, but Nellie knew she wouldn't abide by it. "And, no, thank you, it's fine. I'm planning to write a few more, so perhaps once those are done

I'll have you send them along." Nellie tucked the envelope inside the front cover of the most recent issue of *Ladies' Home Journal*.

"Anything else I can get for you before I go, ma'am?"

"I'm fine for now," Nellie said. "Also, I was thinking about cold lamb sandwiches with mint sauce for dinner this evening. Maybe with a green salad? Do we still have some lamb left?"

"Enough for at least one sandwich." Helen reached behind Nellie and fluffed up her pillows, coming close in a way that made Nellie uncomfortable. The bruise across her jaw was merely a shadow now, but Nellie still tucked her chin to the side and out of Helen's sight.

"Are you done with your lunch?" Helen asked.

"I am, thank you. It was delicious, but my appetite isn't quite back yet." She smiled in apology. "Save the lamb for Richard. It's one of his favorites."

Helen nodded. "I'll prepare it when I'm back from the marketing. What about your supper?"

"I'll have a small salad, maybe some broth. Thank you, Helen. That's all for now."

"Knock-knock!" Miriam's voice echoed from the front door.

"Oh, could you see Miriam in, please?" Nellie asked.

"Of course, Mrs. Murdoch," Helen replied, to which Nellie sighed softly. "I'll leave that sandwich there for you in case you get hungry later."

"Fine, thank you." Nellie fought to keep the irritation from her tone. Helen's near constant presence and fussing made Nellie claustrophobic and unsettled. She needed the help but had grown used to being alone in her house. However, Richard had been quite insistent: Helen would stay with them until Nellie could manage things on her own, whether she liked it or not.

"How's our patient doing?" Miriam moved slowly, clearly suffering with her swollen joints today. She chose a chair across from Nellie and gave a warm smile. "You look better, dear. More color in those beautiful cheeks."

"You are too kind," Nellie replied. "But how are you? You seem to be in some pain yourself?"

"Oh, I'm right as rain. Don't fret. You have enough on your plate, dear."

Helen popped her head back into the living room. "Can I get you something to drink, Mrs. Claussen?"

"Oh, that would be lovely. I'll have whatever Nellie is having."

"Iced tea," Helen said, and Miriam nodded. "Sounds perfect, thank you, Helen."

Soon they each had a fresh glass of ice-cold tea and a slice of Miriam's coffee cake, which she'd brought with her, and they discussed the weather (the sun was supposed to make an appearance at some point) and what to do about a recent explosion of voles—furry little rodents that feasted on succulent roots, bulbs, and especially grass—that had left unsightly bare patches crisscrossing Miriam's lawn. Eventually the front door shut when Helen left for town, the two women finally alone.

Miriam took a sip from her glass before placing it on a coaster. "So how are things today, dear?"

"I can't complain," Nellie replied. "Richard has been keeping himself . . . busy." She didn't specify with what, or with whom.

"Well, I suppose that's a blessing, isn't it?" Miriam said. Nellie murmured that it was, strangely thankful to Richard's secretary, Jane, who was keeping him occupied—the how and the what irrelevant now.

"Are you still able to help me with my herbs today?" Nellie asked.

"I'd be delighted. Lord knows you've helped me plenty."

"I promise it won't be too taxing on those hands of yours."

"My hands are perfectly fine," Miriam replied. Nellie knew

that wasn't true, but she wouldn't have asked for her friend's assistance if she was able to do it herself.

"On that note, I think it's time to get to work," Miriam said, slapping her palms against her skirted thighs. "Tell me what to do."

"Oh, there's one other small thing." Nellie retrieved the envelope from the front of the magazine. "Would you take this for me?"

"Same as the others?"

"Yes, please," Nellie said, and Miriam tucked the envelope into her purse. Nellie was grateful for Miriam's endlessly supportive presence. The older woman never asked questions Nellie couldn't bear to answer, understanding that some things were better left unsaid. Despite their age difference, Miriam was Nellie's most trusted friend.

"Now, is everything in the kitchen?" Miriam asked.

"Yes. The herbs are wrapped in a newsprint bundle on top of the refrigerator. Are you all right on a step stool?" Miriam assured her she was. "You need to pull off the dried leaves and seed pods and put them in the mixing bowl. There's a pestle in the top drawer beside the sink, and two glass shakers on the countertop to store the herbs in once they've been crushed. But I can help with that part. My arms aren't broken."

But Miriam wouldn't hear of it. "Nellie, you stay put. Rest while you're able, dear. I may be old and a touch rickety, but I most certainly can crush a few herbs."

"Thank you, Miriam. And don't forget to use the rubber gloves," Nellie added. "Some of those stems are rough, and I'd hate for you to nick yourself. There's a set hanging over the faucet."

"You just lie back and relax." Miriam tutted, patting Nellie's good leg. "I'll have this done in a jiffy, and afterward we'll finish our chat and cake. Sound good?"

"Sounds good." Nellie smiled. "I've left the recipe inside my mother's cookbook, behind the cover. And would you tuck it back inside when you're done? It's an old family recipe and I'd like to keep it between us, if you don't mind."

"Of course," Miriam replied, giving a wink. "Every woman needs a good secret or two."

23

Serving something new? It's a good idea to try the recipe first. Unless you know your guests well, it's best not to serve anything that's too unusual. As a rule, men like simple food and women take to "something different."

—*Better Homes & Gardens Holiday Cook Book* (1959)

Alice

.....

JULY 14, 2018

"Still in a time warp, I see." Bronwyn fingered a fraying edge of the kitchen's floral wallpaper and crinkled her nose, taking in the peach-hued cabinets, ancient fridge, and chrome-legged Formica table. "I thought you'd have it done by now. Actually, I thought you'd be back in the city already. Aren't you losing your mind out here?" She clutched Alice's elbow. "Come back. Please, Ali."

Alice smiled at Bronwyn's plea, continued stirring the sauce, and double-checked the recipe. "I miss you too." She added the peas, cubed cooked chicken, egg, and onion juice. She had never "juiced" an onion before and had no intentions of doing it again. Her eyes had only just stopped watering half an hour before Bronwyn and her boyfriend, Darren, arrived. "And I know it's hard to believe, but it's okay out here. Different, but not in a bad way."

Bronwyn groaned, leaning against the tattered wallpaper with flair. "God, we've lost you. I told Darren I was worried you'd change. That the suburbs would take you prisoner and that would be that. *The end.*" Alice bristled at Bronwyn's assessment, yet couldn't bring herself to admit that was precisely how she felt, at times.

"I'm hardly a prisoner, Bron." Alice rolled her eyes, gave a short laugh. "I just think I've finally figured out this 'adulting' thing." To be fair, Bronwyn's decision to live in Manhattan and work more hours a week than she slept was no less adult than Alice transforming into a suburban housewife and part-time novelist.

Bronwyn huffed, mumbling something about "adulting" being overrated, then got distracted by a purse hanging over one of the chairs. She whistled, ran her fingers along the quilted black leather. "Where did you get this?" she asked, slipping the gold chain strap over her shoulder and striking a pose.

"It was in one of those boxes I found in the basement. The previous owner's old stuff." Along with the purse Alice had also uncovered a dainty gold watch that still worked when she wound it, and a mother-of-pearl hollow tube that, thanks to Google, she'd learned was an antique cigarette holder.

"Ali, this is an original Chanel 2.55. Like, the real deal. Coco Chanel designed it herself."

Whereas Alice was somewhat indifferent when it came to fashion, Bronwyn was a connoisseur; she slept on a Murphy bed in the living room of her small apartment so she could turn her bedroom into a giant closet. "I figured you'd know," Alice said, glad they had shifted to a less onerous topic of conversation. "That's why I left it out for you."

"Damn. This is gorgeous." Bronwyn hummed lightly as she sashayed from side to side, the bag swinging against her hip.

"So why is it called '2.55'?"

"It's the bag's birthday. First made in February 1955. Hand stitched too. And this one looks like it's never been used." Bronwyn opened the flaps, peered inside. Sighed with longing. "Whoever owned this—what was her name again?"

"Nellie. Nellie Murdoch."

"Right. Well, Nellie Murdoch may not have had great taste in kitchen decor, but her choice of handbags was flawless."

"It's yours if you want it." Alice licked a drip of sauce from her finger.

"What? No. No way, lady. I mean, yes, I want it. But you *do not* give away a vintage Chanel 2.55, Alice Hale. No." Bronwyn took the purse from her shoulder and set it on the table, touching the stitching with envious fingers one last time. "But promise me you'll use it, okay? It should get out there, be seen. It's a crime to keep a bag like this in a dark basement. Or on such an ugly table."

Alice laughed and promised to give the purse a "good time."

"Did you also find that outfit in your magical basement box of treasures?" Bronwyn gestured to the full circle skirt of Alice's vintage pale pink cocktail dress. "I have to say, I'm loving this look on you. Especially those." She pointed to Alice's stockings.

Alice's retro stockings were nude, with a black seam snaking down the back that ended in a bow at the top of her heel. She'd bought the stockings, dress, and simple glass-bead necklace at a vintage shop in Scarsdale and had added a pair of glossy red heels from her publicist days to complete the look. Alice turned and raised one leg, looking at the stocking seam and bow. "I do sort of love these," she said. "But can I still be a feminist if I wear pantyhose?"

"Hey, if you like wearing them, then you bet." Bronwyn

smirked. "Nate's gonna like taking those babies off later. *With his teeth*." She wiggled her eyebrows, and Alice laughed easily. She really had missed Bronwyn—the closest thing Alice had to a friend in Greenville was Sally—and the deep bite of homesickness gripped her.

"So, speaking of significant others . . . how's it going with Darren?" Alice asked. Nate had Darren on a tour of the house, where he was surely peppering Bronwyn's newish, architect boyfriend with questions about the renovations. "Nate's probably holding him hostage upstairs, forcing him to determine which walls are load-bearing and which ones we could take the sledgehammer to."

"Darren lives for that shit." Bronwyn pulled out a chair and sat cross-legged in her slim black pants, which she'd paired with an off-white lace top. "He'd move us out here in a second. Into a house that would slowly suck out my life force, one wallpapered room at a time." She pointedly looked around the kitchen, frown in place, which Alice chose to ignore.

"Moving in, huh? Sounds like things are going well?"

"Ali, you know how I feel about sharing closet space—I don't." Bronwyn twirled her wineglass between her fingers, a small smile taking shape. "But he's okay."

"You know, there's a house for sale down the block. Loads of wallpaper. I'll make sure to mention it to Darren at dinner."

Bronwyn swatted at her. "Don't you dare. I told you, I'm never leaving the island." She picked up a potato chip from the bowl and held it over a glass dip dish on the table. "What's this?"

"It's called 'Hollywood Dunk.' An appetizer from the fifties."

Bronwyn dipped the chip into the white creamy spread speckled with green dots and popped it in her mouth. She chewed slowly, her face moving through a variety of expressions—none of them good.

"Yeah, I know." Alice laughed as she watched her best friend try to get the chip and dip down.

A giant swig of wine later, Bronwyn sputtered, "What's in that?"

"Deviled ham. Chives. Onion. Horseradish."

Bronwyn stared at her, mouthed, *Deviled ham?*

"It's chopped up deli ham mixed with mayonnaise, mustard, hot pepper sauce, and salt and pepper, and then you blend it a bit. Then you add the chives, onion, and horseradish. Oh, and the last thing is whipped cream. Can't forget that," Alice added.

"Why would you make this? *To eat?*" Bronwyn pressed a napkin to her lips and squeezed her eyes shut. "Whipped cream and ham should never mingle. Never ever, never."

Alice placed the still-full dip dish in the sink. "Agreed. That's why it wasn't out. I was curious, but it's disgusting."

"Thanks for the warning," Bronwyn murmured, now drinking wine directly from the bottle.

"You didn't give me a chance!" Alice replied.

"I was hungry. I've been on a stupid juice cleanse," Bronwyn retorted, and they both laughed.

"You're lucky I didn't serve the bananas wrapped in ham, baked with hollandaise sauce on top."

Bronwyn made a retching sound and took another swig of wine. Then she rested her chin on the bottle's top. "Did I mention I've missed you?"

"Me too, Bron." She used to share everything with Bronwyn. But lately there was more her best friend didn't know—about the lawsuit, her frustrations with Nate and his schedule, her inability to write, how she missed her old job so much some days she had a hard time dragging herself out of bed. Bronwyn tried, responding to texts when she could, promising catch-up calls that didn't materialize, but the chasm seemed to widen with each passing week.

"I know you said it isn't so bad, but are you *happy* out here, Ali?"

Alice considered the question. "I'm, like, seventy percent happy."

"And the other thirty percent?"

"Lonely, bored, certain I've made a big fucking mistake. Ten percent each."

Bronwyn snorted. "Hey, that's not so bad." She refilled Alice's wineglass. "Here's to your seventy percent suburban happiness, even if it has you making revolting dips to feed to your city friends."

After they'd finished their meal, which was well received by all, the group settled into the living room to have dessert. Alice was full and too warm from the wine, but she felt relaxed and pleased with the success of her first dinner party.

"This has been great, you guys. Except for that Hollywood Dunk crap." Bronwyn shuddered, and Alice laughed, handing her a slice of chocolate cake.

"Thanks for coming all the way out here," Alice replied, cutting a last sliver of cake for herself. "It has been way too long since we've hung out."

"I know! I can't believe I haven't seen you in, like, almost two months." Bronwyn and Alice used to have a standing Tuesday-night drinks-and-dinner date, and rarely went two days without talking. "Wait. Has it actually been two whole months?"

"Not that long," Nate said, pressing his fork's tines into the cake. "You guys went to Trattoria Dell'Arte, what, like three or four weeks ago?" He popped the morsel of cake in his mouth and looked at Alice for confirmation. Fluttery panic filled her belly.

"Right. That was only a few weeks ago." Alice locked eyes

with Bronwyn, who paused to take a sip from her wine. "I'd forgotten about that."

"Yeah, me too," Bronwyn said slowly. "It feels like longer. Doesn't it, Ali?"

"It really does," Alice replied, a flush filling her cheeks. Bronwyn gave her a quizzical look, and Alice stood quickly. "Who wants coffee?"

Nate gently pressed her shoulders, forcing her back to the couch. "You stay put. Enjoy your cake. I'll get it," he said.

"Can I help?" Darren asked.

"Sure," Nate replied. "I can pick your brain about the kitchen."

Once the two men left the room Bronwyn turned on Alice. "Okay. So why did we go to Trattoria for lunch when we didn't go to Trattoria for lunch?"

Alice sighed. "I'll fill you in later."

"Why not now?" Bronwyn asked, topping up her wineglass. "Darren is long-winded when it comes to renovations. Those two won't be back for ages."

"It's a long, complicated story."

"Those are my favorite kind," Bronwyn said, swinging her feet up to rest on Alice's lap.

Alice glanced toward the kitchen, then lowered her voice. "It's no big deal, but I had to go in and meet with Georgia, and I didn't want to tell Nate because, well, he's got so much going on with work and he doesn't need anything else to worry about."

"Why did Georgia want to meet with you?"

"Shhhh. Bronwyn, you can hear everything in this old house."

Bronwyn cringed. "Sorry," she whispered, leaned closer to Alice. "But what did the Queen Bitch want?"

Alice paused. She could tell Bronwyn—*should* tell her. And she'd be happy to, actually, because Alice felt quite victorious about how things had sorted themselves out. "It was James

Dorian." She spoke softly, and Bronwyn's eyes widened. "There was this lawsuit—"

Darren popped his head back into the living room. "Hey, Ali, where's the sugar?"

"Um, in the right-hand cupboard. Bottom shelf," Alice replied, her voice suddenly too loud.

"Thanks," Darren said, retreating back to the kitchen.

Bronwyn grabbed Alice's free hand. "What lawsuit?" she hissed. "What the hell, Ali? Are you okay? Why didn't you tell me any of this?"

Alice only had time to tell Bronwyn the lawsuit had thankfully been dropped—without going into detail—as a moment later Nate and Darren were back with a tray of mugs, along with the sugar and creamer. "Coffee will be ready momentarily," Nate said, putting the tray down. "So, what did we miss?"

Bronwyn looked at Alice, opened her mouth, then shut it. Then put on a big smile and turned to Nate. "We were just discussing opening another bottle of wine. It's only eleven, which is too soon for coffee, don't you think?"

Darren shrugged and Nate said, "That works for me."

"All righty, then." Bronwyn pushed up from the couch, taking a full bottle of wine from the stand by the dining room table. "Shall I open this?"

"You shall," said Alice, nodding affirmatively, grateful for the reprieve.

Coffee forgotten and wineglasses full, conversation soon turned back to the renovations, and Alice groaned and lay her head back against the couch. "Nate, come on. Darren, what's your hourly rate? I think we've about maxed out on the free advice at this point."

Darren and Bronwyn smirked, and Nate looked appropriately sheepish. "I know, I know. Sorry," he said. "But, Ali, Darren had some great ideas for upstairs." He perched on the edge of his chair. "Like putting in a Jack and Jill bathroom between our room and the nursery. What do you think?"

"Nursery, huh?" Bronwyn asked, eyes locked on Alice.

"Our next little project," Nate said, his grin wide, emphasis on the word "little." "I think barefoot and pregnant will look good on Ali, don't you guys agree?" He laughed, too hard, a bit drunk, and Darren joined in. Until Bronwyn, who had quietly uttered, "Oh boy . . . ," at Nate's terrible joke, gave her boyfriend a look, and it petered out.

Nate, sensing the joke hadn't landed the way he'd hoped, leaned forward and kissed Alice on her cheek. "Ali, come on. I'm kidding. You can be a great mom *and* a *New York Times* bestselling author."

Bronwyn whispered, "No pressure," and Alice gave a quick shake of her head. Her heart hammered with irritation, and a hint of resentment toward Nate. Why did he have to bring it up now, and like that? As though these considerable milestones could be summarized in a lame punch line?

But expressing that would surely have led to an awkward scene. So instead Alice cleared her throat and raised her glass, though she hated herself for playing along. "To a bestselling novel *and* getting knocked up!"

There was a group "Cheers!" and then Nate started in again on the house and Alice sipped her wine, thinking—with only a smidgen of remorse—how grateful she was that Nate couldn't read her mind.

24

Nellie

········

JULY 30, 1956

Tuna Casserole

···

2 cans cream of mushroom soup

1 cup milk

2 7-ounce cans tuna, drained

3 hard-cooked eggs, sliced

2 cups cooked peas

2 teaspoons salt

1 teaspoon pepper

1 cup crushed potato chips

In a casserole dish, blend mushroom soup and milk, stir in tuna, sliced eggs, cooked peas, and salt and pepper. Bake at 350°F for 25 minutes. Top with potato chips and bake 5 minutes longer.

Richard would be home soon, and Nellie—though she was getting better at moving about with the plaster cast—was behind schedule. She placed her index finger on the recipe, double-checking the ingredients, and grimaced as an overwhelming itch crawled up the shin of her casted leg.

Swiveling in her kitchen chair away from the worktable, Nellie grabbed the knitting needles from the counter. She slid one needle into the front of her cast and scratched, groaning with the relief. There was no longer pain in her ankle, now that it had been casted for a few weeks, but the itching was awful.

Scratch finally managed, Nellie went back to her recipe. The tabletop had been wiped clean and the casserole was ready for the oven, but the cookbook remained open in front of her. She glanced at the notation her mother had written in the margin (*a generous sprinkle of spices after cooking as needed*) and hopped over to the cabinets near the sink. Nellie set the jar of herb mix Miriam had helped her prepare on the counter, near the water glasses, so she'd remember to put it out with dinner.

The clock above the door sang its on-the-hour tune, and a fresh wave of anxiety moved through her. She was a disheveled mess; her pinned hair was loosening, her makeup had sweated off due to the heat of the stove and the effort of preparing dinner while on crutches. Supporting her weight on the sink's edge, Nellie turned on the tap and wet a dish towel to wipe her face.

She probably should have shortened her earlier visit with Miriam to prevent the scrambling she was doing now. But Miriam had been a lifesaver recently. In many ways, she was the mother Nellie had never had. Nellie loved Elsie, who was brilliant and side-stitch funny and could bake the most delicious cake with her eyes closed and grow beautiful things as if by magic. But she could be difficult to be around. Nellie understood, even from a young age, that her mother had an illness—a darkness of mind that never allowed her to reach her full potential. Elsie Swann constantly struggled to keep her head above those charcoal-black waters threatening to drown her.

Miriam, by comparison, was easy to be with because she was filled with sunbeams; Elsie had little more than thunderclouds inside her.

Oftentimes throughout her childhood it seemed as though Nellie was the one mothering Elsie. While her schoolmates arrived with bagged lunches made by their mothers, Nellie not only prepared her own lunch but also left something in the fridge for her mother each day. As well as a note on a still-asleep Elsie's bedside table with instructions for how long to heat it, even though many days Nellie came home to Elsie still in bed, lunch untouched in the fridge. She did the household chores—the washing, cleaning, marketing when she was old enough to go on her own—and managed the bills, which were a puzzle to sort out some months when money was tight. Nellie was independent and capable of taking care of the home by the time she was twelve years old and probably could have done anything she set her mind to. But instead she married Richard, in part because that's what young women did—becoming a "Mrs." was what proper girls aspired to. But it also meant there would be someone to take care of Nellie for a change.

Nellie set the timer as the front door opened, ten minutes earlier than expected. She chided herself again for not watching the time more carefully. One hand still on the countertop for balance, Nellie scrambled to prepare Richard's old-fashioned. In her haste, the cocktail glass slipped while she muddled the sugar cube with the bitters and it smashed on the floor. At the sound of the breaking glass, Richard came to the kitchen and saw the shards of glass and scowled.

"Where's Helen?" he asked, his tone sharp. He was in a terrible mood; it must not have been a good day at the plant.

"I sent her home this morning," Nellie replied, wondering how to clean up the glass without being able to crouch. The now familiar feeling of helplessness she loathed swept through her. "She's been here nearly every day, Richard, and she has a family to look after, too."

Richard took off his hat and coat and set them on the kitchen chair, sighing with annoyance. He didn't much care for Helen (he found her timid nature unbecoming and her height intimidating, though he would never have used that word), but he also wanted his house pristine, his meals hot, his drink handed to him rather than in a puddle on the kitchen floor. "I'll do it. Move."

She did as he asked, backing up with her crutches and sitting in a chair on the other side of the kitchen. Richard grumbled as he bent to pick up the glass, using the kitchen cloth to clean up the small puddle of bitters and sugar. Nellie didn't comment that there was a cloth for the floor under the sink, that he was using the one for washing dishes and wiping counters. She would have to throw it away now or risk cut hands, the tiny shards of glass nestling firmly into the cloth's woven surface with every pass on the floor.

"I'm sorry. I'm clumsy with these crutches."

Richard said nothing, continued wiping with her good cloth.

"Dinner is in the oven and I can make you another drink," she added.

The silence in the Murdochs' kitchen stretched, punctuated only by Richard's grunts and sighs, the sound of running water from the tap. He left the balled-up cloth in the sink and took another glass from the shelf, made himself a drink without asking Nellie if she wanted anything.

Frustration simmered in Nellie's chest as she watched him, oblivious to his invalid wife sitting two feet away. It was a burn she recognized—anger at being dismissed, at being ignored. Oh, if she could only go back to that night they met, when Richard made her swoon with his attention, his money such a nice change from her frugal upbringing, and not give in to his charm. But it was far too late for such wishful thinking.

Richard drank his cocktail quickly and made another. Again, not asking Nellie if she wanted or needed anything. Finally, he settled somewhat and loosened his tie, taking a seat at the table.

"What's for dinner?" he asked, shaking his glass to distribute the ice cubes.

"Tuna casserole. With buttered carrots and fruit salad."

He finished the last inch of his drink, nodded. "Fine. How much time do we have?"

"About fifteen minutes?" Nellie glanced at the timer. "It's difficult with this leg, to get things done as quickly as I'm used to."

"Should be long enough." Richard stood and headed into the living room. "Come with me."

"Where?" Nellie asked. "For what? I'd like to rest here for a few minutes before I need to get dinner out of the oven."

"Follow me, Eleanor." There was no mistaking his tone, or the use of her full name—this was not a request.

Nellie settled her crutches into her armpits and hobbled after him. "What is this about, Richard?" she asked, once she made it into the living room.

His back was to her at first, but when he turned she saw him undoing his belt buckle. "Lie down on the sofa." He jerked his head toward the green Kroehler sofa Nellie had chosen when they first moved into the house, the color reminding her of vibrant springtime leaves.

She stared at him. "Why?"

Suddenly he was right in front of her, and though Nellie's instincts told her to *Run! Get away!* she stayed put. She was slow on her crutches and wouldn't get out of the room before he caught up. "Lie down on the sofa, Eleanor. And take them off."

"Take what off?"

"Your panties, Nellie. Take them off." Her mouth dropped open. Surely he didn't intend to do what she thought he was suggesting? Her heart pounded, and she wanted to cry. But she did as he asked and didn't shed a tear, because what was the alternative? She set her crutches to the side and sat somewhat clumsily on the sofa's edge, removing her panties from under her skirt. She took an extra moment to fold them and set them on the coffee table before lying back and closing her eyes.

"Open your eyes," Richard said gruffly as he settled his heaviness between her thighs, shifting and moving her skirt up. Roughly pushing her legs apart with one hand as he opened his fly with the other. His tie remained on and his shirt collar, Nellie noticed, was still freshly laundered white—absent a lipstick stain. Perhaps today's black mood had more to do with that than anything else.

"Richard, my ankle!" Nellie gasped as he shoved her plastered leg deep into the back of the Kroehler. It didn't hurt, but it seemed the only rebellion she could get away with. He didn't apologize or seem concerned about her comfort—or the open drapes framing the picture window that faced the street—as he pushed himself inside her. She wasn't ready for him, her anxiety making his passage uncomfortable. Nellie bit her lip and turned her head.

Richard abruptly stopped his rough movements, grabbed her chin, and forced her gaze back. "Look at me, Eleanor."

She did, and had never hated her husband more.

As he thrust and grunted and writhed over her, the sofa springs groaning with the force, Nellie's body stayed still. Quiet and contemplative in a battle she couldn't win. Her arms useless by her sides, the only clue to the tension swirling inside her found in her fists, clenched so tightly there would be bloodred marks left on her palms from her nails. She briefly wished she had not sent Helen home, because then dinner would have been ready and Nellie wouldn't have broken the glass and Richard would never have forced himself on her like this.

She drove her mind out of her living room, away from her husband's face so close to hers she could smell the whiskey on his breath, and thought about her garden. About how she needed to cull more herbs, maybe cut some flowers for Miriam. Perhaps a collection of roses—Miriam loved Nellie's roses. She imagined Elsie in the garden, singing church hymns to the roses, lilies, even the tiny forget-me-nots, encouraging Nellie to sing aloud with her. "God gave you the voice of an angel, Nell-baby. Never be shy to use it, my girl." Her body went numb as her mind wandered, one of the hymns coming back to her as she softly hummed its tune in time to Richard's cruel thrusting.

He moved quickly, and soon his eyes rolled back and he went limp, releasing his weight fully onto her chest as he shuddered in waves. Nellie couldn't take a proper breath but didn't dare say a word, knowing it would only delay things. Richard was spiteful that way. She understood she was still being punished, and so she took it like the dutiful wife she was supposed to be.

Soon enough he rolled off her, zipping up his trousers though he didn't bother tucking his shirt in. "Stay like that for now, Nellie." He leaned down and kissed her on the lips—gently, the way a good husband would. Tugging the edge of her skirt, he pulled the hem over her bare thighs, using such care in covering her back up, unlike the way he had exposed her only minutes ago. He smiled and the hatred inside her grew to a rolling boil. "We want to make sure there's a baby, don't we?"

Nellie nodded and smiled, though she remained still and otherwise detached so Richard would leave her be.

"Would you like a cigarette?" he asked. "Apparently you were right about that. The doc did say it helps relax women."

"Yes, please," Nellie said, her voice steady.

"Coming right up." Richard patted her hip before he went to the kitchen. She heard him fixing a drink, and knowing it was a risk to do so—but perhaps riskier not to—Nellie got up, taking her weight on her good leg. She hopped one-legged, her eyes never leaving the doorway, hoping to dispel what Richard had left inside of her before he returned. Because even though Nellie's longing for motherhood endured, burned in her like a fever that wouldn't break, she couldn't be sure how deeply rooted the evil was in her husband. And as a result, Nellie would not be responsible for bringing a son, another man like Richard Murdoch, into this world. Or worse, a baby girl, for Richard would see it as his absolute right to control her the way he did Nellie. Ensuring he raised an obedient daughter who would grow into a submissive wife, without a moment's concern for her own wishes.

After some one-legged bouncing, there was a wetness between her thighs, and knowing she had done all she could, Nellie settled back on the green sofa and waited for her cigarette.

25

From the wedding day, the young matron should shape her life to the probable and desired contingency of conception and maternity. Otherwise she has no right or title to wifehood.

—Emma Frances Angell Drake,
What a Young Wife Ought to Know (1902)

Alice

.....

JULY 19, 2018

*D*id you take the ibuprofen?"

Alice nodded, the paper crinkling under her head as she did. She stared at the ceiling, at the track of fluorescent lighting running over the procedure table she lay on. The light hurt her eyes but it was better than focusing on what was happening down below.

"What do you do for work, Alice?"

"I used to be in PR, but now I'm a writer." *At least I'm trying to be.* Alice stared at the lights, then blinked and dots appeared in her vision. *Can you call yourself a writer if you don't actually write?*

"Oh yeah? What sort of writing do you do?"

"This and that. I'm working on a novel right now." She thought of her book. Every morning she woke up eager to work, but within a couple of hours her hopes were dashed and she closed her laptop with a promise the next day would be better. It had become a predictable yet concerning cycle, and she wasn't sure what to do about it. "That's, uh, why I'm here. I need to get my book finished before I get pregnant." *Why had she said that?*

"Birthing a book *and* a baby? Yeah, that would be a lot of work." The doctor sounded sympathetic. "I used to be a voracious reader but don't have much time these days. But I have a stack of books on my nightstand waiting for my next vacation!"

Alice smiled, but it was closemouthed and quick.

"Okay, I'm placing the speculum . . . there we go. Try to relax, let your knees fall a bit more to the side. There, perfect." Dr. Yasmine Sterling, the Scarsdale gynecologist Alice had found through a quick Google search, was hunched between Alice's legs. She looked up and smiled. "All good, Alice?"

"I'm great." Alice tucked her chin to her chest so she could see the doctor. She returned her smile before looking back to the ceiling. Though she was confident this was the right decision (*one year and then I'll have it taken out*)—especially after Nate's joking but thoughtless "barefoot and pregnant" comment—a wiggle of guilt moved through her abdomen and her muscles tensed. The speculum slipped slightly and the doctor told her again to try to relax. "Sorry. I'm just . . . I'm fine."

"I know how uncomfortable this is, but it won't take me long. Hang tight," Dr. Sterling said, then laughed. "Actually, don't hang 'tight'—loose would be better. Hang *loose*." Dr. Sterling repositioned the light and grabbed something off the table beside her.

"Now I'm going to clean your cervix with an antiseptic and we'll be on our way." The doctor had blond hair in need of a root touch-up, but her part was pin straight—not a hair out of place, all pulled back into a low, tight ponytail. Somehow this made Alice feel better about the gynecologist's ability to place the IUD. If she was that precise with her part, she would definitely get the device in exactly the right spot in Alice's uterus.

"I love your purse, by the way. My grandmother used to have a similar Chanel bag."

Alice glanced over at the small, rectangular black quilted handbag sitting on top of her clothes. She had promised Bronwyn she would use it and she had to admit she liked the simplicity of it. The purse wasn't large, so she wasn't endlessly losing her keys or lip gloss in its depths. "We recently moved into this old house, and the previous owner left it behind. It's from the fifties, I think."

"Lucky you," Dr. Sterling said. "It's in great condition, too." Alice jerked at the sharp clang of metal on metal as Dr. Sterling set something on the tray beside her, where a variety of items were lined up, including the IUD, its arms looking like a little white anchor at the top of the tube. "We're almost ready here. Now, you may feel some cramping when I insert the tube and release the IUD. Perfectly normal and it will pass."

Alice nodded, trying not to tense up again with anticipation.

"Take a deep breath. Let it out. Good, good. And one more . . ."

There was pressure, a flutter of sharp pain in her lower abdomen—which deepened quickly and made her suck in her breath, her heels pressing hard into the foot beds of the stirrups. She felt dizzy, but it might have been because her breathing had gone shallow. It hurt a lot more than she expected.

The gynecologist didn't look up. "Keep breathing, Alice. Almost done. I've put the tube through your cervix and am about to release the IUD. A few seconds more. Okay . . . there we go. You okay?"

The cramping continued, and Alice took a deep breath. "A bit of cramping, but I'm okay."

"Good. Last step. Going to remove the tube . . . there we go . . . and now I'm trimming the strings, a couple centimeters below the cervix." A few seconds later it was over, and Dr. Sterling put the empty tube on the tray. "You'll need to check the strings once a month, just to make sure the IUD is still in position. If you don't feel them, come back right away. It's not common, but an IUD can fall out, which means you won't be protected against pregnancy."

Dr. Sterling set the scissors back on the tray and turned off the spotlight pointed between Alice's legs before helping her get her feet out of the stirrups. She snapped off her gloves and pushed her rolling stool back against the wall.

"I'm going to leave this pamphlet here for you." Dr. Sterling set the folded paper on top of Alice's Chanel purse. "It gives you the ins and outs about possible side effects and anything else you need to look out for, like infections or pain. If you get any unbearable pain, or excessive bleeding or a fever"—she put her fist to her ear, mimicking making a phone call—"you call my service right away, okay?"

Alice nodded, a small flutter of cramps continuing to roam through her pelvis. "Now, we can leave this in for five years, and you may not actually have periods. But it won't protect you from sexually transmitted infections, so you'll still need to use condoms."

Dr. Sterling washed her hands in the sink. She lathered twice, rinsed, and ripped some paper towel from the dispenser. "Any other questions?"

"I think I'm good. Can I sit up now?"

"You can." Dr. Sterling nodded. "Nice to meet you, Alice. And like I said, any questions or concerns, don't hesitate to give us a call. My nurse's name and number are on the back of the pamphlet. But I don't expect you to have any problems. You're young and healthy." She started to close the door behind her, then popped her head back in. "Oh, and good luck with that novel. I'll keep my eye out for it!"

26

Eat proper food for health and vitality. Every morning before breakfast, comb hair, apply make-up, a dash of cologne, and perhaps some simple earrings. Does wonders for your morale.

—*Betty Crocker's Picture Cook Book*, revised and enlarged (1956)

Alice

.....

AUGUST 7, 2018

What's all this?" Nate worked the knot into his tie as he surveyed the food spread across the table. Freshly squeezed orange juice. Sunny-side-up eggs. Toast. Bacon and sausage. All of it displayed on the vintage platters that had come with the house. Alice wore a sundress and sheer stockings, her hair in a loose bun, a dab of lipstick and some mascara to complete the look.

"This is breakfast, obviously." Alice pulled out a chair for him. "Sit. Eat. While it's still hot."

"You don't have to tell me twice." Nate carefully tucked his tie into the space between two of his shirt buttons, tidy and precise. Alice thought if she were the one keeping a tie out of her eggs she'd merely toss it over one shoulder and dig in. Nate dusted his eggs with the paprika she'd recently purchased—it seemed a frequently used spice in the cookbook's recipes, and so good to have on hand—while Alice poured the juice, sitting across from him.

"Thanks, babe." Nate buttered a piece of toast and Alice cut into her egg, the sunny yolk pooling onto her plate. "But I have to ask—and don't take this the wrong way—what's the occasion?" Alice typically wasn't up for breakfast, Nate flying out the door before seven with a flask of green smoothie or a coffee and a quickly grabbed banana.

Alice shrugged, cut another triangle of egg with the edge of her fork. *I got an IUD and sorry I didn't tell you about it first?* She had planned to confess over breakfast, but the words wouldn't come. *He will forgive you,* she assured herself. But maybe she'd wait until after they'd eaten so breakfast wasn't ruined. "You're working really hard and I'm . . . not. I mean, I know I'm writing the book." Even though she wasn't. "But I want to do more. 'Earn my keep' so you don't toss me to the curb on garbage day."

Even though her tone carried the lilt of humor, Nate stopped cutting the sausage link and lay his silverware down. "Ali, I hope I'm not doing something to—"

"No. Sorry. That was a bad joke," she replied. "All I meant was we're a team and I can do more. Especially with your exam coming up. Besides, I'm kind of getting into this whole housewife thing." Not the whole truth, but there were aspects of it Alice minded less these days. Like cooking and baking, which helped pass the time and produced something tangible. She dipped a toast finger into her egg yolk, and the fridge emitted its soft hum into the kitchen. It hadn't rattled in weeks.

"Well, if you're happy, I'm happy." Nate took a sip of the juice and smiled again, though it was quick and soon gone.

Are you really, Nate? Can it actually be that simple? Alice thought to ask, but instead she crunched on her yolk-sodden toast.

"So, what do you have going on for the rest of the day?" Nate asked, silverware back in hand.

"Mostly writing, I hope. I've been reading those magazines and Sally gave me a bunch of letters that belonged to the woman who used to live here, Nellie, to help me with my book. And I'm sort of inspired. I think she'd make a great protagonist."

"How so?" Nate asked, genuinely curious.

"I don't know if I can explain it," Alice replied, which was true. Nellie had revealed little more than the day-to-day details of a 1950s housewife schedule, which involved gardening, meal preparation, and Tupperware parties ad nauseam. There was frequent concern over Richard's stomach ulcer, news of babies born to the couple's friends. But despite the predictability of Nellie's life, Alice sensed an untold story between the lines in those letters, penned in the housewife's pristine cursive. "Just a hunch, at this point."

Nate seemed interested, so Alice pressed on.

"Related, and you probably aren't going to believe me when I say this, but I'm not sure I want to change things."

"What do you mean by 'things'?"

"Well, maybe we can leave the kitchen as is? I know we'll need a new fridge and stove eventually, and I'm not sure how long this baby blue will feel charming, but for right now I like it. It's good for me. For my writing, I mean, because I've sort of switched gears, with the book idea. I'm going to set it in 1955, and we're basically living that decade with this decor. I can be immersed in it, you know? Especially with all this vintage stuff. It just fits. With my vision. If that makes sense."

Alice spoke too fast, her body humming with nervous energy. Worried she'd blurt out the truth about the IUD between talk of Formica tabletops and floral wallpaper. No, she needed to tell

Nate properly—the way she had planned. Calmly, the explanation rational so her logical husband could see the benefits of waiting. Career ambitions aside (though his would be unencumbered by a pregnancy), they could focus on making the house safer for a baby, without eliminating its vintage charm. Like, replacing the wiring and removing the asbestos. Getting rid of the lead paint on the non-wallpapered surfaces. Nate would surely respond positively, if Alice framed the conversation properly.

"Baby blue and ancient appliances it is." Nate rinsed his plate and silverware in the sink, following suit with hers before putting them in the dishwasher. This small gesture, which she wouldn't have noticed in Murray Hill, felt meaningful to Alice, and another bubble of guilt bloomed. She would tell him over dinner—she had to.

"Hate to eat and run, babe, but I have to go." He bent to kiss Alice. "Thanks for breakfast."

"Hang on." Alice opened the fridge and took out a reusable bag. "Lunch."

"You made me lunch, too?"

"Turkey and cheese croissant, chocolate chip cookies, and an apple," Alice said.

"Are you feeling okay?" He laughed, pretending to check her temperature with the back of his hand against her forehead.

"Ha. Have to keep you on your toes, throw in a surprise every now and then." Alice playfully pushed him toward the front door. "Now, go, before you miss your train. Hope you have a good day."

Nate kissed her again, more deeply this time. "You too. Hope you get lots of words written."

"Thanks. Going to start right after I clean up."

He pulled her close. "I don't know if I said this, but you look beautiful. Lipstick and stockings for breakfast may be my new favorite thing."

"Even better than bacon and eggs and freshly squeezed orange juice?"

"Yes." Nate ran his hand along her side and tucked it up under her sundress's skirt, letting his fingers slide the length of her stocking-covered inner thigh as he pressed her against their front door. "I wasn't expecting to see you this morning. But I'm happy I did."

"I can tell . . ." Alice's breath caught and she felt a warmth between her legs. It had been longer than usual since they'd had sex—Nate's schedule meant they were rarely awake and available at the same time.

"And your timing couldn't be better," he said, his lips grazing her jaw. "You know what day it is, right?"

"Uh . . ." She was having trouble concentrating. "Tuesday?"

He nuzzled her ear, whispered, "Day twelve, babe."

Alice pressed her eyes closed, her body tightening reflexively. She grew cold and uncomfortable in her center, like she'd swallowed an ice cube whole. But Nate didn't seem to notice the shift, crouching as he rolled her stockings down her legs, grinning up at her. Commenting how he was planning to save this for tonight, but, well, here they were . . .

She watched him as though observing the scene from a distance. Considered her part in all of this. If she'd been honest with him weeks ago, this day would be just another Tuesday. Yet Alice wondered . . . did other husbands track their wives' cycles with such precision when they weren't asked to? Was it fair to feel manipulated by Nate, even though she was guilty of much the same?

Alice reached down and stayed Nate's hands. "You'll miss your train," she murmured, gently pulling him back to standing. Her stockings were in a ball at their feet—later she'd have to throw them out, realizing Nate had ripped the seam.

He gave a ragged sigh, pressed his forehead to hers. "Damn train."

"I know." Alice smiled, then stepped out of his embrace to open the front door. "Besides, it's not as much fun if we need to rush." A breeze wafted under her skirt, reminding her she had no underwear on.

"You're right." Nate took one last, longing glance at her outfit as he snapped on his bike helmet. "Maybe stay like that until I get home?"

"I'll see what I can do," Alice replied, though she was quite certain she'd be asleep in pajamas by that time.

Alice cleaned up from breakfast and poured another coffee. She'd just opened her·laptop when her phone rang. Thinking it was likely her mom—she was the only person who called, typically—Alice ignored it. But then her phone buzzed with a text, and she glanced down.

Can you chat?

Three little dots wiggled below, then disappeared as Bronwyn typed something else but didn't send. Finally, a second line.

Call me. Need to chat!

Concerned, Alice dialed Bronwyn's number. The last in-depth conversation they'd had was a few weeks earlier, when Alice had filled her in on the lawsuit fiasco story, after which Bronwyn had texted her a dozen high-five emoticons and the words, Queen Bitch: 0, Alice Hale: 1. There had been a smattering of texts back and forth since, but Bronwyn was swamped with a new project and relatively absent.

"Hey," Alice said, when her friend answered. "Everything okay?"

"Hey! Yes. All good."

"What's up?"

"Do you have a sec?" Bronwyn asked.

"At least one." Alice pushed back from the desk and sat on

the more comfortable sofa, sipping her now lukewarm coffee. "Though I am a very busy writer, you know."

"Right. Right." Bronwyn was distracted. There was a long pause; only the sound of traffic was audible.

Alice frowned. "Are you sure everything is okay?"

"Hang on." Bronwyn's voice was muffled, but Alice heard her greet someone. "Sorry, getting into my Uber."

"No problem. And good timing. I also need to talk to you about something—"

"I got married."

"Ha, ha, very funny," Alice said.

"I'm serious, Ali. I'm married." Stunned silence from Alice's end; honks and traffic sounds, and then an excited squeal from Bronwyn's, followed by, "Can you believe it?"

"What? To who?" Alice shot up off the couch, knocking the coffee table. Her mug teetered on the edge and Alice caught it before it fell, but not before it spilled all over the rug.

"To Darren, obviously! I had a conference in Vegas and Darren came with me because he's never been and he has this weird thing for Céline Dion—did I tell you he's half-Canadian? His mom is from Montreal, and she met his dad and they moved to Connecticut and he was born there." Bronwyn paused to take a breath. "Anyway, his mom was a big Céline fan—he pronounces her name like, *Cé-lin,* which I guess is how they say it in French? Or in Canada? Anyway, he used to listen to her growing up, and I don't know. You love what you love, right?"

Bronwyn, married? Bronwyn, who believed marriage was okay, *for other people.* Who ended relationships at the two-month mark because that was when things shifted from casual to meaningful. Who swore to Alice she would "never, ever, never" get married, and who had joked that Alice's own wedding had required her to double up on her Xanax.

"It was totally spontaneous. Oh my God, it was *so* spontaneous. Like, one second we were gambling and the next the Elvis dude was pronouncing us husband and wife. Oh my God, Ali, *I'm married*."

Alice sat down on the rug, beside the coffee stain. "Are you pregnant?"

Bronwyn laughed. "Fuck you! No, I am not pregnant. God. You're worse than my mother. I mean, I wouldn't even get married just because I was pregnant. We aren't our grandmothers."

Alice put a hand to her forehead, took a deep breath. "I'm sorry. That was . . . I didn't mean for it to come out like that. You caught me off guard."

"I know. It's shocking, right? Me, married?" Bronwyn sounded jittery, like she'd had too many espressos that morning. "The only person I've promised forever to is my waxer, Zara, because, honestly, that's the most intimate relationship—"

"Wait. When did this happen?" Alice thought back to the last time she'd seen Bronwyn, three weeks earlier.

"Oh, um, on the weekend."

"But . . . it's Tuesday. Why didn't you call me, like, right away?"

"I did!" Bronwyn replied, somewhat defensively. Alice was sure she'd have noticed a call from Bronwyn. It wasn't as though her days were busy. "But you didn't pick up and I didn't want to leave a message and I had to go to Boston for meetings yesterday and, well, I'm calling you now.

"Look, I know it seems crazy. We've only been together for a few months, but I really think this is it. I mean, everyone is getting married. And coming out there that weekend, well, it got me thinking. Like, life is short, you know? And if I only focus on my career, what am I missing out on? I don't want to wake up in five years successful but still single while everyone else has moved on."

"So, wait . . . you got married because of *fear of missing out*?" Alice snorted, couldn't help herself. "Talk about being a millennial cliché, Bron."

Now there was silence from Bronwyn's end.

"You must hear how nuts that sounds." Alice pressed on. "It's not like deciding to get your eyebrows microbladed because you don't want to be the only thin-eyebrowed woman left in Manhattan." She tried to bring her voice down to a less screechy level. "It's a commitment *for life,* Bronwyn. Like, 'til death do us part."

"Look, not everyone gets your fairy-tale meet-cute, okay? We don't all find a Nate running in Central Park, Ali. Some of us say yes to a great guy who, sure, we may not have known forever but we definitely love. And then we cross our fingers." Bronwyn exhaled, then added, more softly, "You don't know how lucky you are."

"Bronwyn, I'm sorry. I really like Darren, I do, it's just that—"

"It feels right when I'm with him. Like, I couldn't imagine *not* being with him. I thought you of all people would understand that," Bronwyn said. "I thought you'd be happy for me, Ali."

"I am. I am!" Alice wished she could back up ten minutes and have a completely different reaction to her best friend's news.

"Listen, I have to go. I'm almost at my meeting."

"Um, okay. Can we chat more later?" Alice said in a rush, feeling upended. "And, hey, congratulations. Sorry. I really should have started with that."

"Yeah, okay." Bronwyn paused, then: "Bye, Ali."

Alice debated calling back but knew Bronwyn likely wouldn't pick up. She wouldn't if she were her. Instead, she riffled through the desk drawer with shaking fingers and pulled out the cigarette pack, unwrapping the plastic casing. In the kitchen, Alice took the matches Nate used to light the barbecue and perched on the countertop facing the window, which she opened wide. She was about to strike the match when she remembered the antique mother-of-pearl cigarette holder in the back of her desk.

Alice broke the first cigarette trying to use the holder but managed the second one fine. She placed the tip in her mouth and set the flame to the cigarette's end. She imagined Nellie smoking just like this, perched in her skirt and pearls on the countertop, the cigarette holder tight between her fingers, blowing lazy circles of smoke out the very same window.

Taking in a deep, smoke-heavy breath, Alice coughed hard, tears pooling in her eyes. Pulling in another drag, light-headed now, Alice blew it out through the screen, though some wafted past her and into the kitchen with the breeze.

She finished the cigarette quickly, nauseated yet clearheaded from the nicotine, and had two distinct thoughts: one, she was a terrible friend who had no right to judge anyone's marriage, especially after her recent actions within her own; and two, maybe Bronwyn had the right idea. Perhaps marriage *should* be spontaneous, based more on feeling than on thinking. Maybe the harder someone worked to create a perfect union, the more power one gave the institution of marriage, rather than the relationship itself, which is where the focus should be.

Shortly after they moved to California, preteen Alice had asked Jaclyn when she was going to marry Steve. Alice's father and Jaclyn had never officially married, living as common-law spouses through their tumultuous decade-long relationship, and Alice desperately wanted her mother to wear a wedding band so she was more like the other moms. Commit officially this time, so Steve wouldn't leave them and they wouldn't have to move again.

Jaclyn had cupped Alice's little chin in her palm and gave

her a quite serious look. "Alice, there are plenty of reasons to marry that have nothing to do with love. And you can be head over heels in love and *not* get married. But no matter what, you should never marry someone unless you believe you'll die—one way or another—without that person. They should feel more important to you than oxygen. Otherwise you'll suffocate, one damn anniversary at a time."

27

Nellie

....

AUGUST 28, 1956

Boiled Chocolate Cookie

....

2 cups granulated sugar

½ cup milk

½ cup cocoa

1 tablespoon butter

2 cups quick oats

1 cup coconut

1 teaspoon vanilla extract

Boil sugar, milk, cocoa, and butter for five minutes. Remove from heat. Add oats, coconut, and vanilla and, working quickly, stir well and drop by spoonful onto waxed paper. Let cool.

The cookies were cooling, and Nellie had finished placing the salmon and dill-pickle roll sandwiches on a serving tray when her first two guests—Kitty Goldman and Martha Graves—arrived, both never a moment late for anything. Helen answered the door, and Nellie heard Kitty first. "These are ready for the table, right in the center if you don't mind. Oh, careful there. You should probably use two hands. That tray was my mother's. *Quite priceless.*" She emphasized the last part in a theatrical whisper, and Nellie chuckled at Kitty's dramatics as she hung her apron. "Nellie! We're here!"

It was their monthly neighborhood-watch meeting, and while it was usually held at Kitty's home—she was the group's president—she'd begrudgingly agreed to move it to Nellie's place this time, due to her injury. The cast had been off for almost two weeks, but Nellie was still slow walking, her ankle stiff and her leg emaciated from being imprisoned by plaster.

Nellie greeted the two women in the front hall as Helen carried (carefully, with two hands and a small scowl on her face) the plate of cookies and bars Kitty had brought. Martha, who rested a plate of deviled eggs on her expansive belly, huffed as she leaned in to kiss Nellie on the cheek. She was swollen and ruddy-skinned with child and looked like an overripe plum, ready to fall off the tree. When Helen came back to take the plate from Martha, she told her she could manage fine and offered her a genuine, warm smile. Kitty rolled her eyes.

"Let me take it, Martha." Nellie felt how taut Martha's pregnant belly was as she reached over her to take the plate. It was like she was carrying a tenpins bowling ball in there. "Would you mind washing up the last of the dishes, Helen?"

"Why would she mind?" Kitty asked, answering before Helen could. "That's exactly why she's here." She cocked her head and gave Helen a pointed smile—part condescension and part amusement.

Helen retreated to the kitchen, and Nellie said, "Kitty, was that necessary?"

"What?" Kitty set her purse on the long table at the

entrance of the living room. She held a notepad in her hands. "She's your girl! She's here to help *you*."

Martha nodded but said nothing, and Nellie resisted saying anything further as she ushered them into the living room, where Helen had set up jugs of iced tea and lemonade, along with the sandwiches and cooling chocolate cookies.

"Oh, I love your boiled chocolate cookies," Martha said, looking enviously at the tray on the sideboard. "But I can barely fit a sip of water in here these days." She rubbed a hand over her bulging stomach.

"How much longer now?" Nellie asked, pouring iced tea as they waited for the others to arrive. Out of all the women in her church and neighborhood-watch groups, Nellie was probably closest to Martha, who was simple and kind and easy to spend time with. But she was cautious about her friendships with the wives, understanding the hierarchy. A wife yielded to her husband, which meant whatever she shared with Martha or Kitty would surely find its way back to Richard.

"Not long, God willing." Martha shifted awkwardly on the sofa—Nellie no longer sat on the sofa, after what Richard had done to her there—and leaned against a pillow, her face contorting in a flash of pain. "I'm not sure how much longer I can last. The back pain is terrible this time. It's really quite unpleasant." Martha already had one child, a boy named Arthur who was sweet and soft-spoken, much like his mother.

Kitty raised her eyebrows but said nothing, thankfully. She was mother to three, the youngest only thirteen months, but had bounced back from pregnancy like it had never happened— her body slim and her face unlined. She *was* only twenty-six, and the Goldmans had a live-in girl who helped with the children and the home. Kitty focused on her charitable responsibilities to the church and the neighborhood-watch group, as well as hosting Tupperware parties every chance she got.

Nellie set a hand on Martha's shoulder and handed her the tea. "You look lovely, Martha. Pregnancy really suits you."

Martha grinned, but it soon faded as she remembered Nellie's recent miscarriage. "Oh, leave it to me to complain about such a miraculous thing." She gave Nellie a sad smile. "I'm sorry. It's quite thoughtless of me, Nellie, with what you've been through."

"Good grief, Martha," Kitty said, her tone scolding, as though she was speaking with one of her children. "I'm sure Nellie doesn't need any such reminders."

Martha looked pained, and Nellie offered a reassuring smile. "It's fine. Don't you give it another thought."

"You're too kind, Nellie," Martha replied, her relief palpable.

"You are," Kitty said, somewhat under her breath, but clear enough that they all heard it. Suddenly Kitty gasped.

"Nellie Murdoch, what is this?" Kitty stood at the small writing table by the window. She spun around, holding a handbag, her mouth open and her eyes wide.

"A gift from Richard," Nellie replied keeping her voice even. The Chanel 2.55 handbag, with its black, hand-stitched, butter-soft quilted leather, and gold chain strap, was a much-coveted purse among Nellie's circle of friends. It had been designed by Coco Chanel herself.

"Oh my," Martha said, slightly breathlessly. "It's so lovely."

Kitty walked back to her armchair still holding the bag. She opened it without asking if she could, which Nellie found rude, and fingered the interior's red fabric. "It looks like you haven't even used it." She looked up at Nellie. "Why on earth not? If Charles gave me this bag I would wear it to bed!" She laughed and Martha joined in.

Nellie shrugged. "I haven't had the occasion yet."

"Oh, sweetie. You don't need an occasion. That's the beauty

of a bag like this." Kitty slid the chain over one shoulder. "It goes everywhere, with everything."

"May I see it?" Martha asked.

"You have sticky tea on your hands," Kitty said, and Martha self-consciously wiped her hands on the napkin. Kitty sighed impatiently as she watched her, holding the bag out of reach.

"Do tell," Kitty said, reluctantly passing the purse to Martha. "Is it your anniversary?"

Nellie paused, and was grateful for the doorbell's ring. "Oh, looks like everyone's arriving," she said, rising and moving toward the door with only a slight limp. "Why don't you help yourselves to some sandwiches? I'll be right back."

Soon her living room was full of women, chattering about mundane neighborhood issues such as someone's lawn not being trimmed often enough, and a barking dog keeping children up at night, and the safety of a particular crumbling section of sidewalk. Nellie sipped her tea and participated in the conversation only when directly asked something, unable to take her eyes off the Chanel purse Kitty had left in plain sight for all the women to fawn over. As they swooned and told her they wished their husbands could be more like Richard, she smiled politely and thought about the reason for his extravagant gift. Her reward.

Nellie was pregnant.

28

After you marry him—study him. If he is secretive—trust him.
When he is talkative—listen to him. If he is jealous—cure him.
If he favours society—accompany him. Let him think you un-
derstand him—but never let him think you manage him.

—*Western Gazette* (August 1, 1930)

Alice

.....

AUGUST 12, 2018

*N*ate was inside stripping the last of the wallpaper in the third
bedroom, which he continued to refer to as "the nursery." He'd
insisted Alice get out of the house, was worried about the fumes
from the heavy-duty glue stripper. "What if you're already
pregnant?" he asked when she protested, saying if they worked on
it together it would be done much faster.

"I'm not." She laid a sheet over the narrow bed, which they'd
moved to the center of the room. The bedroom wasn't large and
she had barely enough clearance to walk past the ladder Nate was
setting up against one wall. Though it was Sunday, Alice had yet
to reveal what she'd done, and so the charade continued. *Just say*

it, she thought as she straightened the sheet so it was even on all sides. *Nate, I'm not ready for a nursery.*

"How do you know?" Nate pulled a mask over his head, settling it temporarily against his Adam's apple. Then he opened the window as wide as it would go, stuck a paint stir stick in to keep it propped open. She knew he was thinking about Tuesday. *It's day twelve, babe.* He'd come home earlier than normal that night and her guilt had softened her resolve. Besides, it didn't matter . . . she wouldn't get pregnant. "I'll feel guilty forever if our kid comes out with eleven toes."

"You shouldn't joke about that," she said, to which he replied, "I'm not!"

Nate was adamant, even when she offered to wear two masks, suggesting she tackle the weeds instead. So, while Nate set to work on the wallpaper, Alice toiled in the back garden. She was soon hot and dirty, her muscles screaming for a rest. Though she'd only been at it for about an hour, Alice decided she deserved a break, and settled into one of the garden chairs with the second stack of Nellie's letters.

She *was* trying to like gardening, or at least appreciate its benefits, but was more interested in Nellie's letters than she ever would be in weeding. Especially since she'd abandoned her first idea—did the world really need another *Devil Wears Prada*? So, she needed to dedicate time to the letters and the magazines because if she couldn't get traction on the writing, at least she could research, thanks to Nellie Murdoch. Alice unwrapped the elastic from the stack and opened the delicate folds of the top letter.

From the desk of Eleanor Murdoch

August 30, 1956

Dearest Mother,

I miss you terribly. It feels like far too long since we've seen each other, but I will visit soon. Once my ankle fully heals and I can find some time to get away for a few days. The business continues keeping Richard busy—who knew chewing gum could be so time-consuming?—so I do need to be here right now. Speaking of my ankle, it has improved greatly and I'm up and about more easily these days. My garden isn't doing as well as my leg, I'm sorry to say, but thankfully a neighborhood boy has been helping with the weeding and pruning. The hostas are, as usual, taking over like the bullies they are, but my roses continue to do well. I will bring you some when I come next.

I have some news to share, Mother. I'm expecting.

Alice sat up straight and reread the line. *Nellie was pregnant?* But what happened to the Murdochs being childless?

I'm feeling well, and so far, pregnancy seems to agree with me. Richard is over the moon, as you can imagine. It did come as a surprise, and I must tell you . . .

"Whatcha reading?"

Alice jumped in her seat, the letter falling to the grass below. The bottle of water she'd been holding in her other hand slipped, drenching the letter at her feet as the liquid glugged from the bottle.

"Shit!" Alice quickly retrieved the sopping pages, hoping they weren't ruined. Too late—the old paper was no match for the washing it had been given, and the ink was blurred. "Shit," she said again.

"Sorry." Nate glanced at the soggy paper in Alice's hand. He tilted his ball cap so the peak shaded his eyes to the sun. He had red indentations under each eye and on the bridge of his nose, where the mask had pinched his skin. "Was that important?"

"Not really," Alice mumbled, laying the paper on the table. Some of the ink had transferred to her fingers and she rubbed them against her denim shorts.

Nate perused the garden beds, the few small piles of weeds. "Taking a break already?"

"I was doing some research."

"Right," he said, sitting in the chair beside her. He gestured to the pile of letters on the table. "Is this it?"

"Yeah. The letters I told you about the other morning. The ones Nellie wrote to her mother, in the fifties? Sally gave them to me."

Nate nodded. "Cool." He leaned back in the chair, stretched out his legs. "So how's the garden? Where are we at?"

Alice bristled at the "we," because Nate had yet to do anything in the garden. But he was tackling plenty of unpleasant tasks inside the house. Plus, he left every morning at seven and wasn't home much before eleven most nights so they could afford the house and everything that came with it. The least she could do, she reminded herself, was to pull the damn weeds without complaint. "Turns out gardening is actually weeding. Endless weeding." She sighed, placed the elastic back around the remaining letters. "How's the wallpaper removal going?"

"Slow. There's a lot of it to get off." He leaned forward,

moved to get up. "Can I help? I'm feeling a bit high from the glue remover. Could use some fresh air."

"Sure," Alice said, grabbing her gloves and following Nate to the garden. He stood with hands on hips, lips pursed as he glanced around.

"What's next?"

"Honestly, I'm still not sure what's a plant and what's a weed. So maybe let's pull the stuff that looks like it doesn't belong? Like these." She crouched in front of a small patch of dandelion. "These I know are weeds. Want gloves?"

"Nah, I'm good."

Alice took the spade and dug around one of the dandelion's roots, lifting it out with a large chunk of dirt attached. She shook it to release the earth and tossed the weed onto the lawn behind her. Nate stepped to the right and started moving some of the large hosta leaves to the side so he could look for more dandelions. Alice was focused on getting the spade deep enough to avoid cutting the root too high, like Sally had showed her, when Nate said, "These are nice. What are they?"

Nate stood beside one of the foxglove plants, reaching toward the flowers. "Don't touch that!" Alice exclaimed.

He jerked his hand back. "Why not?"

"That's foxglove. Sally told me it's poisonous."

Nate rubbed his hand quickly on his shorts and looked back to the plant, the flowers sprouting like hanging bells along the length of the thick green stalk. "What do you mean, 'poisonous'?"

"What I mean is, you shouldn't touch it with your bare hands." Alice tossed the dandelion to the side.

Nate's hands were back on his hips as he looked between the plant and Alice. "We have a poisonous flower in our garden? Like, how poisonous are we talking?"

"Sally said it can cause heart problems. Apparently, it's used to make some sort of heart medication, but the whole thing—stem, flowers, seeds—toxic."

He walked the length of the garden, murmuring under his breath, and turned back to Alice with wide eyes. "Jesus. Ali. *It's all over the place.*" There were three bunches of the foxglove plant, which to Alice hardly constituted "all over the place." Nate's mouth tightened and he held out a hand. "Give me your gloves."

"Why?"

"Ali, gloves." Alice took off her gloves and handed them to Nate. He put them on, though they were small, and grabbed the garden shears Alice used for pruning. In one quick motion, he sliced right through a foxglove stem, near the bottom, and it fell sideways. He picked it up with the too-small gloves and tossed it on the pile of weeds.

"What are you doing?" Alice watched him repeat the process on the next stalk of foxglove. "Those are one of the few things the deer won't eat! And now there's going to be empty holes in the garden. What can we plant there now? Summer's half over." She had little appreciation for this garden but felt a strange responsibility to take care of something Nellie had nurtured and loved so much.

Nate ignored her questions, grunting as he dug in and around the base of the cut foxglove stem. "I don't care. Put in some shrubs."

Shrubs? Alice rolled her eyes.

Nate grumbled, yanking on the stem to try to pull it out by the root. "Who cares about the deer? No way am I letting some deadly plant live in this garden."

"I didn't say it was 'deadly.'" Alice crossed her arms while she watched him remove the second foxglove plant. "And *I care* about the deer."

"Why aren't you more worried about our inevitable baby and

what happens if she gets into the garden and eats one of these toxic leaves?" Nate lost his balance as the stem yanked free, spraying the two of them with a shower of black earth. "It's all coming out. Today."

"She?"

Nate gathered the newly dug-up foxglove into a pile, careful to avoid it touching his skin. He stood and swiped his brow with his forearm. "I'd love a little girl," he said. "Wouldn't you? A mini Alice?"

"Sure," Alice said, the pang of guilt slicing through her. She almost confessed then, right there beside the growing pile of fox-glove, what she had done. Nate loved her and would understand. They were young! Plenty of time still for a mini Alice, or even more than one.

"Here, hold this." Nate handed her a yard-waste bag.

"What if it doesn't work?" Alice asked, holding the bag open wide for Nate to dispose of the foxglove remnants. He was careful to keep the stems from touching Alice's hands.

"If what doesn't work?"

"This." She withdrew one hand, drew circles in the air in front of her stomach. "A baby."

"Why? Is something wrong?" He was crouched, gathering another pile, but he stopped and squinted up at her.

"No." But she had paused too long, and Nate noticed. He took off the gloves, dropping them to the grass, and pulled the bag away from her. Then he stood in front of her and his palms were warm and sweaty on her upper arms. "You know you can tell me anything, right?"

"I know."

Nate's hands squeezed her arms gently. "I get that it has been a tough couple of months. I've had a lot of late nights re-cently and I'm tired, and maybe a bit distracted when I'm home, but I promise, it's temporary."

"Maybe you could study more at home?" Alice said. "There are probably fewer distractions. Especially if I work at the same time. It will be like old times." Back when Nate was studying for his earlier exams and Alice had endless press releases to write, and they'd set themselves up in bed with a bowl of Cheetos between them.

He smiled, though it didn't reach his eyes. "It's just easier to study at the office, babe. Everything is there."

Alice shifted slightly away from him, and he let her.

"Not much longer, okay?" She nodded.

"Now, can we go back to getting rid of these evil plants?" Nate asked.

"Sure." Nate put the gloves back on, and she held the waste bag, opening it as wide as it would go. As Nate tossed the remaining foxglove and other weeds into the bag, Alice thought about everything she was keeping from Nate—the truth about her job and James Dorian, the smoking, the IUD, how little she'd been writing—and wondered what he might be keeping from her as well.

29

Nellie

....

SEPTEMBER 1, 1956

Herbed Cheese Popovers

....

1 cup sifted flour

½ teaspoon salt

1 cup sweet milk

1 tablespoon melted butter

2 eggs

⅓ cup grated cheese

2 tablespoons fresh chives, or other dried herbs of choice

Beat together just until smooth the flour, salt, milk, melted butter, and eggs. Add cheese and chives, and stir to combine. Pour into greased muffin tins to half full, then bake in hot oven (400°F) until popovers are golden brown (about 20–25 minutes). Serve immediately.

*N*ellie smoked a Lucky, eyeing the teenager from behind her sunglasses as he crouched in her garden. Peter Pellosi, the neighborhood boy who did yard work to earn money through the summer, was young—only seventeen—but looked like a man already with his bulging biceps and strong shoulders. While still sweet-cheeked, he had a few shaving nicks on his chin and around his Adam's apple.

"What would you like done with the hostas?" Peter asked, turning to Nellie and squinting in the bright sunshine. His shorts showed off muscled legs, trickles of sweat mixing with the dirt and dripping into his socks and high-top sneakers. Nellie set the magazine on her lap and put hand to forehead to block the light so she could see the plants. Normally Nellie's garden would be in tiptop shape, but her broken ankle meant she had done next to nothing these past eight weeks.

"Darn pushy, those hostas are," she said. "I'd like to wait a few weeks longer to cut them back, but fall is nearly here." She took out another cigarette, holding the pack out to Peter. "Would you like one?"

He paused for a moment. "Thank you, ma'am." Wiping his hands on his shorts, he pulled his Zippo lighter from his back pocket and took the cigarette from Nellie, even though he had his own pack rolled under his shirtsleeve. He sparked the lighter, and Nellie placed the mother-of-pearl cigarette holder to her lips, leaning the Lucky's tip into the flame. She inhaled and tapped the chair beside her. Peter obliged, taking a long drag and exhaling into the warm, late-summer air.

"You're back to school next week, aren't you?" Nellie asked. He nodded. "Looking forward to it?"

"Yes, ma'am."

She watched him as she took another pull on her cigarette. "Are you going steady with anyone, Peter?"

He blushed to the tips of his ears, his knees bouncing with youthful energy. "No, ma'am."

"Well, Peter Pellosi, I can't believe that." His blush deepened, and he looked delighted and uncertain all at once. They smoked in silence for a few moments before Nellie pointed her cigarette toward one of the hostas, which was particularly overgrown. "Cut that one right down its center. And don't be gentle. The roots are stronger than you think they'll be."

"Yes, ma'am." Peter stubbed out his smoke and picked up the hoe, piled with the other tools on the patio stones. Even though he was out of range now, back in the depths of garden, his scent remained—clean sweat, plus a hint of the laundry soap his mother used.

"Good heavens, it's warm today." Nellie fanned herself with the magazine. She glanced at her watch, noted the time, and smiled. Not long now. "I'm going to get us a cold drink. All right?"

"That would be swell." Peter positioned the hoe over the center of the hosta. "Thanks, Mrs. Murdoch." He brought the hoe's tip down hard, grunting, cutting the plant clean through the middle.

Inside, Nellie hummed as she poured two ice-filled glasses of lemonade, dotting the surfaces with fresh mint leaves. Opening the refrigerator, she put the jug back and took out two of Richard's beers—hooking her fingers around the green bottles on the top shelf. Singing softly, Nellie set the beers on the tray beside the glasses of lemonade and nudged the fridge door closed with her hip.

"I have lemonade but thought you might like one of these as well?" Nellie said, holding up one of the bottles once she was back outside.

"Oh, I probably shouldn't." Peter stared at the bottle in Nellie's hands, licked a drip of sweat from his lips.

"I won't tell anyone." She used the opener to pop off the lid, handing him the bottle. "I believe you've earned this. Go on, our little secret."

He grinned, took it from her. "Thank you, ma'am."

Peter put the beer bottle to his mouth and tipped it back. His nicked Adam's apple bobbed as he drank the sparkling amber liquid. A little escaped his lips and dribbled down his chin as the screen door banged shut, and Richard—pausing to take in the scene—appeared on the back patio. Nellie wiped the dripping beer from Peter's chin with a napkin.

"There you go," she said, letting her fingers linger longer than they needed to on Peter's chin, making sure Richard could see. Peter appeared to stop breathing, very aware of Mr. Murdoch standing only a foot away and looking none too pleased about the exchange young Peter was having with his wife.

Nellie turned, pretending to only then notice Richard. "Oh, hello there! How was bowling today?" She opened her own bottle of beer, taking a long sip. The glass rim was wonderfully chilled against her lips. Peter's eyes widened—she expected he'd never seen a woman drink beer right from the bottle, his own mother a teetotaler—and Richard's eyes narrowed, arms crossed. His red-and-black bowling shirt stretched across his chest, the buttons straining.

Peter squinted, glancing between the couple, and put his beer on the table before reaching out to shake Richard's hand. "Good afternoon, Mr. Murdoch." His Adam's apple wiggled with nervousness.

"Peter," Richard said, returning the handshake with extra force. Peter winced but held his own. "How's your father doing?"

"Just fine, sir." Peter looked over at the hostas, wanting to be anywhere but standing between the Murdochs. "Uh, I guess I'll get back to it?"

"Good idea," Richard said, sitting in the chair Peter had occupied only moments before and scowling at the teenager. He picked up the glass of lemonade intended for Peter and plucked out the mint, flinging it onto the grass. Peter glanced back and Nellie smiled reassuringly. "Right down the middle of that one too, Peter. Don't let that little old plant give you any trouble."

Nellie settled back in her own chair, watching Peter jam the hoe into the earth. "Can you believe he's not going steady with anyone? A boy like that?" She shook her head, gingerly sipped the beer. The flavor wasn't her favorite, but with Richard watching so disapprovingly, gosh darn it, she would drink the whole thing. "Though he's grown into quite a man this past year."

Richard glared at her. "I thought we were paying him to clean up the garden, not talk your ear off."

"Never mind that." Nellie leaned toward Richard, and in a stage whisper said, "I think I may have given young Peter his first beer!"

Richard scrubbed a hand through his hair. "For Christ's sake, Nellie," he mumbled.

He was frustrated. Richard was used to Nellie being the sort of wife who did as her husband asked; who was demure and prettier than his friends' wives and would never drink a beer, let alone from a bottle or with a strapping young man (who was, to be clear, closer in age to Nellie than Richard was). Nellie Murdoch was—or had been to now—the flawless wife. But lately she had been impudent, and Nellie knew that made Richard uneasy. But he wouldn't punish her for it, being un-willing to take any chances this time when it came to the baby, and Nellie was quite aware of the power this afforded her. Hence her shameless flirting with Peter Pellosi, which would tie Richard up in knots.

"I made cheese popovers and a Waldorf salad for lunch," Nellie said, her mood brightening as Richard's darkened. She took out another cigarette, lit it, and opened her magazine on her lap. Nellie peeked at Richard, relished the look of consternation on her husband's face. "Why don't you go ahead and eat? I had something not long ago, and I don't want to leave young Peter all alone out here."

30

Don't be jealous of your husband's acquaintance with other women. You don't want him to think you are the nicest woman in the world because he never sees any others, but because he sees plenty, and still feels that you are the only one in the world for him. Have nice girls about the house pretty frequently.

—Blanche Ebbutt, *Don'ts for Wives* (1913)

Alice

.....

AUGUST 13, 2018

I was reading through Nellie's letters to her mother, for my book research, and found something I wasn't expecting." It was Monday afternoon, and Alice was on her knees in the garden, patting the earth around the newly planted shrubs she'd bought to fill the holes from yesterday's foxglove removal.

Sally was clipping off roses for a friend in Stamford with a broken hip she was visiting later. "What was it?"

"You said Nellie and Richard never had children, right?"

"They didn't. Not as far as I know." Sally pulled back to squint at the rose bouquet in her gloved hand, then, satisfied with its fullness, lay the roses on her patio table so she could trim the thorns.

"Those are so pretty," Alice said, looking at Sally's roses. She glanced back at her own garden. "I wonder if I'll ever be good at this."

"You need to give it a couple of full cycles of the seasons before you'll know for sure." Sally snipped at the stems, the spiky thorns dropping to the table. "I think your garden is looking lovely, though. You've obviously been working hard at it." She pointed to the shrub Alice had nested into the earth, her handprints still evident around its base in the dark, damp soil. "I hate to tell you this, dear, but that will likely not fare well there."

Alice looked at the squat shrub. "How come?"

"It doesn't have enough room. For its roots," Sally replied. "You might need to choose something else for that spot. What was there before?"

"The foxglove. I told Nate it was toxic and he yanked it all out. Was worried about our hypothetical child making a salad of the leaves." Alice rolled her eyes. "Which is ridiculous because, one, we have no idea when and if this child will manifest, and, two, name me a toddler who eats salad."

Sally laughed. "You have a point there, Miss Alice."

"So, should I dig this out? Put it somewhere else where it won't feel crowded?"

The older woman brought a finger to her upper lip, scanned the garden bed. She pointed to the back corner, which did have more space. "There, beside the echinacea, maybe. The one that looks like a purple daisy."

"Let's be clear," Alice replied, crouching in front of the shrub and beginning to dig it out. "I don't want to put it anywhere. I was happy with the foxglove."

"You can always get more foxglove at the garden center.

Children can be trained. So can husbands, I suspect." Sally winked, winding golden twine around the thorn-free stems. "I should be on my way, but before I go, what did you come across in Nellie's letter?"

Alice dug at the dirt with her gloved fingers, creating a doughnut of space around the roots. She started to tug, but it wouldn't give. "Nellie wrote to her mother that she was pregnant, but I remember you saying she never had a child." She grasped the base of the shrub and pulled, hard—too hard, because she ended up on her back with the shrub on her chest, her face sprinkled with dirt. She spat earth off her lips and started laughing.

"Oh dear, are you all right?" Sally asked, covering her mouth with one hand to hide the chuckle.

"Everything but my ego." Alice laughed as she stood, shaking off the dirt. "Anyway, I was curious about what happened, if Nellie had been pregnant but never had the baby."

"Hmm," Sally said. "No children, I'm sure of it. But I am sorry to hear that, as I'm sure it was difficult for Nellie. I remember Mother saying she would have been an excellent mother." Sally picked up the bundle of roses. "It wasn't easy to be married and childless in those days. The social expectations around family were rigid. "

"I can only imagine," Alice said. "They're still fairly rigid now, if you ask me."

"Yes, I suppose they are," Sally replied, giving Alice a long look and a gentle smile.

One of the ovulation kit's test strips had been on the bathroom counter that morning, right beside Alice's toothbrush. Nate had slapped a sticky note with a smiley face and the insinuative words *Drink lots of water!* next to it. Alice had completely forgotten about the kit, her housewarming gift from Nate, but clearly her husband had not. She knew she should hand Nate the unopened test strip when he got home and finally tell him the truth. But annoyed and wearied by the reemergence of the ovulation kit (and Nate's stupid sticky note), Alice had decided it was easier to play along for now. She'd dropped her pajama shorts, opened the strip, and peed on its end. Then she brushed her teeth and set the urine-drenched test on the counter beside the water glass for Nate to find later that evening.

"Alice? Where'd you go there, honey?"

Alice shook her head. "Sorry, I'm distracted today. Not enough coffee, I think." She smiled at Sally, but then gasped and clutched her side as an intense pain gripped her abdomen. Sally dropped her bundle of roses and leaned toward Alice, her arms outstretched as if she intended to try to catch her despite the distance between them. "Alice! What is it?"

"I'm not sure, I . . ." Alice took in a deep breath, the pain gone as quickly as it had come. "Maybe I pulled something when I yanked that bush out." She was light-headed and mildly nauseated.

Sally's wrinkles deepened as she watched her younger neighbor rub at her side. "Where's the pain, exactly?"

Alice pointed to her left side, near her hip. "It's gone now. I think I'm okay." She arched her back, then stretched from side to side. "I'm good."

"You sure?"

"A muscle spasm, I think," Alice said. "See? I told you I'm not cut out for gardening."

Sally smiled, bending somewhat gingerly the way older people do, and picked up the fallen roses. "Maybe no more gardening for you today. Go put your feet up and get something cold to drink. Doctor's orders."

"Yes, ma'am."

"I'm spending the night with my friend, but I'll see you

tomorrow," Sally said. "We'll figure out what else to put in those foxglove holes then."

After Sally left, Alice absentmindedly rubbed her side, staring at the three holes in the garden, which she decided to just fill in with dirt and call it a day.

"Did you call your mom back?" They were in bed, Alice flipping through a *Ladies' Home Journal* magazine from a new stack she'd brought up from the basement, Nate with Alice's laptop propped on his thighs. She didn't love him using her computer—worried he'd discover how unproductive she had been with her book—but his was going through an update and he wanted to research bathroom tiles.

"Not yet. I'll call her tomorrow," Alice said. Nate had mentioned it wasn't urgent. Something to do with them taking a trip to California for Thanksgiving. Alice had been on the couch most of the afternoon—a heating pad on her still sore side—and so they'd had leftovers for dinner and were in bed earlier than normal. Nate had obviously found the test strip Alice had left out, because it wasn't on the countertop when she went in to wash her face. But he hadn't said anything about it, and she didn't mention it either.

"What do you think of this black-and-white honeycomb?" Nate asked, squinting at the tile thumbnails on the screen. "Do you want a neutral scheme, or something with color?"

"Sure. Okay." Alice was immersed in an article about the value of simple white vinegar in a housewife's pantry (*poaching eggs, cleaning windows, a rinse for shiny hair*). She remained bothered by Nate's note and the test strip, and her maddening inability to talk with him about it, and so had been quiet all evening. Though he believed she was subdued because she wasn't feeling great—the lingering pain of her "pulled muscle" from gardening casting a shadow on her mood.

"Ali, are you even listening to me?"

"Hmm, what? I am. Just reading about the miracles of vinegar. Big news for women in the fifties."

He put the laptop to the side—at least a dozen tabs remained open, a DIY bathroom tiling step-by-step blog on the screen—and nestled beside her, resting his chin on her shoulder and glancing at the magazine page. He flipped the magazine shut, Alice's finger marking the spot, to see the cover.

"Is this responsible for that?" he asked, pointing to Alice's head. She had wrapped strands of hair using sections of an old T-shirt she'd cut up, tying up the pieces in small balls all over her head. The technique promised a cascade of shiny curls by morning, at least according to the old magazine.

"It is." Alice patted a few of the hair balls, which felt springy under her fingers.

"It's a good look on you," Nate said, and Alice smirked. It wasn't a good look on anyone. Then he set his palm on her side, rubbing it gently a couple of times. "Feeling okay?" Nate pressed closer, and his breath tickled her neck. His hands came around her body to cup her breasts, her nipples hardening under his touch. Alice then realized what the test strip must have shown—she was about to ovulate.

Despite her determination not to participate—annoyed by Nate's presumptive move that morning and his transparent agenda now—her body betrayed her, stirring at his touch. Nate's roving hands massaged her body through the thin fabric of her nightshirt, and his lips continued their descent down the side of her neck, pausing on her shoulder blade. Alice lifted her arms to allow him to pull her shirt over her head. But the neckline got caught on her homemade fabric hair curlers.

"Tug," Alice said, her voice muffled by the shirt. Nate was

being too gentle, trying to peel the shirt over her head. Not long after, they were naked on the duvet, and Nate rolled her so she was on top.

"It's better if you orgasm," he said. *Of course it is.* But Alice knew he meant in reference to her getting pregnant, and tried to ignore his comment.

He held her hips and closed his eyes, his chin tipping back as she moved over him, quickening her pace with every breath, a tingling pressure building in her pelvis as Nate groaned under her.

"Oh!" Alice gasped, slamming her hands to Nate's chest as her fingernails dug into his skin. A fiery swath of pain stabbed her abdomen. Nate winced and reached for her hands, chuckling, not yet understanding what was going on. "Easy, babe," he murmured. "That's going to leave a mark."

Alice couldn't catch her breath—the pain far more intense than it had been in the garden, as though she were being cut in half. She bucked off him and curled into a tight ball at the foot of the bed, the way she'd seen potato bugs do in the garden when sensing imminent danger.

Nate, catching up to the seriousness of what was happening, sprang over to where she writhed, her knees up to her chest. She was sweating profusely, a low hum of a moan coming out of her. "Ali! What's wrong? Is it your side?" Nate's hands roamed the parts of her body he could get to, trying to figure out what was causing her extreme pain. For one delirious moment Alice understood she was being punished. But for what, exactly? *For all of it,* she thought.

"Talk to me, babe. What's wrong?"

She screamed, clawed at her side, and Nate held on to her. "Should I call 911?" He fumbled with his phone, swearing loudly as it dropped to the floor. He managed to keep one hand firmly on Alice's hip as he stretched for the phone. "Hang on. I'm calling 911."

"No. Don't call," she managed, sucking in shallow breaths. "Just give me a minute." The pain was subsiding a bit, maybe. At least she could draw in a full breath.

Nate, phone in trembling hand, rubbed her side—too hard—and she wished he would stop because the motion combined with the waves of pain was making her sick to her stomach. She focused on her breathing. *In. Out. In. Out.*

"Better?" he asked, his voice high, his breathing nearly as ragged as hers.

She nodded, but the pain had yet to abate. Hand leaving her side, Nate placed it momentarily against his chest, where red crescents remained from her fingernails. "Are you okay? You scared the shit out of me."

"Sorry. Me too." She sat up, slowly, with Nate's help. She regretted it instantly, though, and pressed her hands deeply into her left side, sucking in a breath as waves of pain coursed through her.

"Still bad?" he asked, his eyebrows knitting together. He placed a hand behind her shoulders, bending to see her face. "Maybe we should go to the ER. This can't be from a pulled muscle."

"It's getting better." But the pain was picking up again, impatient for its grand finale. Alice's heart raced. *Maybe I'm dying.* Could it be her appendix? That was on the right side, she was pretty sure. Wait . . . had she touched the foxglove plant? No, Nate had pulled it out and she had only held the yard-waste bag. She was wildly confused, unsure of the order of events.

"Nate?" she whispered, turning to him. His eyes seemed too big for his head, his mouth working but no sound coming out. "What's wrong with me?" He didn't even have time to answer before she screamed as the pain ripped through her again, so forcefully this time it was as though her insides had liquefied.

"I'm going to be sick," she mumbled, knowing with such

clarity it was the only way to get the blackness out of her. She scrambled off the bed and Nate held her up as her legs buckled, his panic evident. They'd only taken one step toward the door, Nate trying to get her to the washroom, when she violently threw up, the new bedroom rug taking the brunt of it.

Nate cursed repeatedly as he propped her naked body against his, his one arm tight across her chest and under her armpits, crushing her breasts while she sagged against him. He dialed with his other hand and tried to get her back on the bed, but she resisted him.

"I don't want to mess up the duvet," Alice said, a temporary feeling of relief filling her. "I'm sorry about the rug. I'll clean it up."

"Alice, stop. Stop. Just let me get you . . . Ali, stay with me, okay? Keep your eyes open. Yes, hello? My wife . . . she needs an ambulance . . ." Nate's voice hitched and Alice wanted to tell him she was fine, not to worry. But she soon gave up, too dizzy to do anything but let Nate lay her on the bed. Alice tried to hang on, but sleep promised a reprieve from the pain and nightmare happening in their bedroom, and so she closed her eyes and succumbed. The house hummed softly to her through its cracks, like a mother serenading her child with a soothing lullaby, and she drifted away, Nate's frantic shouts disappearing into the void.

31

Nellie

....

SEPTEMBER 8, 1956

Rose Caramels

....

2½ cups sweet milk

1 teaspoon vanilla extract

2 teaspoons chopped dried rose petals

½ cup molasses

1 cup granulated sugar

Heat milk, vanilla, and rose petals in a small saucepan and simmer for 5 minutes. Strain petals and cool milk mixture. Then in separate saucepan boil molasses, sugar, and milk mixture for 15 to 20 minutes. Pour mixture into greased tin and cut into small squares once cooled. An excellent hostess gift!

Richard had vomited into the front hedge only moments before he and Nellie got into the Studebaker. They were expected at the Goldmans' in less than ten minutes, having already pushed things as late as possible due to Richard's upset stomach. He seemed unsteady on his feet, too, and Nellie wasn't sure he should even be driving. But when she suggested he lie down for a while—they could easily cancel—he insisted he was fine and told her to leave it be. A moment later he was doubled over, gagging into Nellie's front garden shrub.

"You obviously are *not* fine," Nellie said, setting the bouquet of roses she'd cut and prepared for Kitty, along with the tin of rose caramels, on the stoop to rummage through her purse. She handed him a tissue to wipe his mouth, but he pushed it away. Slugging back some Pepto-Bismol he had tucked into his jacket pocket, he unwrapped a stick of gum and marched toward the car. But Nellie noticed he leaned heavily on the car's door, pausing for a few breaths before opening it for her.

"Why don't I go alone? I'm sure they'll understand you're not well." She had already tried to convince Richard, unsuccessfully, to call Dr. Johnson to see if he could make a house call.

"Cool it, Nellie," Richard said. "It's probably something I ate. It will pass." Nellie didn't bother commenting how they'd eaten the same meals and her stomach was fine, understanding that would only incite him further. Richard Murdoch would not want to appear weak in front of their friends, especially Charles Goldman. "We are going. Together." His limp voice belied his assurances.

Richard hung his head out the window as he drove, hugging the curb in case he needed to pull over. Nellie had offered to drive, but he wouldn't hear of it. A few minutes later they pulled up outside the Goldmans' home and Richard leaned his head back, closing his eyes and breathing deeply in through his nose and out through his mouth. Fine droplets of sweat clustered near his hairline, outlining the dark widow's peak.

"Are you ready to go in?" Nellie asked.

He didn't answer, simply got out and came around to

Nellie's side to open her door. He offered his arm and she took it, though if anyone needed help, it was Richard. He swayed as they started up the Goldmans' walkway, and Nellie tightened the muscles in her legs to counteract his wobbling.

"We can leave whenever you like," Nellie said. "I don't mind." In fact, she'd welcome it. Putting on the charade of things being well and good between them was unpleasant and arduous.

"Enough, Nellie!" Richard's tone was snappish. "And don't you breathe a word of this to anyone tonight. Do you understand?"

Richard rang the bell, and Kitty opened the door, dressed to the nines and wearing a bright coral lipstick that didn't suit her coloring. "Nellie, Richard, welcome!"

They were ushered inside, and Kitty commented on what a lovely idea the rose caramels were. ("Oh! You made them yourself? How fancy, though I don't have much of a sweet tooth," Kitty added.) She also initially fawned over the bundled yellow roses, though she soon dropped them onto the kitchen table without so much as a second glance. The yellow rose was a flower of friendship, and while Nellie doubted much could help Kitty become a more thoughtful friend, she was not one to doubt a bloom's prophecy. Though, if she were being frank, a more suitable flower for tonight's hostess might have been the narcissus, but they were harbingers of spring and so were long gone from the garden by now.

After settling into the living room, Kitty fetched cocktails, and Nellie's eyebrows rose when Richard accepted an old-fashioned, a grimace painting his sweaty, green-tinged face with his first sip. *Stubborn bastard.* She only hoped he was ill all over Kitty's living room rug, which looked new and probably cost quite a lot—two details Kitty would share shortly, once all her guests had arrived and she had an audience.

The mood was gay, the cocktails flowing, and Richard did perk up, though the gray pallor remained. No one but Nellie realized he wasn't well, and as promised, she made no mention of it. She stuck with the women on one side of the room, discussing the next neighborhood-watch meeting and Kitty's new rug and Martha's baby boy, Bobby, who had been born a few days earlier.

"She's still the size of a ship," Kitty exclaimed. "But the baby is quite sweet, even though I personally don't care for the name Bobby. She's going to have her hands full with the two of them, without a live-in girl. Better her than me!" Kitty laughed, and the other women joined in. Except for Nellie, who escaped with the excuse that she needed to powder her nose.

When she came back to the living room, a shout erupted, Kitty especially gleeful, like she'd just received the best news. She squealed as she strode toward Nellie, who was unsure about what had transpired in the few minutes she'd been gone. Until she caught Richard's eye and his triumphant smirk told her everything.

"Nellie, you sly fox! Why didn't you tell us?" Kitty grabbed her arms, pulled her into a hug. The other women gathered around and fussed over her, asking how she was feeling, if her ankles were swelling yet. The men pumped Richard's hand, slapped him on the shoulder in congratulations. Nellie fumed but hid her anger behind a practiced smile. Richard had assured her they wouldn't make the announcement tonight—Nellie had said she wanted to let the women know first, at their next meeting (though she had a different plan in mind) and he'd agreed to wait. But Nellie shouldn't have been surprised. Richard would exert his control wherever he could.

Soon the hubbub died down and they were seated for dinner, and Nellie found herself beside the widower Norman Woodrow, a sweet, quiet man whose wife, Kathleen, had died only six months earlier. Kathleen had been in their neighborhood-watch club and was president of the church knitting circle before she fell ill, the cancer taking her so suddenly she went from vision of health to deathbed skeleton in mere weeks.

Nellie had always liked Kathleen—she was a good mother and friend, never gossiping about the other women or their husbands, and had boundless energy for church fund-raisers and bake sales. She also wore flatties exclusively, most assumed because she was quite tall, but she once confessed to Nellie she found heels excruciating and "life is too short for miserable shoes!" She had been quite right, especially about the life-being-too-short part.

Nellie hadn't seen Norman since the funeral but had heard he was keeping to himself, busy caring for their two young children with the help of Kathleen's mother, who had moved in. She thought Norman looked well; better rested and not as grief-thin as the last time she had seen him.

They chatted through the meal, and she found Norman to have a lovely sense of humor. She laughed at the few jokes he shared during the lulls in the larger group conversations and he seemed delighted by the attention. Richard, however, was displeased with Nellie's interest in Norman, which only made her want to give him more. At one point, she put a hand on Norman's arm, gushing about how wonderful it was that he was doing "so very well these days," which was the moment Richard snapped.

It was a quiet jealousy—no one else at the table would see it—but Nellie felt it rolling off him. She raised her eyes to Richard's but didn't remove her hand from Norman's arm.

"You're making a fool of yourself," Richard hissed. Kitty was clearing the dinner plates, and drinks were being refreshed, so Richard's mumbled comment went mostly unnoticed. Except by Nellie, for whom it was intended. The other guests were focused on the iced chocolate cake Kitty presented, and even Norman, seated beside Nellie and certainly within range to hear what Richard had said, seemed distracted by the dessert's pomp and circumstance.

Nellie—her voice at full volume—calmly retorted, "It takes one to know one, Richard." She picked up her dessert fork, lavished Kitty with an appreciative smile as the hostess set a piece of cake in front of her. "This looks absolutely delicious, Kitty." In truth, it looked dry, had obviously been baked too long.

"Why, thank you, Nellie. Coming from you, our master baker, that's high praise!" She continued slicing and plating another piece. "It's a new recipe from—"

"Eleanor," Richard said, interrupting Kitty. Everyone looked at him in surprise—Richard Murdoch had impeccable manners, would never be so rude at a party, nor speak to his wife in such a tone. "You would do well to be quiet. Now is not the time." The other guests detected it then, the taut band of tension between husband and wife perilously close to snapping, and were perplexed. *What on earth is going on with Richard and Nellie?*

"No, it isn't." Nellie licked the chocolate crumbs from her fork. "So perhaps *you* should be quiet, Richard."

A small gasp came from one of the women—*Kitty? Judith?*—Nellie wasn't sure, but it sent a surge of power through her. She smiled at Kitty. "Dinner was excellent, as always." She pushed back her chair and the men politely followed suit. Except for Richard, who was statue still in his seat. "But I'm sorry we have to be leaving now. I find myself exhausted." She laid a hand to her stomach. "You all understand, surely."

Kitty was about to say something in response, but everyone had turned to Richard as a strange, choking noise erupted from his throat. His face was no longer pale but poppy red, as though he had been holding his breath for too long.

"Richard? Are you quite well?" Kitty, seated at the head of

the table and nearest to Richard, put a hand on his arm, which trembled violently against the tablecloth. She frowned at her husband. "Charles, perhaps you should take Richard outside for some air?"

"Let's take a walk, Dick." Charles Goldman set his napkin on the table and came to stand behind Richard, who opened his mouth seemingly to respond. But it wasn't a flurry of words that spewed forth—rather, it was a loud belch, followed by an ejection of the old-fashioned and Pepto-Bismol and the small amount of food he'd managed at dinner. As Richard's stomach contents splattered across Kitty's arm, covering the beautiful tablecloth and the remainder of the cake, everyone jumped back, gasping with shock at the frothy pink mess. Kitty looked as though she might faint, and for a moment no one knew quite what to do.

Before Nellie endured the put-on role of caring wife, getting Richard cleaned up and into the car, she turned to Norman and said, "It was lovely talking with you tonight. I do hope we see each other again soon." He nodded, though he remained startled by what had happened, much like the rest of the guests at the table. Nellie resisted the triumphant smile that threatened to betray her as she took in Richard's livid, sick-covered face.

32

Don't mope and cry because you are ill, and don't get any fun;
the man goes out to get all the fun, and your laugh comes in
when he gets home again and tells you about it—some of it. As
for being ill, women should never be ill.

—"Advice to Wives," *The Isle of Man Times* (October 12, 1895)

Alice

.....

AUGUST 14, 2018

*P*lease, talk to me," Alice said for what must have been the
tenth time since they'd arrived home from the hospital an hour
earlier. Nate didn't respond. "So, what . . . are you planning to
ignore me indefinitely?"

He threw his phone onto the coffee table, hard enough that
it slid off and to the ground. Alice reached over from her re-
clined position on the sofa to pick it up.

"Stop," Nate said, his voice taut with exhaustion and frustration. "Would you just fucking lie there and rest, *please*?"

Chastened, Alice retreated to her prior position, a pillow
tucked behind her head, a soft blanket covering the rest of her

curled-up form. The balls of T-shirt fabric she'd woven into sections of her hair remained, and they pulled on her scalp with uncomfortable pressure.

Nate had helped her settle in the living room, in part because she didn't think she could manage the stairs and in part because there was still a mess to be cleaned up in their bedroom. He was furious, but he also wouldn't leave her alone in this condition, hence the cold shoulder.

She watched Nate pace the living room, took in his outfit and tried not to laugh, for she knew how poorly that would go over. Plus, she was in no position to be laughing right now. But he did look ridiculous—still wearing the sweatpants he'd quickly tugged on after calling 911 along with one of his work shirts, the fabrics and patterns and buttons as mismatched as though he'd chosen the clothes in the dark.

As it turned out, her pain, and the quite dramatic ambulance ride, was the result of a large ovarian cyst rupturing. "Can happen with intercourse," the emergency room resident had said. "You're the second one in as many days, actually."

At first all seemed okay. Alice wasn't dying, as a terrified Nate first thought, and it appeared her ovary was going to make it, too. When the resident said pregnancy shouldn't be a problem, Nate became emotional, until the possible reason for the cyst's existence was revealed. The doctor suspected Alice's hormone-delivering IUD could be the culprit. An IUD that, until that moment, Nate had no clue existed inside Alice's uterus.

Nate had looked confused at first and started protesting the resident's assessment. *Alice doesn't have an IUD . . . we've been trying to get pregnant,* was on the tip of his tongue. But then he looked at her—a look she wouldn't soon forget, full of hurt and disbelief because he suddenly knew it had to be true. He had pressed his lips tightly together and nodded, as though none of this was news to him. After which he promptly walked out of the room.

"Should we wait for your husband?" the doctor had asked. "I have a few things to go over before we spring you."

Alice shook her head, holding back tears. The resident went through the discharge instructions, repeating that she might want to have the IUD removed as a precaution, as she was slightly more at risk now for developing further cysts. Alice said she would, feeling ashamed and embarrassed, finally admitting to herself the magnitude of keeping this secret from her husband. What a mess she'd made of things.

While Alice lay on the sofa, Nate rummaged around the kitchen. The fridge door opened and closed with unnecessary force. Next came the slamming of a cupboard, the echo of something glass set too heavily on the countertop, the pinging of a bottle cap into the depths of the stainless steel sink. A drawn-out sigh (*the house, uneasy with all his banging around*) reached Alice's ears, and she sighed in response. Nate finally re-appeared, a foamy glass of beer in one hand and a bottle of San Pellegrino in the other. She didn't remark on the beer, though it was only seven in the morning.

"You can still make it to the office," she said evenly. "I'll be fine on my own."

Nate ignored the comment. "How's the pain?" He reached into Alice's purse and pulled out two pill bottles, frowning as he read the labels. Still he wouldn't look at her, and she began to feel desperate for him to do so. Why couldn't this have happened while he was at work? He might have never known what she'd done, and she could have undone it without consequence.

"It's not bad," Alice replied, her syllables drawn out from exhaustion and morphine. "So, are you not going in today at all?"

Nate gave her a look suggesting she should leave it alone.

Popping the lid off one bottle, he shook out two small blue pills and handed them to her with the sparkling water. "Here."

Alice didn't protest, set the pills on her tongue, and took a sip of the water, bubbles erupting in her throat. "Why did you leave it out for me?"

"Leave what out?" Nate asked, snapping the lid back onto the pill bottle.

"The test strip. Yesterday morning."

A pause, then a tense: "Does that even fucking matter anymore?"

Alice gave a sloppy wave and leaned her head back, closing her eyes. "You're right. Forget it."

There was a long moment of silence, then, "Obviously you don't want to have a baby."

"I *do* want to have a baby." She opened her eyes, and it was a few seconds before everything stopped moving. Morphine was no joke.

"But not *with me*. Is that it?" He was furious—his mouth a hard line, his hands trembling.

"No! Nate. It's not like that." Alice shook her head, tried to clear her thoughts so she could reassure him and explain things. "Not exactly."

"So, what is it, Ali? *What is it exactly?*" The words exploded out of him, and she recoiled as they did, having never seen him like this: full of vitriol, all directed at her. Nate, too, seemed alarmed at his outburst, a mask of surprise followed by regret settling over his face. Nathan Hale did not—*would never*—yell in such a way at his wife. But everyone had a breaking point.

Alice gingerly rolled on her side to face him. "I made a mistake, Nate. You can't believe how sorry I am."

"A mistake?" he said, and let out a harsh laugh. "Is that what we're calling this? What part was the mistake? Getting the

IUD, or getting caught?" Fair question, and Alice didn't think too hard on it, because she wasn't sure which was more truthful.

"I'm sorry, I—" She winced, and while he surely noticed, he didn't ask her if she was okay. "I was overwhelmed. With the house, and my book." It was hard to read his expression. Alice pressed on. "And you were gone so much. Studying for your exam after work. All the time, it seemed." She didn't add how all the hours he and Drew spent together made her irrationally jealous.

"So this is my fault?" He was incredulous.

"It's no one's fault," she began, then, seeing the look on his face, added, "Fine. It's my fault. I fucked up. But I had these visions of being all alone all the time in our half-finished house with a baby, and . . . I didn't know what to do." She gulped back a sob. "All I can say is how sorry I am. And that I'm going to fix it, okay? I promise."

Nate heaved a sigh before crouching beside the sofa. "This could have been so much worse, Ali." He wiped the tears off her cheeks, his face contorted with worry and the remnants of his anger.

"I know," she whispered, grabbing his hands and holding them tight. Her blinks got longer as the pain medication settled in. "I shouldn't be a mother." This was perhaps the most truthful thing she had said to Nate in weeks. Not everyone could be a decent parent; Alice's own, particularly her father, were good examples of that. Even Jaclyn, whom Alice supposed had done her best based on the circumstances, had proved an inadequate role model. A "good" mother was someone who was selfless and wise and knew how to bake six different types of cookies from scratch. Who tenderly, and regularly, said things like, "You are the very best thing I have ever done with my life."

"Not true," he murmured, kissing her fingers lightly. "When you're ready, you'll be the best mother." He sounded so certain, Alice almost believed it.

Fresh tears pricked her eyes. "You should hate me right now, Nate. Why don't you hate me for this?"

Nate was silent as his fingers kneaded hers. "I could never hate you, Ali. Yes, I'm pissed as hell." He cleared his throat, his gaze focused on their entwined fingers. "Last night was the scariest moment of my life."

"Mine too." She nodded fervently as she said it, which increased her light-headedness and forced her to close her eyes again. "I'm going to get this thing out and then we can start trying again." *Time to pivot, Alice.*

Nate let go of her hands, kneaded his neck as he stood. "I'm not sure that's a good idea."

She sat up, too quickly, and had to place her hands behind her to anchor herself against the dizziness. "Why not? They said my ovary is totally fine. There's no reason to think we—"

"That's not what I meant, Ali."

She tried to focus on him, but everything blurred around the edges, like she had put drops in her eyes. Her elbows quivered trying to hold her position on the couch and she let go, her body collapsing back to the sofa cushions.

"I think we should wait." He puffed out his cheeks before exhaling forcefully. "Look, I've been an idiot. Pushing you, putting on too much pressure. It wasn't fair. I'm the one who should be sorry."

Alice's sluggish brain worked hard, trying to comprehend his words. Nate took her pause as agreement.

"We'll take a break," he said, sitting beside her on the sofa. "We can do what we want in the house and you can finish your book and I can focus on my exam." Nate rested his palms on either side of Alice's body and smiled gently at his wife, who looked better than she had a few hours before but still not well. "Let's not worry about the whole kid thing for now. And we'll see where things are in a bit. Six months, maybe a year. Sound good?"

Alice was shocked, though unable to show it because her emotions were dampened by the medication. Twenty-four hours earlier her husband had been actively trying to get her pregnant— a plan he'd been steadfast about since they'd moved to Greenville. Could Nate really flip the switch that easily? Again, Alice sensed Nate was keeping something from her. The way she had been keeping things from him . . .

But too exhausted and muddled by the pain and medications to confront him, she replied, "Yeah. Okay." She should have been relieved—wasn't that precisely what she wanted? But she was troubled, mind spinning with her predictable husband's sudden change of heart. *What aren't you telling me, Nate? Is this really about logistics and timing, or is it something else altogether?*

33

Remember your most important job is to build up and maintain his ego (which gets bruised plenty in business). Morale is a woman's business.

—Edward Podolsky, *Sex Today in Wedded Life* (1947)

Alice

.....

AUGUST 15, 2018

The doorbell rang, and Alice, fresh from a bath, quickly slipped on her robe. "I'll get it," she shouted down the hall. Normally she would never answer the door with dripping hair and wearing only a bathrobe, but she was antsy. Nate had been hovering, checking on her pain every hour, setting timers for her medication, insisting she be quiet and still. His concern was thoughtful, but it made her restless.

"Stay put," Nate replied, coming out of the bedroom. He had his phone to his ear, and he said, "Nice to talk with you too. Here she is," before handing it to Alice.

"Who is it?"

"Your mom," Nate whispered. Alice grumbled, in no mood to speak with Jaclyn. And it bugged her that Jaclyn had called

Nate's phone—there was a reason she hadn't already answered her mom's three calls. She scowled, holding the phone an arm's length away, and Nate shrugged.

"She's your mother, Ali."

While he headed downstairs to answer the door, Alice reluctantly put the phone to her ear and sat on the top step. "Hi, Mom."

"Hi, honey. How are you feeling?"

"Better, thanks," Alice said, shifting the towel so it wasn't covering her ear. She peered down the stairs, but whoever had rung the bell hadn't stepped inside. "How are you? How's Steve's shoulder?"

"We're good; he's good. Getting ready for our silent meditation retreat in the mountains next week. You and Nate should try this sometime. Maybe if you come for Thanksgiving, take a couple of extra days?"

"Um, maybe. But isn't meditation always silent?" Alice sat on the top step, inspected her DIY painted toenails, which were in serious need of a new polish job. She tried to remember the last time she'd had a pedicure. Couldn't.

"Yes, well, I suppose it is," her mother replied. "But they *do* say—"

Nate laughed loudly, pulling Alice's focus away from her mother, who was droning on about meditation. "Hey, Mom, can I call you back later? Someone's at the door."

"Of course, honey. I'm here all day, except for my yoga class at three. California time, so six your time."

Alice took a deep breath in through her nose, her impatience growing.

"Remember, your body needs a lot of rest right now. And red clover tea is excellent for balancing your hormones. Want me to send you some?"

"Mom, I really have to go."

"Yes, yes. I'll call you before bed," her mother said. "And I'll pop some red clover tea in the mail."

"Okay, bye," Alice said, ending the call before she said, "Always with the goddamn tea!"

"What's that?" Nate asked, at the bottom of the stairs. He held a tinfoil casserole tray in one hand, a bouquet of roses in the other, the stems wrapped in gold twine that Alice recognized as her neighbor's signature decoration. "Sally just dropped off this chicken lasagna for dinner and some flowers."

"You should have invited her in." Alice came down the stairs, thinking a visit with Sally would be the best medicine right now.

"She was on her way out. Said she'd call you later." Nate shifted the lasagna in his hands. "I'm going to stick this in the fridge and put these in water. Can I trust you to rest, or am I going to have to sit on you to make sure you do?" He smiled, but his tone—and suggestion—irritated Alice.

"I'm sick of resting, Nate. This is overkill. I'm *fine*." Alice held out her hands. "Here, let me do it. You have work to do." He relented, passing her the tinfoil tray and roses before heading back to the guest room.

After she put the lasagna in the fridge and the roses in a vase, Alice unwrapped her hair and tousled the wet strands, wishing she could just sit in the garden and have a cigarette. But obviously with Nate home that wasn't an option—one more secret she was keeping from her husband. Sighing, she rummaged through the fridge, looking for a snack to distract her from her nicotine craving. They were down to the staples— milk, bread, one egg, a half-eaten jar of pickles, and three limp carrots. Alice would have to go shopping later, if Nate would let her leave the house.

She pulled the bread and milk out of the fridge and gathered up the other ingredients she needed for milk toast, a dish Nellie mentioned in in one of her letters as a go-to breakfast for Richard when he wasn't feeling well. Though she'd initially thought it sounded disgusting (*toast drenched in warm milk?*), it had proven quite tasty. After she toasted the bread and heated the milk and vanilla until it simmered on the stovetop, she poured the near-scalded liquid over the chunks of toast and liberally sprinkled it all with cinnamon and sugar.

The kitchen smelled delicious, and Alice had just tucked into the milk toast when her phone buzzed. She pulled it from her pocket, expecting it was her mother again with another healing tea suggestion, and saw it was Bronwyn. They hadn't properly spoken since she had called with news of her marriage—a couple of meaningless text exchanges—and Alice wasn't sure when, or even if, Bronwyn might forgive her. She dropped her spoon into the bowl of milk toast and quickly answered the call.

"Hello?"

"Hey, Ali. It's Bronwyn."

"Hey! How are you?" Alice was overeager, her words quick and enthusiastic.

"Good, yeah. Everything's going well. But are you okay? Nate said you were in the hospital?"

"You talked to Nate?" Alice was surprised—Nate hadn't mentioned it.

"Um, yeah. He had a couple of questions for Darren," she said casually. But before Alice could ask what sort of questions, and when they'd talked, Bronwyn continued. "So, what happened?"

"Apparently a very pissed-off ovarian cyst is what happened," Alice replied. She gave a few more details, and Bronwyn responded with appropriate concern. Alice couldn't tell if Bronwyn was feigning ignorance or not—maybe Nate hadn't told her the whole story.

"Yikes. Are you feeling better now?" Bronwyn asked.

"Seem to be." There was a pause, neither woman speaking. "So, how are you doing?" Bronwyn had already answered with a nondescript "good," but Alice was desperate to keep her on the phone. If she ever needed her best friend, it was now.

"Busy, but great. Thanks," Bronwyn replied. Another pause.

Alice waited a beat longer, then said, "Are we okay?"

Bronwyn sighed lightly, and Alice bit her lip, fighting back tears. "We're okay, Ali." It was an olive branch, and Alice clutched at it with both hands.

"I hope you know how sorry I am about the other day. I *am* happy for you and Darren. I'm just an asshole. It's that simple."

"You are sort of an asshole," Bronwyn said, and then she laughed. Alice was relieved. "But I'm kind of an asshole too. I should have told you when it was happening. Before it happened, actually. Even though I didn't really know what was happening until it happened, you know? But you're my best friend and I should have told you. I'm sorry, Ali."

"It's okay. But next time I expect a call before you get to Elvis's chapel, okay?"

"Shut up, you jerk. There isn't going to be a next time." Alice hoped that was true. "Anyway, Darren and I want to have a party, to celebrate. Can you help me plan it? I'm so swamped right now I barely have time to breathe."

"Absolutely. Whatever you need," Alice replied, feeling the creep of envy, imagining Bronwyn's demanding but gratifying schedule. The opposite of her own. "What's your timing?"

"Not sure yet, but I'll let you know. Just meeting Darren for lunch, so I'll text you some details later, okay?"

"Sounds good. Say hi to him for me."

"Will do," Bronwyn said. "And no more hospital trips, lady. I think you aged Nate about a decade." Alice cringed, her guilt blooming. "He's pretty worried about you."

"Yeah, I know."

A pause, then: "Listen, are you sure you're fine?"

"Ahhh, I wish everyone would stop asking me that," Alice said, giving an exaggerated groan. "I'm okay. Ovary too. No permanent damage."

"I didn't mean with your ovary, Ali." Bronwyn's tone was gentle but pointed, and Alice suddenly understood: Nate had told Bronwyn everything, including what caused the cyst to grow and burst. She felt exposed, and stupid for assuming otherwise. Also, she couldn't explain why had she taken things so far, even to Bronwyn, who probably understood her better than anyone. What did it say about her, and her marriage, that she hadn't simply been honest with Nate from the beginning?

"I'm here if you want to talk, okay?"

Alice considered whether perhaps Nate had put Bronwyn up to this call.

"Yeah. Thanks." But she couldn't talk to Bronwyn about this now—Nate had beaten her to it. No matter how she spun it, she would forever be the wife who went to extraordinary, secretive (and some might say irrational) lengths to avoid getting pregnant with her husband.

"I mean it, Ali. Anything, anytime. Well, except right this second because I have to meet *my husband* for lunch. Still getting used to calling him that."

"Off you go, you lovesick newlywed. We'll chat later." Alice kept her tone light, even though her stomach felt like it was filled with cement.

"Bye. Love you."

"Love you too," Alice said, just as Nate came into the kitchen.

"Who was that?"

Alice pushed a piece of sopping toast around her bowl. "My mom."

"Again? What was it this time?"

"She wanted to talk about Thanksgiving. In California."

"Hmm. Maybe we should go. Could be fun." Nate shrugged, then took a fork from the drawer and speared a piece of toast in Alice's bowl. "This stuff is addictive."

"Have the rest. I'm not that hungry." Alice frowned, pushing it toward him.

"You feeling okay?"

"Perfect," she said, smiling for good measure. She had been lying a lot recently, and it was becoming disturbingly easy to do so.

34

Nellie

....

SEPTEMBER 9, 1956

Lemon Lavender Muffins

2 cups flour

3 teaspoons baking powder

1 teaspoon baking soda

½ teaspoon salt

2 beaten eggs

1 cup sweet milk

3 tablespoons honey

3 tablespoons melted butter, cooled

Zest from a lemon

2 teaspoons lavender buds

Sift flour and mix with baking powder, baking soda, and salt. Combine eggs, sweet milk, honey, and butter. Make a well in center of flour mixture and pour in milk mixture. Mix quickly, but not until smooth (mixture should be lumpy). Grate lemon zest into mixture, and add dried lavender. Stir to combine. Fill greased muffin tins until two-thirds full. Bake in hot oven (375°F) for 20 to 25 minutes.

*N*ellie crushed and sprinkled the dried lavender buds into the bowl with her fingers, stirring with a wooden spoon to make sure the flavor would be well balanced throughout. The lavender was meant to be subtle, marrying well with the tart lemon rind, all without being overpowering. Therefore, precision was imperative, or else the muffins would taste like the perfumed satchels Nellie kept in her chest of drawers. She was baking for Martha's baby shower, which wasn't until later in the afternoon, but Nellie had started first thing—right after Richard left for work—so they'd be cooled in time.

Nellie didn't make these lavender muffins often, as they brought forth memories of her mother in better days, which was difficult. Yet, it remained one of her favorite recipes. Lemon the flavor of sunshine, and lavender, a most powerful herb. It symbolized feminine beauty and grace, and Nellie could think of nothing better with which to celebrate Martha's recent delivery.

Martha had confessed, when Nellie called to congratulate her on little Bobby, that she felt like an old, broken-down vessel beyond repair. "Dan hasn't touched me in so long, Nellie. And I can't say I blame him! Everything is just so . . . so lumpy." She had burst into tears, Bobby crying equally hard in the background, and Nellie had done her best to reassure Martha that she was a beautiful woman. *Motherhood has made that only more true,* Nellie soothed. After hanging up with Martha, Nellie thought about the upcoming shower, and lavender immediately came to mind. Poor Martha needed those muffins as much as she needed a good night's sleep, along with a husband who appreciated the sacrifices she had made.

Nostalgia flooded her as she gave the mixture a few more stirs, noting the small clumps that were not to be smoothed out, before she filled the muffin tins. Nellie had made these muffins more times than she could count in the years she lived with Elsie, as it was also one of her mother's favorite recipes. Elsie was forever reminding Nellie about the lumps, and Nellie smiled as she remembered her mother's predictable, "Don't overmix, Nell-girl. Too many stirs and we'll have to throw it out with the burrs!"

She set the timer, and while Martha's muffins baked, Nellie sat at the table and smoked, thinking about the last time she and her mother had made this recipe. It was shortly before Nellie's birthday—her seventeenth—and they were baking for one of her mother's friends, who had the flu. Elsie, seated in their small kitchen, plucked lavender buds from the stems fanned in front of her. Too thin and always cold, Elsie wore a red-and-green winter sweater buttoned to the top, the wide collar high up her neck even though it was summer. She gathered the buds on top of the tea towel she'd laid out across the tabletop. That morning there were other sprigs of herbs on the table as well— oregano, thyme, rosemary, dill, mint, basil, tarragon—set in neat piles, ready to be macerated for future recipes, for satchels to scent closets and drawers, to add to the bathwater.

The herbs had been harvested from what was left of her mother's Victory garden that year, planted three summers earlier after she was inspired by the GROW YOUR OWN, CAN YOUR OWN posters popping up in shops around town. The war garden movement had been amazingly effective, and nearly everyone in the Swanns' neighborhood had planted one, but when the war ended most were abandoned.

Nellie, sitting beside her mother, rolled a lemon between tight palms, loosening the flesh from the rind. Later she would use the juice to make lemonade, but for now she grated the bright yellow zest, the oils from the puckered rind coating her fingers with each turn of the fruit. Soon she had a small heap of the grated rind, which she collected in her palm and plopped on top of the wet mixture.

"Nearly done with the lavender?" she asked her mother. Elsie passed Nellie the buds in a small dish. The recipe called for two teaspoons of dried lavender, and Nellie, after measuring like she knew she was supposed to (especially for this recipe), was amazed, like always, at how her mother could eyeball the precise amount of an ingredient.

"I will never grow tired of the scent of lavender in my kitchen," Elsie had said, pressing her herb-infused fingers to her face. "It smells of contentment, doesn't it?" Contentment was a hard thing to come by for Elsie, so any mention of it had made hope blossom inside Nellie's chest. Elsie began to sing, and Nellie joined in—their voices blending as pleasantly in the small kitchen as the lemon rind and lavender buds within the muffin mixture.

Their frequent cooking sessions in those days weren't only an education in home economics; they were also a housewifery training program passed from mother to daughter. Elsie taught Nellie how to make her own bread yeast, and why one should add a dash of oatmeal to soups (to thicken it), and how vinegar keeps boiling cauliflower pristinely white. And underpinning those lessons was Elsie's wish for Nellie to marry a good man, unlike the one she herself committed to. They lived modestly, without luxuries, but Elsie's love for Nellie was as bountiful as her gardens. "You have been my greatest joy," Elsie would murmur to Nellie when she tucked her into bed, kissing her on the forehead, on her cheeks, her eyelids, smelling of roses and dusty baking flour. "My greatest joy."

"Nellie, I wrote something out for you. Here, darling." Elsie had held out a recipe card, her swooping letters as familiar to Nellie as the sound of her voice, while they waited for the muffins to bake.

"What is it?" Nellie took the card and glanced at the ingredients. "Oh, I know this one, Mother." For a moment, she had worried about Elsie's state of mind, as on the card was a Swann family recipe Nellie already knew by heart.

"I should say your version may in fact be better than mine," Elsie replied, a smile gracing her lips. "I think it might be the dill. It really gave it something special." *Oh, if only that smile would hold,* Nellie thought. Her mother was so beautiful when she smiled.

Elsie leaned forward onto bony elbows, gently cushioned by the thick wool of her sweater, and waited until she had her only child's full attention. Nellie, seated across from her mother at the small table, held the recipe card tightly in her hands. Her fingertips, still dewy with lemon oil, left small prints on the card's edges.

"But there's something else. You're old enough now, my love." Elsie lowered her voice, forcing Nellie to lean in too, so the women's faces were only inches apart. "Something only shared from lips to ears, never to be written down. So listen closely to me now, all right, my girl?"

Nellie's heart had raced at the intensity of her mother's voice. She listened carefully to what Elsie said next, her eyes growing wide for one, sharp moment, before they settled back to normal. Though her heart continued thumping wildly for some time, long after the muffins were cooled enough to pack up and deliver to Elsie's ailing friend.

35

Now, if you are one of those frigid or sexually anesthetic women, don't be in a hurry to inform your husband about it. To the man it makes no difference in the pleasurableness of the act whether you are frigid or not *unless he knows* that you are frigid. And he won't know unless you tell him, and what he doesn't know won't hurt him.

—William J. Robinson, *Married Life and Happiness* (1922)

Alice

.....

AUGUST 20, 2018

After Alice had the IUD removed, which was much simpler than its insertion, and picked up her prescription for the birth control pill, she stopped to browse at the vintage consignment shop close to Dr. Sterling's office. The saleswoman, looking like she'd stepped out of a *Ladies' Home Journal* magazine right down to her sleek pageboy and emerald-green pencil skirt, had been outside on a smoke break. After Alice complimented her on the outfit, the woman, Sarah, offered her a cigarette, with the warning that it was unfiltered.

"Thanks," Alice said. "I've never tried one of these." She set it between her lips.

"Lucky you," Sarah said, extending a lit match to the cigarette's end. "You won't believe the difference." Alice took a drag of the cigarette and promptly started coughing, a raw burn of heat in her throat.

"Yeah, you get used to it." Sarah sucked deeply on her own cigarette before exhaling a long plume of smoke. "I used to cut the filters off myself, which is way cheaper, but it's not quite the same. I buy them online now."

Alice nodded, her eyes watering from coughing, and took a tentative puff. The burn was less, and she didn't cough. Saleswoman Sarah was right: without the filter, the toasted taste of tobacco and its effects were more intense, the nicotine quick to hit Alice's bloodstream. The head rush lingered pleasantly, and after she browsed the vintage shop she headed home and promptly cut the filters off the last of her pack of cigarettes. Rather than write, as she had planned, she sat in her new-to-her vintage dress on the back patio so as not to smell up the house, and blew smoke rings into the air, imagining Nellie Murdoch doing the same half a decade earlier.

The rest of the week flowed easily, Nate, off to the office each morning but home for dinner at night as promised, and Alice, trying to work on her novel. Which mostly meant hours online researching details of life in the 1950s, as well as rereading the magazines and Nellie's letters, and smoking unfiltered cigarettes with the mother-of-pearl holder outside while Nate was at work. She was smoking every day now and knew she'd have to stop soon—she wouldn't be able to hide it from Nate indefinitely. It was tiring, worrying about him finding out. But the cigarettes helped her concentrate and smoothed her frustrations. Plus, it seemed everyone smoked in the fifties—back when even doctors believed it had health benefits—and so it felt almost poetic every time she slid a cigarette into the antique holder; a necessary part of her research.

Sally returned from visiting her ill friend and came over for dinner on Saturday night, which was long overdue. Alice made a simple supper of Welsh rarebit (toast points smothered in a sauce of cheddar, cream, dry mustard, and spices) with tomato slices, from Nellie's cookbook, and barbecued sausages, along with a "fluffy white cake" that turned out not to be that fluffy but was still delicious. The three of them stayed up far too late and had too much wine, as Sally regaled them with stories of her adventures.

When Alice and Nate went to bed, quite drunk and uncharacteristically (these days) cheerful, they hatched a plan to set Sally up, even though they couldn't remember the name of the handsome elderly gentleman who lived on the street and who was always raking his lawn. They had sex for the first time since the ruptured-cyst fiasco, and it was overall a quite pleasant evening, Alice feeling more optimistic about things than she had in some time.

By Monday Alice was back at her desk, feeling bloated and moody thanks to being on the pill and her overall lack of inspiration on the novel. She was staring out the front window, smoking a cigarette and definitely *not* writing, when Nate rode up the driveway on his bike. Panicked, she glanced at the time on her computer screen—3:07 P.M.—and sat paralyzed for a moment, the cigarette burning in her fingers. The window was open, but a thin curl of smoke floated above her like a gauzy veil, and she waved furiously at it, trying to make it disappear. It had been stupid to risk smoking in the living room, but it was pouring rain and Nate was supposed to be late because he was meeting up with a college friend who was in town on business. He wasn't supposed to be home on time, let alone early.

"Shit, shit, shit," she mumbled, tugging the cigarette from the holder and plopping it into her glass of water. She used one of the old magazines to fan the smoke out the open window. The front door slammed shut and then Nate was in the living room, his helmet still on and his messenger bag slung across his chest. He was soaking wet from having biked home in the rain.

"Oh! You should have called me," Alice said. Her tense voice betrayed her nerves. "I could have picked you up at the station."

Nate stared at her, incredulous. "Are you *smoking*?"

Alice held up her hands, tried to think quickly. Denial was not an option. The smell of smoke still hung heavy in the room. "I had *one*. I never told you this, but I used to smoke, in college, for like, *a second*." She sounded a touch hysterical and so took a deep breath.

"I'm sorry, I know this probably seems crazy. But this book . . . it's making me do things I wouldn't normally do. The writing is harder than I thought and the saleswoman at that vintage shop in Scarsdale offered me one and, well, in my research *everyone* smoked in the fifties, so I figured it was part of my due diligence. I mean, I didn't plan to actually smoke the cigarette. I swear, Nate! Please, stop looking at me like that." Nate continued staring at her like he wanted to throttle her.

"I have writer's block and it seemed like maybe it could help? Like, maybe it would give me some insight or something stupid like that. It's only this one. I promise." She pointed to the glass of water, the half-finished cigarette bobbing on the surface, tobacco strewn like loose-leaf tea. Then she noticed the cigarette carton on the edge of the desk, slightly hidden by the stack of magazines. She shifted to block Nate's view.

Nate still hadn't moved. Like a statue in the living room's

doorway, rainwater dripping to the floor under his feet, his expression one of disbelief. "You smoked in college?"

"Barely. Here and there. Come on, Nate. It's just one lousy cigarette."

"What the hell is going on with you, Ali?" Nate asked—yelled, actually—and that was when she realized whatever made him come home early was worse than finding your nonsmoker wife sucking back a midday cigarette.

Alice frowned. "Wait. Why are you home early?"

"You want to know why?" Nate said, his voice rising.

That's why I asked. Alice's hands had started to shake and she clasped them together. "Yes, Nate. I want to know." She quickly ran scenarios in her mind: he was sick (he didn't look sick, not exactly); his dinner got canceled and he decided to work the rest of the day from home; he was still worried about her after the whole cyst incident (except she was perfectly fine now, and they both knew it). However, none of those explained why he was clearly very upset.

Nate fiddled with the clasp on his bike helmet, not taking his eyes off Alice's. "I met Jessica Stalwart at lunch. Remember her? Because she remembers you."

She nodded, kept her face blank and curious even though the picture was taking shape in Alice's mind. "How did that happen?" Nate's and Jessica's paths had never crossed before, and Alice couldn't sort out how this had transpired.

"She's dating Jason Cutler." Jason worked at Nate's firm, and he was a part of Nate's social group. "She came to the office to meet him for lunch."

Jessica Stalwart started at Wittington about six months before Alice was fired. She liked her immediately—a go-getter like Alice, Jessica was quick-witted and confident, and Alice thought they could have been friends if things had turned out differently. Alice heard Jessica got her job as Georgia's lackey after she left, which meant she would without a doubt know things. Private things only Georgia could tell her. Like, say, about a potential lawsuit and a certain famous author. *Damn it.*

"How is she?" Alice finally managed, which was when Nate lost the fight to keep himself contained. He exploded into the living room, threw his messenger bag onto the floor, and unclipped his helmet, tossing it down as well. Alice winced as the helmet hit the hardwood, the floor's tremors of displeasure rolling under her feet.

"Jessica is fine. She recently left Wittington, apparently. But what was most interesting was her concern for how *you* were doing."

"Me?" Alice did her best to look perplexed. "Why?"

"Why didn't you tell me, Ali?" Nate stepped closer, his body tense and fired up. He squeezed his eyes shut and pinched the bridge of his nose with his fingers. "Why didn't you tell me about James Dorian?"

Her mind raced, trying to determine exactly how much Jessica had told him. "Nate, there was nothing to tell."

Nate shook his head, pressed his lips together. "He *assaulted* you, Ali."

Oh. So, this wasn't about Alice exposing James's secret and losing her job and, more important, lying to Nate about it. "It wasn't that serious. I was never in danger or anything. I mean, yes, he put his hand on my knee, and no, I didn't tell him he could. But that was it. As far as things went." She took a breath. "He's a drunk, and a misogynist, but it wasn't anything I couldn't handle."

"Not anything you couldn't handle?" Nate's eyes went wide and his voice dropped. "You need to get the police involved, or something." He huffed, pacing the room in circles. He kicked his helmet by accident, and it skidded farther across the floor. "Sue Georgia, for putting you in that position. And the Wittington Group for lack of employee protection."

He was enraged, but not with her, so Alice relaxed. There would be no police or lawsuit; she had already taken care of that. And it was good he ran into Jessica Stalwart. Her revelation meant Alice could keep up appearances—James Dorian's perverted ways the ideal explanation for why she left Wittington when she did. She would explain her silence on the issue as not wanting to worry Nate about something she had a handle on, but before she could say anything, Nate asked, "Were you fired? Because Jessica said you were fired."

"No. I—"

"Did Georgia fire you over this? Because if so . . ." Nate grabbed at her hands, squeezed her fingers gently in his. God, he looked so sad. And yet, the anger simmered in his eyes, in the way his jaw shifted back and forth, his teeth clenching.

This was the moment to tell Nate. But it was certainly easier not to, Alice decided, the details of what had unfolded with James Dorian and Wittington irrelevant now. Besides, the whole IUD thing was still fresh and raw and Alice wasn't sure either of them could deal with yet another revelation right now. "This is why I couldn't work there anymore. It was a toxic environment and I needed to get away from James Dorian and Georgia and Wittington." She squeezed his fingers back. "I've let it go, so you have to let it go, too. There's nothing to be done. Okay?"

Nate took a deep breath in through his nose and released it with a hiss. "Okay, Ali, okay," he finally said, and Alice whispered a thank-you and leaned into him. "I'm just glad you got out of there."

"Me too." There was a vibration between them, and Alice pulled back as Nate took his phone from his pocket to see who was calling. *Drew Baxter.* Alice noted Nate's sudden but subtle move away from her, eyes on his phone.

"Ah, sorry, I should take this. It's Rob," Nate said, referring to his boss, Rob Thornton. He glanced up from his phone to Alice's face, not realizing she had seen Drew's name on the screen. Nate appeared conflicted about what to do—keep his focus on Alice, who had just verified a serious and upsetting experience, or answer an incoming call from his study partner. It shouldn't have even been a choice. "But I can let it go . . ."

As Nate's phone continued to ring—he clearly wanted to answer it—a numbness moved through Alice's limbs, but she forced a smile. "No, go ahead. You should take it."

He smiled and put the phone to his ear, walking toward the stairs, which he then took two at a time. Alice stood at the base of the stairs, hoping to catch a snippet of the conversation, but all she heard before Nate shut the bedroom door was, "I know this is hard . . . same for me . . . ," in a tone that was too informal, too intimate for Alice to believe it was a work-related call. With a sick drop in her stomach, Alice realized, as she had feared, that something other than studying was going on between Drew Baxter and her husband.

36

Nellie

....

SEPTEMBER 13, 1956

Tansy Tea

....

1 to 2 teaspoons dried tansy flowers
1 teaspoon sugared orange rind
1 cup boiling water
1 teaspoon honey

Steep flowers and orange rind in boiling water until it becomes a
golden hue. Add honey and drink quickly. Repeat as necessary.

ELSIE MATILDE SWANN
BELOVED MOTHER, GONE TOO SOON
SEPTEMBER 2, 1907—OCTOBER 5, 1948

*I*t had been six months since Nellie had last visited her mother,
and things were quite unkempt around the headstone. The grass
grew wildly—some blades longer than others, some greener,

some fatter. It was as though the grass didn't know how to grow uniformly without Elsie Swann, and her green thumb, alive to coax it. Nellie yanked a few unruly tufts from the ground, shaking free the loose earth. She set the bouquet of dahlias—a most harmonious flower, the vivid petals springing from its center like a work of art—at the base of the headstone, the pink and white blooms cheery against the day's overcast dreariness. Dahlias were long bloomers (Nellie had even seen them survive an early frost) and signified an unbreakable commitment between two people. While Nellie found the flower too gay for such a profound meaning, Elsie had insisted that was why dahlias were so enchanting. "Just as powerful as they are pretty. Like you, my sweet girl."

"Hello, Mother. Happy belated birthday." Nellie ran her fingers across her mother's name etched into the cool, mauve-tinted stone, lingering on the date of death. "I'm sorry it has been so long, but it was difficult to get here. Though I do think soon it will be easier to visit more often." She tucked her dress under her and sat beside the grave, the grass prickling her calves. As always, Nellie tried not to think about the last time she had seen her mother, though it never got easier. The horrible scene she'd come home from school to find that day, almost seven years ago. *The bathtub. The water, to the brim.* Her mother fully clothed under its surface with eyes wide yet dull. Nellie was too young to navigate life alone, but her mother had left her no choice in the matter.

Elsie never met Richard, was not at Nellie's wedding, and would never read the letters her daughter had been penning. For whatever reason, it was important to Nellie to keep the truth about Elsie from Richard, even in the beginning, when things were decent between them. Perhaps she was embarrassed—most would agree taking one's own life was a sin, and Nellie didn't want Elsie's memory tarnished. But more likely it was fear that the darkness that took Elsie might one day come for Nellie, too. And if Richard knew this, well, perhaps he would have used it against his wife.

Elsie Swann, Richard believed, was in nursing home care outside Philadelphia, suffering dementia. The nursing home staff recommended brief visits, and Nellie alone, which was why Richard had never accompanied her. However, Nellie had never been to Philadelphia, as her mother was buried in Pleasantville. Only a short trip from where Nellie and Richard now lived.

"Things have become . . . unmanageable with Richard," Nellie said. "But I'm hoping that improves once I go back home." She had told Miriam she would be out of town for the night, visiting her mother in Philadelphia. Miriam had asked if Nellie wanted to take the letters with her on this trip, but Nellie had said, "No, sadly, my mother won't be able to read the letters." Miriam had hugged her tight, her arthritic fingers rubbing Nellie's back in soothing circles. Said maybe Nellie would find her mother more lucid this time, and that she'd pray for her. Nellie didn't enjoy lying to Miriam, but it was easier that way.

Richard had initially resisted the trip, citing the pregnancy and Nellie's responsibilities at home. But she had insisted—her mother wasn't doing well at all. This could be her last visit. Richard finally relented, making her promise to stay only the one night despite the distance.

"I'm pregnant again," Nellie said now, speaking to her mother's headstone. "Richard's over the moon about it." She sighed deeply. "I tried, I really did, Mother, but he was too strong. Too . . . determined." Nellie rearranged the dahlias, though they didn't need it.

"However, not to worry," she added, her voice brightening. "I know what to do and everything will be all right in the end."

Nellie closed her eyes to picture Elsie's beautiful smile,

knowing her mother would be proud of her resilience and courage if she were here. "I was thinking about your friend, Mrs. Powell, the other day." There was a low growl of thunder, and Nellie looked to the sky, where ash-gray clouds clustered together. The hairs on her arms stood on end, the electricity of the looming storm making its presence known. "Remember that gorgeous pearl cigarette holder she gave you? Even though you didn't smoke, you carried it around with you everywhere. . . . It's funny, the things that stay with us, isn't it? Anyway, I use it all the time now. It was a lovely gift."

Betty Ann Powell had been a stunning woman—tall, angular, never without rosy lips or glossy nails or a cigarette in her mother-of-pearl holder—and to Nellie, at thirteen, was the most exotic woman she had ever seen. Nellie had been a mother's helper to the Powells' two young children and had always enjoyed her conversations with Mrs. Powell. She was bright, in both mind and energy, at least until the day she found out she was expecting again. Betty Ann Powell stopped smiling then.

When Nellie asked her mother what was wrong, Elsie explained that while it might be hard for her to understand, Mrs. Powell did not want another child. "Women have so few choices, Nellie. Our gender can be our greatest strength, but it is also our greatest weakness." As her mother predicted, Nellie didn't understand—neither the lack of desire for a child (didn't every woman want children?), nor the comment on strengths and weaknesses—but she'd nodded as though she did.

That was also, perhaps, the moment when Nellie began to see her own mother differently. *Was having Nellie a choice Elsie made, or something her mother had been forced to do?* "My heart continues beating, Nell-girl, only because you can hear it," Elsie had once said. It had scared Nellie—not yet mature enough at the time to comprehend that the heart keeps beating, even through tragedy and grief, though Elsie would teach her that lesson eventually—and it cemented in her a belief that women's survival was ensured only by having children.

Nellie then learned the truth about the heart *and* her mother's illness—realizing, too, that, choice or not, having Nellie had forced Elsie to endure deep, long-standing pain. Without Nellie, Elsie could have succumbed years before she did—to live for another person is no small sacrifice. Soon after her mother's revelation about Mrs. Powell not wanting another child, she and Elsie spent an afternoon at the Powells' home. The women spoke tête-à-tête in hushed tones on the verandah as Mrs. Powell sipped at the golden tansy tea—Elsie's recipe, with flowers from her garden—while Nellie played with the children, thinking about choices and beating hearts.

Two days later Nellie was called on to look after the Powell children again. Elsie explained that Mrs. Powell had caught a bug, a stomach ailment that made her violently ill, and she had lost the baby. Nellie, young and prone to magical thinking back then, thought maybe Mrs. Powell's baby had died because it knew it wasn't wanted, privy to Mrs. Powell's innermost thoughts and regrets. It was only later, when her mother felt her old enough to understand the truth, that she learned the miscarriage had nothing to do with the flu, or wishful thinking.

The wind changed direction, blowing across Nellie's bare calves, and she shivered. "I'm sorry to say I should be going, Mother." She stood and brushed a few blades of grass from the pleats in her skirt. "Don't want to get caught in a miserable downpour."

Nellie bent and pressed her lips to the stone. It started raining, the drops fat and frequent. But she didn't mind the rain or the way her soaked clothes pressed to her skin, making her tremble as she ran back to her hotel, looking forward to a hot cup of tea.

Back in her hotel room, not far from the Pleasantville cemetery where her mother was buried and the home she shared with Richard, Nellie made a cup of tea to fight the chill of the rain-storm she'd been caught in. The tansy flowers, which looked like fuzzy lemon-yellow buttons when they bloomed, were dried and shriveled in the paper bag Nellie pulled out of her handbag. She added some candied orange rind to her cup and poured the steaming water over the mixture of flowers and rind, waiting for it to steep. In went a teaspoon of honey for a little sweetness, as the flowers had a somewhat bitter flavor. Nellie would drink three cups of the tea before resting on the bed, though she did not sleep. She was wide-awake and contemplative after her visit with her mother.

A few hours later Nellie became violently ill. She was sure, as she lay shivering on the tiled washroom floor, that she was dying. Perhaps there was truth to the cadence of a woman's heartbeat. For a moment she welcomed the idea, imagining the next time she threw up her heart would stop and it would all mercifully be over. But by morning the worst had passed and Nellie was awoken by the steady rainfall, filling puddles in the streets.

She stood gingerly, shaky-handed as she clutched the sink, and a fierce cramp rippled through her abdomen. Nellie doubled over, gasping and moaning with the pain as another cramp crested. The relief was nearly as strong as the pain.

Even though she believed it the only way, Nellie sobbed until her uterus stopped contracting and the shards of pain re-ceded. This was not a choice she wished on her worst enemy, but she was grateful to have it. Thankful for the gifts a garden, and its flowers, offered a woman in need.

Afterward, weak and exhausted, Nellie cleaned herself up

and rinsed her teacup, all traces of the tansy flowers washed down the bathroom sink. Smoking one of her Lucky cigarettes through the bathroom window, Nellie watched the rain, wondering when it might stop. The telephone rang as she was packing her small valise on the bed she hadn't slept in. The phone's shrill ring echoed in the small room, and she let it go a few times before picking up.

"Nellie?" Miriam said, slightly breathless. Nellie pressed the handset to her ear, anticipation flooding her. "Oh, honey. You need to come home right away."

Soon after, Nellie was on the train, waiting for it to depart and take her home to Greenville, where nothing would ever be the same again. She was hunched in her seat with arms wrapped tightly around her midsection, the colicky cramping not finished with her yet. The rain was unrelenting, and Nellie leaned her tear-stained cheek against the train's window, eyes tracking the drops as they left streaks down the glass.

Once when Nellie was quite young and helping Elsie prepare the garden beds for planting, it had started to rain—pour, actually. "Seems it's raining cats and dogs, Nell-girl," her mother said, though she stayed put and continued the task, unconcerned by the teeming rain, or the promise of animals falling from the sky. *Cats and dogs?* Young Nellie had glanced up to the sky, blinking repeatedly to move the drops from her eyes, fearful about what was to come. Elsie had laughed hard, tossing her head back and sticking out her tongue to catch a few raindrops.

"It's a saying, Nellie. Only water falls from the sky, my love." Nellie, relieved, also tipped her head back to drink the rain, cool and sweet against her tongue. And as the storm continued and her mother went back to her gardening, she said, "After the rain cometh the fair weather." It came out of her with fervor, as though she believed it a promise the sky wouldn't even imagine not keeping.

However, Elsie didn't do well with stormy skies, and the day Nellie found her mother's lifeless body in the overflowing, blood-tinged bathtub marked the seventh day without a speck of sunshine. It had been a horribly rainy week; flash floods, people going out only when absolutely necessary, hiding under somber umbrellas. The day after Elsie drowned—a half-drunk glass of milk (emerald green in color, thanks to the poisonous Paris green insecticide she had stirred into it to ensure she would never awaken) on the tub's edge—the sun came out, strong and hot and life changing, and Nellie would think about what her mother had said. Would forever wonder why she hadn't been able to believe it that time. The sun always returned . . . as long as you were strong enough to wait for it.

37

Housewives spend so much time alone they often fail to understand that a man's being "left alone" does not imply real loneliness—it just means being set free from all female demands and constraint. Some husbands achieve this illusion by taking a night off to bowl or play pinochle with the boys. Others shut themselves up in the garage and overhaul the car—or read a detective story. Whatever specific use a man makes of these happy moments of aloneness, it's smart for a wife to see that he gets them. No doubt about it, husbands need to slip the leash occasionally.

—Mrs. Dale Carnegie, *How to Help Your Husband
Get Ahead in His Social and Business Life* (1953)

Alice

.....

SEPTEMBER 4, 2018

I think I know why your mom had those letters of Nellie's," Alice said. "Or at least why they were never mailed."

Sally poured coffee into two mugs that read, DOCTORS DO IT BETTER—a gift from a medical student she had worked with years earlier. "Why?"

"Her mother died years before Nellie even met Richard.

Which means there was no one to mail them to." She took a piece of the lemon loaf she'd made when she was supposed to be writing, the sticky icing transferring to her fingers. "I was doing research, for my book, and found a death certificate for an Elsie Swann, from Pleasantville. It had Eleanor Swann written in the informant box."

"You don't say." Sally added cream to her mug, stirred until the coffee was uniformly beige.

"Apparently, she died of poisoning and asphyxiation, and get this, 'drowning from temporary insanity.' Whatever that means."

"Ah. That means it was suicide," Sally said. "'Temporary insanity' under cause of death was the genteel way to say someone killed themselves. Before suicide was decriminalized in the early sixties, you could go to jail if you attempted it."

Suicide. Nellie's mother had taken her own life. A wave of sadness moved through Alice. It was strange to feel so much for a stranger, a woman she had little in common with except for a house. Yet, Alice felt a kinship. She sensed there was more to Nellie than her letters revealed. "I wonder why Nellie kept writing to her mom, after she was gone."

"One can only guess." Sally glanced out her front window. It was raining, so they had been forced inside for their afternoon visit. Six months earlier Alice would have scoffed at the idea of having daily coffee with her elderly neighbor, but now it was the part of her day she looked forward to most. "Perhaps she missed talking with her."

"Do you miss your mom? Being able to talk with her, I mean?"

"I do. Every day. I always felt guilty, leaving her here alone. But she was resilient. After my dad died, she found a way to be happy again. She had a very full life, but I know she would have liked me to live closer. Also, maybe to have had a grandbaby she could knit sweaters for." Sally smiled, looked uncharacteristically regretful for a moment.

"I'm not close with my mom," Alice said. "We're pretty different."

"How so?"

"In nearly every way you can imagine. She's optimistic; I'm realistic. She drinks tea; I prefer coffee. She's thin; I like lemon loaf. She's been doing yoga since before it was trendy and I'm about as unbendy as it gets. I run sometimes, but mostly to compensate for these calories." Alice took a big bite of loaf and raised her eyebrows, prompting Sally to chuckle.

"I don't doubt she loves me, but she was a single mom." Alice shrugged. "I got the sense she resented motherhood a bit, you know? That my life came at the sacrifice of her own, or something like that."

Sally smiled sympathetically. "I can't know for sure, not having had children of my own, but I suspect being a mother is a most complicated role."

Alice sighed. "I suppose she did her best. She doesn't really get me, and I don't get her. But we both know it, so somehow it works well enough."

"What about your father?" Sally asked.

"My stepfather is awesome. Solid, caring, shirt-off-his-back kind of guy. But my biological father left when I was a kid."

Sally didn't say anything, waiting for Alice to go on or to change the subject. And suddenly Alice wanted to talk about her dad, about how terrified she was that she was nothing like her mother because she was *exactly* like her father. "He died almost two months ago."

"I'm very sorry to hear that, Alice. That's a tough pill to swallow no matter what the situation."

"Thanks, though I should add I haven't seen my dad, or talked to him, in twenty years." But Alice knew no matter if your parents were present or absent, good or bad, they remained part of you. Inside you, whether you wanted them there or not. "He was basically a stranger."

"Stranger or not, he was still your father. Relationships are never easy. Especially the ones we're born into." Sally reached out a hand to Alice, and the women held on for a moment. "So, tell me, Miss Alice. How's the book coming along?"

Alice groaned. "It's not. Can I take a pass on that topic too?"

"Writer's block again?"

"Sort of, I guess. I have this idea I'm excited about, and I'm doing research, but I've written so little I'm not even sure it would qualify as a short story at this point."

Sally considered this. "Do you even *want to* write a novel?"

"I think so." Alice stared back at her. "Or I thought I did. But now I'm not sure."

"Then, good heavens, why are you doing it?"

"Because I was fired from my job for doing something stupid and I didn't tell Nate what happened. He wanted to move to the suburbs and I had no paycheck and no more excuses for why we had to stay in Murray Hill, and writing a book was something I always said I wanted to do because it seemed like the sort of thing most people want to do, and it offered as good a distraction as any while I tried to get pregnant." Alice paused, sucking in a breath. If she had gone on she might have confessed the IUD fiasco and her deep regret over it. Or her ambivalence about having a baby, and how it made her feel she was failing her marriage. Or she might have admitted her fear that Nate was keeping his own secrets, and maybe wasn't as good a husband as he seemed.

"My mother always used to say, 'Never ask a simple question if you want a simple answer.'" Sally smiled reassuringly.

"I mostly feel restless. Like I'm waiting for real life to begin, and I'm just putting in time, watching everything fall apart until things make sense again."

"Honey, I wish I had advice to give, but I don't know the first thing about writing a book, or being married, or feeling the pressure to start a family," Sally replied. "Well, I guess I know a little about that last one because Mother was endlessly harping on me to have a child, even on my own. She said I could move in, work at the hospital here, and she would help me raise the baby. She even had a list of eligible bachelors in the neighborhood she updated and mailed to me regularly, with a pro and con column for each. That list always made me laugh. She had things like 'sharp dresser' on the pro side and 'beginning to bald' as a con, as though those attributes were in any way connected to the success of a marital partnership."

They laughed, and then Sally continued. "Yet despite her upbringing, and the pressures of the time for women to be seen but not heard, to have no aspirations outside the home, my mother was actually quite the feminist! One of the greatest gifts she ever gave me—and she was a wonderful mother, so there were many—was to have me answer one question."

"Which was?"

Sally sat up straighter, put on an animated face, and waggled a finger the way Alice assumed her mother must have. "She said, 'Sally, the hardest question we have to ask ourselves in this life is, "Who am I?" Ideally, we answer it for ourselves, but be warned that others will strive to do it for you—so don't let them.'"

There was a lump in Alice's throat; she was on the brink of tears. "Let me offer you the same gift, Alice, and tell you that your only job—more important than any book writing or rosebush tending or meal preparing—is to uncover *your* answer to that question."

"I think I would have liked your mom," Alice said.

Sally laid a hand on Alice's knee. "And she would have liked you. She had a soft spot for the restless ones."

38

But in case of an *occasional* lapse on the part of the husband—there a bit of advice may prove acceptable. And my advice would be: forgive and forget. Or still better—make believe that you know nothing. An occasional lapse from the straight path does not mean that he has ceased to love you. He may love you as much; he may love you a good deal more.

—William J. Robinson, *Married Life and Happiness* (1922)

Alice

.....

SEPTEMBER 23, 2018

*W*hat will it be? My treat." Bronwyn set her notebook on the small corner table at H&H Bagels and pushed back from the table, ready to go order. She had convinced Alice to come to Manhattan for the day, joking that her friend's blood was probably running too suburban, the only fix being an H&H injection and manicure. Bronwyn had planned a full schedule, including a venue visit for her post-wedding party, then dinner and drinks with a few friends from Alice's former life. But nothing would happen until bagels had been consumed, because

Bronwyn was unpleasant when her blood sugar got too low. "The usual?"

Alice had been mildly nauseated all morning but knew she needed to put something in her stomach, which was empty aside from a coffee and banana she'd had early on. "The usual is perfect. Thanks."

While Bronwyn ordered—the number seven for Alice (egg, avocado, and pepper jack cheese on a sesame bagel), and lox and scallion cream cheese on pumpernickel for Bronwyn—Alice glanced out the window, touching the pearls about her neck. She'd chosen black cigarette pants in addition to a polka-dotted sleeveless blouse and the pearls, her hair held back in pin curls. Bronwyn had gushed that she looked amazing—and thin!—and Alice beamed at the compliment, glad she'd chosen this outfit over her usual, more casual picks. She had lost weight since the move—the stress, lack of eating out, and probably her recent smoking habit all contributing to shrinking her to a size she hadn't been for a while.

They tucked into their bagels, Alice taking small bites and assuring Bronwyn she was fine when asked. After a mostly quiet lunch, Bronwyn leaned elbows on the table and looked searchingly at her friend. "Ali, what's up?"

"With what?"

They knew each other well, and Bronwyn could see right through Alice's attempts to feign ignorance. "With you, obviously."

"Nothing new, really. Writing, gardening, trying not to burn the house down when I cook." Alice smiled at her friend, wiping her fingers on a napkin. "All the things a good housewife does."

"See, I know you're making it sound like you're joking, but you're not actually joking." Bronwyn reached out, put a hand on Alice's arm. "Talk to me, Ali."

Alice wasn't in the mood—she wanted to enjoy this blue-skied Sunday and her lunch and skip the probing conversations. Coming in on the train that morning, Alice had believed everything was back on track with her and Bronwyn: she had apologized; Bronwyn had forgiven her. Yet, as soon as she saw her it felt to Alice as though remnants of the fight lingered, the way someone can clean up a sticky spill and still have it grab their socks days later. Despite the hugs and Bronwyn's exclamation of "Now all is right with the world!" when she met Alice at the station, something fundamental had shifted between the women—like the excitement and proclamations were more for show.

"Honestly, there's nothing to tell. I feel good." She sipped her water, wiped the condensation ring from the table with her napkin, thought of Nate and Drew. Held back her scowl. "All is well, Bron. Don't look so worried."

"Well, I am worried. You just seem different."

"How so?"

"For starters, you aren't wearing jeans . . ."

"So it's my outfit?" Alice glanced down at her clothes, shrugged. "I'm immersing myself in the fifties, for my book. It's research. Isn't that what all great authors do?" She hadn't expected to like the vintage clothing as much as she did, but Sarah the saleswoman had a great eye, and Alice felt well put together in her outfit. Besides, because she'd lost some weight none of her old clothes fit quite right anymore.

"I don't know . . ." Bronwyn gesticulated to her pearls, the hair pins. "Don't get me wrong. I like it, but it's not you."

Alice threw up her hands. "You just told me I looked good!"

Bronwyn nodded, murmured that was true, she did.

"It's not really about the clothes, Ali," Bronwyn said, more quietly now. She bit her bottom lip, something she did only when deciding whether to speak freely or not. "And Nate's worried about you too."

Alice narrowed her eyes. "What do you mean, he's 'worried' about me?"

"Okay, look. Full disclosure. Yes, I desperately wanted to see you—I've missed you, and Darren's gluten-free and so he never comes to H&H with me—but Nate called me. Said he wanted to give you a day in the city, that things had been a bit stressful recently." She put air quotes around the word "stressful," which Alice knew referred to the undisclosed IUD and subsequent emergency room visit.

"He asked me to lure you here with bagels and manis and my unfailing charm." Bronwyn smiled wide, but it faded at the look on Alice's face.

"You two are unbelievable," Alice muttered, pushing her chair back quickly. It screeched as she did, and the people at the neighboring tables looked over in surprise.

"What? Wait, Ali. It's not—" But Alice was already at the door. Bronwyn cursed under her breath, following her onto the sidewalk. She watched helplessly as Alice riffled through her handbag looking for something, ignoring Bronwyn's pleas to tell her why she was so pissed off.

"You know what, Bronwyn?" Alice said, head still down as she dug around in her purse, finally pulling out her phone. "Instead of worrying so much about me, you two should be worrying about yourselves."

"What's that supposed to mean?"

Alice let out a harsh laugh, finally looking at Bronwyn. "You married a guy you barely know—in Vegas, no less—because he promised to build you a walk-in closet and you were tired of being single. Marriage is fucking hard, Bronwyn. I give you guys a year, tops." It was a cruel, awful thing to say, but Alice couldn't help herself. She hated the idea of Nate and Bronwyn discussing her, sharing their worries with each other rather than Alice. Like she was a child in need of coddling.

Bronwyn took a step back, her expression one of shock and hurt. "You don't know anything about him."

"You're right. I don't. Because you didn't even tell me you got married—your best friend—until days later. When was I supposed to get to know him?" Alice trembled, and Bronwyn watched her, looking like she might cry. "And Nate should worry more about his study partner and the fact she's clearly trying to break up our marriage, and that he's going along with it."

Bronwyn frowned. "Come on, Ali. Nate wouldn't do anything like that."

Alice snorted. "Because you know *him* so well? I guess maybe you do, as the two of you have been colluding behind my back." Bronwyn started to protest, and Alice interrupted. "He's been lying to me about her. So don't tell me he would never do anything like that. People can surprise you, and not in a good way."

"Nate is one of the good ones. You two are like a flipping storybook romance, okay? He would not cheat on you. Never, ever, never." Bronwyn grabbed for Alice's hands, tried pulling her closer. "She's just his study partner. That's it, Ali. Don't turn this into something it isn't."

"Have you two talked about this? About Drew?" Alice tugged her hands free, took a couple of steps back.

"No! Alice. Stop it. This is ridiculous." But despite her words, Bronwyn looked . . . nervous. What did she know that Alice didn't?

She wanted to go home, to get away from Bronwyn and this conversation that was degrading by the second. Then she remembered Nate was in the house studying—or so he claimed. Alice wondered if when she walked through the front door, early and without warning, she would find him alone. Or if this plan he'd concocted with Bronwyn to get Alice out of the house was about more than simply giving her a stress break. Either way, she needed to know.

"Um, I'm not feeling great. Don't think that bagel agreed with me," Alice said. "Sorry about the spa and everything, but we'll do it another day." She turned and walked away quickly, Bronwyn calling after her to wait up. But she didn't stop.

39

Food prepared with a light heart and in a happy frame of mind is often the best food. Preparing the special foods that are favourites of those you love . . . making just a little effort to garnish the salad with a sprig of parsley, a bit of grated cheese, or a wild strawberry from the nearby meadow. This says "you cared enough to do the little extra things." This makes cooking pleasant and satisfying. Make the food look as pretty as it is good to eat.

—*Betty Crocker's Picture Cook Book, revised and enlarged* (1956)

Alice

.....

SEPTEMBER 23, 2018

*W*hat happened?" Nate asked, putting his computer to the side and standing quickly from the living room sofa, where he had been studying. It had been only a few hours since she had left, and Alice could tell Bronwyn had already called him—he didn't seem surprised to see her. She saw no signs of Drew, though she would have had time to clear out after he got Bronwyn's call.

"Think I'm coming down with something." Alice hung her

coat and took off her shoes, then picked up the stack of Nellie's letters from her desk, along with her laptop, which she tucked under her arm.

"Oh. Can I get you anything?" Nate asked. "Tea maybe?"

But Alice was already at the staircase. "Think I'll just lie down for a while." If Nate said anything else, Alice didn't hear it as she climbed the stairs quickly.

She had fumed all the way back on the train, incensed about Nate and Bronwyn conspiring and trying to make it seem like she was the one to worry about. Her thoughts ping-ponged between Bronwyn's comments and Nate's lie about Drew and the phone call he took from her the other night. *It was hard to know who to trust.*

With Sally away, Alice realized she had no ally, no kind ear to hear her frustrations and anxieties. She would never call her mother to vent, and her other city friends had quickly turned into mere acquaintances once she moved to Greenville.

Desperate for a distraction—she really didn't want to think about Nate, or Bronwyn, or Drew—Alice reached into the stack of *Ladies' Home Journal* magazines beside the bed. She leaned against her pillows and thumbed through one she hadn't yet read. After a dozen pages of advertisements and articles aimed to help the modern housewife be her best self, she came across an envelope. Yellowing, not unlike the pages of the magazine, nestled deep into the crease. Nothing written on its outside.

She sat up and set the magazine beside her, sliding a finger along the envelope's seal. Inside was another "Dearest Mother" letter, from Nellie to Elsie. This one quite short compared to the others, only half a page. Alice's eyes widened as she scanned the words, written in Nellie's flowing hand, and once she got to the end, she read them again. Her breath quickened along with her pulse.

From the desk of Eleanor Murdoch

September 15, 1956

Dearest Mother,

Richard is dead.

I am fine, so please don't worry. There is plenty of money and I have a dear friend, Miriam, to look out for me. I believe I am better alone, Mother, as we both know Richard was not the good man I had hoped for. The one you wished for me. But that matters little now.

I should also thank you for the tansy tea recipe. I was careful, like you taught me to be, and though it made me quite ill both in stomach and at heart, it worked as promised. I am free, which is a great blessing. These truths will follow me to my grave, when I'll see you again.

Your loving daughter, Nellie xx

Alice flipped the paper over, but the back side was blank, offering no further clues. She read it again. *These truths will follow me to my grave . . .*

For whatever reason, Nellie hadn't included this letter in the stack she'd left with Miriam. She had obviously placed it inside this magazine to keep it hidden. Though if she had really wanted it to never be read, Alice thought she would have destroyed it. No, Nellie must have wanted this letter to be found by the right person. Someone like Alice Hale; this letter had been waiting for her all this time.

Alice opened her laptop, the glow of the screen illuminating her face, and typed "tansy tea" into the Google search box. Scanning the results, she read "medicinal" and "digestive tract benefits" and the words "toxic" and "abortifacient herb." Alice typed "abortifacient" into the search box and stopped breathing at what popped up, though she'd had an inkling. Now Alice understood why Nellie had been expecting but never delivered a baby.

An abortifacient is a substance that induces abortion. . . .

Springing to her feet, Alice shut her laptop and grabbed the laundry hamper, setting the most recent letter underneath a pile of towels to be washed. She headed to the basement, taking only a moment as she passed by Nate to tell him that she was going to do a load of laundry. He asked if she was feeling better and she said, "A little," before shutting the basement door.

Undeterred by the shadowy corners and certain arachnids, Alice walked quickly down the stairs and to the laundry machines. She started the load, then crouched in front of the box of magazines and pulled out as many as her hands could hold. It took three dips in to get them all, and she sat on the bottom stair and, one by one, the energy-efficient bulb finally having reached its full potential, flipped through the magazines. Unsure about what she was hunting for, she initially found nothing in the first few magazines and wondered if her instincts had been wrong. Perhaps Nellie had left nothing further for her to find.

But on the eighth magazine—a September 1956 issue with a photo of a chubby-toothed blond toddler, dressed in a blue-and-white seersucker dress on the cover—something fell out of the pages when Alice shook it. It was another envelope, though thicker than the others, its center sturdier. Tucked into the paper's folds was a small card with the words "From the kitchen of Elsie Swann" printed across its top. Her heart racing, Alice quickly read the recipe card.

It listed ingredients and instructions for an herb recipe—

Swann Family Herb Mix—the same mix Alice had seen mentioned so many times throughout the pages of Nellie's cookbook. *Lemon balm, parsley, basil, thyme, marjoram, sage, every herb measured in equal parts (a tablespoon of each).* She recognized Elsie's handwriting, until she came to the final ingredient, which was penned in Nellie's hand and which made Alice lose her breath.

With shaking fingers, she opened the folded paper and read the letter, Nellie's greatest secret, and the one she had intended to take to her grave, finally revealed.

40

Nellie

········

SEPTEMBER 18, 1956

*H*elen can finish up here, Nellie. You should rest, put your feet up." Miriam steered Nellie toward the green sofa in the living room, but Nellie resisted. She would never again sit on that sofa, even with Richard now gone. Miriam's weathered hands fluttered over Nellie's arms as she tried to gently tug her again. "Honey, it's been a long day. Let me take care of you."

"Thank you, Miriam. But I'm all right. I don't need to lie down." The dining room was cluttered with plates of food—sweet squares and tuna casseroles and triangles of egg salad sandwiches dotted with pimentos. Nellie would send it all home with Helen, who had a family to feed and would certainly appreciate the leftovers. Except for the lavender lemon muffins Martha had baked, using Nellie's own recipe, the thoughtfulness of the gesture bringing tears to her eyes. Those she would keep.

While Richard's mourners mingled in the Murdochs' living

room, nibbling squares and offering platitudes and whispering about the poor young milkman who had discovered Richard's body during his morning delivery, slumped on the sofa, his face planted in his plate of shepherd's pie.

"Heart attack, Doc said. He was likely gone before he knew what was happening," Charles Goldman murmured to a small circle of Richard and Nellie's neighbors and friends, running a hand through his dark hair, streaked lightly with silver. *How awful! Poor Nellie!* Their sympathy mattered little to Nellie. She could only imagine what they would say if they knew the truth about Richard's untimely death. About the shepherd's pie Nellie had left for her husband, which he doused liberally with his wife's homemade herb mix.

Nellie sat in the wing-back chair that had been Richard's favorite and listened to the gossiping women, watched their frown-faced husbands shake ice cubes in highball glasses of liquor.

Her situation was *especially tragic*. With a baby on the way who would grow up fatherless, and therefore, these wives assumed, at a great disadvantage. They perked up when one suggested Nellie could find someone else to marry, still young and beautiful as she was. *Perhaps the widower Norman Woodrow could step in?*

Everyone believed Nellie was still pregnant, even Miriam. She would wait one week longer before blaming the miscarriage on Richard's sudden death and her body's inability to deal with the grief. The casseroles would then continue for another few weeks, the hushed and pitying whispers of her women friends when they believed her out of earshot: *Who is she now, if not a mother? If no longer Richard Murdoch's wife?*

"Who am I?" She whispered it back, though not loud enough for any of them to hear her. "I am a survivor."

With shaking hands Nellie took one of her Lucky Strikes and lit it, waving away the first puff of smoke. Miriam sat across from her on another chair, worried eyes scanning Nellie's face. "Nellie, honey. What do you need?"

"You're sweet to worry, but I'm fine, Miriam." Nellie took a long drag of her cigarette.

"I know you are, honey. I know." Miriam pressed her lips together, her hands clasped on her knees.

"Sit with me until Helen goes," Nellie said. She looked tired, dark circles under her eyes and a gauntness that was distressing. She confessed to Miriam she'd been unwell when she went to see her mother; the baby was probably making her ill, as they had a tendency to do in these early months. Nellie assured her she was feeling much better; however, she hadn't ingested a thing except for iced tea and cigarettes.

"Of course I will," Miriam replied, patting Nellie's knee through her black skirt. "I'll get Helen to make us some soup for supper. We'll eat together."

Nellie nodded, finished her cigarette, and immediately lit one more. "I'd like to write my mother a letter. Would you mind getting me my correspondence paper, over there in the top drawer of the desk? And my cookbook from the kitchen? I have a recipe I'd like to share with her."

"I'll leave you to it," Miriam said after she handed Nellie everything she had asked for. "But give a holler if you need anything. I'll be in the kitchen."

Soon a low hum of voices, along with the sounds of running water and dishes being stacked, seeped out from the kitchen. Miriam wouldn't leave her alone for too long, so she hastily started the letter, the last one she would ever write to Elsie.

From the desk of Eleanor Murdoch

September 18, 1956

Dearest Mother,

*I know you told me to never write it down, that
our secret was to only be passed from lips to ears,
but I will not be having a daughter to whisper it to.
Therefore, I have noted the final ingredient on
the recipe card.*

*I have no regrets, Mother. It was the only way to
ensure he would never hurt me again, and in some
ways, it was too easy. I may be a widow now, but I am
fine. There are worse things than being alone, I have
learned.*

*Thank you for your lessons, and for the beautiful
foxglove plant you insisted I take with me for my own
garden one day. I had hoped the plant would be useful
only as a deer deterrent in my garden—another pretty
flower to bolster my spirits! I did believe Richard
would be a good and decent husband, but it appears I
was fooled. Alas, men seem a most predictable beast.
Some must be worthy, but I am not certain how to be
sure of it.*

*I will visit soon. My dahlias continue to bloom,
which has been a lovely end-of-summer surprise.*

Your loving daughter, Nellie xx

Nellie finished writing, then pulled the recipe card—the one
Elsie had given her years earlier, shortly before she died—from
the front of the cookbook, and after making a notation at the

bottom, placed the card into the folds of the letter. She sealed it, then pressed the envelope deep into the crease of the most recent *Ladies' Home Journal* magazine. Later she would box all the magazines up, including the September 1956 issue, which hid this final letter, along with her cookbook. She wouldn't need it again, not now that there was no one to make dinners for. Besides, Nellie knew most of her favorite recipes by heart.

When Miriam came back into the living room, with a fresh coffee and a bowl of soup, she asked Nellie if she wanted her to take the letter and put it with the rest. She didn't comment on the stack of letters she still held for Nellie in her own dresser of drawers, or question why Nellie never seemed to post them.

"I decided I'll write it later, but thank you," Nellie said, closing the cookbook and settling it onto her lap. With a nod Miriam started in on her soup, and Nellie drank her coffee in the quiet living room, both thoughtful in the silence.

41

Don't quarrel with your husband. Remember it takes two to make a quarrel; don't you be one of them. Lovers' quarrels may be all very well, but matrimonial doses are apt to leave a bitter flavour behind.

—Blanche Ebbutt, *Don'ts for Wives* (1913)

Alice

·····

SEPTEMBER 24, 2018

*A*lice awoke in the guest bedroom Monday morning, late enough that the house was quiet and sun-filled. She hadn't slept in bed with Nate because she was still angry, unsure how to proceed normally when she believed he might be having an affair with his study partner (*how had everything become so screwed up?*). But rather than get into the real reason for her distance from her husband, she blamed it on not being well, worried he would get sick just before his big exam. Nate seemed hesitant to accept the excuse but, like Alice, appeared too weary to unpack whatever the real issue might be. After having a bowl of cereal and telling Nate there was a box of macaroni and cheese in the pantry if he got hungry, Alice went up to bed—the newest letter and recipe card hidden inside the magazine under her arm.

Alice wasn't sure how Nate's night went because he was gone by the time she woke up, but she had a restless, fitful sleep. Her mind reeled from the previous afternoon's discovery, which kept her awake but thankfully gave her something to focus on aside from her crumbling relationships. Along with the drone of exhaustion was the pleasurable buzz that Alice had been right: there *was* more to Nellie Murdoch than those earlier letters showed. And it had given her what she needed for her book— she knew precisely the story she wanted to tell now.

She showered and dressed quickly, making a pot of coffee and a piece of toast with butter and jam before sitting in front of her laptop. Alice vibrated with energy, her mind overrun with ideas, her fingers at the ready on her keyboard. Finally, *finally,* she was inspired and ready to knock off some pages. But as she typed her first words, her phone rang.

"Hello?" Alice put the call on speaker so she could continue typing, her eyes not leaving her laptop's screen.

"Alice?"

"Yes, who is this?" She was impatient to get back to it. But the voice was familiar, and she glanced at her phone's screen.

"It's Beverly Dixon, your Realtor."

"Oh, hi, Beverly. What can I do for you?" Alice rolled her eyes at the interruption—Beverly was probably looking for a testimonial or referrals.

"Well, I haven't been able to get ahold of Nate this morning and I need to confirm the copy for the listing. So I thought I'd give you a quick ring to see if you could help."

Alice's fingers stopped. She frowned, then took her phone off speaker and put it to her ear. "What listing?"

"For the house," Beverly said. "It needs to go in by Thursday and I couldn't remember which appliance Nate said you replaced. Was it the oven or the refrigerator?"

"Neither, actually." Alice stood, feeling out of breath.

"Huh. Must have mixed yours up with another listing. Well, that's fine. I'll just strike that note . . . there. Done."

Alice was light-headed—her breaths too rapid—and she crouched, worried she was going to pass out.

"Okay, that's great, Alice. I'm so glad I caught you! Tell Nate not to worry about getting back to me. I'm going to be out at showings for the afternoon and evening, but if he has any other questions, he can leave me a message and I'll respond lickety-split."

"Okay. Thanks." Alice was now lying down, one hand to her forehead, trying to process what was happening.

"I'll let you go, but we'll chat soon about timing for the open houses. I'm sure you have a million things to do before you leave for California. How exciting for Nate, with his new job! For both of you! I've always wanted to learn to surf, though now they say with global warming and ocean temperatures rising the sharks are all coming closer to shore, and—"

"I have to go." Alice ended the call without saying goodbye. Still on the floor, Alice watched as the ceiling spun overhead, the crack moving in circles like a lazy fan. Closing her eyes, she put a hand to her stomach and took several deep breaths, then sat up quickly and waited for the light-headedness to pass.

"Yes, it's an emergency. Can you please pull him out of the meeting?" Alice nibbled at a ragged cuticle. Tucking her phone between her ear and shoulder, she tapped a cigarette out of the package and set it into the holder, lighting it just as Nate came on the line.

"Ali, what's wrong?" He sounded panicked, worried.

She started to cry, though there were no actual tears.

"What's wrong? Are you okay?"

"The kitchen . . . Nate, oh my God. It was terrifying." She blubbered some more, then paused to take a drag of the cigarette.

"Calm down. Take a breath. What about the kitchen?"

"The oven caught fire! I told you we needed to replace it, like, weeks ago!" Hysterical now.

"Holy shit . . . oh my God. Are you okay? Are you hurt?"

"I'm okay. I burned one of my hands, but I don't think it's too bad."

Nate exhaled shakily. "Do you need to go to the hospital? Is Sally home?"

"Sally's in Hartford, visiting a friend." Alice examined her hand, which was just fine. "But I think it's okay. I have ice on it."

"Good, okay. What about the kitchen? How much damage?"

"Pretty bad." Alice whispered now, pausing again to take another drag. "Can you come home? I know you were in a meeting, and I'm sorry to—"

"I'm on my way. Just need to gather my stuff. Uh . . . I think I can catch the next train, but if not I'll grab an Uber."

"You don't have to rush. Just wait for the train. I'm okay," Alice said, sniffling. "I got the fire out with the extinguisher. But the whole wall behind the oven is black."

"Oh my God . . ." Nate was hoarse, perhaps just at that moment thinking about how the house—*her house*—was supposed to list on Thursday. The tiniest part of Alice felt guilty for feigning the scenario, but then she remembered her conversation with Beverly and the fact that Nate had taken a job—in California!—that he had not mentioned. "I'm just glad you're okay. Everything else can be fixed."

"Yes, it can," Alice said, taking a final pull on the cigarette.

When Nate came racing through the house an hour and a half later, Alice was in the garden, patting earth around three newly planted flowers. "Alice! Where are you?" he shouted.

"Out here!" she replied loudly, having left the back door open so he would hear her from the yard. She finished the planting, then stood, wiping deep brown earth from her knees. A moment later Nate came flying out the door and down the back steps.

"The kitchen looks fine," he said, sounding both perplexed and relieved. She noted he'd gone into the kitchen first, before coming to check on her. His messenger bag was still across his chest, and it bounced against his hip as he ran the few steps across the lawn to reach her. "Let me see your hand."

She took off her gardening gloves and let him take one hand, flipping it over to see her palm. Then he grabbed the other hand, did the same. "Where's the burn?" he asked, continuing to flip her hands over, searching for the injury. He looked up at her, his forehead creasing with confusion.

Alice took her hands back and slid them into the gloves. "Like I said, I'm fine."

Nate stood there for a moment, mouth open. "What the hell is going on, Alice?" He rarely used her full name, and it sounded formal and odd.

"I was doing some late-summer planting," she said, gesturing to the new flowers, which stood tall like soldiers guarding the hostas. "The deer have been treating our garden like a buffet." Nate took in the plants, the tube-shaped flowers hanging from the green stalks, trying to place why they looked familiar . . .

"It's foxglove." Alice picked up the spade and rake, then stood back and admired her handiwork. "I went to the garden center this morning and picked them out. I would have preferred something brighter, but the guy said this Camelot Cream—that's its name—could flower until November, which is amazing."

"But . . . you said foxglove is toxic. We pulled it all out." Nate was bewildered. "Why would you plant more?"

"I told you," Alice said, voice calm. "The deer are eating all our hostas."

Nate grunted with anger and struggled to get his messenger bag from around his neck, before throwing it to the ground forcefully. "What the hell is wrong with you!"

"Beverly called."

At that Nate became still, his face going from angry red to ashen pale, though the small apples of his cheeks remained rosy. "What?"

"Beverly Dixon? Our Realtor?" Alice put the rake and spade into the shed, closing the door and sliding the bolt into the lock to keep it shut. "She was working on the listing and wasn't sure if we had replaced the fridge or the stove, but not to worry. I straightened things out for her."

Nate hung his head, hands on his hips, and took a deep breath. "Let me explain."

"I figured, the deer are ruining the garden and I'm not pregnant and we're apparently moving to California soon, so even if there was a baby it won't be eating any of these flowers or leaves, so might as well plant the foxglove again. We can leave a note for whoever buys the house that it's poisonous but a great deer repellent."

"Jesus Christ," Nate muttered, his tone thick with guilt. "This is not how you were supposed to find out."

A sharp laugh exploded from Alice. "You think?" she said. "Fuck you, Nate. I'm not going anywhere." And with that she took off her gloves and threw them at him, then strode into the house.

42

Nagging is a devastating emotional disease. If you are in doubt about having it, ask your husband. If he should tell you that you are a nag, don't react by violent denial—that only proves he is right.

—Mrs. Dale Carnegie, *How to Help Your Husband Get Ahead in His Social and Business Life* (1953)

Alice

.....

SEPTEMBER 27, 2018

*N*ate and Alice didn't speak for three full days, even though he tried more than once. They slept in separate rooms, shared no meals together, stayed out of each other's way. It was awkward and unnerving, but from Alice's perspective, quite necessary.

Then on Thursday morning Alice was at her laptop writing when an email popped up. It was from Beverly, and it was the listing for their house. *Wanted to send this along,* Beverly wrote. *Already getting some interest, so we'll chat soon about an agents' open house.*

Alice stared at the email, at the listing, for a long while. There were pictures of the house that had obviously been taken recently—the walls paper-free, the freshly painted front door and improved walkway, the beige office (previously the nursery)—and Alice wondered how Nate had managed that without her knowing. Her fury grew, until she was consumed. She called Nate, and to his credit, he answered right away.

"Why is Beverly sending me a listing for our house, Nate? I told you, I'm not moving. I told her too, but obviously you've made other plans?"

Nate spoke to someone nearby but muffled the phone with his hand so Alice couldn't tell what he said. "Ali, we're selling the house." She heard a door shut, the ambient noise of the office disappearing as it did. "Look, I didn't want to do this over the phone, but you've made it pretty clear you don't want to be in the same room as me these past few days, so here it is."

Alice lit a cigarette, didn't even bother to open a window. She trembled as she held it, brought a shaky hand to her mouth to inhale. "Is this about Drew, Nate?"

"What?"

She exhaled impatiently. "Is. This. About. Drew. Baxter?"

"Ali, I have no idea what—"

"Does she even care that you're married? *Do you?*"

"What the hell is that supposed to mean?"

"I think you know exactly what I mean." Alice snorted, but then something bubbled up to smother her anger. It was fear. She didn't want to be anywhere near Nate right now, but she also needed him. "Are you sleeping with her?"

A sharp inhalation from Nate. "Have you gone insane, Ali? You actually think I'm having an affair? With Drew?"

"I know she called you that day, when you told me it was Rob. So don't be so fucking righteous. You lied to me about her."

Nate sighed, his frustration seeping through the phone. "I told you it was Rob because I didn't want to get into it right then. We were talking about James Dorian and what happened, and, well, it didn't seem like the right time."

"So what was that call about, then, if not a check-in from your lover?"

"Stop it, Ali." Nate was angry now too. Good. At least he was taking her seriously. "I would never . . . God, is that how little you think of me?"

She shrugged, forgetting Nate couldn't see her.

"Drew and I were both offered positions in the L.A. office. But I didn't want to say anything to you until I knew it was a for-sure thing. And that afternoon Drew called because her mom is recovering from cancer treatment and she was worried about leaving New York. I was trying to help her with the decision, which we had to give by the end of the day. She's a friend, Ali. That's it." Alice couldn't be sure Nate was telling the truth about Drew, but there was a different sort of betrayal to focus on—that he had unilaterally decided to take a job across the country and expected Alice would fall in line behind him.

"And when did you make *your* decision, Nate?"

A pause. "I accepted the week before."

"Without talking to me first?" Alice's body quaked, and she stubbed out the cigarette, feeling nauseated. "Why are you doing this to me? To us?"

"Ali, listen to me." He softened his voice, pleading with her to understand. "It's a big promotion. A lot—like, *a lot*—more money, and even more when I pass the exam. A chance to run my own team! And the timing seemed good, because I know we just moved, but you can write anywhere and we can get settled and then do the whole baby thing down there." *The "whole baby thing"?* Alice closed her eyes tightly, set her forehead into her hands. "Your mom and Steve will be close enough to help out. I honestly thought you'd be relieved."

"Relieved?!"

"I know you were stressed about money, and how much the house was costing us. And the move has been extra-hard on you. I get it. It's a big change." Nate paused, took a breath. "Things haven't been the same between us lately, and I hoped this might get us back on track."

Alice sighed. "When are you supposed to be in L.A.?"

"End of October." Nate's voice was subdued, his tone conveying his regret. That was a month and a half away. "Right after my exam. But everything will be paid for. And they hire a company to come and do all the packing up, so you'll have help." *Go to hell, Nate.*

"What if I don't want to go?"

He huffed with exasperation. "What's the alternative? You're going to stay here in Greenville, alone? I can't afford to carry our place and something else in L.A., so how would that work? I know I should have said something earlier, but this is good for us. Now we can really get ahead."

Get ahead to where? Then Alice thought about Sally's question. *Who am I?* The answer—a flailing, unemployed writer; a mediocre housewife; a woman forced to bend to her husband's ambition—made her sick to her stomach.

Nate had stopped talking, was waiting for her to say this was fine, she forgave him for not telling her until now, understood the money mattered, as did his future success with the company (he was the breadwinner of the family, after all), and didn't blame him for wanting more. *We're a team,* she knew he expected her to say. *We stick together.*

"I'll have dinner ready at seven thirty. Don't be late." Then she ended the call.

Alice spent the rest of the day working on a plan, and by the time Nate came home—walking through the door at 7:20 P.M.—she was ready.

She had made a simple supper of pork chops, mashed potatoes, and salad and had a bottle of wine breathing when he came to stand at the kitchen door. He glanced at her and sensed a shift, and hope bloomed on his face.

"Come and sit down," she said, pouring them both wine. He sat across from her at the Formica table and took the wineglass she offered him. "First, I need you to know I'm really upset," Alice said. "This is a big deal, and I still can't believe you took the job without telling me."

"I know, and again, I'm sorry," Nate said, then added evenly, "We haven't been good at telling each other the truth recently, have we?" The scent of cigarette smoke—faint but undeniable—lingered in the living room, and Nate had undoubtedly noticed. Alice had tried to quit, but the cigarettes were like a salve she desperately needed at the moment. She'd stop, eventually.

Alice didn't react to Nate's comment. He was right (and her lies certainly outnumbered his), but she didn't want to have a discussion, which would certainly lead to an argument about it; she needed to focus on resolving the problem at hand.

"I was thinking about things today, about what I want, and I have a proposition for you," Alice said.

Nate raised an eyebrow, curious though wary. "I'm listening."

"I made a few calls, one to Megan Tooley, my friend who's a literary agent? Remember her?" Nate nodded. "I pitched her my book idea, and she was interested. Like, *really* interested. Said the premise was fantastic and that she could think of a half-dozen editors who would jump for a book like that."

"Okay," Nate said, his voice even. "That's great news."

"It is." Alice went to the oven to pull out the pork chops, unable to sit still. "So, I was thinking . . . let me have six months. I can finish the book and then Megan can sell it. If it all works out, we can stay because my book advance—and then the royalties, once it publishes—can help with expenses. If it doesn't sell, I'll go with you to L.A." Alice was plating the meat, so she didn't see Nate's expression, which had shifted from curiosity to disbelief.

"What do you think?" she asked, setting the plates in front of them. She finally looked at Nate, and her stomach dropped.

"I already took the job, Ali. Papers are signed. It's a done deal."

"But if it's about the money, I'm telling you in a few months—a year, tops—I can contribute! Or I'll get another job. It won't be all on you." She sat back and away from her dinner, her appetite gone. "Ask for an extension for the promotion. They love you and know you're brilliant. They'll hold the job if you say you can't leave for another few months."

"No, they won't." Nate's tone was incredulous. "Maybe if you had suggested this earlier, like in June or July, I could have made it work. But now? It's too late, Ali. We have to go."

"Too late? How could I have suggested anything when I had no idea! California is thousands of miles away."

Nate crossed his arms over his chest, his voice rising. "Thousands of miles away from what, Ali? It's not like there's a job you're leaving behind. What exactly is holding you here?"

Alice narrowed her eyes, then took her wine and got up from the table. She left the kitchen and went into the living room, sitting at her desk, her muscles tense and vibrating with adrenaline. Nate was right behind her.

"Okay, you want to play it this way?" he said, his tone challenging. "Show me your book."

"What?"

He gestured to her laptop. "Open it. Let me see what you've been working on."

She shook her head.

He gave a mock look of surprise. "Why not? I mean, if you want me to turn down this promotion and stay here so you can sell it, you must be feeling pretty confident about your work."

"*No.*"

"Come on, Ali. Just a chapter. One little chapter!"

"Stop it, Nate. I'm not ready to—"

But he was quick, reaching around her to grab the laptop from the desk, and before she could react he had the screen open and tapped a few keys. Alice regretted ever giving him her password. She was shocked by his behavior; it was so unlike him—or at least so unlike the old Nate.

Alice made one last attempt to take the laptop back from him, but he was taller than she was and held it over his head. And then she saw he'd managed to open the Word document titled "Novel" and, breathing heavily, she let her arms fall to her sides.

Nate looked at the first page, scrolled down for a few moments, then locked eyes with his wife. The first page remained on the screen and showed the title, written in bold caps in a large font so it stood out against the brightness of the screen:

RECIPE FOR A PERFECT WIFE, and then: *by Alice Hale.*

Alice's heart beat as fast as hummingbird wings.

"Is this all of it?" Nate asked, scrolling down the page. The cursor soon stopped, reaching the bottom of the document, which was only two pages long. He minimized the document, started looking around the computer's desktop. "Is there another file?"

"Give it to me, Nate."

"Alice, where the hell is your book?" Nate turned to her.

"That's it."

"This is it?" He looked back at the screen. "But there's hardly anything here."

"I know," she said.

"What have you been working on?"

"I've done a ton of research. I've got websites bookmarked. . . ." She was breathless, high-strung with adrenaline. "I've been trying, honestly. But . . . it's been more complicated than I expected."

"You've been lying to me, *again,* this whole time?" Nate lowered the computer. "What's happened to you?" He scrubbed his free hand through his hair, distraught. "Maybe we never should have moved here. . . . It's not good for you, or me. . . . This goddamn house . . ."

Alice snapped. With an anguished grunt, she ripped the laptop from Nate's hands and sprinted to the back door. Nate was on her heels, telling her to stop. She pushed open the door and threw the laptop as hard as she could against the stone patio steps, where it broke apart, the keyboard bouncing erratically before settling onto the lush green lawn. Alice was glad Sally was away, especially when Nate screamed, "Have you lost your fucking mind?" at her once the pieces of the laptop settled. Arguments this volatile between a couple belonged inside the four walls of a house. It was the neighborly thing to do.

The fight fizzled shortly after the scene on the patio. Alice was drained to the point of being ill, and Nate didn't look much better. Their meal was cold by the time they returned to the kitchen, and Alice reheated both plates in silence, though she was unable to eat anything. Not long after, she scraped her uneaten dinner into the garbage and went upstairs, exchanging not a single word with Nate. Soon, she heard the back door squeak open, a thin stream of light illuminating a swath of patio stones. Alice looked out the bedroom window to see Nate sweeping up the bits of laptop casing, holding a small flashlight in his mouth so he could see and sweep at the same time. Then he turned off the flashlight and stared for a while at the shadowed garden, statue still in the moonlight.

43

Just as the vampire sucks the blood of its victims in their sleep while they are alive, so does the woman vampire suck the life and exhaust the vitality of her male partner—or victim.

—William J. Robinson, *Married Life and Happiness* (1922)

Alice

.....

SEPTEMBER 28, 2018

*N*ate knocked on the bathroom door. "You okay?"

It was early. Nate was up for work, and Alice was on hands and knees, dry heaving into the toilet.

"Ali?" He knocked again. She tried to answer through her gagging but couldn't catch her breath.

"I'm coming in," Nate said, the door handle starting to turn, and Alice managed to gasp, "No, don't. Give me a minute." The door handle stopped turning, and Alice heard Nate's footsteps retreat down the hall. She flushed the toilet and splashed water on her face.

Nate was sitting on the guest room bed, where she had been sleeping now for nearly a week, waiting for her. He was still in boxers and a T-shirt, and he looked concerned and exhausted.

Alice cleared her throat, happy at least the horrible nausea she'd woken up with—that had sent her bolting for the washroom— was mostly gone. "I'm fine," she said, pulling on leggings and a sweatshirt. No way she was going back to sleep now.

"Didn't sound like it." Nate fiddled with the drawstring of his boxers. "Are you sick?"

"Probably something I ate. I feel better now." Alice suspected her weak stomach had more to do with what had transpired the day before. She thought about the in-pieces laptop and cringed with the memory; she'd lost her temper, and so had Nate, and things were worse than ever.

"Okay, well, I need to hop in the shower. If you're sure you don't need . . . ?"

"Go ahead." Nate nodded, got up from the bed, and brushed past Alice, who moved slightly to the side so there was no chance they'd touch. She heard the shower go on; then a minute later Nate called out for her.

"Could you grab some soap?" he asked, his dripping-wet head sticking out from behind the shower curtain. "None left in here."

"Sure," Alice said, going to the linen closet to find the large package of soap she'd bought on her last trip to Costco. At least they were being civil—she wasn't sure that would even be an option today. Alice reached for the package, then stopped, glancing at the box beside the soap. Tampons—the package unopened. She frowned, her hand hovering.

"Ali?" Nate was getting impatient.

"Just a second," she shouted, needing more like a minute to figure things out. To do the math, because that box of tampons should not be unopened. A strange sense of prickly warmth filled her as she began counting backward in her head, her eyes widening as she did. *Holy hell.* It seemed impossible, and yet . . .

She took the soap and shut the linen closet door, her hand

lingering there for a moment as she pulled herself together. Then she took it in to Nate and said she was going out.

"It's barely six," he said, wiping the water from his eyes as he watched her brush her teeth. She spat into the sink, then said, "I have something to do," before leaving the bathroom and a puzzled Nate to his shower.

Alice was locked in the washroom at the Scarsdale Starbucks, the only place open that time of morning aside from the pharmacy where she'd bought the pregnancy test. Someone knocked on the door and she shouted, "I'm in here!" and stared at the stick on the sink's counter. With shaky fingers, she held it close to her face, but there was no need—staring back at her was the undeniable plus sign in the test's small round window.

Who am I? Alice thought, looking into the coffee shop's bathroom mirror, eyes a bit wild, though clear and bright. *A mother, and that changes everything. . . .*

After dinner, after Alice handed him the test stick, after Nate's face transformed from frown to beaming smile, they sat together on the living room couch, as close as they'd been in more than a week.

"I can't believe it," Nate said. Rubbing her socked feet, which were on his lap, distractedly. It tickled, but she didn't pull away. "I mean, I know it's possible—nothing's perfect—but still. Wow."

While one *could* get pregnant on the pill (especially if one forgets to take it at the same time each day, which Alice had), the chances were minuscule. Because Nate lived and breathed statistics and risk, he was always prepared for the tiny percentage—no matter how unlikely—for in his line of work that typically ended up being the thing with the greatest impact. However, he remained stunned, if not deliriously happy, by the news.

"Do you think it's a boy or girl?" he asked.

"I haven't even been to the doctor yet, so let's not get ahead of ourselves."

Alice lay her head back against the sofa cushion, the ceiling crack yawning above her. "We should get that fixed."

"What?" Nate asked, and Alice pointed up.

"Probably a good idea, especially before the open houses. I'll call Beverly to find out if she knows a good plasterer."

Alice nodded, then said, "I think we should get it fixed, but not for the open houses."

"Huh?" Nate had laid his head back as well, and now turned toward her. "How come?"

She lifted her head, so they were facing each other. "Because we're not moving."

"Ali, come on. Don't start this again." Nate's jaw tensed and his hands dropped from her feet. He looked back to the ceiling.

"Sorry, I should have said, *I'm* not moving."

Nate sat up straight and shifted his body to face hers. "Yes, you are. We're having a baby, Ali."

Alice sat up too. "I'm aware, and I'm not leaving the house. This is where our baby should be raised, Nate. Not in California, where we have no friends and nothing is familiar and the epicenter of the publishing world is a five-hour plane ride and there's only one season. You were raised on the East Coast so you don't know how depressing it is to put a Christmas tree up in eighty-degree weather," she said. "I'm staying here, and you're welcome to stay with me. Or not."

He pushed her feet off his lap and stood quickly. "Why are

you being so difficult about this? It's not like you really see your old friends anymore. And publishing? I mean . . . come on, Ali. Starting a new career with a baby in tow? It's not exactly realistic." He gave her a pointed look. "Don't do this, okay? Not now."

"*Now* is exactly when this has to happen." She got off the couch as well, went over to the desk and pulled a pen and notepad from the drawer. A half-finished pack of cigarettes peeked out from the back of the drawer, and Alice reminded herself to throw them out later. She would never again smoke another cigarette— the desire disappearing the moment that positive sign showed itself. The sudden sense of responsibility, along with a burst of protectionist love, that she'd felt staring at the test strip had both shaken and anchored Alice.

Alice wrote on the notepad, then handed it to Nate. "The way I see it, you have two options."

"Are you serious?" he asked, his face contorting with his exasperation as he read from the notepad. "One, stay in Greenville with Alice and baby, or two, go to L.A., alone." He looked up at her, and his expression hardened. "You forgot number three: move to L.A. with Alice and baby."

She shook her head, taking the notepad back from him. "No, Nate, that isn't an option."

His rage rolled off him in waves, and he clenched his fists and took a step toward her. Too close for Alice's comfort, based on how angry he was. For a brief moment Alice wondered if she might have pushed him too far. "We are moving, and that's final."

She stepped back from him but kept her voice calm, her tone serene and matter-of-fact. "If you decide to go to L.A., you are going alone. I will stay here and finish my book, take care of this house, raise our child. You're welcome to be a part of that, or not. Your choice."

"That is hardly a choice!" His voice boomed through the living room, seeping into the ceiling crack, into the bones of the house.

Alice shrugged, unmoved by his distress or forceful tone, though she did cross her arms over her stomach in a protective fashion that was not lost on either of them. "You always have a choice, Nate."

44

The average man marries a woman who is slightly less intelligent than he is. That's why many brilliant women never marry. They do not come in contact with sufficiently brilliant men, or fail to disguise their brilliance in order to win a man of somewhat less intelligence.

—Dr. Clifford R. Adams, *Modern Bride* (1952)

Alice

.....

OCTOBER 30, 2018

*A*lice tied the apron slightly above her waist to accommodate the small bulge of her stomach. It was supposed to be moving day, but the house remained as it had been for the past few months. No boxes packed and ready to ship; half-finished home-improvement projects everywhere; no sign the Hales were leaving anytime soon. Instead, Alice was up early baking for her visit with Sally later that day and Nate was at the kitchen table eating breakfast before catching his train. The scent of lemon filled the kitchen as Alice grated rind into a bowl, then cut and juiced the fruit.

"Feeling better?" Nate asked, dragging a bit of egg through

the hot sauce on his plate. He was surprised to see her up and without her reliable green mask of illness.

"Much." Alice's morning sickness had been awful the past few weeks. But she rarely complained, even though it was miserable. And Nate, seeing how ill she was, seemed somewhat less angry than he had been. No matter what had transpired between them, or how Alice had forced Nate's hand, she was carrying his baby. Still, they were far from good, the cracks between them as evident as those in the ceiling they had yet to fix.

Alice wiped her lemon-drenched fingers on her apron, reaching for the coffeepot. "Want a warm-up?"

"Sure." She poured the steaming coffee, and Nate put a hand up when the mug was half-full. "Thanks." He took a sip of his coffee, eyes back to whatever news story he had been reading on his phone.

"Think you'll be home for dinner?" Alice read through the recipe, then measured out a quarter cup of poppy seeds.

"Hope so. But if you don't feel like making anything I can just grab something on my way."

"Should be fine. I'll do something easy."

Nate nodded, not looking up from his phone. She scraped down the sides of the bowl, giving one final stir before pouring the black-speckled yellow batter into the loaf pans.

"Still planning to paint the nursery this weekend?" she asked, taking hold of the edges of one loaf pan and banging it hard once, twice, on the countertop, to get any air bubbles out before baking. Then she did it with the second one.

Nate glanced up sharply at the banging, his forehead creased with annoyance. "Probably Sunday. I may need to go into the office on Saturday for a few hours." With a final sip of his coffee, he rinsed his cup and plate in the sink before stacking them in the dishwasher.

"I'll get the paint today," Alice said, squeezing around Nate to slide the loaf pans into the oven. "Oops, sorry about that." She had jostled him, and he set his hands on her hips to keep either of them from stumbling. Nate's fingers lingered for a moment, then retreated to shut the dishwasher. It had been a long time since his hands had been on her body—four weeks, by her latest count. "Unless you want to wait? Maybe pick a gender-specific color?"

"Up to you," Nate replied nonchalantly, untucking his tie from between the buttons of his shirt. He smoothed the tie flat to his chest, then shrugged on his suit jacket, which was hanging over the back of the chair.

"I think I'd rather get it done now. So maybe a soft yellow? Or mint green could work."

"Either is fine with me." Nate reached for his messenger bag from the chair beside him, slipping the strap overhead and across his chest.

"It's supposed to be cold today," Alice said over her shoulder as she rinsed the bowl and set it on the drying rack. "You might want your coat, too."

Nate frowned, perhaps thinking about how if they were living in L.A. he wouldn't need a coat in October. Alice wondered how many times a day Nate's turned-down promotion came to mind, or the fact that Drew was already in warm and sunny California, mobilizing her new team. He was doing fine in New York—he'd passed his exam and had received the requisite bump in salary. But with no positions open in upper management in the Manhattan office (though they expected there might be, within a year or so), he essentially held the same job with a slightly higher paycheck. His aspirations stifled and his work ethic questioned when he reneged on the offer, Alice knew none of this made her ambitious husband very happy.

"I'll be okay without it." Nate took the travel mug of coffee

Alice handed him and in return gave her a perfunctory peck on the cheek. "Ali, I . . ."

For a moment, they locked eyes and Alice waited for Nate to finish. But whatever it was seemed lodged in his throat, which he cleared with a quick cough before taking a step away from her. "I'm glad you're feeling better. Don't forget your folic acid."

"Already took it," she said. "And my multivitamin, too." Nate said he'd call if he was going to be later than seven, and Alice wished him a good day. Then she shut the door behind him and for the first time that morning her shoulders relaxed. If they were to be honest with each other, she sensed that Nate would admit to feeling the same relief when he left the house as she did to have him gone. Alice much preferred being home alone, without the constant hum of disappointment that flowed off her husband.

It was a lot of work, this tiresome, superficial back-and-forth they engaged in daily. How long could they keep it up? Maybe the baby would bring with it a truce of sorts, Alice thought, or at least a distraction from their marital ennui.

As Alice was making another pot of coffee, a text from Bronwyn arrived.

What's the vomit count this morning?

She chuckled, typed back,

Morning sickness: 0. Hale: 1

The friends had reconciled after the disastrous H&H lunch, with Bronwyn forgiving Alice for being a "psycho bitch" that afternoon, as she put it. And Alice promised to re-create the day, complete with bagels and manicures, when she could stomach more than chicken broth. She was grateful for Bronwyn—aside from Sally, the one constant in her life at the moment—and couldn't believe she'd almost allowed Nate and the drama around Drew to come between them. Though when she thought about it now, she didn't feel like that same person who had lied about the IUD and started smoking again and accused her husband of cheating on her. That had been a different version of Alice Hale—one who had been weakened by a lack of purpose, who hadn't been able to see her own potential. She was relieved that Alice Hale was gone for good, now that she had more important things to focus on, like her book. And the baby.

She rubbed her tiny belly bump and smiled, adding cream to her fresh mug of coffee. Alice, finally hungry, couldn't wait to eat the lemon poppy seed loaf—it would be a relief to put something in her stomach and have it stay there.

Late afternoon, after sharing her baking and a long chat with Sally, Alice came home fatigued and longing for a nap. It was mind-boggling, how much energy a baby—currently only the size of a fig, according to Nate—required. But while crawling back into bed was tempting, her manuscript was calling to her more insistently. So, resigned the nap would have to wait, Alice decided a cup of tea might perk her up. She was filling the kettle when her phone vibrated on the kitchen countertop, and Nate's name illuminated the screen. Alice sighed, let it ring four times before she picked up.

"Hello?"

"Hey," Nate said. "How's your day?"

Alice finished with the kettle, then reached for the box of tea in the cupboard. "Good, thanks. You?"

"Good. Yeah. But apparently there's something going on at Williams Bridge. The trains aren't getting through."

"Huh. Wonder what happened." She checked the kettle, noticed she'd forgotten to turn it on.

"They're saying someone got pushed," Nate said.

"Oh God. That's horrible." Alice laid a hand to her stomach. "Who would do something like that?"

"I can't even imagine. Brutal." He paused. "So I figured I'd stay in the city for dinner. Avoid the delays. As long as that's okay with you?"

"Totally fine." Alice was glad to have the evening to herself. "Thanks for calling," she added.

"Um, yeah. You're welcome," Nate replied, before hanging up.

Turning off her ringer, she glanced out the window at the back garden, waiting for the water to boil. Though the bright, gregarious flowers were long gone, there remained plenty of green foliage, and the foxglove—which as promised continued to showcase its vanilla-colored blooms well into the fall—had kept the deer away. She thought of Nellie, as she often did, and imagined the housewife would have been pleased to see how well her beloved gardens were faring.

Alice's mind drifted—another side effect of early pregnancy, as if the baby was siphoning all her focus—and it slipped back to her conversation with Nate. For a moment, her thoughts going there without intention, Alice indulged a macabre musing . . . what *if* it had been Nate who was pushed from the train's platform? He always stood too close to the safety line, which was an oddity to his otherwise predictable personality. Then she would be alone in this house not only this evening, but forever. All decisions would be hers alone.

She suddenly envisioned Nellie, standing where Alice was now, staring at her cherished garden, the kitchen filled with mourning casseroles and funeral cakes and her hypothetical grief. The fantasy was provocative purely because if a marriage ends in such tragedy—one person departing through no fault of either party—it is blameless. No failure, no compromises, no expectations. And while Alice would never wish to be a single mother, at least her own mother showed her it was possible. If Alice had to do it alone, she would be fine.

A sharp crack rattled the kitchen window—a bird that had

gone off course—and Alice yelped and jumped, only then noticing the rolling boil of the kettle. Taking a breath, her heart pounding in her throat, she turned off the kettle, then went on her toes at the window to look for the bird on the grass below, but it must have managed to fly away, uninjured.

Shaking off the last vestiges of her daydreaming, Alice poured boiling water into her mug and padded over to her desk. The constant nausea had wreaked havoc on her creativity, but now that she wasn't distracted by the incessant need to vomit, she felt ready to work. Sliding her chair closer, she opened the desk's drawer and pulled out a picture frame, placing it on the desktop in front of her.

In it, a young, vibrant-looking Nellie stood in the front garden, slender arms, legs bare in quite-short shorts, with her gloved hands wrapped around a fresh-cut bouquet of pink peonies. If one looked closely, one could see dirt smears on her knees. The snapshot caught Nellie mid-laugh, her head tilted back slightly, though her eyes were bright and focused on the camera's lens. Alice had found the picture upside down in the cardboard box, tucked deep into a flap and therefore previously hidden. On its back was penned *Nellie, 173 Oakwood Drive, June 1957.* It had been taken only months after Richard died, and Nellie looked—at least to Alice—happy and carefree. Whoever had taken the photo had captured the real Nellie Murdoch.

Alice gingerly sipped her too-hot tea, rereading the last couple of pages she'd managed the previous day. Then, as Nellie looked on, Alice ducked her head and let her mind go, invoking the housewife's ghost, the tapping of keys filling the otherwise quiet, contented house.

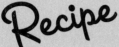 

FROM THE KITCHEN OF *Elsie Swann*

Swann Family Herb Mix

A dry tablespoon each of:

Lemon Balm

Parsley

Basil

Thyme

Marjoram

Sage

Foxglove (flowers and leaves)
*1 dry teaspoon

Dry herbs on newspaper in a cool spot. Using mortar and pestle, grind dried herbs one at a time until almost a fine dust, then combine in a bowl and mix well. Store in a glass shaker and sprinkle on your favorite recipes, like meatloaf and toasted cheese sandwiches! Can also be baked into biscuits and used in salad dressings. A family favorite!

Acknowledgments

I own a lot of cookbooks: Baking, vegetarian, vegan, classic, French, Italian, barbecue, and one Paleo cookbook I bought on a whim (I liked the cover) and never used, because I've since returned to vegetarianism and it's full of meat-based recipes that make me weepy for the cows and pigs and chickens of the world. In this large stack are also a number of vintage cookbooks, some bought at secondhand bookstores and others passed down through the generations by the women in my family. Those are my most prized, and while some of the recipes can be . . . unappetizing, for lack of a better word (jelly salads were the bomb back then) . . . I treasure those books for their legacy. They represent strong, capable, and interesting women whose great skills were only showcased in some cases—because of the times—in their kitchens and via these cookbooks.

Like the ingredients in a recipe, there are many elements to writing a book. Furthermore, if you leave one ingredient out, or get the measurements wrong, you can end up with something unpalatable and only fit for the trash bin. Novels can be finicky like soufflé and piecrust, satisfying like stew and potpie, and mesmerizing like pavlova and Baked Alaska. But unlike nailing a recipe, nailing a book takes more than a list of ingredients mixed together. And so here, friends, is my recipe for this novel (please note, measurements are random and for fun, so 2 cups of one thing is no more significant than 1 teaspoon of another).

Recipe for a Perfect Wife, the Novel

....

INGREDIENTS

3 cups editors extraordinaire: Maya Ziv, Lara Hinchberger,
  Helen Smith

2 cups agent-I-couldn't-do-this-without: Carolyn Forde
  (and the Transatlantic Literary Agency)

1½ cup highly skilled publishing teams: Dutton US,
  Penguin Random House Canada (Viking)

1 cup PR and marketing wizards: Kathleen Carter (Kathleen Carter
  Communications), Ruta Liormonas, Elina Vaysbeyn, Maria
  Whelan, Claire Zaya

1 cup women of writing coven: Marissa Stapley, Jennifer Robson, Kate
  Hilton, Chantel Guertin, Kerry Clare, Liz Renzetti

½ cup author-friends-who-keep-me-sane: Mary Kubica, Taylor Jenkins
  Reid, Amy E. Reichert, Colleen Oakley, Rachel Goodman,
  Hannah Mary McKinnon, Rosey Lim

½ cup friends-with-talents-I-do-not-have: Dr. Kendra Newell,
  Claire Tansey

¼ cup original creators of the Karma Brown Fan Club: my family and
  friends, including my late grandmother Miriam Christie, who
  inspired Miriam Claussen; my mom, who is a spectacular cook
  and mother; and my dad, for being the wonderful feminist he is

1 tablespoon of the inner circle: Adam and Addison, the loves of my
  life

½ tablespoon book bloggers, bookstagrammers, authors, and readers:
  including Andrea Katz, Jenny O'Regan, Pamela Klinger-Horn,

Melissa Amster, Susan Peterson, Kristy Barrett, Lisa Steinke, Liz Fenton

1 teaspoon vintage cookbooks: particularly the *Purity Cookbook*, for the spark of inspiration

1 teaspoon loyal Labradoodle: Fred Licorice Brown, furry writing companion

Dash of Google: so I could visit the 1950s without a time machine

METHOD: Combine all ingredients into a Scrivener file, making sure to hit Save after each addition. Stir and stir and stir for what feels like an eternity but is likely about six months to three years, give or take. Move to a fresh Word document and beat until smooth. Pour into well-greased pans provided by publisher, and bake for approximately one year. Take out of oven and let cool briefly, then serve, perhaps with a side of ice cream. Enjoy!

Credits

COOKBOOK SOURCES

Betty Crocker's Picture Cook Book, revised and enlarged [City]: McGraw-Hill, 2nd ed., 1956.

Lake of the Wood Milling Company. *Five Roses Cook Book*. Montreal: [Company], 1913.

Purity Flour Mills. *Purity Cookbook*, 3rd ed. Illustrated by A. J. Casson R.C.A. [City]: [Pub. Co.], 1945.

About the Author

Karma Brown is an award-winning journalist and bestselling author of the novels *Come Away with Me, The Choices We Make, In This Moment,* and *The Life Lucy Knew.* In addition to her novels, Brown's writing has appeared in publications such as *Self, Redbook, Canadian Living, Today's Parent,* and *Chatelaine.*